Praise for *The Shehnai Virtuoso*

"[Jenny Bhatt's] translation of Dhumketu's prose is relaxed and even-toned, never slipping into performativity. The translator is deeply engaged with the context of each story and follows each dip and tremor in the narrative flow with practised ease and linguistic flair . . . With this collection, Jenny Bhatt drives home a fact that is not often recognized in the milieu, that the translator is also a literary explorer and evangelist whose initiative in selecting works of important writers and presenting them in another language is unique in the world of publishing, and deserves acknowledgement and recognition."

—N. Kalyan Raman, translator of *Stories of a Goat*

"[A] revelation: we hope that several other writers like Dhumketu, who are almost unknown to the English-speaking world, will soon be made available in translation." —*The Hindu*

"Dhumketu coming to the US in English is a wonder I am thrilled to witness. In these stories, writer and translator Jenny Bhatt transposes the lushness of life as described by the author—adept in both rural and urban settings where life folds and unfolds. As Dhumketu says, 'dexterity, humility and imagination' are required of the writer, but we see these clearly as the translator's work as Bhatt ushers in new, important, florid, and disciplined renderings."

—Rajiv Mohabir, author of *Cutlish* and *Antiman*

"Dhumketu's stories appeared in Gujarati literature like sparks, or comets, lighting up the sky, creating desire to hear more, and see more. Generations in Gujarat have grown up on Dhumketu's stories. Although not the first, Dhumketu is the most renowned short story writer. Jenny Bhatt's labor in understanding, contextualizing, interpreting and translating him deserves our gratitude and attention."

—**Rita Kothari, editor of** *The Greatest Gujarati Stories Ever Told*

"The brilliant and prolific writer Dhumketu is an integral part of the Gujarati canon. Jenny Bhatt's empathetic and intuitive translations convey the signature and nuance of his short stories, and make this iconic voice available for readers around the world."

—**Namita Gokhale, author of** *The Blind Matriarch*

"Dhumketu wrote nearly 500 short stories and this beautifully translated, brilliant and glittering collection from his oevre will go a long way in reminding readers about one of the finest short-story writers from India."

—**Aruni Kashyap, author of** *The House with a Thousand Stories*

"A comet that flew through other linguistic skies now visits the Anglophone firmament. Train your telescopes, ladies and gentlemen, Dhumketu is here!" —**Jerry Pinto**

The Shehnai Virtuoso

The Best Stories of Dhumketu

Translated from the Gujarati by Jenny Bhatt

DEEP VELLUM PUBLISHING
DALLAS, TEXAS

Deep Vellum Publishing
3000 Commerce St., Dallas, Texas 75226
deepvellum.org · @deepvellum

Deep Vellum is a 501c3 nonprofit literary arts organization
founded in 2013 with the mission to bring
the world into conversation through literature.

First published in English in India as *Ratno Dholi: The Best
Stories of Dhumketu* in 2020 by Harper Perennial
An imprint of HarperCollins Publishers.
Originally published in Gujarati as *Dhumketu Ni Tunki Vartao*
by Gurjar Prakashan
English translation © Jenny Bhatt, 2020

First Deep Vellum Edition, 2022

LIBRARY OF CONGRESS CATALOGING-IN-PUBLICATION DATA

Names: Dhūmaketu, 1892–1965, author. | Bhatt, Jenny, translator.
Title: The shehnai virtuoso : the best stories of Dhumketu / Dhumketu ;
   translated from the Gujarati by Jenny Bhatt.
Other titles: Dhūmaketu nī ṭūṅkī vārtāo. English
Description: First Deep Vellum edition. | Dallas, Texas : Deep Vellum
   Publishing, 2022.
Identifiers: LCCN 2022005647 | ISBN 9781646051687 (trade paperback) |
   ISBN 9781646051694 (ebook)
Subjects: LCSH: Dhūmaketu, 1892–1965—Translations into English. |
   LCGFT:
   Short stories.
Classification: LCC PK1859.D535 D4813 2022 | DDC
   891.4/736--dc23/eng/20220301
LC record available at https://lccn.loc.gov/2022005647

ISBN 978-1-64605-168-7 (TPB) | 978-1-64605-169-4 (Ebook)

Cover design by Harshad Marathe
Interior layout and typesetting by KGT

PRINTED IN THE UNITED STATES OF AMERICA

મા તે મા, ને સહુ તે વા

There's simply no one like one's mother.

For my mother, who taught me Gujarati, passed on her love for Gujarati literature, and introduced me to her favourite short-story writer, Dhumketu. Though she could not do this project with me, she was with me throughout the process.

ગણ્યા ગણાય નહિ, વિણ્યા વિણાય નહિ
Cannot be counted, cannot be measured.

For my father, who has supported the journey of this first translation work in immeasurable ways.

– Jenny Bhatt

Contents

Translator's Introduction

Dhumketu, one of the towering figures of Gujarati literature, often described the short-story form as an incomparable flower in the garden of literature, as delicate as the juhi, as exquisitely beautiful as a golden bird, as electrifying as a bolt of lightning. For him, the short story roused the imagination and emotions by saying what it must through only allusions or sparks. This last idea was so important to him that he titled his first collection *Tankha*, meaning 'sparks'. Later, he released three more short-story collections with the same title.

To accomplish so much through allusions or sparks, writers need more than imaginative invention in their short stories. What's indispensable is a deeply insightful observance of one's world with a superior technical skill for capturing the hidden, nuanced and unusual details. Stefan Zweig once wrote about Tolstoy: 'One who sees so much and so well does not need to invent; one who observes imaginatively does not need to create imagination.' This is also an apt description of Dhumketu's art and craft.

Had this writer been more widely translated and read, his

stature and skill as a pioneer of the literary short-story form in Gujarati would have been acknowledged as equal to that of Tolstoy, Chekhov, Tagore, and Premchand in their respective cultures and languages. Perhaps this translated volume of some of Dhumketu's finest short stories will go some distance towards building that reputation.

The Evolution of the Gujarati Short Story

The short-story form has existed for a long time across the Indian subcontinent. Though not formally identified as such, our ancient mythological and religious texts have always been a series of short stories woven together into long multilayered epics. That most of these were written in verse form rather than prose means that they continue to be technically recognised as mostly poetry.

The modern Gujarati short story owes a lot more to the European, Russian and American short story of the nineteenth and early twentieth centuries than to those ancient epics. Much of Indian literature across all regions was being influenced by or adapted from works from Europe, Russia and America during that time. However, for a long time, both prose and verse forms of Gujarati literature were dominated by themes of religion or nationalism. Before Dhumketu, writers like Dalpatram, Narmad (widely considered the founder of modern Gujarati literature), and a few others had studied Western literature closely to aid their own craft. Still, the short works that were written during their time were mostly fable- or folktale-like, or satirical, and had the primary goal of enabling sociopolitical change or providing simple entertainment.

A major milestone was achieved when Bhogindra Divetia

translated Tolstoy's short stories into Gujarati. This set off a wave of more literary translations into Gujarati from other cultures and languages, including Bengali, Hindi and Urdu. Along with this new exposure, there were even essays in major magazines and periodicals about the form's literary merits and techniques. This led to an enlightened appreciation of the short story as an independent literary form and several Gujarati writers began approaching it with more concerted efforts. As a result, this era also saw many short stories adapted from popular Western ones by writers like Maxim Gorky, Guy de Maupassant, Nathaniel Hawthorne, Edgar Allan Poe, O. Henry, and others. However, given the political climate at the time, the works continued to favour instruction and didacticism at the expense of aesthetics and craft.

Eventually, due to the works of stalwarts like Ranjitram Mehta, Dhansukhlal Mehta and K.M. Munshi, the Gujarati short story came into its own as a literary art form. In 1918, Malayanil (pen name of Kanchanlal Vasudev Mehta) was credited with having written the first modern Gujarati short story, 'Govalani', which showcased all the classic elements of the form at the time.

This pre-Dhumketu evolution of the Gujarati short story was predominantly characterised by translations from and adaptations of Western short stories. Original creations were somewhat uneven in their craft and technique, and biased towards easy entertainment or heavy-handed morality.

Dhumketu's Pioneering Short Stories

Dhumketu was born as Gaurishankar Govardhanram Joshi in 1892 to a Brahmin family in Gujarat. In his memoirs, *The Path of Life* and *The Colour of Life*, he writes about how stories came to flow in his blood from an early age: through the oral storytelling of his parents and his own fascination with the lives of historical figures. As was common for most Gujarati writers of his time, he was heavily influenced by Narmad's heroic tales, the ancient epics of Vyas and Valmiki, and the innumerable Gujarati folktales passed down orally from generation to generation.

Throughout his schooling, his years studying Sanskrit and literature at university, and his career as a schoolteacher, Dhumketu had access to many literary works, especially through the private libraries of certain wealthy patrons and educational institutions. Early in his teaching career, he was assigned the task of reading biographies and historical novels to a nobleman's wife – an activity that fed both his reading habit and writing aspirations. While teaching at a private Ahmedabad school – owned by Vikram Sarabhai's father, Ambalal Sarabhai – he gained an even wider exposure to all forms of art and culture – music, drama, sculpture, poetry, etc.

He started writing while still in middle school and gained a reputation as an essayist and poet. While studying for his matriculation, he used a couple of different nom de plumes like 'Vihaar' and 'Paagal'. The adoption of 'Dhumketu', meaning comet, came later during his university years of trying and failing (initially) to get his early short stories published.

Considered one of the pioneers of the Gujarati short story, Dhumketu wrote more than 500, collected in twenty-four volumes. These were accompanied by twenty-nine historical novels, seven social novels, numerous plays, travelogues, essays, literary criticism, and memoirs, not to mention the painstaking translations of writers and poets like Kahlil Gibran, Rabindranath Tagore, and others.

His most well-known and frequently anthologised short story in English translation is 'The Post Office'. An early version was published in 1923 and, while it is not his best in terms of technique and craft, it still appeals to a wide readership in terms of age, geography and culture because of its simplicity and pathos. A lonely old man waits, in vain, for his daughter's letter. Through this one circumstance drawn on an intimate canvas, Dhumketu gives us the universal: a father's longing for a lost daughter's love and the world's indifference to, even derision of, such a deeply personal need.

The first collection, *Tankha I*, followed in 1926. Using all the variegated raw materials from the short stories before him – techniques, social issues, prose styles, themes, exposition approaches – Dhumketu took full advantage of the readers' cultivated fondness for the short-story form to put forth many skilful original and adapted creations. So much so that his name became synonymous with short stories in Gujarati literary culture.

His work was notable then, as it is even now, for three standout aspects. These set him apart from his major contemporaries – K.M. Munshi and Jhaverchand Meghani – in Gujarati literature at the time. While the other two, like many other prominent writers of their time, were also on the frontlines of India's social reformation movements and its fight for freedom from the British, Dhumketu chose to allow his writing to do all the speaking. In his story, 'The Creator of Life's Ruins', he demonstrates this belief: 'Someone has said correctly that society is shaped by individuals. But an individual is shaped by work.'

The first differentiating aspect was how he explored the inner worlds of his characters through their experience of external events. To that end, the events portrayed in Dhumketu's stories were much more than a sequentially linked chain. They were a means to illustrate deeper nuances of human nature and evoke particular emotions and ideas within his readers. Plot, character, action, setting, dialogue, theme – all of these were employed to make his readers live within those characters' inner worlds.

The second important divergence from the short stories of his time was his focus on people from all walks of life – rural to royal, young to old. Frequently, his characters were from the lower classes and castes – a section that had been largely neglected or caricatured in Gujarati literature until then. Dhumketu's depictions of village and family life were not as influenced by Gandhi's teachings and exhortations of moral and humble grassroots living as were those of his contemporaries. And, while he certainly explored the familiar themes of sacrifice, love, individualism and patriotism in both his social and historical fiction, he often preferred to do so through the lives, joys and sorrows of commoners. One of his deeply held beliefs, mentioned variously and often throughout his works, was as follows (quoted from 'The Noble Daughters-in-law'): 'That a man is a king only due to the circumstances of birth should be considered just as terrible as when a man is untouchable only due to the accident of his birth.'

The third exceptional characteristic of Dhumketu's works was how his strong, independent-minded women and emotionally sensitive men were well ahead of their time. Before we achieved independence, when nationalistic and religious fervour called for traditional gender roles in not just the real world but also in those created by artists, Dhumketu deviated from the norm in ways that make his stories even more relevant during our times.

The Selected Stories in This Collection

To choose a 'best of' selection from a writer's works when the oeuvre is as wide-ranging and vast as Dhumketu's is an impossible project. Beyond the question of how 'best' should be defined, we have the typical dilemma faced by all writers or translators of short-story collections or anthologies: of trying to make every story appeal to every reader.

For this project, I wanted to ensure the following: enable an understanding of Dhumketu's chronological progression as a short-story writer; showcase his range and skills with different themes and styles; whet the reader's appetite for more of his works.

So, it made sense to select at least one significant story from each of the twenty-four published volumes. There are two additional stories here: the most anthologised 'The Post Office', which was included since it is the most recognised of his works; and 'Kailas', which can only be justified as this translator's whimsy because of a personal connection. That both stories feature aged fathers grieving the absence of a child is an interesting coincidence but, given Dhumketu's own life, not entirely a surprising writerly preoccupation.

Two stories, 'The Dispenser of Justice' and 'The Worst of the Worst', have the same main plot point: a poor man is wronged by a powerful, rich one. However, while one is about exacting revenge, the other is about extracting justice. Most importantly, the two stories are different in narrative voice, point of view and literary style, and highlight something that many short-story writers do even today: adapt their own works to revisit certain themes or issues they feel compelled to re-present to their readers.

As a translator and a short-story writer myself, I was keen to unpack the nuances and layers of these two similar stories to understand why Dhumketu was compelled to revisit them with different narrative voices, points of view, and styles. As a literary critic, I was driven to comparative criticism to understand how the writer worked at honing both his craft and his message with these two stories. As a reader, I was curious to see how a man went from considering revenge as a way to restore balance in one story to showing how justice is the way to right a wrong. That journey – from vindictiveness to vindication, emotionality to rationality, personal to impersonal, resolution to closure, and retaliation to righteousness – could not have been easy as it involved switching from the low road to the high road.

Only one of the short stories in this collection is historical while all the other selections centre on sociocultural issues, several of which prevail in Gujarati society even today. 'Tears of the Soul' is based on the story of Amrapali, the royal courtesan of the ancient kingdom of Vaishali (present-day Bihar). As with all of Dhumketu's historical works, this story is well-researched for accurate period details (with a number of authorial footnotes) and fictionalised like a theatrical drama. In keeping with the 'variations on a theme' approach mentioned earlier, Dhumketu wrote this short story about Amrapali and then went on to write an entire novel about her.

A majority of the stories are set in rural Gujarat, which Dhumketu felt was underrepresented in Gujarati literature of the time. And a number of them are set in India's northeast rather than

Gujarat. These showcase not only how Dhumketu's wanderlust and creativity fed off each other, but also his fascination with and close observation of the cultures of other regions.

While more stories here have male protagonists, it's the women protagonists who are more singularly memorable. Dhumketu was certainly not free of the gender biases of his time; however, he took care to portray his female protagonists as complex human beings in their own right. He also did not hesitate to poke fun at the classist pomposities and self-inflicted pain of the male characters who were often based on his own professions: teacher, writer, poet, government employee, etc.

In his literary criticism, Dhumketu often mentioned that the real beauty of the Gujarati language had barely been revealed by the literary works of his era. His narrative style was in the somewhat effusive, romantic tradition of his time. From his essays, memoirs, travelogues and his own introduction (translated later here), it is evident that he was more influenced – in terms of technique and style – by Western, European, and Russian short-story writers (Tolstoy, Gorky, Chekhov, Maupassant, Hawthorne, Kipling, to name a few) than his Gujarati predecessors or contemporaries. As a literary translator himself, he favoured poets like Kahlil Gibran and poetic prose like that of Rabindranath Tagore. That said, his stories are tautly structured and intricately detailed. There is very little superfluity in his exposition.

Overall, it is possible that the contemporary reader might find stereotypical and caricatural depictions in some of these works. However, we must acknowledge that we have the benefit of hindsight about our past societies while Dhumketu had the unavoidable biases and prejudices of a middle-class man of his time. This is not to excuse the writer's judgement flaws but to acknowledge them as part of the man's sociocultural limitations.

A Note on the Translation

All of us, readers and writers alike, are translators. The very act of reading involves translating and interpreting the writer's meaning and intent. The act of writing involves interpreting and giving voice to our own thoughts, which are often guided by the things we have read, seen, heard, experienced. So, translation is not simply the act of converting words from Language A to Language B. Also, language is not merely words, phrases, idioms, etc. Languages contain entire cultures within them; entire ways of thinking and being too.

Growing up in India, I spoke Gujarati at home, English at school, Hindi with friends, and Marathi with pretty much everyone else (since we lived in the state of Maharashtra.) At university in England, I studied German for two years and wrote my major thesis in the language. During my first two years as a full-time manufacturing engineer, I studied and worked for a certain time in French. So, while this is my first literary translation from Gujarati to English, I have always been drawn, both formally and informally, to translation work because it allows me to explore the ideas and emotions of people from another time or culture. The transformation of something foreign into something familiar deepens my own awareness of the world, past and present.

Translation involves understanding and leveraging the subtexts, cultural implications and stylistic choices made by the original writer in Language A so that they can be recreated in Language B without losing any literary merit in terms of plot, story, dialogue, insight, action, character, setting, etc. It is about being a close reader in Language A and a skilled writer in Language B, both of which require deep cultural understanding, literary sensitivity, and a writer's intuition.

Given all of the above, while I have aimed for fidelity to the writer's meaning, I have also aimed for a critical interpretation of his works. Due to their accretions of tradition and culture over centuries, no two languages can be seamlessly transposed. I hope I have been faithful to Dhumketu's tone and intention while ensuring le mot juste in my choices of English words and syntax. For ease of reading, I have added a glossary of Gujarati terms for readers who wish to understand certain words, phrases and cultural nuances.

Throughout this journey, I've learnt new or nuanced meanings of words and phrases in both Gujarati and English, discovered certain beautiful rhythms and cadences of both languages. I've seen how particular words and phrases in these languages, while seeming like they correspond to each other, can actually mean different things. Above all, I have discovered parts of my own Gujarati culture and history that I would never have otherwise. It would be entirely fair to say, paraphrasing a Dhumketu statement from the story 'Mungo Gungo' and from his memoirs (where he attributes the original to Kahlil Gibran): 'The translator was creating her artwork, but the artwork was creating the translator.'

Conclusion

Within the Indian literary translation community, there is ongoing frustration about the lack of adequate readership for the sheer volume of works in regional languages and how, as a result, many are being forgotten. I have also often railed and ranted on social media and in essays about how, even when such works manage to get translated and published, there is ridiculously low compensation and visibility. During such times, I find myself viewing writers like Dhumketu with renewed respect. Despite having encountered much censure for pursuing a literary career over other more lucrative opportunities, he persevered and, eventually, left a significant, lasting mark on the landscape of Gujarati literature. However, this was never his primary goal. For him, the work was always its own reward as the story 'A Happy Delusion' illustrates.

In this story, Dhumketu writes about a young man, Manmohan, who sees his literary journal as his life's work, his dharma, his ideal. (There were many during Dhumketu's time who worked hard at such monthly journals to promote Gujarati literature. Dhumketu himself received a lot of encouragement when they published his short stories and essays. In his memoirs, he refers to the founders of such journals as the unknown and unsung heroes of literature.) He's put a lot of effort into his journal and wants to publish it. His widowed mother gives him her life's savings while he himself borrows money and works at another job to pay it off so he can keep the journal running and continue writing. People think he's delusional to carry on. The story's narrator, a respected writer rather like Dhumketu himself, says the journal is not that good: 'there was no vision, no life experience, nor any grand ideas that could move the nation'. However, he concludes that the man's determination to put his entire life into the project despite the many hardships is remarkable.

Towards the end of the story, the narrator visits Manmohan in his home. He sees the physical impoverishment, the intellectual richness, and the bliss of the man's existence. He asks himself: 'What was the outcome of this man's lifetime of labour?' He answers this himself: 'Nothing at all, was the answer. But wasn't his hard work the highest possible degree of his achievement?' The final words, which sum up everything about all literary endeavours, resound timelessly. So here's giving Dhumketu the last, glorious word in this introduction:

> While returning home, the entire way, I was recalling this Manmohan's entire life story. And a stanza from one of Mirabai's bhajans arose in my mind:

> > 'Chhota sa mandir banaun
> > Main apna bhagwan bithaun.'
> > ['I will make a small temple
> > I will place my own god within it.']

> A question was surging in my mind: those who build their own little temples, the small people with such happy delusions – are they not really greater than those who make big-big propaganda-driven proclamations about seeking the truth? Who can say?

Author's Introduction

Introduction to *Tankha I*, First Edition

The stories in this collection have appeared in various monthly journals over the last three to four years. About four or so entirely new stories will be seen for the first time in this collection. Pretty much none of the stories – with the exception of 'One Mistake' – is a transcription, translation, adaptation of, or allusion to any other creation. Zola's influence has marked 'One Mistake'. Of course, just as even a supremely powerful artist like Kalidasa was indebted to the first poet, Valmiki, so is every writer indebted to his ancestors. There cannot be even a hint of a denial of this indisputable principle here. On the contrary, what Emerson says is much closer to the truth: 'The most original man is the most indebted man.'

America is the motherland of the short story. But, during the last twenty years of the nineteenth century, mainly from the time that Rudyard Kipling began writing in *The Allahabad Pioneer*, the art of the short story progressed more. After Kipling, writers such as Conrad, Barry, Galsworthy, Wells, Hardy, et al., greatly elevated the short story as a suggestive art form.

Before universally accepted principles about the art of the short story are established, the handful of mistaken ideas that have become prevalent must be pushed away.

The short story is not the miniature form of the novel. The art of the short story is entirely independent. In that same vein, there is no novel-writing tradition that especially governs the short story.

The idea that the short story can only be considered ideal if it is filled with entertainment is also not right. A work of art can be entertaining, and yet filled with implied meaning. So it is difficult to ascertain whether a story is artistic based simply on whether it is purpose-driven, emotion-driven, or entertainment-driven. The dexterity, humility and imagination required while presenting a story, and controlling emotions and ideas by giving free rein to and harnessing them – these require the discipline of a good horseback rider. Wherever all this exists, it can be said that an artistic creation is being designed. Various women might wear the same fine garment. But, among all of them, only one will wear it with such attitude, simplicity, decency, display and draping, that an observer might proclaim there's 'something' in her style that is unmatched. That 'something' is the essence of art and it only comes about through inspiration. Whoever can generate such inspiration within themselves will always have art and a deep, mystic wisdom within.

That a sad ending is necessary for an art form is also putting forward a half-truth or an untruth. It is not compulsory that the ending be sad, and the art of the short story does not have any compulsion to have a particular type of ending.

'A short story must be of two or three thousand words only, and must be read in one sitting' – this math has also not been proven to be accurate. First of all, the word 'sitting' can take on different manifestations from person to person. A good writer can draw in even the most efficient reader for hours on end with the pleasures of his creations, while another reader might get bored in an instant. So many of Chekhov's short stories have barely a thousand words, while Meredith's story, 'The Tale of Chloe', has about nine chapters and is still considered a short story. Balzac, Turgenev, Maupassant and Arnold Bennett blossom properly only in entertainment-driven stories. In Maupassant's most beautiful creation, 'Boule de Suif', it seems as if the only point of the story is entertainment. In contrast, Tolstoy always has some key purpose. Encompassing deep wisdom within even a short story has made Anatole France an incomparably superior artist. While, in Tagore's art, the design of the implied meaning appears in a beautiful manner. Actually, every creation of genuine art has its own traditions. New traditions will continue to be established from whatever works inspiration-driven, ever-evolving artists create. Creativity and life rely more on one's environment than traditions – this truth will also continue to be universally applicable to the art of the short story.

The short story is that which, like a flash of lightning, pierces right through while establishing a viewpoint; without any other machinations, simply gestures with a finger to awaken dormant emotions; creates an entirely new imaginary world around the reader. The novel says whatever it wants. The short story, by rousing the imagination and emotions, only alludes to or provides a spark of whatever it wants to say. This is why the writer of the short story needs a reader who is impressible, emotional, swift and intelligent; to such a reader, he will be forever in debt.

This is not the place to further debate the structure of the short story, so these simple ideas are enough.

Temperament is not judgement. The unreasoned expression of a personal like or dislike is not analytical criticism.

From the Introduction to *Tankha I*, Second Edition

Whoever has had the opportunity to get acquainted with our society will have seen that there are heaps of short stories everywhere. Anywhere, at any time, by familiarising ourselves with our community, we are able to learn a lot of new things. Not only that, a new insight and a new world come into being. Within this beautiful world, the numerous root causes of the joys, sorrows, beliefs, ignorance, innocence, and damaging traditions of the lives of the masses are so clearly evident that, from them, the new clarity and insight one gains can play an important role in new creations.

A friend had once said that, when there is a most beautiful crop of short stories, it should be understood that there is a transformation in the lives of the masses. This principle can apply as much to any work of literature as to the short story. Despite that, it can be said without any exaggeration that the straightforward, simple, on-point, small body of a short story can contain much more essential vitality than the proportions of its size.

The Post Office

The hazy dawn sky was glittering with the previous night's stars – big and small – like happy memories shimmering in a person's life. Wrapping his old, tattered shirt tighter around his body to protect against the blasting wind, an old man was making his way through the centre of the city. At this time, the unrestrained, rhythmic sounds of mills grinding, along with the delicate voices of women, could be heard from many homes. The odd dog's bark, some early riser's footsteps heard from a distance, or some prematurely awakened bird's tone – except for these, the city was entirely silent. People were snoring in sweet slumber and the night was more dense thanks to the cold of winter. Bearing the pleasing temperament of a man who can kill without uttering a word, the cold was spreading its tentacles all over, like a deadly weapon. Shivering and tottering quietly, the old man exited the city's gates to reach a straight path and, very slowly, continued walking with the support of his old cane.

On one side of the street was a row of trees, while the city gardens stood on the other. Here, it was more chilly and the night was more velvety. The wind pierced right through and the fine brilliance of the morning star, Venus, fell on earth like an icy flake of falling snow. At the very end, near the edge of the gardens, there was a beautiful building. And lamplight was spilling from its closed windows and door.

As a devout person experiences a reverential joy on catching a glimpse of his pilgrimage destination, so did this old man feel happy upon spotting the wooden arch of the building. The arch had the words 'Post Office' painted on an ancient signboard.

The old man sat outside, on the verandah. There was no discernible sound from inside but he could hear some indistinct whispering, as if some people were busy at work.

'Police superintendent!' a voice called from inside. The old man startled, but sat back down quietly again. Faith and affection were, in such cold weather, giving him warmth.

The noises inside began to rise in intensity. The clerk was reading out the English names on letters and tossing them towards the postman. Commissioner, superintendent, diwan saheb, librarian – calling out such names one after the other in a practised manner, the clerk was flinging the letters rapidly.

During that time, a playful voice called from inside: 'Old coachman Ali!'

The old man sat up where he was, looked up at the sky fervently, moved forward, and placed a hand on the door.

'Gokalbhai!'

'Who is it?'

'You said old Coachman Ali's letter, right? I'm here!'

In response, there was merciless laughter.

'Saheb! This is a crazy old man. Does a futile round of the post office to collect his letter every day.'

As the clerk said this to the postmaster, the old man sat back in his place. Over the past five years, he'd developed a habit of sitting in that spot.

Ali had been a skilled hunter. And, gradually, he had become so proficient that, like the addict needs opium, Ali needed to hunt. As soon as his eye spotted the colourful partridge, which could somehow still blend like dust within dust, it would be within his hands! His sharp scrutiny could reach into a rabbit's warren. Sometimes even the hunting dogs couldn't separate the dirty grey colouring of a clever rabbit sitting hidden with cocked ears in the nearby dry, yellow wild sugarcane or thatching grasses. The dogs would carry on forward and the rabbit would be saved. But Ali's sight, like that of an Italian eagle, would land precisely on the rabbit's ears and, in the next moment, it would be no more.

Then, sometimes, Ali would team up with the fisherman to hunt in the water.

But when the twilight of life seemed to be approaching, the hunter abruptly turned in another direction. His only daughter, Mariam, got married and left for her in-laws' home. Her husband worked in the army, so she went to Punjab with him. From that Mariam — for whom he had been holding on to life — there had been no news for the past five years. Now Ali had learnt what affection and separation meant.

Earlier, one of the pleasures of the hunt was the baby partridges running around in bewilderment once he had shot and killed the parent. The delight of hunting had permeated every nerve. But, since the day Mariam left and loneliness engulfed him, Ali had forgotten the hunt and begun staring steadfastly at the brilliant green fields teeming with grain. And, for the first time in life, he understood that a universe of love and tears of separation, both exist in nature.

One day, Ali sat under a palash tree and cried his heart out. From that time on, he would awake at 4:00 AM every morning to arrive at the post office. There was never a letter for him but, with fervent devotion and hope-filled cheer that his daughter's letter would arrive one day, he always showed up before anyone else and sat waiting outside the post office.

The post office – perhaps the most uninteresting building in the world – became his holy land and place of pilgrimage. He always sat in the same spot, in the same corner. Seeing him, everyone would laugh. The postmen would make jokes and sometimes, in jest, call out his name even though there was no letter, making him come running to the door of the post office in vain. As if possessing an endless faith and resolve, he came every day and returned empty-handed.

While he sat, peons came one after another to pick up their office documents. Mostly, these twentieth-century peons were like the secret confidantes of their officers' wives. So the private history of every officer in the entire city was recited now.

Someone sported a turban. Another one had sparkling boots on his feet. In this manner, each one displayed his unique status. Just then, the door opened and, in the lamplight, the postmaster sat in the front-facing chair with his pumpkin-like head and displeasure-filled, unsympathetic face. With no radiance on the forehead or face or eyes, the clerk and postmaster of this century are rather like Goldsmith's village schoolmaster.

Ali did not shift from his spot.

'Police commissioner!' the clerk boomed and a young man reached his hand out impatiently for the police commissioner's letters.

'Superintendent!'

Another peon came forward.

And, in this manner, the clerk always read out the entire list of names like a Vishnu devotee.

Eventually, they all left. Ali got up. As if there had been some miracle in the post office, he offered his salutations to them and left. Arrey! Like some bumpkin from ancient times!

'Is this man crazy?' the postmaster asked.

'Yes, who? Ali, na? Yes, saheb. Five years have passed and, no matter the weather, he comes to collect a letter. It's very rare for him to receive a letter,' the clerk replied.

'Who's got that much free time? How can there be a letter every time?'

'Arrey, saheb! But his mind has slipped away. Before this, he committed many sins. And then he did some wrong somewhere. Bhai, one must suffer for one's actions.' The postman offered support.

'The crazy ones are very strange.'

'Yes, I had once seen a madman in Ahmedabad. He made piles of dirt all day. Bas, nothing else. Another one had a habit of going to the riverbank every evening and pouring water on a stone.'

'Arrey, I know of one who walked back and forth all day. Another kept singing a poem. Yet another kept slapping his own cheek. And then, believing that someone else was hitting him, he would keep crying.'

Today, a mythology about the mad people had come forth in

the post office. Giving examples like these and talking about them for a few minutes at leisure has become an established habit for pretty much every working person – much like an alcohol habit.

Finally, the postmaster got up and, while leaving, commented, laughing: 'Gosh, the mad folks also have their own world. The crazy must consider us crazy and their universe must seem like a poet's universe.'

One of the clerks would, when time allowed, enact some behaviours of madmen. Speaking these last words in the direction of the clerk who often caricatured the actions of madmen, the postmaster went away laughing. The post office became as quiet as before.

Once, Ali did not show up for two or three days. There was no one in the post office with the empathy or perceptiveness to understand Ali's state of mind. But everyone was curious as to why he had not come. Then, the day that Ali came, he was panting and there were clear signs of the end of life on his face.

That day, Ali became impatient and asked the postmaster, 'Master saheb, is there a letter from my Mariam?'

The postmaster was in a hurry to go to his village and his mind was not sufficiently at ease to entertain a question.

'Bhai, what kind of a man are you?'

'My name is Ali!' Ali's irrelevant reply was received.

'Yes, but is your Mariam's name registered here?'

'Please register it, ne, bhai! In time, if a letter arrives and I am not here, you will need it.' For one who had spent three-quarters of his life hunting, what did he know about how, besides her own father, Mariam's name barely carried the worth of two paise for any other?

The postmaster got fired up. 'Are you mad or what? Go, go. If your letter arrives, no one is going to eat it up!'

The man left in a hurry and Ali went outside with slow footsteps. As he was leaving, he turned around once to look at the post office. Today, there was a glimmer of the orphan's tears in his eyes. There wasn't a lack of faith but his resolve had come to an end. Arrey! Now where will Mariam's letter come from?

A clerk seemed to be following him. Ali turned to him, 'Bhai!'

The clerk was startled. But he was a good man. 'Why?'

'See, I have this with me.' So saying, Ali removed five guineas from an old metal tin.

Seeing this, the clerk got angry.

'Don't get angry. This is a thing of use to you. I have no use for it. But will you do one thing?'

'What?'

'What do you see on top here?' Ali pointed a finger towards the empty sky.

'The sky.'

'Allah is there above and, with him as witness, I am giving you this money. If my Mariam's letter arrives, you must deliver it.'

The clerk stood still in astonishment. 'Where must it be delivered?'

'On my grave!'

'Huh?'

'I am speaking the truth. Today is the last day. Arrey re, the last! I did not meet Mariam, did not receive a letter!' There was a drowsiness in Ali's eyes. The clerk slowly moved away from Ali and walked away. There were three tolas of gold in his pockets.

After that, Ali was never seen again and no one bothered to check on him.

One day, the postmaster was grieving a bit. His daughter was ill in a faraway country and he was sitting, woebegone, in wait of news from her.

The mail came and he took hold of the pile of letters. Based on the colour, he assumed an envelope to be his and quickly picked it up. But the name on it was 'Old Coachman Ali'!

As if struck by lightning, he threw it onto the floor. Due to distress and worry, within a few moments, his authoritative demeanour had disappeared and his human side had emerged. He suddenly recalled that it must be that old man's envelope. Perhaps his daughter Mariam had finally written to him.

'Lakshmidas!' he immediately yelled out.

Lakshmidas was the same peon to whom Ali had, in the final hours, given money.

'What, saheb?'

'Your old coachman Ali … whereabouts is he these days?'

'We'll search.'

That day, there was no news of his daughter for the postmaster. He spent the entire night in doubt. The next morning at 3:00 AM, he was sitting in the office. When old Ali comes at 4:00 AM, I will give him the envelope myself – such was his plan today.

Now the postmaster understood the old man's plight. He had spent the entire night for the morning to arrive, and with it, the letter. For the first time, his heart was overflowing with emotions for the person who had spent five long years suffering such endless nights. At precisely 5:00 AM, there was a knock on the door. The postmen hadn't arrived yet. It could be Ali knocking! The postmaster got up. As if a father's heart recognised another father's, he ran today and opened the door.

'Come, Ali bhai! Here's your letter!'

In the doorway, a poor old man stood, leaning over his cane. The tracks of his last tears were still fresh on his cheeks and, over his coarse colouring, the wrinkles of his face were awash with kindness. He looked at the postmaster and the postmaster became somewhat disturbed. There was no life in the old man's eyes!

'Who, saheb? Old Ali?' so saying, Lakshmidas slid sideways and came to the door.

The postmaster did not pay any attention to him and kept looking towards the door – but it didn't seem like anyone was there. The postmaster's eyes widened. What was this, there was no one at all in the doorway! He turned towards Lakshmidas and answered the question, 'Yes, old Ali, that's who! It was him, right?'

'Ji, old Ali is dead! But let me have his letter!'

'What? When? Lakshmidas!'

'Ji, it's been three months!' A postman just entering the building gave this second response.

The postmaster was stunned. Mariam's letter was still in the doorway. The image of Ali was floating before his eyes. Lakshmidas also told him how he'd last met Ali. That knock rang in the postmaster's ears and Ali's image remained before his eyes. A doubt rose in his mind: 'Did I see Ali or did I simply imagine it or was it Lakshmidas?'

Again, the daily routine continued: 'Police commissioner, superintendent, librarian…' the clerk threw the letters in rapid succession.

But, as if there was a beating heart within each letter, the postmaster was staring steadily in their direction today. An envelope means one anna and a postcard, two anna – that awareness had disappeared. What does a widow's only son's letter all the way from Africa mean? The postmaster sank deeper and deeper.

If a man could put aside his own perceptions and look through another's viewpoint, then at least half the world would be at rest.

That evening, Lakshmidas and the postmaster walked with slow steps towards Ali's grave. They had Mariam's letter with them. Placing the precious mail on the grave, the postmaster and Lakshmidas turned back.

'Lakshmidas, this morning, you were the first to arrive, right?'
'Ji, yes.'
'And you said that old Ali…'
'Ji.'
'But then … then … I don't understand…'
'What?'
'Yes, all right. It's nothing!' The postmaster quickly changed the subject. On reaching the threshold of the post office, the postmaster separated from Lakshmidas and went inside, pondering. It was stinging him that he had not understood Ali's heart as a father himself. And, having received no news of his daughter yet

again today, he was going to spend another night worrying about getting news of her. Set aflame by the three kinds of fires of surprise, doubt and repentance, he sat in his living room. And a sweet warmth began to radiate from the nearby coal stove.

Tears of the Soul

There was considerable chaos in Vaishali's town hall[1] today. Many elderly statesmen had sat themselves on the clean marble steps of the town hall. Many were in the open field, holding their chariot reins, listening to the uproar inside. Holding massive spears in their hands, many young men were strolling about as they liked. There was disorder in the assembly. It was as if no one was listening to anyone. Everyone talked however they liked.

Just then, a chariot was seen coming from the bazaar ahead. Craning their necks with eagerness and curiosity to know who was coming, everyone began to get impatient. In a short while, the chariot came close.

'It is Mahaanman,' one youth yelled out. Hearing that, many young men left the steps of the town hall for the field and stood right in the path of Mahaanman's chariot.

'It looks like Mahaanman has arrived alone!' 'So? Then Amrapali has not come?' all the young men babbled together.

---

1. Vaishali had a republican democracy. So this town hall also functioned as a court.

One of them stamped his foot in anger and thrust his spear into the ground.

'So then she intends to disobey royalty and the law?'

They stepped aside a little to give way to a beautiful rider. From another direction, a couple of horsemen arrived. They were dressed as hunters. Dogs with smooth, glossy and shiny coats were running to and fro around their horses. In the meantime, Mahaanman got down from his chariot, climbed the smooth marble steps and stood in the royal temple.

As if a magic wand had been waved, the excited crowd became completely quiet. Everyone was curious to hear what Mahaanman had to say.

'Noble folks! My adopted daughter, Amrapali...' his voice faltered a bit. He cleared his throat and went on: 'Amrapali, whom you have disallowed marriage per the Lichhavi clan laws,[2] and whom I have kept unmarried so that the Lichhavis do not slice each other dead amongst themselves...'

People got impatient to hear the end.

'... there has been no trace of her for eight days!'

'Treason! An insult of the Assembly! Utterly false talk!' many shouted.

---

2. In Vaishali, the republican state had a rule that any extremely beautiful woman should remain unmarried to 'entertain' the men of the city. A rich man named Mahaanman had a daughter named Amrapali. Due to her beauty, if she married anyone, the youth of Vaishali would compete amongst themselves and get sliced to death. Sinh Nayak, who was like the 'president' of the administrative General Assembly, had understood the problem and tried to resolve it.

Mahaanman, as if he could not hear the murmurs and the shouts, continued speaking. 'No trace … and, though there was no trace, today she herself has suddenly arrived!'

People heaved a breath of relief. Many called with joy: 'And now…'

Just then, there was a hubbub in the middle of the field. A majestic horseback-rider could be seen cutting a path through the crowd. Folding both hands, citizens in all four directions were greeting him.

'But there, the Nayak is arriving. He will tell you everything.'

People looked towards the open field with curiosity. The rider had descended from the horse and placed a foot on the steps of the royal temple. Settling his horse beside a sentry, he moved forward.

'Jai Vaishali! Jai Lichhavi Clan! Jai Sinh Nayak!' Triumphant cries rose immediately from the crowd.

Laughing softly, keeping his hands folded before the masses, he continued climbing the steps with a careful agility. When he entered the royal temple, the lords stood and paid their respects. He went and sat beside Mahaanman. If anyone had dropped even a pebble, it would have been heard, such was the deep silence among the congregation. The people were now restless to hear what Sinh Nayak would say.

Sinh Nayak stood. He threw a fleeting glance at the people.

It seemed as if, confronted by the majesty of this man, the entire crowd had grown smaller. Softly, but in a clear voice, he began speaking: 'Noble people! I have come to you only after Amrapali agreed to come here from Neelpadmabhavan. If the

General Assembly strongly desires to abide by Vaishali's law to the letter, they will have to accept whatever stipulations Amrapali puts forward.'

'That's all right! That's all right! What are the stipulations, tell us.'

'Amrapali says that her house will be considered a secure fort; no one will be allowed inside it without permission. Her main work will be to please the masses with music.'

'That stipulation is all right,' many said. The statesmen, noblemen and people's representatives sitting in the royal temple said only 'that is fine', and signalled the Nayak to inform them of the other stipulations.

'The General Assembly will have to give her a beautiful palace to live in Pushpavihaar – a Saptabhumika[3] palace.'

Many among the General Assembly glanced at each other.

'The third condition is that there will be no searching or checking of who's coming and who's exiting from Amrapali's home.'

With this, the General Assembly began to hum with voices. The faces of several elderly statesmen turned red, like heated copper plates, with anger. Many navkotinarayans[4] knitted their brows. One of the princes[5] of the state sat up erect and said

---

3. Saptabhumika: Pertains to ancient Indian architecture and involves a complex, ornately designed system of spire-like and podium-like structures. It was found only in royal palaces and important temples.
4. Navkotinarayan: The word is used to denote 'crorepati' or the owner of a crore of rupees. The literal meaning is 'owner of nine crores.'
5. Eighteen such kings/princes were also in the General Assembly.

out loud, 'That would be an insult of the General Assembly's authority.'

But, before all those displays of consternation could play out fully, everyone's eyes turned and fixated on the steps of the royal temple. Wrapped in clothes as white as moonlight, a woman's person could be seen there. There was a huge uproar brewing in the field and people were pushing and shoving to come forward. Many young men were clearing their path by threatening people with their spears.

The woman entered the town hall. In a short while, a silence spread all over again. She gathered up the ends of her fine, silky garments and looked at the General Assembly in a manner of issuing orders. Her small nose was flaring with pride and her brows were raised with anger and disdain. Many were rankled by this look and the insult to the republic's authority contained within it. But her charming beauty, like a poison-filled arrow, pierced their hearts.

'Noblemen! And Brahmins!' There was clear scorn in her words. 'The evil law that you are preserving in Vaishali…'

'Evil! An insult of the law!' said someone in the assembly.

'Yes,' she emphasised, 'that evil law you are preserving, I accept it. If you agree to my stipulations. Otherwise, I will say no to being subjected to the authority of the General Assembly. God has given me beauty so that I do not have to submit to any earthly authority.'

She stood, her body tall and her head held high while she adjusted the string of pearls that adorned her head.

A storm cloud seemed to gather. Amrapali's words sent a bolt of lightning through the General Assembly. The rule that visitors to Amrapali's house couldn't be inspected rankled many.

A murmur could be heard in the assembly.

'That means, simply, that any enemy can come and stay safe and sound at her place.'

'That rule absolutely cannot be accepted.'

'It's as if she herself is the leader of the General Assembly!'

She saw the situation was tempestuous. 'You make the decision,' saying this, Amrapali walked away. Her father, Mahaanman, left the assembly after her.

In the end, everyone responded in one voice to Sinh Nayak: 'The republic will not accept such a condition. And Mahaanman will have to accept the rule of the republic.'

Lines of worry began forming on Sinh Nayak's forehead. He ran his hand over his forehead briefly, improved his voice by clearing his throat, and said to the assembly: 'Noblemen! Around Vaishali are many kingdoms standing ready to devour her. To make enemies of such Shatkotiyadhipati[6] as are in this assembly is against our philosophy of civil governance.'

'Lichhavi youth have also gone to Takshashila and studied archery,[7] many young members retorted, 'and we are ready to successfully resist an attack from any kingdom!'

Nayak laughed softly – a dismissive laughter that embarrassed the speakers.

---

6. Shatkotiyadhipati: A 'crorepati' a hundred times over. The literal meaning is 'owner of one hundred crores.'

7. This is not an exaggeration. An 80-crore nobleman had a son who studied at the second-ranked Kashi Mahavidyalaya in Takshashila and gave this account. See 'Vishwabharati' (1-3) by Professor Radhakumud. [Note: This is Dhumketu's own footnote, not the translator's.]

'The fame of your archery skills reaches far and wide, and a time will come when a head will be demanded by every young Lichhavi in exchange for freedom. But a state weakened by civil war is like rotten fruit – it will destroy itself. Stay safe from civil war.'

Many elderly and wise assembly members fell into thought.

'How to be safe? For Amrapali…'

'There is one solution. Without giving Amrapali advance notice of eight days, her home cannot be searched – will the assembly agree to such a condition?' Sinh said.

'With that, Vaishali will be destroyed,' many said.

'That destruction will not be more horrible than a civil war in Vaishali.'

'Does Amrapali accept that condition?'

'I will see to that. But does the assembly agree to it?'

'Yes, yes,' so saying, the General Assembly rose.

Below, many young people were eager to know the outcome. They gathered in a large crowd by Sinh Nayak's horse. As soon as Sinh came, the masses encircled him, chanting, 'Jai Vaishali!'

'What was said? What does Mahaanman say?' enquired one man.

'That you have heard,' responded another.

'Tomorrow, with the Sannipaatbheri,[8] everyone will be informed.' Saying this, Sinh Nayak climbed his horse in haste

---

8. Sannipaatbheri: The drum-like instrument played to gather a crowd of people. Here, the reference is likely to the daily ritual of gathering a crowd using this instrument to share important news and announcements from the government.

and, as evening was about to descend, galloped to wander amongst Vaishali's battalions. Gazing at the gem-inlaid windows of the many majestic houses along the way, he reached Vaishali's vast battlefield. Thousands of horseback-riders and chariot warriors were, per the rules and regulations, studying archery there. Foreigners, merchants and princes from far-away places were standing and observing the Lichhavi youth in wonder. In one area, chariot warriors had busied themselves in a competition. With purple, silky reins, charioteers were exerting significant efforts to keep the speeding chariots under control. Sitting in chariots with horses as white as a swan's wing, many dignitaries were watching all this.

Sinh Nayak, keeping an eye on all this, moved forward. Wherever he looked, beautiful young men, as exquisite as Ashwinikumar,[9] were wandering about on horses or chariots. In all sections, valour and regulated training could be seen. Thinking of Vaishali, his chest swelled with pride and joy. 'What clout is there in Bimbisaar or Kosal or Avanti or anyone that they could hold Lichhavi's young men in subjection for even a moment?' With the force of passion, he spurred on his horse.

He arrived at the banks of the Neelpadma Lake. The colours of the twilight were spreading golden hues over the water and, partially and secretly, exulting to see the emerging moon. At the lake's edge, there was Vaishali's pleasure palace, Pushpavihaar, in

---

9. Ashwinikumar: The divine twin horsemen in the Rigveda. They were the physicians to the gods in Hindu mythology. They also symbolise the light of sunrise and sunset, appearing in the sky before dawn in a golden chariot, bringing treasures to men, and averting misfortune and sickness.

a semicircle. In the water below, the reflections of marble canopies were swaying. Here and there, melodious voices could be heard in glorious form. Adorned with rows of lights, many boats were being readied to cruise the lake. Sinh stopped there. This part of Vaishali was extremely beautiful. He cast a look towards the rest of Vaishali. With copper, silver and golden domes, the city had assumed variegated colours. After a moment's pause there, Sinh turned back. But, at this time, his countenance had fallen a bit, his enthusiasm dimmed, and his pace had slowed. Deep within his conscience, a thought had just awakened: 'So much glory and pleasure will not give birth to the element that will destroy the state, right? Would the people of Lichhavi want to trade their hard wooden pillows for soft silk?'

Pondering, he turned his horse homeward, from where he went on foot in the direction of Amrapali's home, Neelpadmabhavan.

Sinh drew closer to Neelpadmabhavan. He had seen Amrapali's obstinate nature. At the royal temple today, in the assembly, he had seen her in her true form. If the General Assembly would not let go of their opinion and if Amrapali would not accept the rule of a house inspection after an advance notice of eight days, the fire that could erupt from that spark could set Vaishali ablaze – the thought today made him tremble.

If Mahaanman decides to marry Amrapali to some youth, then thousands of young men will race their chariots to win her by engaging in war on Vaishali's battlefield and possibly even near Neelpadmabhavan. The godlike Lichhavis, twanging their bows, will fight each other face to face. To win Amrapali's hand, every young man will spill his blood, and then…? Sinh Nayak pressed his head with anxiety. After this kind of devastating civil war, any enemy could rise and ruin Vaishali. Nayak was so shaken by this thought that his vision swam and he sat on a nearby marble veran-dah. With vacant eyes, he stared towards the deep, sky-coloured Neelpadmabhavan.

Vaishali! Vaishali! As long as he has breath, Sinh will do every-thing in his power to keep your domes whole ... This resolve gave him renewed strength, and he calmed down as he came to a halt at the door of Neelpadmabhavan.

As he entered through the door, the maids, like sculpted dream statues, welcomed him. Passing through many beautiful Indrabhavan-like chambers, he arrived at Amrapali's residence. Sitting on a swing, deep in thought, Amrapali swayed it to and fro with light kicks of her feet. Seeing Sinh, she sat up and, folding her hands together in obeisance, stood. Sinh sat on a nearby seat of red sandalwood. Amrapali moved the veena to one side and sat before him on the other seat.

'Amrapali, the General Assembly has not agreed to any of your stipulations,' Sinh said after a brief pause.

Amrapali stared at him with steadiness.

'But it has accepted this much: that your house will not be inspected without giving you a notice of eight days. There should be no problem accepting that much of a stipulation,' Sinh said further.

'But I don't even accept your evil rules!' Amrapali said. 'I had put forth certain stipulations in the town hall only due to your insistence.'

Sinh ran a hand from his eyes to his forehead to absorb the insult. It rankled him that a woman should insult the General Assembly's rules, but he was accustomed to working with patience.

'Amrapali! That rule may be evil – it is. But, right now, Vaishali's future hangs on it.'

'Why don't you get rid of that rule? Does such an evil rule exist in any other place? Does it give you joy to bear women being insulted like this?'

'Such a time will come when the rule is cancelled.'

'When?'

'If you save Vaishali now, then – '

'To save Vaishali, should I live a disgraceful life?'

'For the deliverance of her people, this much self-sacrifice – of youth and reputation – I ask of you on behalf of Vaishali.'

Amrapali's tempestuousness softened completely. She felt this man was completely intertwined with Vaishali's greatness. Hearing Vaishali's name, an aspiration to become great awoke within her too.

'Nayak,' she said in a calm voice, 'for the deliverance of the people, is solely my womanhood, which is invaluable to a woman, necessary? Is there just no other way?'

'The self-sacrifice of one who wishes to be great can only be great. Vaishali's women have not hesitated to offer up their Kanhaiyya-like handsome young husbands, sons and brothers to sacrificial fires. Drinking their sweet blood, this soil has bloomed to fulfil all wishes. Today, the land is asking for an offering that has not been offered anywhere else in Bharat – of womanhood,' Sinh replied. Every word of his was filled with encouragement.

Each nerve in her body pulsing, Amrapali shouted, 'Vaishali! Vaishali! What if I gave Vaishali my life?'

'No, that will provoke a civil war. Your father will lose his daughter. There are many families on his side and they will all scorn the authority of the General Assembly. Vaishali asks for your womanhood. For the sake of the people, it is not your dead body but your living one that is required.'

Like a withering flower, Amrapali turned pale. She said in a despondent voice, 'Nayak! A holy state like Vaishali will take such an unholy sacrifice?'

'In this world, things by themselves are unchangeable, untainted. Only emotions make them holy or unholy.'

'Nayak! I am a woman. I will not give up my woman-hood,' Amrapali replied with firmness. 'Not even if the General Assembly accepts my stipulations. God has made me a woman; to remedy that is also in his hands alone!'

'So then Vaishali – which now can fight against Takshashila, Rajgriha, Kashi, and Avanti, all of them – will, in a short time, be reduced to nothing.' Nayak spoke sadly. 'Her unique republi-can democracy, Neelpadmabhavan, Pushpavihaar, all the glories – everything will slip away soon.'

'Why? How?'

'How? Do you know that, at present, the fear of Magadha weighs heavy on Vaishali? In the middle of four large kingdoms with absolute authorities, Vaishali, which is the size of two hands cupped together, has been preserving her democracy. To save all statehood, Vaishali has pushed forward with a new message. This is the message of its republican state governance. And who all are against this message? Three great kingdoms like Kosal, Vats and Magadh who have surrounded Vaishali from three directions. And the fourth, Avanti.'

'Who? Kosal too? But Prasenjit is an ally of Vaishali!'

Sinh shook his head. 'Na, baapu, na. They are all advocates of sovereign rule, which is why they have become allies. Except for Vaishali, no one else is likely to obstruct Magadh's Bimbisaar. Now, Magadh has teamed up with Kosal and Avanti for political purposes. It has taken the easternmost Angdesh to ensure a situation where a blow cannot land from the back. To move forward, Raja Bimbisaar will, sooner or later, build a fort at the confluence of the Gomti and Gandaki rivers. Then Vaishali will also tremble. And what will happen if Vaishali falls? The absolute authority of the kings will rise again. Amrapali! In another state, a king committed an outrage on a Brahmin girl. By themselves, the masses murdered the king in a filled market and declared a republican state. It is the result of the desire for a democratic order as spread by the Lichhavis. In Kapilavastu, in Raamgaam, in Keshaputtata, and in Bhag, arrangements are also being made to convene general assemblies. In opposition to Magadh, which is fond of sovereign rule, Vaishali is trumpeting the new message of a people's democracy.'

'Will Vaishali be successful in that? And what if she doesn't succeed?'

'Successful? Who knows? Magadh is extremely powerful. Our house is broken. My brother, Gopal, is Raja Bimbisaar's chief minister. If Vaishali doesn't succeed, then Kosal, Vats, and many other states that are now Magadh's allies will fall to Magadh. Magadh's ambition is to reach all the way to Avanti. So, when Vaishali falls, Magadh's royal standard will immediately start for Avanti. Right now, only Vaishali is protecting the sovereignty of several nation states!'

'Kosal will also fall?'

'Yes. All will fall. Vaishali will fall, several nations will fall, republican democracies will fall. Only Magadh's sun will burn bright – from Angdesh to Avanti!'

Amrapali stared at this noble man's vision. He wanted to save many other nations like Vaishali. He wanted to introduce the order of people's democracies in place of sovereign monarchies. He wanted to make Vaishali's glory eternal.

'Nayak!' Blinded by his grandeur, she said, 'how can this path to the well-being of the nations be kept open?'

'If you keep it open, only then. Your youth, reputation, and marital status – if you give the great offering of these three for the holy purpose.'

'Hai, Vaishali! You will take my womanhood? Then what do I have left?'

'What is left then? A body made impure for the people's welfare – but, living within it, a virtuous soul. The soul does not reside in the body but in the mind.'

It was as if an arrow had pierced Amrapali's heart. For a moment, she was quiet. Then, in firm and clear words, she said, 'Nayak! All this conjecture is terrible. But go, I offer up my youth, reputation and shot at marital bliss, all three, to Vaishali! From tomorrow, I will go and live in Pushpavihaar. To my mind, there is no man left. Whoever can keep his restraint upon seeing a woman, he is a man, and whoever trembles is an animal. Give the Lichhavi people this final message from me too: that if they want Amrapali's head for the study of eyesight and hair, then they just have to ask for it! And Nayak, also remember: since Lichhavis have become pleasure-seekers, their ruination is near!' Saying this, Amrapali, with the speed of lightning, sat up and bolted. As soon as she entered the inner chamber, the sound of her suppressed weeping could be heard.

Sinh's foot, raised to leave, pulled back. 'Devi! Vaishali will only take an offering given gladly. Amrapali! I free you from the bond. This kind of offering cannot be taken!'

Amrapali immediately came out to the doorway. Her face was hard and fierce.

'An offering given with tears cannot be accepted, Amrapali,' Sinh said in a clear voice.

'Tears?' Amrapali said. 'What tears?' She stood upright. 'Tears, Nayak! Now they are nowhere in the body. They are in the soul. And they will always fall for dear Vaishali!' Not waiting to hear Sinh's response, she rushed back inside.

Walking past golden lamps fragrant with sweet-smelling sandalwood oil, Nayak left with slow footsteps.

Many days passed. Amrapali's veena still held the inhabitants of Vaishali in thrall. From Takshashila all the way to Champa, merchants spoke about Vaishali and Amrapali. Once, the king of Magadh, Bimbisaar, got eager to meet Amrapali, and made enquiries through his chief minister, Gopal.

Amrapali said, 'Come as you wish. But leave your royal politics back there. For eight days, at least, you will be safe and secure in my home.'

Raja Bimbisaar descended at Pushpavihaar seated in a carriage drawn by oxen as beautiful and white as swans. That day, there was a festival in Vaishali. The banks of the Neelpadma Lake were resounding with raas by women, chariot competitions by young Lichhavi men, and various sorts of light-filled boats. Watching all this, and comparing Vaishali with his royal home, Bimbisaar entered the Indrabhavan-like Saptabhumika Palace where Amrapali resided.

On entering, there was a large open courtyard, around which were many chambers spread across two storeys. At the very top, golden pinnacles adorned marble canopies.

Raja Bimbisaar stood there and, immediately, lovely hand-maids arrived and stood before him with their hands folded. Bimbisaar indicated a wish to meet Amrapali. On a path sprinkled with scented water, he proceeded with the beautiful hand-maids. Beside a beautiful marble basin enamelled with meenakari bows, a handmaid was ready with perfumed water in a golden pitcher. After a massage and a bath, he walked through many chambers to the top.

'Amrapali will come here,' so saying, laughing and giggling, the handmaids went away.

The raja stood alone in the chamber, which was made entirely of marble. Pictures were hanging on the walls. The scent of incense was dispersing from a golden censer placed in a corner on a sandalwood stool. In the light of lamps burning with sandalwood oil in another corner, the gem-bright floor had the colour of a blue lotus. The floor was like a pool of clear water with many-coloured fish swimming in it.

The raja stopped in his tracks. Seeing the floor glimmer with fish swimming in it made him suspicious. 'What if there is water?' He removed his precious stone ring and threw it down. A clear, ringing sound was heard. He placed a foot forward.

Just then, laughter and then words – melodious, languid, and like the tinkling of small golden bells – could be heard: 'That is the palace sculptor's creation. It's not water, it's a composition of light. And the fish also move because of machines.'

The raja looked up. Having opened the door of the chamber before him, Amrapali stood there laughing. She was wearing a fine garment of Malabari gaaj. A petticoat of Chinese silk, translucent like water, covered half her body. A necklace made of Lanka's large, lustrous pearls hung from her neck. Girdle, diamond earrings, gem-encrusted anklets – with this ornamentation, Amrapali's beauty was incomparable. With a soft laugh, she told the raja to come forward and herself went and sat on the swing. With strings of jewels on its golden bars, the swing had been made very pretty. Raja Bimbisaar moved forward and, momentarily forgetting the enmity between Magadh and Vaishali, sat on the unique swing. It swayed and a few handmaids appeared beside them to fan a breeze. On a charming yellow brocade cushion, a bejewelled lotus and swan looked becoming. On the pillow was a string of pearls. The fragrance was spreading from a small, golden, pearl-filled censer on a sandalwood stool nearby. The light of the lamp fell on Amrapali's face, which was peaceful like a new dawn but fresh, dazzling, and filled with enchantment. One by one, the handmaids cooling them with horsehair fans that had handles carved from ivory slipped away. Like Rajni[10] is alluring when set among many stars, so Amrapali alone was becoming in that chamber.

Raja Bimbisaar went away on the eighth day.

---

10. Rajni: Vedic goddess of the night.

Six years passed after this event. In the same house, on that swing, a five-year-old boy was in deep slumber. This was the son Amrapali had with Bimbisaar.

Amrapali sat nearby on a low seat. Today, a heavy sadness had spread across her face. The light of the lamps grew dim and the dogs started barking. As if some massive shock had occurred, Amrapali pressed both her hands to her head and, with a down-cast face, remained seated. In a short while, the door opened. Amrapali looked up with indifference.

Her handmaid entered. 'Bhojal says the chariot is ready.'

Amrapali signalled with her hand for the handmaid to leave and, again, sat with a crestfallen face.

'Two ghatikas remain before nightfall,' the handmaid said as she left.

In a little while, the door opened again and a man's deep voice sounded: 'Amrapali!'

Amrapali sat upright. She shook off her anguish as if shaking off dust. Her face became hard, fierce, and resolute.

'Come, Sinh Nayak,' she said, sliding a seat in his direction.

'Is Kumar sleeping?'

'Yes, but now the chariot is ready to leave. But … are you certain that Kumar going to his father in Magadh is in Vaishali's interest? Is there simply no other way? Yesterday, you said, for the sake of Vaishali, leave Kumar. Today, I am ready to do that. But is it only for Vaishali's welfare?'

'Yes, for many reasons. His going to Magadh will create two opposing sides. This Kumar of yours will become a competitor of Raja Bimbisaar's crown prince, Ajatashatru. And if, perchance, he succeeds, he will retain an affection for Vaishali. Who knows about the future? If he does not succeed, Vaishali will gather him back into her folds.'

'Will this Kumar be able to survive the royal politics? Nayak, to give this tender child such a cup of poison with my own hands makes me shudder.'

'Have you not taken a promise from Raja Bimbisaar that he should raise his son?'

The horses joined to the chariot began to whinny. Amrapali, from extreme sorrow, did not speak for a couple of moments. 'Yes, I have taken a promise.'

'All right, then. The raja of Magadh is certainly true to his word. He is an enemy but his virtues are worthy of praise. Also, is Ajatashatru's mother – Vaidehi – not there? She is my daughter and, if nothing else, she will definitely keep Kumar safe.[11] When Bimbisaar came to your place, did you not also make that pact from the beginning with Gopal?'[12]

---

11. Dhumketu seems to be foreshadowing history here. Ajatashatru is one of the worst royal sons in ancient history. He did a lot of terrible things from childhood onwards to his parents. As an adult, he imprisoned Bimbisaar and took over Magadh. Vaidehi was more likely to be loyal to her father's charge, Kumar, than to Ajatashatru. Sinh Nayak has this confidence because he knows of Ajatashatru's ways as a child with his own parents.

12. When Gopal, the chief minister, was negotiating Bimbisaar's visit with Amrapali, she laid down stipulations about how, if she had a child with Bimbisaar, the child would always be protected no matter what happened politically between Magadh and Vaishali. Dhumketu and

Kumar turned to the other side. The light of the lamp was falling on his face. Amrapali's gaze remained there.

Sinh, as if forewarned, sat up immediately. 'Amrapali, it must now be barely one and a half ghatika to nightfall.'

Amrapali sat up. The handmaid came and began to lift Kumar. Pushing her aside with a hand, Amrapali picked Kumar up. His eyes were shut. In his sleep, he placed his head on his mother's shoulder. Tears began falling from Amrapali's eyes but she forced herself to go forward.

In the courtyard, the chariot was ready. Placing Kumar gently on a soft cushion, Amrapali sat next to him. Two handmaids climbed onto the back.

'Who is going with him?'

'Vaasvi and Mallika. I will go a little distance and turn back.'

The chariot's reins loosened, the horses became restless to move.

Suddenly, as if startled, Amrapali sat up. 'Arrey! Arrey! Nayak, what is this?'

Sinh had fallen to Amrapali's feet. He placed her silk slippers on his head. 'Amrapali, you are not a woman, you are the goddess of liberty! You are the embodiment of Vaishali! If Kumar has any difficulty, then I have made all preparations to deal with Magadh. Now leave with peace of mind.' Sinh Nayak ran a hand over the sleeping boy with affection. 'Son, may you live long to establish a republican democracy in Magadh.'

---

several other historians believed she was as smart as, if not more than, as all the political and royal men around her.

That mighty man's chest was also choked with emotion. His eyes filled up at the thought that he was sending an innocent child, who chirped happily with laughter, abroad while he slept – all the way to Magadh – alone, helpless.

'Amrapali! You will return from part-distance, right?'

'Yes, from the border.'

The chariot began moving. In the dark, its sound felt very harsh. Nayak, wiping his tears, went away alone into the dark. Vaishali's Nayak kept listening, with utter concentration, to the clap of horse-shoes that were growing faint with each step. When the sound had completely drowned, he stood there for a moment and said to himself, 'As long as Vaishali has such women, she will remain invincible!'

When the chariot reached the border, the sun was rising. Kumar's face was visible in the dim light. Amrapali took him into her lap once and, brushing his hair away, kissed his forehead, kissed it again and, to satisfy her thirsty soul, kissed him one more time. At that moment, Kumar opened his eyes from sleep. 'Ba,' saying only so much, he fell asleep again.

In a short while, the horsemen sent by Sinh arrived. 'Sinh Nayak has sent us to protect the chariot.' Saying this, they stood ready near Amrapali.

It was not wise to stay even a moment longer. She needed to leave before Kumar awoke. She climbed down and, as she was descending, she took the boy once more into her lap.

'As soon as you reach there, go straight to Gopal's place. Okay, Bhojal? And Vaasvi, Mallika! Take care of him like he is your life!' Deeming it better that she shed no tears while the hand-maids were watching, she turned her face and wiped them away.

'Gopal has been told everything ahead of time; so there is no problem. Vaasvi! Mallika! Take care of Kumar, alright?'

'Devi! We will take care of him like we do our lives!'

'And send news from time to time, alright?'

A little further, the crows began to call from the trees. Daylight was advancing.

Amrapali observed Kumar closely one more time. With a signal of the hand, she gave permission for the chariot to carry on. The handmaids folded their hands in obeisance.

The chariot began moving. Amrapali stood there and gazed at the retreating vehicle as if she was made of stone.

When the chariot could no longer be seen, nor its sound heard, Amrapali gazed at the dust it had left in its wake. When that too was gone, she turned back with intense grief. Ahead, Vaishali's temples were glinting in the morning light. Touching one of her earlobes, she stared at the temples: 'Who is more dear to me? Vaishali or Kumar?'

The terrible sorrow she had suppressed with considerable strength began to show on her face all over again. Her firm resolve melted in the heat of love.

Like a madwoman, she ran along the chariot's path. The birds were chirping; the sun's rays were bursting through. And Usha[13] had come and hidden the covers of Rajni.

'Hai! Hai! He must be asking, "Where is my ba? Where is my mother?" Oh, my flower!'

Falling on the jungle grass, she wept copiously. The jungle resounded with her distressed cries and, finally, even the tears

---

13. Usha: Vedic goddess of dawn.

were exhausted. With nothing else to do, she turned back with slow steps.

Vaishali's golden, silver and copper domes were beginning to become visible. Her own palace, desert-like without Kumar, caught her sight. With an anguished cry, she fell on the ground.

'Vaishali! Oh, Vaishali! I gave you my womanhood, gave you my motherhood. Now what do you want? Tell me, what should I offer you next?'

It was as if the jungle were speaking from all four directions: 'Your soul!'

On the Banks of the Sarayu

After the rainfall, the sky had cleared up a bit. The clouds lay scattered about and a soft moonlight was shining. It was a night to rouse the imagination.

It was nearly 9:00 PM. The lawyer, Harshvadan, reclined sideways on a swing, making it sway back and forth with light kicks of his foot. Across from him, on an armchair, sat his wife, Vijayagauri. On the floor, on a mat, his son of five or six years, Prasannvadan, was writing something with a blunt pencil in the pages of a notebook. From the street below, a horse carriage driver's harsh cries of 'Haiyo-oh-haiyo' and 'Hey, Black Cap' could be heard. On the verandah across the street, women sat talking. But the barking of the dogs drowned out their voices.

Suddenly, Harshvadan said, 'Come, come, Prasannvadan. Let me tell you a fine story.'

The boy immediately threw the blunt pencil away and, wiping his nose, stood up.

'What's the story about?' he asked as he came to sit by his father on the swing.

'See.'

From below, the house help yelled, 'Bai saheb! Where should I put the wheat flour?'

'In the cabinet.'

Harshvadan continued, 'See…'

Downstairs, the door rattled: 'Vakil saheb!'

'Who is it?' Harshvadan said and craned his neck. Two or three people had come to meet him. 'Who is it? Doctor saheb! Welcome, welcome. I was just waiting for you.'

Prasannvadan pulled his father's dhoti. 'Then what happened?'

'Prasannvadan!' Vijayagauri called as she went inside, 'I will tell you the rest.'

Prasannvadan pulled his father's hand. He wanted to hear more.

The poor father, faced with the town's various current and past affairs, did not have the time to recall a five-thousand-year-old story. He patted the child's head with affection and said, 'See … the rest, later. I'll tell you later, alright?'

'But tell me a little bit.'

'Alright then, on the banks of the Sarayu River – '

As if a terrible calamity was upon them, Prasannvadan looked in the direction of the stairs. Having climbed the stairs, Doctor Anantprasad's figure – tall, fat, shapeless, wearing an odd, wide pair of trousers and half-coat – stood in the drawing room. Behind him were two lean, stick-like men. This alliance of very fat and very thin men was the kind that could provide some amusement.

'Prasannvadan!' Vijayagauri called out.

He ran inside.

As soon as the child left the scene, the men sat to discuss

everything – from Ahmedabad's municipality to the latest vegetables becoming available – in its entirety.

Prasann ran in and leaned against his mother's back, draping
his arms around her neck. Vijayagauri was counting her bodices
and blouses.

'Hey, hey, what are you doing? Leave it be. Look, my silk bodice is getting creased.'

But Prasannvadan did not loosen his grip.

'Vijayaben, tell me, what happened to the Sarayu River, then?'

'I will tell you that tomorrow. Now go to bed. Come on.'

'Where is Sarayu River?'

'For now, go to bed. Go on.'

'Vijuben! Are there crocodiles in that river? Do steamboats
go on it? Who lives there?'

'Come on. Are you going to bed now or should I call your
father?'

Prasannvadan went to lie in his bed quietly. But his tiny mind
was caught up in the flights of his imagination. He fantasised that
a cool, sweet river, large as an ocean, was flowing. A bridge like
Ellis Bridge crossed above it. Below, in the river, a steamboat was
chugging. On the river's banks was a big city. In it, there was a
king. He had a queen. And they did not have a child … and …
and then what else did they not have?

From what existed to what did not exist – his child's heart sped
along on this theme. 'There will be no school there, no master, no
tests. Also, there will be no mathematics … and there will only be
playing about in the river! Truly, Sarayu River is so beautiful.'

He recalled that first phrase: 'On the banks of the Sarayu
River.' What was to follow?

He could not solve the puzzle and fell into a dream-filled sleep. He dreamt he was wandering alone about a riverbank ... of the Sarayu. At the edge of the river was a forest. From that forest, a lion – like the one he had seen at the circus – fixed his yellow eyes on Prasannvadan ... and he shouted out: 'Oh, Papa!'

Opening the door, Harshvadan came inside. The visitors had left. Only after all the important conversations are done is a man free to turn his attention to his most precious asset, his child.

'Prasannvadan!' Vakil saheb, having heard the boy's cry, shook him. But the boy had turned on his side and fallen back to sleep.

When the child woke up in the morning, the first question he asked was: 'Papa! On the banks of the Sarayu River...'

Harshvadan laughed with fondness. 'Arrey, silly. "On the banks of the Sarayu River" – have you been memorising that all night?'

Sipping the cup of tea in her hand, Vijayagauri said: 'The Master will come now. Have you done your sums?'

Like a flower wilting, Prasannvadan's face fell. Just then, the sound of shoes was heard from outside and the pale, middle-aged master, wearing a white khadi cap and a white shirt, entered.

Smiling, Harshvadan greeted him with a namaskaar and said, 'Be quick. See, Master saheb has arrived. What, Master saheb! Prasann must be doing good work now?'

Outside, there was the noise of a car arriving and two or three shouts of Vakil saheb's name. The Master, having opened his mouth to speak, bit his upper lip to stop himself as Harshvadan's attention was drawn elsewhere.

Prasannvadan's 'On the banks of the Sarayu River' riddle remained unfinished. He went along with the teacher to study, but his first question was about the Sarayu. 'Master saheb! What is on the banks of the Sarayu?'

'On the banks of the Sarayu? On the banks of the Sarayu is a beautiful city.'

'What is it called?'

At that moment, Vijayagauri entered: 'Master saheb, Prasann has totally forgotten his sums. Look, you ask and see.'

'Tell me, seventeen times nine?'

'Sarayu River,' Prasann blurted out but he corrected himself immediately, 'Seventeen times nine … seventeen times nine – '

Vijayagauri looked at him sternly: 'Prasannvadan!'

And, forgetting Sarayu River for a while, he battled with his sums.

Now, every evening, when Prasannvadan was let out from school, he daydreamed about Sarayu River during the walk back home. Then, one day, due to a public lecture at Premabhai Hall, the second day due to a municipality meeting, the third day due to a useful case, the fourth day since he was tired, the fifth day because Vijayagauri had to go out, for some reason or the other, Prasannvadan was left without the beautiful Ayodhya on the banks of the Sarayu. The little child fell asleep imagining, and he dreamt as he slept, but he never got to actually hear the magnificent story connected with the Sarayu.

Then came test time. During such days, test questions occupy all of one's attention. So Prasann was focused on his test and, for a while, it seemed as if he would no longer remember the Sarayu. But some names and some stories became dear to children for no apparent reason and they are never forgotten.

Once the tests were over, Prasannvadan had a severe attack

of a strong fever. In time, after the bout abated and he was feeling somewhat rested, he sat on his verandah. In that moment, the sweet morning heat seemed gold-coloured to him. The dust from the street seemed more fascinating than usual. He gazed happily at the cows roaming about the pol. Seeing the dogs frolic after each other, he sensed the sweetness of life. He observed everything with great absorption. Then he saw a trickle of water run out from the house … and, with an inconceivable quickness, he recalled Sa…r… yu River. And the joy of childhood began to flow again in his life.

After that, he began going to the pol to play. Even though he was not actually able to play, he observed closely and enjoyed watching others play and chat.

One day, he was standing at the edge of the pol while two or three boys were chatting excitedly. He stood and listened. They were all so engrossed in their discussion that, if there had been news of the entire world drowning, not one of them would have moved.

At that time, Vakil Harshvadan came walking from the other direction. He was stealthily headed home before anyone could waylay him. But then, this sentence: 'With one arrow from Arjun, Karna would be blown to dust', by one of the boys, caught his attention. The boy added to the theatricality, thundering, 'Arjun is so strong! Oh-ho-ho!'

Vakil Harshvadan saw his weak, lean, pale son standing there, looking on with a steady gaze and an intense yearning – a thirsty soul standing to catch precious drops from the holy sea of nectar.

Walking up to him, the father asked dotingly: 'Son, Prasann. What are you listening to?'

The tests, Master, and the river, these three had easily slipped Prasann's mind. Listening to such conversations was the opposite of what he was required to do for test-taking, that much he was aware of. So he trembled as he spoke: 'Oh, it's nothing, nothing; this Vinod is talking, but I'm not listening. I've still got to do my sums.'

As if someone had shot an arrow piercing his heart, Harshvadan was distraught on hearing this. But he said, lovingly, 'What was the talk about?'

'What? About? Eh, Master saheb has come.' Prasann pointed ahead at the Master coming through the pol.

Harshvadan turned to the teacher politely: 'Master saheb, will you give Prasann a holiday today?'

A ripple of happiness swept across Prasann's face.

The father took his son along by the hand. He seated Prasann beside him with tenderness. 'What story were you listening to with such interest?'

'About Arjun and Karna.'

From below, a voice called, 'Vakil saheb!'

'Who is it? Moti, just see who it is.'

The maid stuck her head out to see. Two or three people were standing outside.

'What do you want?' Moti asked.

'Tomorrow, we have a meeting, so we wanted to see about that,' came the reply.

The Vakil gestured at Moti.

'He's not at home,' Moti replied to them and went back to her work.

'You know, you were saying the other day?'

'About what?'

'That Sarayu River, and so on?'

'Yes.'

'Could you talk about that again today?'

Harshvadan let out a sigh. 'Arrey re!' He recalled a song some-one had sung in Premabhai Hall:

> You have been given to me by my god.
> You are my true treasure.
> Come and be immortal forever.

He bit his finger: 'False, false, absolutely false. No one believes that. It's just a song to be sung.'

From below, another cry came: 'Vakil saheb! Harshvadan bhai!'

'Moti, just see who it is.'

Moti glanced down: 'Doctor saheb.'

'Is he in? Is Harshvadan bhai in?' The visitor asked a second time.

Per the Vakil's indication, Moti answered: 'No, he has gone out.'

'When will he return?'

'I don't know.' Moti went back to her work again.

'Yes, Prasann. I will tell you that story today. So listen. On the banks of the Sarayu River – '

'Vakil saheb!' a voice called from downstairs.

'Moti, shut that door,' Harshvadan said. 'And tell anyone who comes that I am not at home today.'

Moti followed his orders and, staring at the father and son with wonder, went on slowly with her work.

'Don't you want to go today?' So saying, Vijayagauri came out. 'Why are you sitting? Do you not want to go?'

'Where?'

'Where, what? Have you forgotten? Today, it's your turn to be the chairman of the caste-community meeting, no?'

'Arrey! Yes, yes, I remember. Prasann! On the banks of the Sarayu River,' Harshvadan said, as he stood and took his turban from the wall-peg.

'On the banks of the Sarayu River, there was a beautiful city called Ayodhya. Dharmatma Dashrath Raja ruled there. The king had three queens.'

'You will be late, see.'

'Yes, I'm leaving.'

'Then what? Then what?'

Harshvadan started down the stairs: 'The king had three queens. But not one of them had a child.'

'Ah ha … Then?'

'Vakil saheb! Eh, Harshvadan bhai, are you coming?' From below, some caste-brother called as he walked on by.

'Coming, coming, Navnidhrai! Coming. Then, the king held a sacrificial rite.' Harshvadan descended the first step. 'Will you tell him the rest of the story?'

'No, I have a women's association lecture tomorrow. But I will tell you the story later, alright, Prasann?' Vijayagauri responded.

Teary-eyed, Prasann looked on.

Slowly, Harshvadan went down. In the square, the sound of his shoes was drowned out by the song of the wandering women who were singing:

> You have been given to me by my god.
> You are my true treasure.

Kailas

[1]

Have you ever been alone on an evening at the edge of a river by a village and turned to look? Its small stretch, like an old solitary wayfarer, is filled with melancholic charm: the birds have turned back, the dust raised by cattle has settled down, the evening's westbound sun has cast its last rays and gone. And this emptiness by the riverbank is also like the desolation woven into the life of a certain old man.

No one knows where he came from. No one knows what he used to do either. The secrets of his life are unknown too. There is only this dim, hazy memory of when Manohar once had a debate with Sunderji Sheth about how, with a constant motion of his fingers – and if the fingers stopped moving, it would be considered defeat – he could gobble up two and a half ser of penda. This old man had been sitting there and, on hearing such talk, had burst out laughing. The people there, who had never in their lives seen him so much as smile gently, had been amazed to see him laugh so much.

Ramgar Bawa, who sits at the crossroads, had said once that Kailas maharaj never laughs; the only time he did, a disease had erupted across the entire village. But Ramgar Bawa was somewhat jealous of Kailas, so no one had paid heed to his insinuations. Though, after maharaj left, when Punjiyo Bhangi had said he had seen maharaj picking through the bones of the dead at the Mahakhandi three days earlier, everyone had turned grave for a while.

Manohar completed his bet by eating the two and a half ser of penda. Once done, belching comfortably, he set off on a stroll around the village, boasting as if he had scored some great victory. This was not Manohar's first win. During Holi, only Manohar could leap the breadth of the entire riverbank with a single leap. Once, he polished off two-and-a-half ser of dates along with their seeds. He could break a sugarcane stalk into four pieces with just one blow. He could crack open a coconut still in its shell with one fist. During the rainy season, crossing the Kalwa River was not a job for any black-haired man and, yet, Manohar once succeeded even in this. This youth was joyful, ever-smiling, sportive, dutiful, and accomplished in many small things: sometimes, you could even catch him intensely debating matters of religion.

Every morning, when Manohar went to the river for a bath, he would stop by maharaj's hut for a visit.

Kailas had built a small hut by the side of the river, a shelter made from a few large stone slabs. On all four sides, he had planted white and yellow oleander to protect the pathway. Along the inner path, he had created a display of various interesting flora, like bili trees, beds of holy basil, rose shrubs, gulbas flowers, datura, etc. But right in front of his hut, he had planted a single shrub of red oleander. A part of his eccentricity was that he would often sit and stare at that shrub in silence. On the odd occasion, he would remark, 'That jasmine smells nice, those roses are lovely too, but oleander is oleander.'

But such talk from maharaj was dismissed with amusement. Except for Manohar, no one could even imagine that maharaj's love for the plant had been born from the seed of severe grief.

[2]

One morning, per his usual habit, Manohar came to visit Kailas and gave him the news about the stormy happenings that had the entire village trembling and shaking. In the nearby villages, lathi charges had been underway. In some places, even unweaned infants had fallen in the fights.

Usually taking great interest in such discussions, today, Kailas did not ask Manohar for more information.

Manohar began to tell him without being asked: 'Maharaj, they burned fifteen large stacks of unthreshed grain. What will the cattle eat now? There will be nothing left to gain from this land now. Maharaj, an old woman gave a stinging comeback: how will anything grow on blood-soaked land? Even a cactus stalk would be ashamed to grow on it.'

'Have all those villagers left?'

'Haan ji. They have all left. In one village, even the dogs and donkeys have gone elsewhere.'

'Is that so?'

'Ji haan. And that youth who left for the war, he sacrificed his body for the country.'

'Alright. Har Bhola, Har Bhola. Manohar, what other news do you have?'

'Maharaj, that youth who was fasting in prison – that Punjabi youth – he has also died.'

'Is that so?'

'Yes, maharaj.'

'Alright. Har Bhola, Har Bhola. Rudra has begun his dance of terror. Kalika is asking for an offer of sacrifice. He who gives blood will now attain immortality.' Kailas, who had been subdued so far, now spoke with some enthusiasm. When Manohar took his leave, he said with his usual calmness, 'Manohar, this evening, my food and drink account with this land will end. So, if you could stop by this way in the evening, that would be good.'

Manohar stared. Kailas had spoken like this many times before, but his voice today was peculiar. He had spoken from some visceral, vital part of himself.

[3]

That evening, when Manohar went to visit Kailas, he saw the place in entirely different hues: the hut was illuminated with several ghee-filled lamps; coconuts, sugar and baskets of flowers were lying close at hand. The red tilak – with a few grains of rice interspersed in it – on Kailas' forehead shone like pure blood; a garland of red oleander flowers bloomed about his neck; like a peaceful and quiet sadhu, like an embodiment of sacrifice, Kailas sat firm and resolute.

'Maharaj, that youth – Punjab wallah – the one who died … there is a beautiful portrait of him in this paper.'

'Is there a portrait?'

'Haan, maharaj. A portrait. Look, what a beautiful youth.'
Manohar began to open the paper.

'Leave it, leave it be. Don't show me, don't show me,' said
Kailas, rising.

'Why? Why?'

'Sit. Sit,' Kailas said to Manohar, 'I have a true, beautiful portrait of that youth in my heart – sit, sit. Listen.' He kept looking at Manohar.

Manohar did not understand. But Kailas's changed expression was heart-rending.

Kailas did not speak for a moment. Then, softly, he said,
'Manohar, I look like a gangster, don't I?'

Manohar shook his head.

'I look like a sadhu but I am worse than a gangster.'

'Maharaj!'

'Understand, understand … wait, wait, Manohar. Hear me
out. I had a firm belief in the ethics of violence…'

Suddenly, Kailas placed a hand on Manohar's shoulder. 'Son,
like you … my young son is about your age.'

Manohar kept staring at him. 'Maharaj, you? A sadhu – '

Kailas continued to speak. 'Son, I … I am no sadhu. I have
made bombs, successfully thrown them and caused immeasurable damage. But when an entire population is weaponless, it is
like playing with fireworks, and each player leaves behind many
dead. To ensure the safety and security of my family, to prevent
my deeds from affecting them, I had run away and come here.'

Holding his breath, Manohar listened to him with
consternation.

'I am not a sadhu, nor a sanyasi; I am a worldly man. I have a wife and children – they must be waiting for me. The boys must always be biding time hoping that, tonight, their father will return home.' Kailas' voice trembled slightly. He wiped away an unseen tear. 'But since the day I left home, I have not turned back to look at even its threshold. Today is exactly twelve years since that day. But, just as a leech latches on to you suddenly and sucks up your blood without you even realising it, there is no knowing when the CID will catch hold of me and suck me up. The last sweet memory of my home is still fresh in my mind.'

A small village by a small river and this matter of great significance. It was as if the night had become doubly sombre and more deathly quiet.

'There's our village. At the edge of the village, there are trees of sweet jamun. A beautiful, calm river flows by – as if a pure stream of Gangaji. Our soil is dark as an unclouded night. In my youth, I have sown wheat in it, planted jowar and bajri in it. But this system is no longer one that allows a farmer to be contented or a labourer to eat his bread. The small village moneylender is sucking him dry. Debt, bribery of petty officials, courts of big officials, and, to make matters worse, the lawyers – the injustices become long-standing traditions, but justice is not given. If it is given, it comes after five to fifteen years, when it has no value. So many young men of our village got tired and joined the bomb-makers. I joined them too – and then large-scale arrests, killings and hangings occurred. I ran away. I have a sweet memory of the night I ran away…'

Kailas paused for a few moments. His voice, burdened with sorrow, became slower. 'My oldest son – about eleven to twelve years old – had come to see me off. We were standing by the riverbank. Moonlight gleamed above us. I looked at his dear, mournful, tender face from time to time and absorbed it deep inside of me. He remained standing there while I alighted on this shore.'

Manohar was unable to control his own tears.

Kailas, sitting before him, continued in a shaking voice: 'That beloved, lovely, fair face … fair face … like that of a happily smiling, beautiful Radha … like that of the flute-playing Kanhaiyya … It still shimmers deep inside me.' As if the words 'fair face' were a visible image before him, Kailas kept repeating them: 'Fair face!'

Kailas turned a vacant gaze towards the oleander bushes. Manohar shivered. As if some age-old, churning inner torment now stood upright, the shrubs too stood still, solicitously, not letting a single leaf stir.

Kailas kept his eyes fixed in their direction and continued speaking: 'And today, that young man behind bars who quietly offered up his life, whose wordless sacrifice has shaken me to my very core – that youth is like my own Kanhaiyyo, standing before me again as he was at twelve years old! Look, Manohar, it is as if that same river, those same trees and bushes, that same night, and that same beloved face is before us … Manohar!'

Pressing both hands to his eyes, Manohar bent his head low. He did not have the strength to look at Kailas.

'Manohar! Look! That river, those shrubs, that night, and my dear flute-playing Kanhaiyyo…' Kailas raved madly. 'Ahaha! That sweet, alluring, beloved, woeful face is still etched inside of me!'

Who could look? Manohar's suppressed sobs became audible.

'And that image buried within me – that beautiful image must not disappear from my memory, which is why I had refused to see that youth's portrait earlier. But – see…'

Manohar looked up. Kailas' face now showed only faint traces of the previous moment's fathomless anguish. In an instant, he had changed so completely that the figure now sitting before him was steady, luminous, determined, and like an unflappable gambler playing with his life clenched in his fist. The garland of red oleander flowers around Kailas' neck seemed like a phantasm of sacrifice.

'Today, I will return to my home. A desire has awakened in me to meet everyone – greet them Ram-Ram, to wish them well – and throw myself anew into the war. What path this desire will take me on, god only knows.'

Kailas stood. He took hold of Manohar's hand. 'Come, brother, see me off part of the way and then you can return.'

One last time, Kailas took a turn about the small path. The trees were bent low as if in mute mourning. A solemn quiet had spread all over. Both men went out. After they had gone a little distance, Kailas stopped Manohar and hugged him. Manohar, speechless, touched his feet. The tears still flowed from his eyes. Kailas raised his foot to go on. Manohar watched with a steady gaze till all he could see was Kailas' faint shadow. Perhaps that Kanhaiyya-like boy had, on a lonely night just like this, observed this solitary traveller. Manohar's soul swooned deep inside. It felt as if, rather than Kailas, it was his own father leaving alone to meet death ... alone.

[4]

At dawn the next day, it was discovered that two people had gone missing from the village – Kailas and Manohar.

The Queen of Nepal

A tender dawn was blooming. It had rained the previous night.
The hills looked cleansed and the greenery had a particular
freshness. Clouds lay like heaps of cotton in the valleys between
those hills and their long rows filled those valleys as if a flowing
river had stopped and frozen there. Several stray clouds rested
in the laps of the hills, like children in a comfortable, deep sleep.

At that time, about six miles from Darjeeling, the small forest of Badamtam had awakened. Along the footpaths from all
directions, their dungri and umbrellas swaying, dressed in bril-
liant-hued velvet costumes, Nepali, Lepcha and Bhutanese
women emerged to walk towards Darjeeling's main road. Among
the lush green tea plantations, their colourful clothes created an
extraordinary pattern.

As it was the day for Darjeeling's Sunday bazaar, the women
had left their homes clad in their finest. Gopi had also departed
Badamtam wearing her newest purple velvet bodice, odhni, and
above her black skirt, a green scarf wrapped around her waist.
With kalli around her ankles, kantha around her neck, her
favourite mudri and chuchi adorning her nose, and the dungri

and umbrella in hand, she walked with a leisurely gait. At some
point, from a secluded lane by the road, Dalbahadur joined her
and, chatting, they reached Darjeeling together.

Near Badamtam, Dalbahadur had his own field. With the
corn grown on it, he managed to support his family and two bullocks, which were of vital importance. He also planted cabbage,
carrots, chillies, etc. To sell these in the Sunday bazaar, he took a
regular weekly trip to Darjeeling. Today too, he was headed there
for the same reason.

Gopi went to the tea plantations near Badamtam every day,
bringing back ten paise. Her husband earned fourteen paise.
Having collected six anna each day, over the rest of the six days,
Gopi would go to Darjeeling on Sunday, the seventh day, to buy
corn, rice, potatoes and other sundries. And just so, week by week,
she had got into the habit of seeing her life's years go by.

Today, Dalbahadur and Gopi were walking together. Despite
being neighbours, they were separated by a thousand-foot-high
hill and a valley just as deep. So, while they knew of each other,
they were not on familiar terms. Dalbahadur was quite a fun-
loving youth and Gopi was a rather lively woman; these similar-
ities of character were immediately apparent as they went along.
So, enjoying the sweet breeze, they continued forward together
to Darjeeling.

The first week, they got acquainted with each other. By the
second Sunday, Dalbahadur was teasing Gopi warmly as he
accompanied her, while Gopi gave witty replies to his jokes as
she went along.

In both homes, an unrest was spreading: Gopi was speaking to
her husband, Nobhu, with a heated temper and Dalbahadur was

behaving carelessly towards his young wife, Parvati. As Sunday after Sunday went by, the peace within their homes was being destroyed more and more.

On the sixth or seventh Sunday, Dalbahadur went with Gopi to the tea-house to drink tea. Both ate paan and reddened their mouths. And, with an entire day's wages, Dalbahadur sat in Marwadi Raimal's shop to buy a piece of vibrant purple velvet. At 4:00 PM, when they headed back to Badamtam, both had the intoxicated look of passion in their eyes.

In both homes, the discord was growing. At every step, there was sharp acridity to be seen. Parvati suspected that Dalbahadur returned every Sunday with his mouth stinking of alcohol. And, even before the next Sunday arrived, his mouth would reek again, two to four times. While letting the bullocks graze on the hill, he would gaze steadily at the hut on the opposite hill. Sometimes, late in the evening, when the green bloom of the trees turned the colour of the evening sky, he would take a hidden path to climb that other hill. Parvati was noticing these early signs of marital breakup, but that woman was true-hearted and suffered all of Dalbahadur's negligence while always preserving the sweetness of life within their home.

[2]

The next weekend was terrible.

Gopi's face had an astonishing brightness. She had covered her young beauty in a deep purple-coloured velvet bodice. Wrapping a pleasing yellow silk scarf around a chintz skirt, she had draped herself with a rose-pink odhni. Her face, like a blood-red rose, also shone with the radiance of healthy youth.

Gopi was certain that Dalbahadur would not be able to survive this assault today, and that is exactly what happened. When Gopi reddened her lips by chewing paan, Dalbahadur was almost overcome. They made a secret deal that, at three that night, Gopi would come to Dalbahadur's house and, without anyone ever knowing, they would live forever with each other. They had discussed this with passion-filled eyes. An assignation spot had also been determined. The plan was ready and, again, Dalbahadur bought Gopi the best of the best pieces of velvet cloth from Raimal's shop.

At 4:00 PM, as they were heading back, Dalbahadur talked about watching a play. Gopi needed to get things ready; so she did not linger. Though the road to Badamtam must have seemed longer that day, she went back alone. Dalbahadur stayed on to watch the play. He was going to return home at night.

When he entered the playhouse, it was 9:00 PM. *Sita's Exile* was playing, and Ram's name had drawn people from the highest to the lowest ranks of society. Dalbahadur had spent some time in Kolkata at a babu's place and, though he was not proficient in the Bengali language, he had a serviceable knowledge to get by.

Sita is sleeping, and Ramchandra is sitting by her, fanning her with great affection – the drama opened with this scene. The audience was very quiet and, like the steady patter of raindrops falling from a dark sky on a cold night, the words could be picked out lucidly. At the end of the first act, when Sita is exiled to the forest, and Ram, calling out 'Sita, Sita' walks into the pale darkness and disappears behind the curtain, tears flowed from the eyes of every child, youth, and old person. Women were crying, men let out sobs, and the children kept looking at the curtain, watery-eyed.

Outside, a single melody from a lamenting voice:

> 'Where is the light, where is the light?
> The sky is so black, so black – '

The night was unexpectedly and uncommonly clear. For the brief moments that Dalbahadur stepped outside, several coquettish Chinese women were roaming about selling packets of peanuts; but his attention was captivated by the silent music of the stars above and the elegiac strains of the shehnai below. Everywhere, there was only one mood: sadness.

After the tears had dried, the second act began and, finally, the third act arrived.

Following Sita's example, Ramchandra himself is living in solitude. At that time, Luv, having learnt of Sita's exile and being filled with fury, runs out of the forest to meet the Lord of Ayodhya.

Lakshman and Bharat are standing guard for Ramchandra. The impudent Luv calls out, 'Where is Raghav? Raghav?' Lost in his own thoughts, Ramchandra hears this and thinks Sitaji has arrived and called out to him.

So he comes right out: 'Whose voice? This long-familiar voice, whose is it?'

This is the first father-son meeting but, when Luv leaves Ram completely disappointed, the unsettled and lonely Ram's sorrowful cry cuts right through the audience. Despite being well aware of the story, people wept their hearts out, as if their tears could wash away all the evil and restore all that is right.

But there was more. At the end of the third act, Ramchandra, in his royal court, gets more eager by the minute to meet Sita as she returns from the forest. With the frequent announcements of Sita getting closer and closer, even Dalbahadur sat up on his seat.

'Sita has arrived at the banks of the Sarayu ... in Ayodhya ... inside the Royal Square ... inside the Royal Hall ... She has arrived ... arrived...'

Message upon message is received; the audience was just as excited as the Royal Court to see Sita.

Buuut...

And Sitaji is seen.

The entire audience was as still as a drawn portrait, engrossed in this great grief-filled love story.

Vasishtha urges the court to test Sita; silence falls like a lightning strike. But when, with a woeful sound, Sita begins praying, 'Bhootdhatri dharni, Janani,' to Mother Earth to take her into Her protection, then, already privy to the love story's tragic end, the audience's tears could not be stopped. Dalbahadur covered his face with both hands and sobbed. Not able to watch the last scene, he ran right out. He had heard 'Sita' and his own adulterous behaviour was stinging him.

Outside, the air was filled with strains of mourning.

He ran through the teeming bazaar, past its vibrantly coloured street, and on to his route.

Since having exited the playhouse, Dalbahadur had remained in thrall of that pure word: 'Sita...' He was walking rapidly towards his home – to meet 'Sita' and fall at her feet.

A fine moonlight shone through little clouds and fell on the surroundings. The tea plantations nearby stood utterly quiet. Not a thing could be heard. Ahead, rows and rows of hills were covered by a hazy, dark sky and, in the moon's glow, a few snow-topped Himalayan peaks stood out, visibly lustrous, like milk teeth.

When Dalbahadur reached his corn fields in Badamtam, the hour of the rendezvous had begun. Walking through papaya and banana groves, he came to his small street. Two or three larks were flying about on the grass-covered thatch of his hut. Half-open oleander flowers infused the breeze with a new kind of fragrance. Decorated with a metal sheet, the doorway to his home was shut. From within, there was no other sound besides the flapping of the rooster's wings. He held his ear to the door and felt something rattling. Surprised, he stepped back. Then, with a single leap, he bounded further away. From behind, someone's hand had touched his and the man who was not afraid of sin jumped up, afraid of ghosts.

Just then, with a low, sweet laugh, Gopi shook his shoulder.

That's when Dalbahadur recalled the night's secret promise made to Gopi, their assignation spot, their plan. Alongside, he also remembered Sita. As he stood beside Gopi, the effect of that word on Dalbahadur was like the touch of holiness that makes evil melt away, prompting him to move further and further away from her.

He kept staring at Gopi; she had taken on the form of a spectacular enchantress. The quiet hills were beckoning. The breeze was gentle. They were alone. It was night-time. The cool moonlight was delightful.

Suddenly, a cock crowed inside and they heard Parvati turning to her side.

As if this sound had helped him make up his mind, Dalbahadur signalled to Gopi to follow him and walked out right away.

Where they were going, Gopi did not know; Dalbahadur moved forward and Gopi walked behind him.

Cautiously, both descended the hilly pathway, reaching lower and lower into the valley.

In all four directions, light had begun to dawn. The Himalayan peaks gradually became more visible.

When they reached the valley, Gopi paused for breath: 'Dalbahadur! Where are you going?'

Dalbahadur simply gestured with his hand for her to move forward. He began climbing the road that went through the tea plantations. When he reached the hill's summit, the sun's first ray had emerged over Kanchenjunga like a rising hope, like a smile of love, like a holy crest. And, in an instant, the soft pink and gold hues spread over two or three hilltops.

Dalbahadur stopped there. He beckoned Gopi to come nearer.

Gopi came to him, laughing. But … but, what was this?

Dalbahadur suddenly fell at Gopi's feet. Gathering the dust under her feet, he raised it to his head and said, in a muted but distinct voice: 'Gopi! We have made a mistake. You become my … sister, I will be your brother!'

Without saying a word, Gopi threw him a single look of contempt and walked away.

The next day, it was discovered that Gopi had abandoned Nobhu.

[3]

A reasonable distance from Badamtam, near a beautiful stream, there is a modest tea-house.

Set at an elevation, the window of the establishment is highly attractive to passers-by on the road below. One reason is that there are several lovely flowers and plants rooted around it; the other reason is the shining brass mugs arranged in tall rows that give the intimation of sweet tea to be had.

In that window, with half her face showing and the rest of it hidden, sat The Queen of Nepal. The nearby Bhutia and Lepcha people called the Gurkha owner of the tea-house 'The Queen of Nepal'. And, if any traveller asked, they would be pointed to the 'The Queen of Nepal's Tea-house'.

But The Queen of Nepal was even more beautiful than the place itself. With the tall, robust, curvaceous proportions of her fair figure, she personified the richness of natural beauty in the forest. Her body was so well-formed that it was as if some dream-sculptor had carefully measured every limb when creating her and then dusted her all over with a fine radiance.

'The Queen of Nepal' sat there like a half-opened, half-closed blossom. And the three powerful attractions of the place, the hour and her beauty lured every wayfarer to go there for a drink of tea or coffee even if he may not have desired it.

One day, a handsome youth climbed up for some tea. He was wearing an army officer's uniform. An ornamental gold crest rose from the turban on his head. It suited his fair face. Every now and then, and for no apparent reason, he tapped the cane he held in his hand against his tall, shiny leather boots. Entering the tea-house, he sat down.

The Queen of Nepal put her knitting aside and stepped out. As per usual, she asked with a sweet, easy smile: 'What would you like? Tea? Coffee?'

The young officer stared at her.

The Queen of Nepal stared back: 'Arrey! This is Dalbahadur!'

'What, Gopi? You have become a queen now?'

Gopi came forward, laughing gently. 'Dalbahadur! Where did you come from? You had gone to war, right?'

'I went to the war and returned.'

Dalbahadur had left to fight in France. All of Badamtam had gone to fight. Gopi's husband, Nobhu, had gone too. As per the reports Gopi received, the young men who had gone had all been mowed down.

'Have you come from Badamtam?'

'Yes.'

Gopi went into the kitchen, fetched a tall brass mug of tea, and sat before Dalbahadur. In the time that had passed, she had grown even prettier.

'What do you do here?'

'I run this tea house. I knit. I keep a few pigs and chickens too.'

'You know about poor Nobhu, don't you?' Dalbahadur asked Gopi.

Gopi gazed at him without saying a word but the utterance of Nobhu's name made her soften. She guessed there was some bad news.

'Parvati is dead, Bhagirathi is dead, Kukkuchin died at war. So many have died.'

'Who is left in Badamtam now?'

'Among the young, only you and I,' Dalbahadur said. 'The remaining are children, elderly, the disabled, and the weak.'

'The entire village must appear desolate?'

'Yes, so much that it would consume you alive. The fields sit empty. I cannot see a single young person in the village and don't know who to talk with. In every home, the beds are filled with injured men.'

Gopi was lost in thought. She was remembering Nobhu. Whatever else he may have been, he had been a good man. He had never betrayed her. He had been simple and true. Today, his death was troubling Gopi. And Nobhu's simplicity was stinging her. 'So simple and true!' a voice kept repeating in her mind.

'What are you thinking?'

'Did Nobhu remember me?' Gopi asked in a choked voice.

'You? Arrey, that miserable man repeated your name as if reciting Ram's name in constant prayer. Said, "Once I am back in Badamtam, once I see Gopi, once she comes to me…" mumbling this, he died on the steamer. The helpless thing was too weak, though.'

'And then?'

'Then we cast him off at sea. What else could we do?'

Gopi placed a hand to her chin and exhaled deeply. Both of them stared wordlessly at each other for a few moments.

Eventually, Dalbahadur said, 'Gopi, I have come to ask you. In Badamtam now, you and I are the only young people left. Parvati is dead, and Nobhu is no more.'

Gopi did not say anything for a bit, only looked down and nodded her head. 'Poor Nobhu is dead, isn't he?'

'You left him when he was alive. Now you are pining away? Nobhu is dead. Who remains alive forever? What's the use of remembering all that? Gopi, now come back to Badamtam.'

Gopi did not answer. She stood, picked up the mug of tea and went inside the house.

Dalbahadur sat there, smoking cigarettes.

When Gopi returned, Dalbahadur asked, 'What, Gopi! What are you thinking? You want to come to Badamtam, na?'

Gopi stared at him for a while. 'I will let you know tomorrow.'

Dalbahadur puffed on his cigarette slowly and, promising to return the next day, left.

The next day, when Dalbahadur came back to visit, he found that Gopi had handed over the tea-house to someone else and gone off to Nobhu's mother's village.

The Rebirth of Poetry

[1]

Many years of the twentieth century had flown past. Society had transformed completely.

A social system where no one was rich or poor had come into existence.

No master was to be found, no labourer, no servant. All were simply human beings. All worked and lived off their work. They found joy in work alone. No one had a house of their own. No one was especially important, nor had any individuality. All awoke in the morning to the sound of a great bell; before 6:30, they assembled for common prayer.

In those prayers, those who had created that world were commemorated. There was an absolutely open challenge to God that if He dried up the great oceans, they would create a new ocean. If He sent an epidemic, they would destroy and remove it. Helplessness and humility were seen as weaknesses; modesty was seen as a lack of education.

No one was above anyone and none saw himself as below

anyone. Everyone was free. But they lived by the rules and regulations of the state. The individual had been destroyed; the collective had been birthed.

All had the same tastes, pleasures, desires, affections and aspirations. They watched movies and plays together, ate together, sat in a gathering, went about together.

Nobody spoke words such as 'secret'.

Nobody had any secret ownership of anything. Their bodies belonged to the state. To talk of the existence of the soul was considered a crime.

A human being was just a part of society as a wave is a part of the ocean. A man of that era arose punctually, worked habitually, could only meet with a woman at fixed times, watched movies per schedule, listened to lectures and plays, all according to the rules. Instead of calling him a man, it would be more fitting to call him a set of rules.

Based on certain rules and regulations, each person could travel in the state's aeroplane; in the skies, mansions hung midair and held dance and music festivals. At such times, everyone went to attend. No one thought of anything else but the 'rules'.

The word 'poor' existed only in poetry; virtues, morality, beauty existed only in the imagination. To remove beauty's claim to superiority, the ugly and deformed people were made good-looking using scientific and technological methods.

Women could, of their own volition, become men. And men could take on womanly appearances. For some time, this self-rule caused some mismanagement and the number of men began to exceed that of women. So, a six-month prior notice was made compulsory. And another rule was made to ensure only a specific number of gender changes per year. In the meantime, the scientific experts were moving heaven and earth to design a single, middle-of-the-road solution so they could get rid of separate male and female genders altogether.

Forms of virtue and morality change with time; so, the circumstances that allowed human beings to earn their daily bread were accepted as those with the highest virtues and morals. Special rules were made to ensure no one deviated from the current rules with any kind of dreamy, passionate or lively talk.

To place the motto of 'order is humanity' above everything and to avoid having any cripples, lepers, blind or disabled people in the society, only wholly healthy women and men were allowed physical relations and offspring from any other unions were killed immediately.

In the celestial mansions, common women had been placed in common halls and every man could while away his leisure time delightfully there.

In this systematic, organised, science-driven country, homes, parks and gardens, roads, and boys and girls – all were found in singular versions. Beauty makes the world crazy and poets have written in praise of it. Given this, to ensure that the germ of such a grievous disease does not enter any person, surgery was done to give all men and women identical faces.

Houses, furniture, parks and gardens, trees, streets, all were created identical so that the desire for ownership would not arise. Similarly, to eradicate such a mindset, the naming ceremony ritual for men and women was abandoned too.

If, on a moonlit night, someone were to wander out into the skies, they would see thousands of men and women, having quickly attached invisible beams of light to their own wings, fly-ing along happily, moving about the clear skies like human birds. But, amongst all of them, it would be hard to find even a single face that looked different from the rest.

To keep track of the population, the society had developed a top-notch approach. After the destruction of the naming custom, each person was recognised by his number, so no mistakes could be made. In this manner, for any person, you needed to remember three numbers: person number, room number and street number.

The street and person number were written onto an easily accessible spot: right on the wings. So, for example, if you said, 'number 3750612, room number 1750621, street number 731', you could get in touch with the right person.

[2]

The night was blossoming. Despite all the romantic words of poets, artists and foolish lovers having been destroyed, the moon-light that had finely draped this night was so attractive that it held the world in thrall. With this kind of enchantment, people grow passionate and fanciful. A scientist (no. 63751) had endeavoured to prevent such effects, but the efforts had not been successful yet. His scheme had been to spread many points of light, like hun-dreds of thousands of stars, across the night sky in such a way as to blot out its supernatural beauty so that, like any man-made cre-ation, it would seem to be another contraption to light the world.

This plan had been undertaken for the main reason that a wandering couple had landed on some stray island. Seeing all things arranged in singular patterns and observing the lack of any diversity seemed oddly new to them. During the first few days, they appreciated the preciseness – like that of identically cut henna plants. But then the environment felt so artificial and uniform that they played a sad song about missing their forsaken land of birth on their worn-out veena!

Initially, thinking it was just part of the communal song that was played from the skies daily at five and ten, no one paid attention. Then, because they had not heard such melodious, sweet, alluring rising and falling music in years, an illicitly joyful passion grew in the souls of thousands. In many, inexplicable inner fancies came to life. For some, a longing arose to leave their homes and go wandering to far-off lands. A number of them closed their eyes, entirely absorbed in the notes of the captivating composition. To a few, some inner part of themselves, hidden and never heard before, became discernible.

Where order, rules, discipline and clear ideologies had shaped people uniformly – physically and mentally – seeing such tumult among the population, the state authorities could not initially understand how to end the calamity. In the end, they operated surgically on the people who had shown weaknesses to destroy the glands that caused the disruption and replaced them with new glands.

Once again, there was quiet everywhere. The wandering couple was taken to the coastline and placed in a boat. They were sent off on the endless journey to their whimsical country.

[3]

After technological contact with the inhabitants of the moon and of the planet Mars had been made, on some moonlit nights, stray couples from those places sometimes visited Earth. One day, an interesting woman and man from the moon landed on Earth to take in the winsome sights.

The woman was wearing a rainbow-coloured, finely woven, silvery cloud-like sari. A brilliant golden-belled girdle made by the inhabitants of Venus adorned her body. Real flowers of paradise were strung into her braided hair. A pearl with the essence of moon nectar decorated her delicate nose. In her hands were bracelets made with the imprint of the Milky Way. Her face was seductive; her eyes were intoxicating; her walk was proud; the lines of her body were clear and clean.

The man with her was just as charming. But the serenity on his face was astonishing. To look upon his handsome face without noticing that was impossible.

This couple, while roaming about, saw a pleasing garden at the edge of a dainty little stream and stopped there.

Inside the garden was a small cottage. All around it were flowering plants; the ground in front was covered with green grass. From the mountain behind, a dancing, tumbling stream flowed. At a little distance, deer roamed fearlessly. To one side, the birds sat, linking wing with wing trustfully. Flowers bloomed as much as one might desire on all the exquisite plants in the garden. The atmosphere was clean, calm and pretty.

But there was only atmosphere in the garden – there was no sign of any human being around. As if someone had renounced their body and chosen a solitary, lovely spot as a resting place for their soul! While on Earth, they had seen things like sky-high palaces, airplanes, bioluminescent paths, wings, people, machines, sounds and roads. But seeing this solitary place in an almost hidden spot made the moon couple happy. They sat there quietly, listening carefully for the sound of any footstep.

The only thing in the cottage was a single veena. Everything was still, like the soundless veena inside. There was no noise anywhere, no disturbance, no disorder. Only, there was a sense that someone had relinquished his body here and left his words. Leaving his inner song locked inside the mute veena, some poet had succumbed to death. Rules – rules – to escape from rules, a wandering, independent, self-respecting, wilful, odd-minded, carefree, wild poet had once reached here from that governed nation. Then, to get out of that controlled circle of life of 'sing this much' and 'write in this manner' and to compose his own free-spirited songs, he had settled here.

In that verse, he sang about living, anguish, the curse of mechanical union, the absence of satisfaction from pleasure; about the comforts, resources, and unrest derived from technology. Then he wrote about the importance of living life; about birds and nature, the streams. He also sang about the moon people and about the existence of an internal turmoil despite an external organised system. He took everything from the outer world and the inner world, and sang about the greatness of a new life formed from the synthesis of both. To his mind, humankind had only one class. He had tried to make every being an 'individual'. Progress is only possible if each person becomes 'individualised' – he sang of this notion of his. In the end, his body was gone. The words remained. All his silent songs lay scattered about the garden.

Today, as if from the touch of the moon couple, several notes arose from the hitherto-mute veena. To the world, to the beauty pervasive in the world, to man and to humanity, to nature and to life – from the silent veena, notes emerged like the embodiment of life, order, and the evolution of life. They began to emerge, began to sweep across and, rising to the skies, they began to touch each home and each heart.

[4]

Now came the critical test.

This time, it was not simply a few people suffering from glandular weakness who felt their imagination awaken, sensed their desire for beauty stir, felt a longing for something unknown. The wives and children of the superior-gland carriers and thousands of young and old were enraptured by those notes. 'Give us something out of the ordinary', 'Give us some variety', 'Something is incomplete', 'Give us the something that is missing in our lives' – so saying, they ran in the direction of the music. They felt their lives were orderly but not vitally new. They ran towards the poet's garden to receive the meaning of life.

There, seeing the magnificent statue-like moon couple, people broke all rules and began dancing like maniacs! Today, for the first time, they had seen other people with faces different from theirs. Shortly, the authorities and the superior-gland carriers arrived with the surgeons. But everyone was saying as if with one voice: 'Give us diversity! Give us beauty! Give us dreams! Give us some fancifulness. This regulated life is destroying us. Give us a new life.'

'You're asking for dreams? You want to talk about things that do not exist? Dance, music, art, poetry, literature – haven't these intoxicants made beggars of you in the past? You are asking for them again today?'

'We may well become beggars again, but the poverty of this emotionless life is unbearable. Instead of making us strong like thunderbolts, you are making us dull as inanimate objects!'

From the hitherto-mute veena, the dead poet's song in honour of the moon couple gained strength. The superb woman wearing the rainbow-coloured sari began to dance. The man clapped to the beat of the music.

With voices that pierced the skies, the people said only one thing: 'Do not turn us into emotionless machines. Give us dreams! They may well be false; they may well be vain! But when is life itself real?'

And all were engrossed, single-mindedly, in the dance.

The dead poet's veena issued forth the song about the importance of living life!

From a thousand throats, voices rose: 'Glorious woman! Say your name. Tell us your name. Tell us, because we only know numbers. Tell us your name. We want to hear you speak.'

'My name … my name … Anaami!' The words received in response were clear, clean, sweet, and peaceful like a stream of moon nectar: 'My name is Anaami!'

Ebb and Flow

Nine bosses had come and gone, but all nine had seemed like fruits from the same tree to Bhogilal. The first boss came and always chose Bhogilal to accompany his wife; the second one lessened that kindness but preferred only Bhogilal for his mundane errands. To be polite by nature, to be sweet-spoken, or to be practical-minded – these are not, by any means, terrible faults. Yet, for Bhogilal, under the auspices of these three kinds of virtues, pounding away at a railway job for twenty-one years under each of the nine bosses had worn him down in nine different ways. It is just as well that the first shloka in the second-year Sanskrit text is about how, even after being rubbed again and again over a stone slab, sandalwood maintains its sweet fragrance. And Bhogilal had studied exactly that. Otherwise, if it had been some other person, the chafing of these twenty-one years would have set him aflame.

Bhogilal was filling gasoline in the hurricane lamp. Chandulal, his oldest son, was sitting by the second lamp and memorising some Sanskrit forms. The other three children – numbers two, three and four – were lying about on the bed showing the baby the moon and singing 'chanda-poli, puran-poli' to her. And with number six, a future guest, in her belly, Manivahu lay sleeping on one side of the bed. Her time was due, so the poor woman, tired from the day's work, lay utterly exhausted.

'What's for dinner, Chandu?' Bhogilal asked as he continued filling gasoline in the hurricane lamp.

'Khichdi.'

'What vegetables have been prepared?'

'Your father wants sweets of seventeen flavours. He has no shame. Here, this boy Chandu is barely managing to cook and there, on top of that, "what vegetables have been prepared"? As if he's some big millionaire!' Manivahu said.

Instead of entering the hurricane lamp, the stream of gasoline fell to the floor. So Bhogilal took Chandu to task.

'Eh-la! Chaandiya! Stand up. You are not to study. Fill this gasoline first.' Forgetting that he had spilt the gasoline, Bhogilal rebuked Chandulal.

'But you being so grown-up and spilling it – are you not embarrassed?' asked Manivahu.

'Now you just lie there on the bed, or you'll hear a couple of choice words,' replied Bhogilal.

'Make me hear them, na? What else is there to listen to? Since casting my lot with yours, I haven't ever eaten a morsel of food at leisure. One after another, there's been a child, without respite. Five cannot be supported, how will a sixth be taken care of?'

Bhogilal, with the thought of the upcoming sixth, turned quiet. Chandu placed his book to one side and silently filled the gasoline. The boy then served plates of food for all. About that time, the cowherd came by, calling out 'milk'.

After supper, a man gets into an imaginative mood. Bhogilal

too sat fanning his body. Before him, Manivahu slept stretched out. One child in the lap, one nearby, one between the husband and wife, they all lolled about getting ready for bed.

'The village is better than this city. Here, you get a hundred rupees, but can you ever sit comfortably cross-legged to enjoy a morsel of food?'

'It might seem like that. Go to the village, then you will know. Mathuradas went and returned, did you not see?' Manivahu responded.

Mathuradas was also from Bhogilal's workplace. Taking a six-month vacation, he had gone to his village to produce grain from his little piece of land. But, after incurring a debt of 125 rupees, he had returned.

'But now I must get a divorce from this job. For how long can one live at Shankarlal's mercy?'

Shankarlal was the head clerk. All the clerks under him believed that all the bosses were good when they arrived, but then Shankarlal spoiled them by pandering to their whims. In Hindu culture, relationships between a mother-in-law, a wife, and a sister-in-law have been (in)famous since ancient times. To those, modern times have added the new relationships of clerks and head clerks, and assistant masters and headmasters.

'After leaving the job, what will you eat?'

'Arrey, we'll do physical labour; we'll do freelance work.'

Her physical-labour-aspiring husband would not even exert himself to fill a pot of water. Manivahu was certainly not oblivious to this.

'Physical labour, na? Of course. You will get physical labour work indeed.'

'Arrey, we'll go to the village and take care of properties. At least our health will improve.'

Having just given the example of Mathuradas, Manivahu did not say anything. The children had slowly fallen asleep and Chandu had moved a bit further away to read. Seeing this opportunity, Manivahu landed a blow: 'This is my sixth pregnancy. It's been this bad and now, after six months of bearing this child, you are troubled by the idea of how to support the family.'

Bhogilal did not like that the real reason – that he was weary and tired of his job – had revealed itself like this. He used the support of the same false shelter that people hide true faults under: 'But what can you or I do about that? What is set in destiny, we have to endure that much, right?'

Nobody has seen this destiny, but it has seen everyone.

'Then what did Devshankar Bhatt say?'

Devshankar Bhatt was the neighbourhood astrologer. Bhogilal sat with him frequently and had slowly begun to believe in Raahu, Shani and Mangal. This is what happens: difficulty challenges a person's strength of character, and also takes measure of his weakness.

'Devshankar said there will be pain for a month and a quarter.'

'So there, did I not say?'

[2]

A month and a half later, Manivahu gave birth to a son but he died after a few days. Bhogilal's worldly affairs carried on again from 11:00 AM to 5:00 PM. When Manivahu was tired from work, she would beat up one of the boys. Like labourers who drink alcohol when they are tired, some women often use this as a way to relax. The rousing sense of anger can, for some time, make one forget feelings of boredom, fatigue and drudgery.

When Bhogilal got bored with his monotonous life, he would go sit awhile in the library. There, he only read the advertisements, but that helped the time pass. The doctor had told him that, if a seventh pregnancy happened, they should keep both medicine and shroud ready together. So, in Bhogilal's life, that particular kind of diversion had lessened. After fifteen years, the pleasure of married life, as he had understood, had suffered a big blow. Just as the absence of alcohol in an alcoholic's life is felt very keenly, Bhogilal felt a deficiency in his life. Now he did not have the same interest as before in conversations with Manivahu. Previously, he used to gather a crowd when telling stories about his fellow clerks in his inimitable way but that too now gave less cheer. His mind became calm in the library; he would read there for some time, then go to some hotel-botel for tea and refreshments, then return home. Everyone would be asleep, so he would go to bed too.

Despite everything, he talked to a nurse one day and gave Manivahu medicine for a few days. When the women of the neighbourhood often got together to talk, Champi would say, 'Bai, that Manivahu's body was strong and stout but, after that last miscarriage, it has become lean and wasted. That's because the miscarriage did not happen at three months. Don't they say that it is fine to have seven deliveries but one miscarriage is the worst?'

'Arrey, curse you, Champi, who taught you, of all people, this? Let us, ma, speak the truth. What miscarriage happened? It was made to happen. Moreover, it was falsely spread about repeatedly that it simply happened.' So someone would reply to Champi. But Champi would not say anything further. She got three or four rupees for doing housework at Bhogilal's.

[3]

After Manivahu's miscarriage, her body continued to deteriorate. So, she began to stay confined to her bed. Therefore, the load of responsibility on Bhogilal increased. His oldest son, Chandu, also began to carry a share of that load. Bhogilal truly felt that life had become burdensome. To cook from 7:30 AM to 10:30 AM, then from 5:00 PM. to 7:00 PM, to get the beds ready from 7:00 PM to 8:00 PM, and then to go to bed so as to get up early: this awful regularity would weigh heavily on even the most courageous. The kind of punctuality that is maintained not for the sake of principles but for the sake of the clock ruins life. Bhogilal's life was being destroyed. He saw endless exertion in his existence. Manivahu seemed like a huge encumbrance. Chandu and the other children, who once gave him delight, now often seemed life-draining. His feet, when returning home, dragged. Any charm he had left in life was only outside the home.

A couple of moments of diversion at the office; slanderous gossip about the head clerk while walking along the street; examples of the foolishness of the government's management despite drawing a government salary; unsubstantiated criticism of current affairs – these were the only springs of joy left in Bhogilal's life.

Eventually, a death-like regularity draws a man towards bad habits. Just as addictions can form for alcohol, tobacco or cigarettes, so also many other kinds of addictions can happen – like reading journals and books, writing poetry, giving lectures, etc. Not for the sake of principles or pleasure, but the things that people grasp to save themselves from weariness and boredom, the things they seize not because they are good but because they are easy and at hand, these are all bad habits – be it studying the Gita or smoking cigarettes or inspecting cadavers. These addictions appear in ways that cannot be comprehended. The emptiness in Bhogilal's life was filled by journals; and whatever was left was taken care of by the uniformity of life. What is going on at home, what is Chandu doing, or what are the needs at home – the reading material would not shed light on any of these issues. He lost it all in reading. Bas, after waking in the morning and after finishing his work, it was only the library for him.

Before the librarian could even open the shutters, Bhogilal would be standing there. 'Why, you're a bit late today,' saying this, Bhogilal would snatch a paper from his hands.

The librarian got fed up too, and once retorted: 'Bhai, you come before everyone else, you leave after everyone else, you shuffle more papers than anyone else, and you read less than everyone else – what is this craving you have for this place?'

Chandu had grown older and was taking a bit more care of the house. So, having lost interest in his endlessly monotonous existence, Bhogilal had discovered a new pleasure in the library.

The disruption that had occurred in his life's usual rituals, Bhogilal wanted to coax it away with various stimulating substances. The enjoyment of sitting with Manivahu, the gratification from envying others in their community, the glee in making fun of the head clerk and, after all that, the pleasure of placating Manivahu – the void that came with not doing any of these things

was so disagreeable that Bhogilal tried to repair it in many ways:
with chevdo, tea, cinema, journals, libraries. Yet, the dreadful
presence of that disruption stood like a lonely, solitary, dried-up
babul tree before his eyes all the time.

[4]

At the time of Chandu's wedding, a tide of bliss filled that uniform existence. Seeing people from all over coming out to see the
groom's father made Bhogilal as happy as a writer when his first
poem is printed in a corner of a journal. When, on the outskirts
of the village, the pompous watchman took aim at the tamarind
tree and blew it up, Chandu's father wielded his influence like
some lecturer from a podium.

When Chandu's wife, Sumati, older than Chandu by only
three years, came home, the entire house lit up as if a new light
had appeared. As if his life was starting again, Bhogilal began to
observe anew the arrangements of the house. The zest for life
that had become dormant deep inside of him awoke again and he
began to make merry again. The contentment flowed again when
talking with Chandu's mother about the in-laws.

Chandu was young. His wife was older. Bhogilal was an
unfulfilled sensualist. Once, at early dawn, Chandu's wife awoke
and was pouring water in the heating vessel for bathing. Bhogilal
went there to help. But, despite being younger, Sumati had the
innate woman's distrust of that kind of man and had been on her
guard. So, after some effort, when Bhogilal grabbed her arm, her
shrill cry woke up the entire house. And, like a frightened rabbit,
Bhogilal ran away. So Sumati was saved. But, after that, Bhogilal
again began to suffer from a lack of attachment to life.

One time, when he came home at night, a scene as disturbing as the third battle of Panipat met his eyes. Manivahu, like a victorious commander-in-chief, was threatening Chandu and his wife. Chandu stood in a corner, crying, with his head in a book: *Bhartruhari Shatak*.[14] Chandu's wife was crying too.

'I warn you now, if you ever eat bread in my house again! Le, are you not ashamed of making such big talk with such a small mouth?'

Bhogilal, with a bundle of clothes in his hands, came and stood by quietly. 'What is it?'

'What else? Why, your daughter-in-law has gone and spoiled things!'

The guilt lying inside awoke and Bhogilal turned pale. Had his daughter-in-law revealed his sin? This fear made him tremble internally.

'But what is it? Why is Chandu crying?'

'What else? It's all your fault!'

'I will know only if you tell me, na?'

'This know-it-all daughter-in-law of yours went to sit at Mathuradas' ...'

Relieved that the conversation was not about him, Bhogilal said casually, 'Yes, so what?'

---

14. Bhartruhari: Bhartruhari was a king who had grown weary of the world and become a mendicant. He had then written a collection called *Shatak Neeti* (*A Collection of Rules*), which outlined how to live a good, proper life. That Chandu is already reading this book after being newly-married says something about how oppressed he must have been feeling with the weight of looking after that family while his father whiled away time at the library.

'Now listen at least. So what? So what? You keep saying that.'
Bhogilal softened. 'Le, then tell me.'

'Then what? There must have been some talk at Mathuradas'
that some fellow's daughter-in-law is greedy...'

'So what? If someone thinks it is alright to talk like that, they
can.'

'Is that what you think? That it's alright to knowingly defame
others?'

'And what's the matter with Chandu?'

'Chandu came to defend his wife. The know-it-all daughter-
in-law then comes to tell me that confessing one's faults is the biggest virtue – so full of learning.'

Bhogilal was experiencing the deep, exulting glee that every
weak-hearted man gains from the strength of knowing his sin
has not been laid open. Leaving the bundle of clothes right there,
he climbed onto the upper storey. At that moment, his feet were
buoyant with a joy as light as air. Climbing up, he sat for a while
but his manic soul could not rest in one place. He sat up, took
a pen in hand, and drew up a request for a year's leave from his
job. The next moment, he began thinking about what to do now.

The stolen thrill of the library embodied itself in various
forms and began to enchant him. In his imaginative vision, he
began seeing large and beautiful letters. In his mind's eye, he saw
his own journal filled with various attractive captions. At the
top, 'Bhogilal' began to appear as the editor. He formed a plan.
Enclosing his leave request letter in an envelope, he prepared to
mail it. As if there was only one grave question in life, he placed
a finger to his forehead and began to ponder like the poet, Veer
Narmad: 'What should I do? Put out a monthly or a weekly?

Should I write "editor" or "publisher"? And he spent the entire night in search of a name that would usher in a rightful revolution.

[5]

The next morning, near Bhogilal's house, a few scraps of paper were flying about. On these, 'one year without salary', 'the favour', 'otherwise this resignation', and other such words were dashing against the bhangi's broom and being tossed towards the dirty drain.

Unknown Helpers

L ike a star falling from the sky, he arrived in the village on a night overcome with darkness; with calm, noiseless feet; in an imperceptible way.

On his face, there was a clear brightness. In his eyes , there was tranquillity. On his lips, there was an unbeatable smile.

He stayed at the dharamshala. Nobody from the village asked him: 'Who are you?' He didn't say: 'I am so and so.' Yet, he found a place in the village. In every village, there is always one vacant spot. That spot was filled by him.

He corrected the community's mistakes – without any criticism.

He served the community – without any expectation.

He gave the community vitality – without any disruption.

He became a part of the community – the community considered him a part of it.

When there was work to be done, it was only entrusted to him.

The responsibility for all the helpless lay at his doorstep.

The skulduggery of all the rogues was counted against him.

All failures were on his account.

When a new cart rut was being made, the disapproval was directed at him.

With prophecies of fruitless efforts, he was held accountable.

And, in the tales of victories, several shares were cast; his share remained the smallest.

On the day of ashaadhi beej, clouds had darkened the sky. In Sarju's home, like quiet raindrops, an orphan's tears were falling. She was alone. Sick. She had no hope of anyone coming. She was an orphan. Poor. Helping her would not serve anyone's interest. All had given up on her: because she was poor; because she was low; because she was diseased.

The door of the hut flew open suddenly.

Afraid of the dogs, the sick woman said involuntarily: 'Hudh! Hudh!'

Taking a step forward, the man lit a match. He held the hurricane lamp in front of her face.

Sarju's eyes rested on the unknown helper for a moment and she stirred.

When she brought bundles of wood from the mountains of Gir, with sweat dripping and heart hammering, instead of paying her properly, they harassed her improperly. Because the wood was dry but she was beautiful with the essence of life; the wood was aged but she was in the fullness of her youth. She was herself an untouchable dhedh but her youth felt touchable to all. The young man who followed her around at that time was the same one who had circled back today.

But the earlier desire did not light up his face today. His eyes did not have the former intoxication. His gestures did not have the old passion. With slow, steady steps, he moved forward. He sat beside Sarju's bedding and took her hand in his. He placed her head in his lap.

'Arrey! Arrey! Your being will become polluted ... people will see, they will ridicule. All will laugh ... you will lose your honour.' She said so many things. But, instead of responding, he began to caress her head.

To impress upon her mind that the unbelievable event would not prove false, the weak woman shut her eyes.

She had caught him sitting like this near her several times before; but all that had been hidden from people's eyes. Goodness was viewed with suspicion by all minds. But today he was sitting openly. He had seen the villagers; the villagers had seen him. He had issued a fearless challenge to them to do what they will. The people had also decided to do everything they could. Before, at that earlier time, her youth had won him over. Today, her awakened soul was drawing him in.

He said softly: 'Sarju! Remember, you would bring the bundles of wood and I would come and fix bogus prices? Sarju, remember, you would bring bales of hay and I would haggle dishonestly about the rates?' Across her face, a quiet, faint smile came and left.

When it was quite late, he turned back towards the village, having received the soul-filling joy of giving aid to the helpless. His figure blended into the grey, dusty twilight. And he was returning, having cleansed his mind of caste, having observed what was considered a sin by the multitudes.

At the point where the banyan branches spread and a thick darkness arrived before all other places, the villagers were waiting.

He came close and, immediately, without any words, the stones began to fall. From above, lumps of earth were falling; from the side, stones were raining; from nearby, there was cruel laughter. He understood.

He did not say anything. There was nothing to say. A person is drawn to a task by two tendencies: compassion or wisdom. If there is compassion in people, then stones won't fall. If there is wisdom, there won't be cruel laughter. To people, between reason and appearance, the latter is of more importance. He bore the assault quietly and went on.

The next day, villagers renounced him as their leader. When he was a secret lover, he was respectable. When he became an open lover, he became worthless. When he sinned in private, he was considered honourable. When he tried to clear his sin away with repentance, he was considered crazy. But, in his mind, service was the path to self-evolution.

And since the injustice done to Sarju had been acute, there would be more growth and evolution in attending to her. He took care of her because she was the lowest of all. Because unrepented sin sets the tree of life afire. Because no sin can be given up until it is confessed with an open heart in the public square of the world.

He was not sad about leaving the village; he did not even have a desire to stay. The village was unimportant. Life was more important. Another village could be found; another life could not be had. The next day, Sarju's health had recovered enough for her to not require his help. So, with the same silence that he had arrived, he left. Like wealth flowing quietly away from the village to foreign lands, he became distant.

Where there was a need for help, he provided. Where no

one recognised him, he resided. Because it gave him pleasure to give assistance anonymously. Because that was the philosophy of his life.

Anaami

Punctually, at six o'clock in the evening, a voice could be heard: 'Bai saheb! Milk.' With the voice, the footfall, the face, and the time, a kind of mechanical regularity had become established so that, exactly at the stroke of six, those feet could be seen approaching in just the same way. Often, to escape them, I would sit with the newspaper at exactly that time. The newspaper also has that sort of usefulness where time can be passed and, along with that, the unwillingness to talk or look can also be beautifully embellished and dressed up. In the train, second- and first-class passengers often make this kind of use of the newspaper. Although I was not a second-class passenger, I always enacted this drama at six o'clock for five minutes. Sometimes, I would get up and even go out; or, sometimes, exactly at the stroke of six, I would go inside to wind up my pocket-watch. Anyhow, I always made an effort to keep the voice and face that belonged to 'Bai saheb! Milk' at a distance.

For what reason, I do not know. Also, who knows why, with just as much care as I tried to keep that voice at a distance, our neighbour's little daughter would come running on hearing it. Perhaps she always heard different voices or perhaps because, for a bit of time, she would get to see a new face. But she always came running immediately. For five minutes, she would stand before the one who said 'Bai saheb.' The owner of the voice possibly smiled gently and went away.

One day, the woman came and went as usual, and then the girl said: 'Might she have a girl my age at her place?'

In the whole world, who has how many children was all in the population census, so I didn't bother with a response.

The next day, indeed, she asked the woman: 'Do you have a girl my age at your place?'

When the young girl and that older woman laughed in tandem as if they had understood each other, the snake of superiority sleeping in my conscience was disturbed.

The woman laughed and replied: 'Arrey, haan re, bai! I have a daughter just your age. Like you, she also has to drink milk.'

'What's her name?'

Before a response could be given, the milk vessel was returned to the woman.

'What is it to you, ben? Come here. Now, you mustn't ask things like that.'

The girl ran back inside laughing and even added before leaving: 'Will ask, so there.'

With the power of the same mysterious imagination with which she had discovered that the woman had a girl as big as her, she had also created a mental image of the unnamed girl.

Day by day, the glories of that unnamed creation grew too. She thought, 'That girl is my age. She must play like me. She has a mother like mine. Like me, she must wait for her mother.' And many such things manifested in that creation.

After that, she formed a habit of waiting for the milk-woman. When the lady came, she would ask one or two questions. The maternal instinct hidden within every woman became a connecting link between the milk-woman and the little girl. And the unnamed child continued to play a principal part in that link.

'Today, the milk-woman will not come,' the girl told me at exactly six o'clock one day.

Psychology is a dear subject of mine and, when it comes to the weakness of emotions, without understanding half of it, muddling in some philosophy and to conceal my own foolishness, I scribble a lot. So now, I was making just such jottings.

The little girl's interest in the milk-woman seemed to mirror my interest in psychology: she was not likely to leave that topic unfinished.

'She must have work back at her home, na?'

I gave no attention to her. But whether the listener lends an ear or gets restless in his chair, like a novice poet who does not let his friends go until he has made them listen to his entire poem, this girl was not likely to set me free.

'She must want to make moong water, bhai. She must be making it right now. Then she will make the daughter drink it.'

Without even nodding my head, I continued further with my own subject.

A grown man, on losing, refuses to concede defeat. How will a little child give up, then? She continued: 'She must have put a thermometer in her daughter, na? Her daughter must be crying! When will the fever subside?'

Immediately, I touched my hand to her cheek. 'Arrey, ben! Do you have a fever?'

'No. That milk-woman, her daughter got a fever yesterday.'

'How did you find out?'

'She had said yesterday, na? A high fever. How much fever could it be?'

'Bai saheb, milk,' the woman's familiar voice called. But today, there was some agitation in that voice. Instead of coming along her regular route, she had taken the shorter one. As she climbed the steps, one could see that her face was a bit pale.

'Here she comes. Has your daughter's fever subsided?'

'No re, bai, that poor one is still lying in fever. It's raging.'

I did not desire to speak but, this time, I blurted out: 'How much is it?'

'How can we figure that out, maadi? But the crown of her head is hurting badly.'

I was preparing to get re-immersed in my subject when the girl asked, 'Can I give you medicine?'

'Na re, maadi, what medicine? We've wrapped bandages around her abdomen.'

I recalled that, just a few days ago in our neighbourhood, a boy had wrapped bandages in ignorance and died. I feared the girl would also end up the same way. An inclination rose to take some interest in the creation. The girl gazed at me.

'Is her stomach alright?' I asked.

'Na re, maadi, it's hard as stone.'

'Then, here, I'll fetch medicine!'

Without saying a word, as if she knew which medicine, the girl ran into her home and brought a bottle from the cabinet. The bottle was empty. But, with the firm belief that the bottle was the medicine itself, and the source of relief rather than the medicine, she held the bottle out towards me.

Thinking I had developed an interest in her life, the milkwoman described all her troubles to me in detail. At the root of her supposedly enormous difficulty, there was only a slight issue – like a blade of grass hidden in the shadow of a mountain.

I gave her an ordinary stomach-purging powder.

The next morning, on returning late from outside, when I was still removing my coat, the girl came running to give the information, 'Her daughter, who's as big as me – her fever has subsided, alright!'

The Noble Daughters-in-Law

For three days and nights, like a dog wandering about the courtyard, the nobleman's daughter-in-law wandered about for refuge.

But, out of the fifty people from whom she had sought help, not one word of kindness was heard; not one look of sympathy was received; not one person moved towards her. As if she were not even alive, everyone remained absorbed in their work.

The older brother-in-law, calling out to the servants, started to leave for the shop without even casting a proper look at the shelterless and wretched woman standing near the door.

The younger brother-in-law passed by too. He was a beautiful, much-loved, good youth, and also a bit of a show-off.

Right then, as his bhabhi, she called to him in an affection-filled voice: 'Eh Vinoobhai, please come here!'

Instead of replying, Vinoo ran off, scaring the dogs.

The help, Ganga, arrived with the filled water pots.

'Eh, Ganga, eh, Ganga – sister!'

As servants accustomed to living in the homes of important people shape their manner of communication from their environment, so Ganga heard Yamuna's pleas but acted as if she had not. Behaving as if she found the burden of her water pots too heavy, and taking advantage of the hand pitcher colliding slightly with the door-frame, saying meaningless words as 'Oh dear, dear!' she went inside without giving a response.

In a short while, the cook came and closed the peep-window. In this manner, many indirect hints continued signaling for her removal from the compound. Eventually, exhausted, Yamuna left the house that night and then there was no trace of her. The rich in-laws felt no need to investigate because her husband had died. And there was no place for a widowed daughter-in-law. She was the daughter of poor parents; so, she had no standing.

Her father was dead and her mother, with her meagre savings from working hard at the grinding mill, had made as many efforts as possible to help her daughter. In the end, they didn't amount to much. There was no news of Yamuna. Eventually, the millstone, which once used to hear the mother Sarla's songs at two or three in the night, was now watching her quiet flow of tears. In a crowded universe, Yamuna had drowned like a pebble sinks in a brimming lake.

When she was born, Yamuna was the daughter of wealthy parents. As she reached maidenhood and came of age, Lakshmi, the goddess of wealth, left their home, as if she had been just a visitor, along with Yamuna's father's death. Yamuna became the daughter of an impoverished widow. This change in a society where money is given limitless prestige is considered of much significance. Nobody could take away the beauty that belonged to her, but the wealthy people who had wished to make Yamuna part of their family because of that beauty now frequently made Sarla aware of her status.

Actually, the betrothal had happened with a rich father's daughter. Now that Yamuna was a poor widow's beautiful daughter, the in-laws were just honouring their word with the wedding. If there had been no beauty, that connection would not have endured. But beauty is such a terrible, ephemeral, fickle thing that whoever chases it does not attain it. Also, that beauty does not even exist the way they imagine it.

Yamuna arrived at her in-laws'. She managed to come, but the millstone-grinding mother had hardly any right to visit since the untouchability established by inequality in wealth is greater than that caused by birth or caste. So Yamuna's true identity was being destroyed, like that of a bird imprisoned in a cage. And the beauty that had bought her a place in this family was losing its value like a desired item does once it's been acquired. Not only that, as if the beauty itself was reason for immorality, everyone wanted to cover it up. In every way possible, they were trying to reduce her to an existence in name only. So her beauty blossomed even more.

When civil unrest spread across the city, it was given a religious hue so that the thugs' knives could take more lives. The police had meagre salaries and children to raise. So, if they got a four-anna or eight-anna coin, a knife could wander freely for a day. Even the police officers understood that this is not the age of Raja Vikram that they had to conceal this. They felt that they had done more than they were required to keep the streets clean.

That violence took the lives of many innocents, Yamuna's husband being one of them.

He who forgets the Gita's teachings about the destruction of killers can only be liberated by dying at the hands of killers. Tyrannical violence and ignorant non-violence – both, in the end, bring the same result: the destruction of social morality.

The entire village had forgotten this creed. Due to this, everyone tried to protect their own neighbourhoods by sending thugs to counter thugs. It was an atmosphere of fear and suspicion. Shripal Sheth's young son and Yamuna's husband became a scapegoat during those circumstances.

Right near the entrance to his home, a thug thrust a dagger into him and he fell. Seeing the attack on him, a poor cart-puller ran; leaving his cart and young wife and child, he ran like the wind. But he was attacked and he too died there. There was a general outcry among the people. A chaotic rush began and, as if nothing had happened, the thug escaped undaunted.

Yamuna got the news. In great adversity, great virtue shines. And so it seemed she was transformed. At first, she did not allow the corpse to be picked up from where it lay. Her voice was different. Her look had altered. Her entire torso had transformed.

'Now, what was to happen has happened, bai, ben! Will being obstinate turn things back? And you make a legal complaint – does the court ever refuse to hand out justice?'

The response was like that of a lioness: 'Who is that coward, who is talking about the court now? In rural regions, what kind of court is there? What kind of law? What kind of order? I am telling you, I myself will lift up and carry this corpse around from house to house!'

The speaking policeman's pride was wounded: 'Bai, we appreciate your sorrow, but you need to be careful with your tongue when speaking.'

The words 'we appreciate' from the inspector's mouth were even more terrible than the thug's dagger.

'Now do me a favour and leave off appreciating me. But I am telling you, na – first get the thug behind bars. After that, this corpse will be lifted from here. Otherwise, instead of one, you will have to lift two corpses!'

Yamuna's heart was filled with sorrow. As her vigour subsided, the cold cruelty of the calamity struck her. She tumbled onto her husband's corpse, screeching, 'Why did you not take me with you?' and burst out crying.

All those standing nearby felt sympathy.

About that time, it seemed that another crowd, shrieking just as pitiably, was going by. The cart-puller's corpse had been picked up and his wife and little boy were following with lamentations. The boy, saying, 'Oh father! Oh … father!' was tripping frequently behind the corpse as it was being carried away.

Where the regime is not driven by a sense of welfare, such sights are inevitable. That a man is made king due to the circumstances of his birth should be considered as terrible as when a person is deemed untouchable due to her birth.

After the incident that day, everyone realised that Yamuna truly had the soul of a lioness. Despite that, Shripal Sheth and his family members felt that there had been a bit too much immodesty shown during the whole business. Normally, during such an event, the women sat inside the house, wailing heartrendingly or preparing their widow's garbs. Instead of that, to be out wandering with her husband's corpse in full splendid attire – this seemed unbecoming to all. But, more than that, it was her shameless behaviour afterwards. That story was revealed later.

It was around nine or ten at night. By herself, so that no one would know, Yamuna accompanied the cart-puller's wife to Panjara Pol's chief minister and administrator, Kiratchand Sheth.

The sheth had fallen into adverse times. So when she got there, the man was half-asleep, making heedless chatter with friends. The soft expanses of their beautiful, silky beds were making them a little too merry. Yamuna arrived there. The cart-puller's grieving wife and her son stood behind her.

Faint lines of surprise spread across everyone's faces. That the city's leading nobleman's daughter-in-law would come at this time to this place in this manner and with such a low woman – reprehensible! Everyone turned quiet.

'Who?'

'Kaka! It's Yamuna.'

Kiratchand Sheth was from her own village. So Yamuna always called him 'kaka'.

'Why at this hour? And that too without any escort?'

'I need some help.'

'What?'

'This woman – she is the wife of the cart-puller who died trying to save us. This is her little boy…'

'Haaaan,' Kiratchand's surprise grew. He did not understand a thing.

'The poor one does not have even a single day's worth of grain in her home. The boy is little. Your Panjara Pol has a fund of hundreds of thousands. If you could give her some decent annual aid from it …'

'Arrey, crazy woman!' Kiratchand burst out laughing. 'You made the trip here for this? At this hour?'

Seeing Kiratchand being supportive of her cause made Yamuna happy. She was also about to enquire about the aid that could be given when Kiratchand's crude laughter ended and his gaze wandered across towards his clerk sitting nearby. Due to the laughter, the narrowing of his eyes had not yet become apparent.

He asked the clerk: 'Right, Abheychand bhai? Heh, what is the need to come here for this kind of thing?'

'No, no, what is the need to take the trouble? And how is this a big thing? As if even the city's leading nobleman, your father-in-law is likely to refuse such a thing? If you had suggested this to him, he would have given six months' worth of grains.'

'No, but there is another objective in this,' Yamuna said.

'What?'

'That we are all with this woman; she will never be without support – I want to reassure her of this. And then, in my home, I am now alone. No one else cares to help. They think that, by helping in this manner, it will become a permanent burden. Further, the wicked will then always have their eye on us.'

Kiratchand yawned: 'We have no other problem. Why, Abheychand bhai, what other problem do we have?'

Abheychand was slow in speaking, 'If one paisa from the mute cattle's hay is spent elsewhere, that does bother me.'

As if they were both ready for this game, Kiratchand immediately picked it up: 'Yes, saalu, that will certainly feel a bit

improper. And not only that, but there will be people question-
ing us, na?'

'It's like taking hay from the mouths of lame, crippled, invalid,
dumb animals.' Vaneychand, who had been completely silent
until now, spoke.

'So then, do this, no, daughter! I will write a note to the city's
leading nobleman for you that…'

Hearing this talk about a note to be sent to her father-in-law,
Yamuna trembled somewhat. For one who, on occasion, became
a lioness, the sense of inferiority from her childhood had gathered such strength that her heroism at times became the size of
three almonds. The bravery she had shown during an occasion
of deep sorrow – once the moment had passed, her fear of her
in-laws' home had started again. Those who take on big, long voy-
ages, even those who are known as the merchants of the oceans,
don't they become drenched in embarrassment when they have
to uproot an old tree-stump lying in a corner of their neighbourhood? Or, when some customary practice within the caste-community has been flouted, don't they stick their hands and tongues
out in dread? The lioness-like Yamuna also, at the mention of any
of her in-laws, shook from fear.

Kiratchand immediately recognised this vulnerability of hers.
'That's how it should be done, na?'

'But her husband gave his life on that day,' Yamuna said.

'I tried so hard to stop him, but maadi! He just shot off like
a rifle and fell into the quarrel. Such was our destiny, what else?'
The cart-puller's wife joined in.

'Yes, baapu, yes. Is fate ever false? Whatever days God has
given, we must endure…' But Kiratchand's sentence remained

incomplete. From within the soft, silky bedding, something was piercing him. He raised himself a bit.

'You see! Abheychand, just mention children and we're done for. My son has hidden, who knows when, a glass marble here under the covers!' Kiratchand, said, pulling out a small glass marble from underneath, using the occasion to change the topic. Holding the glass marble in his hand, he said, gazing at Abheychand: 'You see? Here it is. I'd been feeling it for quite some time, ho!'

'So then, kaka – '

'Yes, daughter, what else? You go on. We cannot spoil the cow-maata's hay – '

'And this is about feed for the lame, dumb cattle – '

'And a human being has speech. Do cattle have speech?'

With the responses that came one after another from all three, Yamuna, turning speechless for a moment, just kept staring.

'But don't you feel that the cart-puller preserved the honour of the higher castes?'

'Preserved honour? Arrey, crazy woman, not only did he preserve our honour, he had his own name recorded in the heavens in golden letters!'

'Then shouldn't we help them a little?'

'Not from the feed of the dumb cattle,' Vaneychand spoke up.

'It is the duty of those who raise. Our duty is to raise dumb cattle. The cart-puller's duty...'

'To die for us, right?' An acidity entered Yamuna's voice. She regained her vigour.

They all burst out laughing: 'Ben, you are getting angry for no reason. God has given everyone arms and legs.'

The response was more insolent than the laughter. Without saying one more word, Yamuna walked away.

'Ben, you don't get nervous, ho. I will do everything I can from my end. It is like this, ben, I have this ornament from my parents' home that, for a long time, has been lying heavy around my neck. So I will get rid of it,' Yamuna said to the cart-puller's wife.

'Na, re, maadi! You are a young, beloved wife – ' the cart-puller's wife protested.

Yamuna was looking at her. She was a labourer and that identity seemed to suffuse her very being and colour her perception of herself and of others. 'Your name? I've seen you somewhere before.'

'Why, of course. I used to wander about near your husband for work – have you forgotten? My name is Vajji.'

'Alright, then. You wait right here. I will return presently.'

So saying, Yamuna disappeared.

Shripal Sheth found out about this. And, with that, the news that Yamuna had sold her family ornaments and given the money to the cart-puller's wife and, on her way back from there late at night, thugs had even harassed her. On receiving this information, his anger knew no bounds. He threatened the servants. He dismissed those providing help. And he drove Yamuna out – this low-life's daughter is not wanted in our home.

Without wavering for a moment, he let Yamuna wander for three days and three nights. Yamuna, who showed a lioness' heroism at times, had a weakness. Memories of her mother would make her lose spirit. That her mother's feeble body should suffer for her,

this thought would make her anxious. To be cast adrift – this sup-
position alone frightened her. As someone without protection, she
would be a burden to her mother – this foreboding would make
her desperate. A person can, on occasion and due to certain circumstances, show bravery. But, within them, there is also the debilitat-
ing inability to fully transcend the effects of conditioning. Even the
most adventurous heroes panic if they have to defy conventions or
customary social practices. Tired, eventually, Yamuna left the home-
stead on the third night. After that, there was no trace of her. No
one felt the need to even search in earnest for the wayward, widowed
daughter-in-law. Actually, if she remained invisible – if she was not
seen or heard of from people's tongues – the deep assurance that
was in such a circumstance, that assurance alone helped them all in
maintaining a complete, studied silence about Yamuna.

Yamuna's real story started from here. After leaving the house,
she had two thoughts: to go to her poor mother's or to commit
suicide.

She would have put one of the two ideas into execution. But
there were many thirsty eyes watching from all over. As soon as
she gave up her home, an organised gang began planning to kid-
nap her. A man followed her to keep her in sight. She ran into
the first urban settlement she came upon. Noticing that the man
was still behind her, without asking or meeting with anyone, she
rushed into the first house she saw open.

Some young man saw her and, saying, 'Eh … doing,' he ran
alongside her. But Yamuna lay down at his feet: 'Bhai, I am poor.
I am alone. Give me a little shelter. The thugs are after me.'

Seeing her beauty, he relented: 'Alright, go, there are utensils lying near that chokdi. Sit there and clean them.'

'Arrey, eh, Dhansukh bhai!'

'Why, bhabhi? Why? Who do you need?'

'Arrey, bhai, you have become so elusive. My tongue is tired and twisted from calling for you constantly.'

'But what is it?'

'This, of course. Today also, that whore of a servant has not come again. Who will go to call her now?'

'Arrey, what need do we have of her? Here, another poor, helpless one from some other village came asking for work, so I have sat her down to it. Have decided on meals and four rupees.'

Yamuna was listening. She understood that she would need to preserve the guise of a servant from another village. In the meantime, bhabhi came out of the kitchen.

The woman's figure was appropriately jolly and heavy. She had an average, unremarkable appearance. She saw the servant.

'Ali, what caste are you from?'

'Ba, I've just come here from another village three or four days ago. By caste, I'm a Sathvaari. If you'll let me stay to work, I'll do good work; if you give me a little room, then I will be here the whole day.'

'What kind of room-voom is here? A room's rent is six rupees. If we could give it to you, would we not keep two people to do the work? But look, if you want to stay under the stairs there, you may. Where are your things?'

'I don't have any things, ma.'

'Ma? Whom are you calling ma? Am I some old woman? Why, Dhansukh bhai, are you not saying anything?'

'Could *anyone* call you *old*, bhabhi?'

Yamuna, as if not understanding anything, continued scrubbing the utensils.

Laughing, bhabhi came over and gave Dhansukh a slap, and he stood up. 'I will make you sorry.' So saying, he ran after her up the stairs.

Yamuna found all this – the atmosphere in the house – strange and suffocating. But she had no desire right now to look for anything else. She kept scrubbing the overturned utensils.

From the upper storey, sounds of laughter could be heard. In a short while, a bhaiya arrived. He sat on a broken table under the stairs: 'You came, na? If I had not warned you, do you know what would have happened?'

As if she had not heard, Yamuna scrubbed the utensils harder and harder.

After waiting a while, the bhaiya spoke again, 'Awful how people are also thoughtless. When they have no use of you, friends become enemies.'

At this point, Yamuna looked at the bhaiya. 'What are you saying? Whom are you saying it to?'

'Oh! Where did *you* come from? I thought it was the servant. The colour of the sari is the same, na? That's why I mistook you for her.' His surprise had no bounds. First, he found Yamuna's features very beautiful. He was also suspicious of whether this woman had come for work or something else. He fell to thinking and became silent.

Just then, the master of the house, the big sheth, arrived. The bhaiya stood and greeted him.

At four in the afternoon, the whole house was empty. There were only two people left: Dhansukh and herself. All the rest had left for the temple. The bhaiya was lying asleep in a nearby room.

Dhansukh came close to Yamuna, who was trembling like a frightened, timid doe.

'See how I talked bhabhi into letting you stay? Do you know why I got you to stay?'

In response, Yamuna shook her head.

'What are you shaking your ten ser for? If you could smile a bit! Will you eat some paan? It's kapuri, ho!'

Yamuna could not look at him; he was such an ill-mannered and lustful man.

'See, now, if you want to stay in this house, you can have your fun. But you will have to take care of me, ho!'

'I will take care,' Yamuna said and immediately added, 'But, sheth, I have a traveller in my belly. You will have to first help me find a suitable place for it, ho! Once I am free of that, then … First, let me be free of it.'

'What? Get away, you whore's daughter! You've brought someone, na?' Then, thinking of the future, he did not say more. 'Beware, if anyone finds out, then consider yourself dead. Bhai will cut you open as you stand, understood?'

That day, at least, Dhansukh went away.

As her trick had been successful, Yamuna's confidence strengthened. She spent a few days there, lying low. And one evening, finding an opportunity, she escaped.

In the second home Yamuna searched out, she felt she would

have some peace. The whole house had an atmosphere of sickness. The man of the house was ill. His wife was ill. Their son was ill. Only the son's newly married bride was healthy. Yamuna thought that woman was filled with love from head to foot. As if her love was overflowing and no one was responding to it. Which is why, in every word she uttered at every moment, there was a sweet, discerning language of love.

There was no end to the wealth in that house. There was no end to mismanagement either. Neither was there any end to sickness and greed. When she stood on the topmost storey of the big, elegant, grand haveli, she thought there was no house in the city that could match this one. Only the newly married wife understood the emptiness of the house. This was just a building and, except for that, there was nothing else in it. Every moment, Yamuna thirsted to do killol[15] with someone – but there were only colourful, empty rooms before her.

After Yamuna had been there awhile, the man of the house passed away – he had been living only for the sake of dying. His wife also left immediately after. And the new owner of the house – the newly married bride's husband – was lying sick with consumption. There was no hope that he would survive.

At this time, a new vitality spread through Yamuna. She began

---

15. Killol: Poetic, rhyming folk songs that children used to learn from an early age, especially in rural Gujarat. Womenfolk would often sing them when gathered together to do chores or for festive occasions. The writer and poet, Jhaverchand Meghani, made them popular again by collecting them from the oral tradition and publishing them in book form. He also created his own rhyming folk songs.

to feel as if God had provided an opportunity to her. She served the sick husband day and night, although there was no expectation that the tide would turn.

It was about ten at night. Yamuna was lying quietly in her room. Outside, gentle drops of a fine rain fell.

Suddenly, the door opened: 'Yamuna!' The sheth's new wife stood before her.

'Ben? Why, Vasant ben? Did you call me?'

'Come here, na. I need your help.'

Yamuna went out. Her uneasiness was unending.

Vasant took her to the topmost storey. Yamuna walked behind her. The place had been decorated with unparalleled elegance. Everywhere you looked, there were rows of erotic paintings. Mirrors faced each other splendidly as if responding to each other's beauty. Everywhere, lovely women lay in water, making a vain effort to hide their comeliness and, despite being painted, left one's emotions aroused. In one spot, there was a charming depiction of ancient Babylon. In another spot, covering their voluptuous limbs, there stood even more alluring, pretty women. In one location, a pleasing young woman appearing like a blooming bud – a beauty drenched as if she had just come out of the water – sat naked on a bare rock. The sight of that body's shape and lines was not as exciting as the sound of silence from her every limb. That silence, it seemed, was saying: 'See, here I am. Forever young, forever yearning, forever new.'

In many places, sculpted beauties stood holding pitchers to their breasts and filling vessels with drink.

Yamuna kept looking. This was the first time she had seen this room. She could only stare. She had also lived a life as the daughter-in-law of a leading city merchant. But here, she saw a rather different scene. So, as if she had understood Vasant's intention somewhat, she spoke: 'Ben, I am seeing this for the first time. You typically sit swaying on the swing here.'

With a terrible impassioned sigh, Vasant shut her eyes and stood before her. Yamuna did not say anything further.

When Vasant opened her eyes, tears were falling profusely from them.

'Ben?'

'Who are you, bai? You seem to be someone like me. You are not an ignorant and uncultured servant. Speak, tell the truth, who are you?'

'Ben...' Yamuna stood without offering information.

'I cannot bear this now. To set myself on fire, to drown myself in water, to commit suicide – this is what I feel like doing. You are someone like me. Even though you won't tell me, I am telling you. This wealth, this restraint that has to be forcibly maintained – I cannot bear either of these. Yamuna! Will you bring me a bit of poison?'

'Arrey, ben! Being so wise, why are you acting like a mad person? Who does not have sorrow? And tomorrow morning, he will be hale and hearty and you – '

'All that hope is false. Yamuna, Narayan forbid, but if anything unfavourable should happen, I will become a wanderer on the streets. If there is no heir after the master, then I will wander in a worse condition than homeless sluts. Yamuna, can you not be of some help?'

'Ben, ba, what should I do?'

'Do you have knowledge of any young man ... While there is

still time – afterwards, nothing can be done. While he is still sick, can we not do something?'

As if stung by a thousand scorpions, Yamuna stumbled backwards. She understood Vasant's misery. But she had not imagined even in her dreams that the mistress of the house would go to such lengths.

'Ben!' She took the support of a nearby couch and sat down.

Vasant fell to her feet. 'Yamuna, you – you be my sister. If you don't want to make me a homeless slut, then this is the only path. It is known from the scriptures. Great men have seen fit to do it. Some true youth…' She could not speak further.

Like a person runs away on spotting a cobra, so Yamuna ran to escape. But Vasant went after her. She caught Yamuna and crushed her in a double arm bind. And, intoxicated by the fervour of the moment, she kissed Yamuna's face.

'But won't you say who you are? You are not a servant. And you are not wandering after some holy man from house to house, are you?'

'Ben, let me go, I'll tell you something.'

'Alright, tell me, dear!' Vasant patted her on the cheek, grabbed her hand, and sat her down. 'What do you want to say? Say it, dear.'

'I am unfortunate just like you. I have been wandering about simply trying to save myself.'

'And still you are not helping to save me from becoming a wanderer?'

'What can I tell you, ben? You are putting yourself, intentionally, into prison.'

'Well done! She is an intelligent one. But dear – '

Just then, there appeared to be some noise downstairs. Taking advantage of that, Yamuna went downstairs.

Going out, Vasant said in her ear, 'Support me. Dear, give me some support, search out some assistance. What else do you need to understand this situation?'

After that, Yamuna evaded the young mistress. After three or four months, the sun of that house set. That day, Vasant did not cry much. But her face was so absorbed with grief that, on seeing it, a person would become grave. It was not the kind of grieving a person does for another person or relative. The indescribable sadness on her face was the kind of sorrow that a person experiences when the time comes to leave the earth.

Vasant woke up in the morning and called the watchman. 'Bhaiya, this is for you...' and she gave him two gold bracelets.

So, remembering every servant, she gave everyone something or the other. Yamuna received a beautiful sari.

Yamuna was bewildered. She thought Vasant was giving gifts to everyone because she had to leave the house soon. She worried about herself. Now she would have to find another home.

After that, Vasant walked through every single room, sitting for a short while in each one. So many rooms were overflowing with wealth. In several, the furniture had been delivered just three days before.

Late in the evening, she went to the uppermost storey. Yamuna followed quietly after Vasant. But she could not see the woman anywhere. The doors were shut. The lights were switched off.

Right at midnight, horrifying shrieks shook the entire building.

Yamuna ran to go upstairs.

Flames of fire could be seen billowing from Vasant's room.

In the meantime, the watchman arrived and kicked open the door. Inside, in the flickering light, Vasant was ablaze. She saw Yamuna, who ran to save her. But, running forward, Vasant embraced Yamuna.

'Ben! You … you … suffering … to me…' Vasant could not say anything more. She tumbled into a heap. Yamuna also fell beside her.

The next day, the pyres of both the noble daughters-in-law, who had been sacrificed in the fire accident, were burning next to each other.

Light and Shade

For such a small girl, this dignified-sounding name was certainly somewhat startling. But even more surprising was her temperament. Until something was broken, she did not believe in fixing it. For one, at such a young age, she took care of a couple of children as if she were a mother. And, on top of that, as a bonus, her mother would beat her up. Being the oldest might have many advantages but, in Chandangauri's share, there had only been disadvantages. Her mother always gave her the last and the smallest portion of food. It was good that Chandan was second to none. So, when Ma wandered away, Chandan would force a bit out of everyone else's portions by yelling at someone, or making another cry, or threatening another sibling. Otherwise, the poor one would have been mired in misfortune.

When Gopaldas' wife, Lakshmi, awoke at 8:30 and sat to clean her teeth, Chandan would stand there with a pot of water. But, if she just stood there with the pot of water, Lakshmi would say, 'Are you stupid? Why are you standing like that? Last night's utensils are lying dirty. Can't you see?' Yet, if she went to clean the dirty

utensils, Lakshmi would say, 'So here comes *bai saheb*! Bring the
pot of water right away. Get the utensils later.'

The constant bickering would hurt Chandan like an arrow
to her heart. But she had committed to memory the fear that her
mother Nandu, who usually did all the housework for Lakshmi,
would intimidate her with at home. And that fear, which had
made a home inside of Chandan, had also made her determined to accept every task with ease. Before sleeping, her mother
always told her, 'Girl, wake up early tomorrow morning and go.
Otherwise, my mother-in-law will strip your hide! And work with
attentiveness, or my precious lady there will kick you out. And
then what will they eat?' So saying, her mother would show her
the four children who had arrived at intervals of a year and a half
each – numbers one, two, three and four. When ranked by age,
they were in the order of six, seven-and-a-quarter, eight-and-a-
half, and ten. Chandan was twelve or thirteen.

So this thing Ma would tell her at night would be in her mind
when she came to work at Gopaldas' house. And, as if she did not
understand anything, she would work like an emotionless puppet.
She would pay only enough attention to know that Gopaldas' wife,
Lakshmi, was definitely not in sight, then get a piece of sopaari[16] or
a piece of clove or a string of wool or sometimes an anni dropped
somewhere by the wandering vaaghran Rudki. Whatever came to
hand, she would take and save it in her huge pocket. In this way,
once, she had gotten an anni. For four days, she had left during her

16. Sopaari: An areca or betel nut that is broken into pieces and
chewed, on its own or wrapped with other ingredients in a betel leaf. It
is a mild stimulant.

afternoon break of noon till 2:00 PM, telling Ma that the saheb's wife had asked her to come early to wash the table. And she had gone out and bought roasted gram, then sat and eaten them on the sands of the Sabarmati, under the bidi leaf tree. At that time, who else would come to eat there in a similar manner but Bhikla?

That secret joy of hers made her quick at her work too, forcing Lakshmi to say once to Chandan's mother, 'Nandudi! Your daughter has become very active nowadays!'

Chandan would not say anything then but, in case she got fortunate with some other wandering anni or a pie paisa, she would take a cloth and start dusting everywhere. And she would do more rounds especially where Gopaldas' architect's scale and other such instruments lay. She was certain Lakshmi was not the kind to leave even a pie lying about anywhere. But Gopaldas had suddenly received the opportunity to increase his 250 engineers to 350. So, sometimes, he would unknowingly drop a stray coin or two.

Lakshmi ran the house, primarily. She had only three years of schooling and said 'cha'ab' since she couldn't say 'saheb'. Being from the village, her physique was large and heavy. Gopaldas had been educated in such poverty that he had developed a natural tendency to underestimate himself. With Lakshmi, he had considered himself insignificant from the start and, in so doing, had truly become insignificant. So, at home, which person to hire or fire, what to do and how to do it – all this management was in Lakshmi's hands. Nandudi and Chandan would sustain the torrent of Lakshmi's words. At 8:30 in the morning, Chandan would always be standing with a pot of lukewarm water. Yet, at least once a day, Lakshmi never failed to threaten to have Nandudi's husband removed from his job at the mill. And there was a reason for that. Where she came from, all elders threatened the younger people to keep them under control. Her father threatened her mother, who in turn threatened their boy; the boy threatened the girls, who went on to threaten the rabaari who went to graze the cattle; the rabaari beat the cattle; and on and on that unhappy circle continued. So, no matter how much Chandan or Nandu worked, it failed to please Lakshmi.

And Lakshmi often told Gopaldas: 'Nandudi hasn't been working; do as you see fit with her husband.'

Despite that, in the end, the threats never materialised. Seeing this, mother and daughter stopped minding the insults. On occasion, when Lakshmi would hit Chandan, Nandu would also reprimand her instead of taking her side, 'Here, whore! You're not doing as bai saheb wants?' and even hit her. After this would happen, and everyone would sit to eat that afternoon at home, then the precious four or five vegetable pieces brought from Gopaldas' would find their way only into Chandan's plate.

Seeing her mother's unspoken love and recalling her actions from the morning, unbidden tears would fall from Chandan's eyes. Then both mother and daughter would start to eat in silence.

Ma's speechless love – which spread its light across even such dark earth – must have taught Chandan this much at least: that, oftentimes, there is something in not thinking only of oneself. Otherwise, why would this girl, who toiled so much for roasted gram worth one paisa, do this now when Nandudi was ill: put aside a biscuit and some tea in a bowl when she went to give the saheb snacks in the afternoon; deliver them to her Ma on the way itself; and, so that she would not lose time, walk so quickly as to become breathless?

During the time that Nandudi was sick, Chandan came to work regularly. And, with her sharp vision, she kept looking, hoping to find a square two-anna and not the uneven one-anna. Nandudi was ill and the young girl was motivated by her innate nurturing tendencies to carry out these different roles, doing all of it as if it were nothing: take care of four children, do the housework, keep Lakshmi happy, steal snacks and give Ma a drink of tea.

She began to do as Nandudi used to do before her. Nandudi had a right to one cup of tea at Lakshmi's house. But, on some rare days, she would get one and a half cups of tea. Nandudi would not drink tea that day. Chandan would get angry that Ma was not drinking tea and was not letting her drink it either. But the mother took the tea home with her so that all the children would get a few drops. Chandan would see that and stop complaining.

Now that she was in Nandudi's place, she had begun to do the same thing. She didn't realise it, but who knows how exactly it suddenly occurred to her: now I will not drink the tea here; I will take it home.

But the real fun came one day when Chandan stole a paavli. Her thought was to keep the coin hidden and, if no one remembered in a few days, take the opportunity to steal it away. But before she could make any decision, Lakshmi arrived and, in a fright, Chandan put the paavli into her pocket.

In the afternoon, when she came to work, her thought was to put the paavli back. There was a reason for that. She was aware that if she did any wrong and lost her job, the tea that her sick mother was getting in the mornings and afternoons would be gone and it would be a big emotional blow for her. So, if possible, she wanted to stay virtuous right now. She would take the opportunity to be wicked afterwards. But now – though, in her mind, this virtue was worthless – she had no option other than to be vigilant.

It so happened that, as she was leaving home, the four children were clinging to their ma, pulling at her. There was no one else at home. So, as Chandan left to go, Ma said, 'Give these children two paise's worth roasted gram before you go so they will leave me in peace!'

Nandudi said this for the sake of saying it, but the children immediately caught onto her words. Then Chandan found out that there weren't even two paise in the house, so she left without saying anything. In the afternoon, somehow, she dropped off roasted gram worth two paise at home. These two paise were from exchanging the paavli.

The next morning too, she bought two paise's worth of roasted gram. These snacks kept the children quiet and, thanks to that, Nandudi got so much rest that her illness also seemed to be receding. So Chandan also resolved to forget about the paavli.

The following morning, when Chandan came to work, as soon as she had placed a foot on the verandah, she jumped with, 'Oy, you're killing me!' Lakshmi had caught her by the lobe of one ear, pulled Chandan towards herself, and landed two blows on the girl's back.

Chandan took no account of the beating, but she trembled in fear that, if Lakshmi had found out about the paavli and was beating her for that reason, she would be removed from the job. Just then, she heard Lakshmi's Gajendramoksh[17]-like voice: 'Saali! You touch a Bhangi and then come into this house without bathing?'

Chandan remembered. Yesterday, to exchange the paavli, rather than going to some nearby shopkeeper who might give evidence if he heard of the matter, she had turned to no other than the Bhangi's son, who had been jingling paisa in his sack. She had exchanged the paavli with paisa from him. Lakshmi's gaze, from the window or who knows how, had fallen on Chandan sitting beside the Bhangi, Bhikuda, and not on her taking the paisa. And Lakshmi had hit her.

On discovering the reason for the beating, Chandan felt it like the light touch of a flower. She spoke with some enthusiasm, 'I will never touch him from now on, ba!'

'Never touch from now on! But what were you doing there yesterday?'

Chandan was sure she would not be able to think up a reason and would make some mistake when, like Vishnu's vimaan,[18] Gopaldas' voice was heard, 'Eh-li! Chandi! Water, bring water! Late, it's getting late!'

'Eh-li, wash your feet before you go.'

'Yes … ba…' So saying, Chandan walked away. No, not walked, ran away.

But the blows that had landed had felt so lovely to her that,

---

17. Gajendramoksh was an elephant, Gajendra, who had been saved by Lord Vishnu from the clutches of a crocodile and given moksha (salvation).

18. Vishnu's vimaan: A reference to Lord Vishnu's heavenly aircraft or divine flying chariot.

if she could have her way, she would go to Lakshmi and say, 'Hit me with two more, maavdi![19] But be so kind as to forget about the paavli!'

But if a vulture could remain without sniffing out a dead beast, only then Lakshmi could remain without sniffing out a paavli. In the evening, she told Chandan, who was leaving for home, 'Girl, send your mother tomorrow.'

'She has a fever, ba!'

'Still, send her. Or she will not stay on. You stole a paavli yesterday, na?'

'Paavli?'

'Yes, yes, paavli, you rich man's daughter! Do I not know of it? Tomorrow, bring back the paavli. And, from tomorrow, don't come to work.'

Chandan felt a mountain of worry weigh on her but she said suddenly, 'The paavli will be wherever you've placed it, ba! I have not taken it.'

'Fine. Go now. We'll see tomorrow.'

Chandan did leave, but it was as if there were shackles weighing a thousand maunds around her ankles. It was evening-time and, in the Ahmedabadi fog, the light from the electric lamps was dim. She walked on but, in her mind, a worry was making its home: where to get the paavli, and how to put it back exactly where it had been so that she would be saved. She was walking absent-mindedly when someone collided into her.

'Alya, who is it?'

_____

19. Maavdi is an affectionate term for mother in some rural Gujarati dialects.

'It is only me, Chandi!'

'Who, Bhikudo?'

'Yes.'

'Alya, why did you run into me?'

'This paavli of yours is no use. Take it back and return my paisa to me!' Bhikuda held out the paavli.

Chandan felt a tremor of joy and quickly snatched the coin from Bhikuda's hand.

'But my paisa?'

'Your paisa … won't I give it to you tomorrow?'

'If you don't – '

'Swear on you.'

'Arrey, get off with you. Swearing on me! What relation are you of mine that you will abide by that oath?'

Chandan had become so upbeat after getting the paavli back that she burst into laughter.

And, believing that there was no other cause for such laughter, Bhikudo fell to laughing too. 'Why are you doing so much khi-khi?'

'Looking at you,' Chandan could not think of another response.

'So you'll give me the paisa tomorrow, na? If you don't? Give me a promise, then.' Bhikuda extended his hand.

Chandan clapped his hand but, before she could pull it back, Bhikuda caught it. 'Chandudi, I don't want the paisa. But you take this road every day, right?'

'Yes. Why?'

'So … look, I'll tell you…' Bhikudo came forward and pinched her cheek. 'Who's all this loveliness for?'

'Ey ... yy!' Chandan moved away.

'Saali, you're standing near him again?' Gopaldas and Lakshmi had come out to take a turn. They saw Chandan standing beside Bhikuda and called out. Lakshmi took her to task severely and properly, 'Come on, saali ... come home. And sit under the faucet.'

Lakshmi walked ahead, Chandan behind her. Their evening walk remained unfinished and Gopaldas stood yelling. Lakshmi sat Chandan under the faucet and bathed her with her clothes on.

As Lakshmi wandered away in a bit, Chandan removed her pomchu,[20] wrung it thoroughly and wore it back on. She washed the other clothes and hung them to dry. After that, she went into the house to ask, 'Ba, is there any work or can I go?' And then, she returned the paavli a little further away from where she had found it. Then she went back to her home.

On her way back, Chandan found Bhikudo standing at a distance. He saw her coming and went to her. 'Chandudi! Why? What happened?'

Chandan laughed. She had been amused by the bathing but, more than that, she was thrilled by the fact that she had put the paavli back properly and had decided that she was not going to work from tomorrow on. In that joy, she kept laughing heartily.

Bhikuda said to her, 'Tomorrow, will you bring my paisa or what?'

'Yes, I told you already!'

---

20. Pomchu is a length of cloth worn around the upper torso by women and used to cover the head when needed. It is also known as odhni, even shawl. Often, it is brightly coloured and embroidered.

'Otherwise, I'll touch you!' And, looking around to see if anyone was watching, he caught Chandan's hand. 'What, did you become impure?'

'No, re!' Drawling thus, Chandan walked away. But a very bad thought came into her mind: 'Tomorrow, I will ask him for two paisa!'

The next day, the paavli was found, so Lakshmi did not punish Chandan any more. But she called her mother and threatened her.

Nandudi went home and thrashed Chandan.

On the third day, instead of stealing tea to give her ma, Chandan asked Bhikuda for two paisa, bought roasted gram, and ran off to eat them.

Gulabvahu

The swing-bed was swaying slowly. Sitting on it, Gulabvahu opened her paan box and made a very fine paan. With the skill of a connoisseur, she moulded it and placed it in her mouth. Just then, as if suddenly hearing something, she got up coolly and peeped into the downstairs verandah. Then, with quick feet, she turned back to the swing-bed. For a moment, she sat there uneasily. Then she shouted with a robust intensity: 'Reshamdi ... eh, Reshamdi!'

In response, 'Ho, ba! Eh ... I'm ... I'm coming, ba!' So saying, a sixteen- or seventeen-year-old, somewhat dark but well-formed beautiful young girl, having climbed the stairs, was seen peeping in. 'What did you say, ba?'

'What did you say, ba? So said Rani saheb standing there: what did you say, ba? Come here, ne!'

Reshamdi entered the room. The entire room took on a new appearance due to her beauty. It was as if even the swing-bed was inclined to say to Gulabvahu: this teenage girl is best suited to sit on me.

She began sounding off. 'First of all, see, these metal rings are making a noise,' Gulab said. 'Get a rag dipped in oil from down-stairs. Then, did Khemaji come?'

Without answering the question, the girl went downstairs to work – in fact, she went running.

'She is just as wicked inside as she looks on the outside!'

But Kishorilal, who had come soft-footed up the back stairs and was standing there, caught these words that she had spoken only to herself.

'What can the poor one do? You want to throw her into a bad situation; she doesn't want to get into a worse situation. You brought her up here, raised her, shaped her mind. Now what can the poor one do?'

Gulabvahu slid to one side of the swing. Kishorilal had barely seated himself there when Reshamdi returned. So, for a moment, there was silence.

[2]

Leaving the three-year-old Reshamdi behind, her mother, Jeevti, had been dead for thirteen or fourteen years. Jeevti was, by caste, a Thaakardi.[21] But she had no family on any side. Who knew from which village she had come to the city? And she stayed here, at Kishorilal's, doing the housework. At the time of death, her breath would simply not give up. The thought of what would happen to little Reshamdi had, it seemed, bound her soul tight to her body,

---

21. Thaakardi: Originally from the Kshatriya or warrior caste, this sub-caste eventually became merchants and traders by profession and were, in previous centuries, considered as belonging to a lower level within the sociocultural hierarchies.

leaving the ailing woman miserable. At that time, Gulabvahu had come forward, taken holy Ganga-water in her hands, and given her word that she would bring up Reshamdi. And Jeevti's soul had departed.

Now, this same Reshamdi had come into her youth. She was somewhat dark – just slightly – and that bit of colour lent her exquisitely beautiful, well-shaped physique another kind of charm. It seemed as if, without that extraordinary complexion, half her loveliness would be lost. For all these years, she had lived with the family as its own child. So manners, behaviour, likes, dislikes, desires, temperament, character, disposition, hygiene, living customs – in all of these aspects, she had adopted the family's traditions as its offspring. No one could say she was a Thaakardi and no one could even tell she was of a different caste. Kishorilal's young son – who was called Babulal by all – had now returned home from abroad and, when he had seen Reshamdi, he had been bowled over. At first, he simply could not believe that the five- or seven-year-old he had last seen was this same Reshamdi.

[3]

Reshamdi got the metal rings to stop squeaking but could hardly stop her own youth from making its presence known, could she? If her youth was alluring or attractive, it wouldn't have posed a problem; but the kind of eloquence her youth had was in keeping with her original tribe and community. As the undulating phrases of their folk songs fill the air completely with resonance, so a new splendour would rise in the air wherever she walked.

Task done, she turned to go downstairs when Gulabvahu called her, 'Reshamdi!'

'Ji! Ba!'

'Is Babubhai downstairs?'

'Yes, ba. Yes. He's downstairs.'

'Send him up here. Then, did Khemaji come today?'

'No, ba,' so saying, Reshamdi ran downstairs.

'When I came, what were you saying?' enquired Kishorilal.

'Who, me?'

'You were saying something like, *just the same inside*.'

'Yes, yes, this girl is something else. Different caste – does that imprint ever leave?'

'Why? Does she steal? And who is this Khemaji?'

'This girl is of Thaakardi stock. Now her youth cannot be safeguarded by us. So I have searched out this Khemaji. He is of her caste-community. Does farming. He has wealth. He likes the girl. But this girl doesn't want to move from here! She doesn't like anyone!'

'I was also telling you this. Let her stay with us.'

'And then? Are you going to sit and guard her youth? Or will I? We also have a young boy in the house. I do not want to be in the eyes and on the tongues of people. Once people start talking, that's the end. I don't want that.'

Just earlier, when she had peered into the verandah, she had thought of Babulal's manner of speaking to Reshamdi as somewhat inappropriate. But, right now, she chose to leave it out of the conversation. Which issue should be mentioned, which issue described, how much – in this matter, she had firm confidence in her own proficiency and was never willing to listen to anyone else about it. Kishorilal knew this, so he didn't proceed further. In the meantime, Babu was on his way up from the lower floor.

[4]

In three days, the small four-person and four-storey house was shaken up with clashes of diverse thoughts. At just the mention of Khemaji's name, Reshamdi would become agitated. That was fine, but there was a huge war coming to the house.

Kishorilal felt: why not let Reshamdi stay on if Babubhai had chosen her too.

Hearing this, Gulabvahu was dumbfounded. Then, in an impatient and anguish-filled voice, she said, 'Oh, what will be done of you? Are you not ashamed of saying something so utterly useless? She's lived with us for fifteen years, so she has become part of our caste, is that so? Do you father–son have any understanding of social customs or not?'

'But just you listen to this point –'

'Now I've heard it. I don't want to listen. You may not have a nose. I want to be able to socialise within the caste-community – you just want to go amongst the elders to sit and talk.'

'But she has been with us since she was three years old. What about that?'

'So what? We considered her an orphan child and kept her. But does that change her caste? If her poor mother was here today, she would be completely offended. Can anyone tell she is a Thaakardi?'

'That is exactly why I am telling you. Thought and conduct, behaviour and manners, speech, etiquette – in all of these, she is completely moulded in our way of being. As if she were born a Brahmin–Vaaniya only! And Babubhai finds her agreeable. Then what is the problem in keeping her here?'

'You father and son – both of you have gone crazy, haven't you? If Khemaji does not interest her right now, then I have another boy in my sights also.'

'Who?'

'Bhikuji's Lakhmanji.'

'Lakhmanji?'

'Have you seen him?'

'You had sent him the other day with tea?'

'Yes.'

'That Lakhman is a rustic dullard!'

'We have to search from whatever is within her caste-community. God has filled these castes as he sees fit. What can I or you do about that?'

'But I'm saying our Babu and Reshamdi are of one mind. Do you consider that worth throwing away?'

'Look, you are saying this here to me, that's fine. But if you say it anywhere else, someone will surely give you a dressing down; and not just that, they will consider you a fool! Which world exactly are you living in?'

'We'll change her name. We'll call her Manjula. And where do we have another child to marry off that we will have need of anyone from the caste-community or their opinion once this marriage is done?'

'Fine, do as you wish. Here I go. A-li, Reshamdi!'

From downstairs, a melodious, bird-like voice came, 'Yes, ba! Here I come.' In a short while, Reshamdi arrived and stood there.

Kishorilal stared at her. A girl so beautiful, accomplished in every task, a young woman who could be considered cultured – to hand her over to just anyone felt like he was committing the great sin of a betrayal of trust.

But, to confront Gulabvahu and have this conversation was impossible. So, in the days that followed, father and son both simply watched the arrangements for Reshamdi's departure to her new life in silent agony.

In a short while, Gulabvahu settled the marriage with Lakhmanji.

When the rituals were completed and Reshamdi came to Kishorilal for the final farewell, the awareness that he had committed an injustice towards this refined, beautiful, bright, introverted, playful woman made his heart quiver. With eyes brimming over, he looked closely at the innocent child falling to his feet. Handing her a bag of a hundred rupees, he said, 'Ben, I am giving you this in case you need it sometime; so keep it safe. And, if you need help in a dark hour, never hesitate to come to this house. Consider this your true parental home. So, now go, beta. Everyone must be waiting downstairs. Your husband seems nice. If you have any unhappiness, then write, alright? Don't hesitate even a bit. Now, go.' Forgetting that Reshamdi was his servant, Kishorilal was addressing her as if she were his own daughter. Reshamdi stepped forward to leave and he watched her go with eyes overflowing.

A huge weight burdened his heart. He had let Reshamdi go and had not been able to do anything. Because his world of only three people – himself, Gulabvahu and Babubhai – would be shattered with Reshamdi's presence and he could not bear that. For years, this four-storey house of his had, in a mechanical fashion, become accustomed to a regular lifestyle. When the very first dilemma arose within it of Reshamdi, everyone naturally took the easy route to avoid friction. He was perplexed and agitated but could not win over Gulabvahu's prejudiced social customs. The result was that Reshamdi was gone.

And Reshamdi was gone for good. Her husband, after just a short while, took off to work at another place. Reshamdi also went with him. She felt a deep mistrust for this upper-class community. Similarly, she developed a distaste for the weak-minded overindulgence of their customs and manners. For her path henceforth, she now saw comfort in her own culture. Her memory did not endure anywhere now except during the rare occasions of general small talk. Such was the stream of life that flowed uniformly in Kishorilal's and Gulabvahu's home.

[5]

But Kishorilal's caste-community was not the kind to forget Reshamdi in a hurry. The enthusiasm with which Gulabvahu had married Reshamdi off meant only one thing.

The chatter went like this: 'What could the woman do? It fell on her head, so how could she escape from doing it? Good that she resolved it quickly. If she hadn't done it, a black mark would have marred her reputation. They say the boy had become persistent: "If I marry, the bride will be Reshamdi!"'

'Hai! Hai! It is said, kalyug will arrive in the fourth age – is that not true? Have you heard anything like it?'

'That which we had not heard of, we have seen with our eyes!'

In this manner, Babubhai and Reshamdi became an interesting subject of conversation. From that, another matter was raised:

'Babubhai was going to marry Reshamdi! Now, no one from the caste-community should invite such a degenerate!'

Despite Gulabvahu's tactful moves, this defeat proved to be too expensive. The caste-community folks developed a united front in the matter. Not one of them would cross over Gulabvahu's threshold. They would make aimless conversation, show politeness, but, on the subject of marriage, there was a big nothing. From the poor to the wealthy, all shunned the family.

Gulabvahu now started to speak of it upfront. Yet, no one came forward. A young woman's marriageable age can elapse – this situation was known within society. But this was Babubhai's marriageable age beginning to lapse.

In the meantime, intimations of a particular law were heard. Men might not now be able to marry women who were a certain number of years younger than them. And the women of the entire caste-community were all younger than Babubhai by at least that many years.

But Gulabvahu met some sort of a pious man who took a philanthropic view of her worries. Khushaalchand, the neighbour, came one day. 'Kaki! There is one girl. Like a ring of gold!'

'But of the caste-community, brother? Is she of the caste-community?'

'Caste-community, caste-community, caste-community – why not, kaki? Fifty years ago, her grandfather went to live in Indore. So did he cease to be of the caste-community? If a trader's son crosses the seven seas, it is nothing. She is not educated – but like a ring of gold! She has no money, but her respectability! Next to her, all the rest are like green sprouts.'

Khushaalchand, in the end, had the ring of gold inlaid with

Babubhai's ruby stone. And Gulabvahu, as if issuing a challenge to the entire caste-community, went to the big haveli[22] for darshan[23] with the new bride. And then all the women of the caste-community just stared with their noses high in the air.

The new daughter-in-law was a treasure trove of beauty. The colouring and looks she possessed made her stand apart in the entire caste-community. On the day she showed her daughter-in-law to the community, on returning from the darshan, Gulabvahu had kansaar[24] put to boil for a second time. In three months, that had been the thirty-third time that kansaar was being cooked.

But, before the kansaar had even fully come to boil, someone's footsteps were heard outside. Gulabvahu stared. This was the first time armed forces had arrived at her doorstep. She was not the kind to be frightened, still she was agitated. In front, there stood a head constable accompanied by two or three policemen. Among them, Gulab saw Khushaal. She gestured to him but the head constable immediately asked: 'Who is Babubhai? Where is he?'

'Why? He has gone out. What do you need from him?' Gulab replied.

'There is a warrant in his name!'

'For what?'

'You don't know for what?'

---

22. Haveli: A big Vaishnava temple.
23. Darshan: A devotional visit to a holy place.
24. Kansaar: A well-known Gujarati sweet made from wheat flour, jaggery and ghee. It is typically made for special occasions like weddings or festivities. Newly-wed couples are given kansaar to bring happiness into their life together.

'Are we God that we would know?'

'If there is any man in the house, call him. He is accused of marrying an already-married woman named Lakshmi and installing her in his house!'

'Lakshmi? Who is Lakshmi? There is no Lakshmi here. Lakshmi or Manjula?'

'Whether she is Lakshmi or Manjula – we are only concerned with this photuwaali bai.' The head constable took out a photo.

Gulabvahu was stunned on seeing the photo. It was the same daughter-in-law whose arrival she was celebrating for the thirty-third time. But she boldly made an assertion: 'There is no Lakshmi here. Manju...'

'Arrey, lady, you are wasting time unnecessarily. We are not concerned with who is Lakshmi or who is Manjula. We are interested in this photuwaali bai of the Vaaghri caste, Mangudi. Then, whether she sits here as Manjula or sits elsewhere as Lakshmi or lives somewhere as Padma or wanders about as Kamla – we have no concern with that. Is there a man in the house? Call him!'

Bewildered, Gulabvahu ran upstairs. Her daughter-in-law was standing on the steps. At the very sight of her, Gulabvahu was overtaken with embarrassment. 'Hai re! This slut is the same – here she is!' Muttering this, she ran up.

Coming down, Kishorilal met her head-on, having fastened his coat buttons anyhow in his nervousness. He stared at Gulabvahu. 'What is it? Why are you frightened? I heard everything!'

'But this slut! She's the same cursed one as in the photo!'

Just then, her daughter-in-law's response was heard: 'Yes, ba, that is me all right. But don't say it now. My wretched man used to beat me!'

'But, whore!' Gulabvahu ground her teeth and, in a low voice, took her to task severely: 'Your baap here – '

'Don't be scared, ba! This is the fifth time this sort of thing has happened with me. Is there an escape path from the cellar or not?'

'Yes, yes,' Kishorilal immediately caught on to that idea. He felt his daughter-in-law would now be their deliverance.

'Then just show it to me.' She put a finger on her lips to silence Gulab, who was about to speak. 'If you speak, you are dead, ba! Just show it to me by signalling – '

Gulab showed her daughter-in-law the path and returned, by which time Kishorilal had rearranged his coat buttons and become calm. Following Gulabvahu slowly, he said, 'You betrayed that innocent girl's trust – this result was inevitable. That's what I feel!'

'Na, but now what should I say if they ask something?'

About then, the head constable's voice came, 'And who is Kishorilal in this house?'

The New Poet

[A Farce Performance]

One day, as Raskalanandanand snored during the day, he had a lightning-like idea. Or, in poetic language, a brilliant idea emerged from his soul.

'What if I became a poet?'

In his case, as happens with all good fools, thought and action ran together. From the next day on, he began to compose poems. Which style to select from the countless styles currently popular in the Gujarati language – this was a big question. Eventually, he took a little bit from every style – a trader at every port.[25] One way or the other, he threw himself into the field of poetry. But then he became aware of the difficulty of good grammar and the terribly tangled question of diction. What should he do now?

Seeing how Gujarat's litterateurs had placed so many challenges for a man to become a poet, he also realised the real reason

---

25. The original Gujarati idiom is 'sab bandar ke vepaari', similar to 'jack of all trades' in English.

for this country's decline. He adopted the mantra of 'all is mine' and even kept his diction the same as everyone else's. Emerging from that experiment, this was his first poem:

Poem No. 1

Agnirath[26] body, where does any[27] consciousness[28] go?
Or if my body is everyone's, where does all the con-
sciousness reside?
You are the consciousness of the eyes; you are the con-
sciousness of consciousness.
You are a beloved blossom; you are the call of the blos-
som's brew.
Or you are the one who entices with the brew,
The flower of the soul has such fragrance,
Has beautiful brew essence.

Poem No. 2

Wherever I wander then –
Whenever we have, among flowers,
Begun a pleasant conversation, in that garden,
The splendid, fresh memories of all those events

---

26. Agnirath: This literally means 'steam engine'; it is unclear what the poet intended here.
27. The original Gujarati word used is 'ko', meaning any or some when used poetically.
28. The original Gujarati word used is 'chaitanya', which can mean any of these: consciousness, life, intelligence, knowledge, spirit, the Supreme Being (considered as the essence of all being), vitality, strength or valour. It is not entirely clear what the poet intended here.

Makes my heart shiver. Your memory is the greatest
Elixir of life![29] Your name is beloved; beyond this
More beloved is your heart.

After writing these poems, he began doing the rounds of his
friends' gatherings. Everyone said the poems were excellent. If
they became well-known, he would become a leading light –
the kind that makes people shut their eyes – in literature. One
friend advised that, since the poems were of a superior kind,
notes be provided with them. Another said to add a preface. A
preface writer was also only obtained at a third visit. A devoted
critic had accepted the task of providing notes for these new
poems.

One day, the monthly journal *Gahan* found its way
into his hands. In it, he read his poems and their criticism.
Raskalanandanand was traveling in the third-class compartment
of a train that had just left Viramgaam. In the seat before him, a
Gujarati gentleman sat reading a pamphlet and, as if entertained,
was shaking his head. Raskalanandanand had a terrible doubt.
What if this amusement was flowing due to his writing? Near the
gentleman's head, a young man was bending over and reading. In
the seats nearby, two to four merchants were digging through the
entire history of the declining prices of cotton. A little towards
the end of the seat, a fashionable dandy was getting high on the
pleasure of a ghazal.

---

29. The original Gujarati word used here is 'rasaayan', which could mean
chemistry or medicinal preparation or elixir of life. Given the context,
the third seems most relevant.

To attract the attention of the two pamphlet-wallah literature lovers, Raskalanandanand cleared his throat loudly. He said
softly, 'What are you? Brahmin?'

No matter the topic of the conversation, it must start with a
question about caste – he preserved this custom.

'Ji, yes.' The reader raised his head from his reading and gave
him a sideways look.

'You must be from around Surat?'

'How did you know?' the young man asked with some surprise.

'Why, that's our business, na?' Raskalanandanand said.

'Are you from around Surat?'

'Na, na, there is an implied suggestion in my speech. Due to
much practice, I use poetic language even in general conversation,
so forgive me. But I am a poet and the close observation of human
behaviour is our very business.'

'Oh-ho!' the young man said in a jocular way. Then, as if struck
by lightning, that youth kept staring at Raskalanandanand. He sat
up in his seat and, as if in wonder, he said, 'Your name?'

'I write only with a pseudonym. If I give my real name, people
visit frequently to get poems written.'

The merchants fell quiet, possibly interested to know where
the conversation was going.

'Did you see the last issue of *Gahan*?' Raskalanandanand's
inner aesthete put forth the question.

'*Gahan*? What is that?'

'It's a reputed monthly journal. They include all my writings. Look, this is one of my poems.' He took out an issue of the
monthly and opened to his poem. 'These days, a "European War"
has been raging among the Narmad style, Naval style, Dalpat

style, and recently, the Nanalal style. So, to maintain the "balance of power" and through equal ownership and weightage, I have applied all the styles! And yet, the reader will see that, like a black line running amongst white clouds, my individuality shines brightly. Listen!'

The merchants gazed expectantly at Raskalanandanand in the hope of some delightful reading material. His discourse continued. 'Now the poet creates poems targeted primarily at the soul. Man does all his work with the help of machines, but there is no soul in it – have you experienced such a situation?'

'Yes, yes. Many times. Right now,' the youth chimed in.

But Raskalanandanand was not able to understand the sarcasm within that. He continued: 'Agnirath body, where does any consciousness go?/Or if my body is everyone's, where does everyone's consciousness reside?'

He continued: 'Agnirath body – you will not understand unless you take it one word at a time. This is a coconut. Its meat can only be eaten after breaking the shell. Our body is a steam engine. Just like the one we are traveling in. It works, but in the separated state, it often seems that there is "no consciousness" – to make so much emotion sound mystic, the word "any" has been inserted.'

Having spoken, he looked around triumphantly.

The poor merchants looked baffled. One of them, acting as if their earlier conversation was still going on, said to his colleagues, 'If these prices had not fallen, then I wanted to undertake Jaggu's wedding this year itself!'

Another, with some politeness, asked Raskalanandanand, 'Bhai, forgive us. This is not our work; it is for the Pundit folk.'

'No worries,' Raskalanandanand said. 'This is not your field. Big, powerful people get tripped up with this subject matter. What can you do!'

And, from that superior posture, he moved forward. 'Now here starts another style. Like that of the great poet, Kalidasa's "Athava mrdu vastu hinsitum"[30] – you know it, na?'

'Ji!'

'So this next line is of that kind. But the sentiment is still high.'

'No, bhai, the price[31] is toppling!' a merchant asserted.

Everyone burst out laughing.

'Bhai!' Raskalanandanand spoke as if reprimanding, 'This is about the essence of sentiment found in poetry!'

'Huh. Keep going, keep going, king of poets!' That youth was quite a match for Raskalanandanand. He was nodding his head as if deriving a great deal of pleasure.

'"Or if my body is everyone's, where does all the consciousness reside?" "All" – by adding that word, the poet has indicated that his mind has now achieved freedom from even Indriya-vyaapaar.[32] There is a deep implied meaning in that word.'

---

30. Athava mrdu vastu hinsitum – This is the start of the 45th verse of Canto 8 from Kalidasa's epic poem, Raghuvansha. The entire verse: 'Or, tender things destroyed by means of tender things alone – such acts the god of death (literally, destroyer of the people) undertakes. The lotus plant which is destroyed by frost – I consider as the first instance of this.' It is really quite meaningless in context here, as with most of our poet's prattling.

31. Bhaav: In Gujarati, the word 'bhaav' means sentiment as well as price.

32. The literal translation of 'Indriya' is 'organ of sense, sense-organ; organ of reproduction'; 'vyaapaar' means business or activity or business

'Although, the word seems a bit shallow,' that youth said to instigate him a bit.

'That is its very ingenuity. A small word has infinite depth.'

'King of poets, you have surpassed expectations with this second line!'

'It is now that the sentiments will rise!' the king of poets said with elation.

The Surti gentleman squinted at the merchants.

'Look at this, Kalaapi![33] From every limb, life has come to reside right here. In my second line, there is more of the "Soul's Cry" – aatmanaad. But now comes a new style. So that those taking the path of Apadyaagadya[34] will consider me theirs for even a moment, and those writing in the styles of Dalpat, Narmad or Kalaapi will not make faces as if they've swallowed castor oil, this is a new experiment! There is no song in it, but there is a rhythm! Look at these swinging letters! "You are the consciousness of the eyes; you are the consciousness of consciousness." Do you see now? There is a rhythm here. "The consciousness of consciousness." With these words, the entire line is dancing – as when we strike a filament at one end and the entire filament vibrates. And, with that, the entire line takes on a poetic beauty!'

---

or occupation. So, we might assume the poet is describing a rest from the activity of the senses but with a double meaning, as his next line suggests.

33. Kalaapi: The pseudonym of a nineteenth-century Gujarati poet and the Thakor (prince) of Lathi state in Gujarat. He is mostly known for his poems depicting his own pathos.

34. Apadyagadya: The innovative, rhyming, lyrical prose of Nanalal Dalpatram Kavi, a poet and playwright and son of the famous poet, Dalpatram.

He continued: 'Now "You are a beloved blossom; you are the call of the blossom's brew!" This isn't just poetry, this is art. The effect grows more and more, such is the wealth of words. Look: beloved blossom, blossom and brew. So they are all words beginning with B. Again, the blossom is beloved; moreover, there is the call of the blossom.'

'Call of the blossom?' the youth asked. 'Not of the aamli,[35] right?'

'That, you will not understand,' Raskalanandanand said hastily. He did not have time to pause in the middle now to explain the depth of his poem.

'Look: "You are my life; you are my heart itself." Did you see? Bhavabhuti's[36] sentiments. Now the poet is flying even higher! The flower's fragrance is still crude. Its subtle secret is its essence. That's why "Or you are the one who entices with the brew…" has been included. Besides, the other ingenuity there is that it becomes an embellishment. In this poem, there is old, there is new, there is dance, there is music – so this is a beautiful poem! I am not writing nowadays, otherwise I'd write poems that would easily put Gujarati literature on the literary map of the world.'

'Can this poem be sung?'

---

35. Aamli: Literally, tamarind. However, in Gujarati, there are a couple of idioms which this youth could be referring to as a way of making fun of the poet. First, 'aamli ramaadvi' translated as 'to play with the tamarind' and meaning 'to deceive/fool/confuse' someone. Second, 'aamli na paan ma sui ja' translated as 'go sleep in the aamli leaves' and meaning 'be gone; away with you.'

36. Bhavabhuti: An ancient, well-known Sanskrit poet.

'Yes, why not? Read with a somewhat higher note. Essentially, singing is just talking at a higher register, what else? See this last poem about a dove that I have called "Dove's Joy": The dove's eyes are pure; pure is its gaze;/As a holy statue/As a likeness of the soul/As an ideal image of joy/As if making music 'Ghu Ghu'/ Pure dove of the garden of the world/It is a flower! A flower of the bird society!'

Elated, he continued: 'There is imagination here. Moreover, the poet, each time, flies higher and higher! Finally, establishing the dove's position, connecting it with worldly customs, he flies so high in his imagination that people cannot see with their human eyes!'

'Oh-ho! This is just as expressive as Shelley's "Skylark". However, it is even more similar to Keats. Such poems are rare in Gujarati literature,' the Surti gentleman said somewhat jokingly.

Raskalanandanandji would have continued further but, just then, the next station arrived and a handful of men got on. It was such that he could barely keep his seat. So, putting poetry discourse aside, the king of poets descended to the lower level. Hoping that the new men would recognise him as a poet too, he waved *Gahan* about a few times. But poetic talk on the topic of the gold market had spread in such a manner that he now had to observe silence.

But can such an aesthete remain without creating a literary atmosphere? After a short while, he asked the newcomers: 'Bhai, your name?'

'Amrutlal.'

'What caste are you?'

'Vaaniya.'

'What, you must be a Shroff?'

'Yes.'

'Any interest at all in literature?'

'If it's easy to understand and interesting, then I certainly read it.'

'Read the latest poets?'

'Yes.'

'Who all?' Raskalanandanandji became impatient.

The man replied, 'Have read Tulsidas' Ramayan, Premanand's Dashamskandh, Shyamal Kavi's stories – '

'Those are all old. What about the new?' Raskalanandanandji cut in.

'Bhai, please forgive. The new poets either fly so high that they seem like birds rather than people, or they fly so low that they seem like rabbits hiding from people. Cannot understand anything there.'

'The subject is deep, na? It's not your subject!' Raskalanandanandji said, as if taking pride in his self-created superior disposition.

But that jocular youth could not remain quiet. 'This bhai is also a poet!'

'Is that so?'

'Then let us hear one of your poems, na?'

'Here, read this. *Gahan*.'

The gentleman took the journal but, within a moment, cast it aside and applied himself to market chatter. The Surti gentleman was noting, with squinty eyes, Raskalanandanandji's despair.

All this while, I had kept my peace. Now, I decided to chat with this Surti gentleman. I called to him but he was being overtaken by sleep. He gave a joking response: 'His poems awaken a honeyed imagination and send one to sweet sleep!'

Raskalanandanandji laughed and said, 'But *I* am not sleepy.'

'Now that can be cured,' I said. 'Read your own poetry, na? You will promptly fall asleep. It's as if you are carrying sleeping pills with you already.'

Everyone burst out laughing.

The Shehnai Virtuoso

Hassan village, which looks so shabby during the day, alters its appearance in such a way at night that it doesn't seem like its daytime self at all. On a moonlit night, when both its water-filled lakes look like serene skies and begin to make the night lotuses sway lovingly – that vision is one of life's invaluable privileges. In the slow and gentle ripples of the breeze, the waters of both peaceful lakes do a twinkling dance, like some divine beauty's smile. Unintelligible, lovely, secret sounds emerge from within the playful interweave of shadow and light in the nearby coconut grove. Further back, the forest, sleeping in the countless mid-sized green hills, assumes a kind of all-pervasive formless beauty that is not recognised visibly but perceived within. And at the lake's edge, from far away in that coffee-house, stray voices bring across an unusual sweetness because of the remoteness. Then, to stop there for a moment or two, by chance, is rare fortune like some sacred sighting.

I had received that good fortune once but it is so embedded into my memories that, even now, whenever I open my mind's eye, it feels as if Hassan's splendour is inside of me or I am myself in Hassan.

During the day too, the forest canopies on that reddish soil of Mysore can make you forget all the cares of the world for a moment or two. But due to them, the village takes on a kind of ethereal look at night, which is truly wonderful against the skyline.

Once, I had spent a night in that village. Suddenly today, that memory arises from within me. The night was well underway and it was a moonlit one. I thought, to continue sleeping would be a sin. Such a lovely night had blossomed. I sat up in bed and called out to Havaiyo.[37] Havaiyo was none other than a talkative youth from the village. As soon as I had arrived in the guest house during the day, he had shown up talking about far-off places. I devised the name Havaiya based on his business – God only knows his real name. Who knows what it might be? Here, in this unknown land, there was a need for someone knowledgeable. So, while drinking tea, he had spoken of the sky, wind, birds, etcetera; from the famous south Indian sculptures of Jakanacharya[38] to Keshav Mandir.[39] Due to this flighty talk, I had named him Havaiyo.

He had said to me, 'It doesn't seem like anyone is going to be able to sleep tonight in the village.'

37. Havaiyo: A slang term for someone who makes insubstantial or fanciful talk. 'Hava' literally means air or wind.
38. Amarashilpi Jakanacharya: A legendary sculptor credited with building many fine temples for the Kalyani Chalukyas and Hoysalas – the tenth–twelfth century rulers of what is present-day Karnataka and more.
39. Keshav Mandir: This most likely refers to the Chennakeshava Temple, also referred to as Keshava, Kesava or Vijayanarayana Temple of Belur. It is a twelfth-century Hindu temple in the Hassan district of Karnataka state, India.

'Why? What is it?'

'You'll see for yourself. The blooming vision at night of Hassan village – this little piece of earth – it's the beauty queen of south India.'

I laughed inwardly. This was a clear example of how man is a compulsive slave to his own emotions. In his mind, his village was unique. In my mind, there was no beauty like that of Sabarmati's vast sand-filled shores on a moonlit night.

But the night progressed a bit further and Havaiya's point began to seem a hundred percent true. Hassan village stood like such a vision! As if some heavenly angel. Such charm could not be had even in that Ghantvad village settled on the banks of Shingoda river of the Girnar jungle. Otherwise, under the canopy of the forest, the shimmer of a moonlit night is something else. So I thought: to spend this night sleeping in bed would be a real pity. I called out to Havaiya.

He was lying awake. 'Why, sa'ab? Had I not told you?' So saying, he immediately sat up. 'Every year on this day, no one sleeps in Hassan village.'

Then, without saying anything more, we went out for a walk. We strolled towards the lake.

[2]

After going a bit further, Havaiya suddenly said, 'Sa'ab, today is the very day. You are very fortunate. Now, for all your life, you will not be able to forget this village.'

'Alya, you're not mad, are you?' I said. 'This shabby village of yours, where there aren't even a full five nice shops – you keep praising it for no reason. Nature has provided quite a few places with such splendour. Your hamlet doesn't even feature in the count.'

'But this isn't about what splendour nature has given to the village, sa'ab!' Havaiya insisted. 'Here, nature has poured out beauty. But this is about another thing...' Saying this, he suddenly stood still.

'Why, what is it?' I asked.

'That's what it is. Surely it is. Without that, there wouldn't be such a flurry.'

'But what is it?'

'We are going towards this lake. There, every year, on this very day – exactly on this day, not on any other day – a shehnai[40] player arrives.'

'Who is he?'

'A shehnai player. There's a story about him ... worth hearing. In the olden times, in those backwoods, he had a coconut grove. Had a small house. And he was contented living in his small world. When there was a festive occasion and he was called for, he would go and play the shehnai. He got a couple of paise from it, with which his happy, peaceful, steady life continued. He had a respect and pride that he was the master of this auspicious instrument. An artist's pride. As a shehnai player, it was as if he did not even get to witness unhappy events. He was content. There was no other master of the instrument like him in these parts.

'He had a son. In this land, no one had ever seen a boy so fair,

---

40. Shehnai: A musical instrument similar to the oboe and common in India, Pakistan, and Bangladesh. It is made of wood with a double reed at one end and a metal or wooden flared bell at the other end.

lovely, like a statue carved by a sculptor. But he was blind from birth. As if having decided to give the boy the inheritance of all his knowledge, the shehnai player worked hard day and night to make his son a wonderful shehnai player too.

'He was considered a great performer. But this boy of his? It was as if he had become the musical embodiment of some forgotten divine power of nature. Sometimes, he manifested an invisible, extraordinary and secret expression of sorrowful emotion from his auspicious shehnai, such that tears streamed down from the eyes of the listeners. As if, in the destiny of every festive occasion, he had foreseen the markings of grief that nature had hidden in God Shiva's matted hair. So it emerged from his shehnai-playing. After that, all the listeners would fall into praise for his artful offering and forget the scales of sorrow that had risen from the shehnai. Yet, who knows where the sound of this boy's instrument came from. The sad tunes that arose from his auspicious instrument on some occasions were considered the most amazing. When the tragic gloom, like the doleful, lamenting strains of jogiya[41] music, would advance from that shehnai, then even his own father would lay a hand on his and be able to say only this much in a grief-drenched voice: "Son! Enough now. Enough. Any more than this will not be bearable." At that time, it would seem as if even the atmosphere would not have the energy to endure any greater sorrow.

'When this happened, the boy would put away the shehnai.

---

41. Jogiya music: Refers to the classical Jogiya raag in Hindustani music. It's usually sung or played before sunrise (during the first prahaar) to evoke a heavy mood of devotion.

But, as if the silhouettes of sorrow were still visible in the air, all the listeners would continue to perceive the music in their hearts for a few more moments.

'He was an astonishing boy!

'Once, it so happened that a landowner was celebrating a festive occasion at his place. To ensure that such an important man would not have even the slightest bit of suspicion, the shehnai player did not take his son with him that day. He knew that capturing incredibly tragic melodies in the auspicious instrument was not the work of any human ability. It was a unique gift given to his boy. But, where the event was festive and only happy things were being exchanged in the passing midnight, if his boy raised sounds of the lamenting jogiya, echoing the sadness of the lonely devotee, then the mood of the occasion would be ruined unnecessarily. And, in time, the dark shadows of people's suspicions would fall over the festive mood.

'So, that day, he went alone. The boy's mother had died during his early childhood. So, father and son, who always went together everywhere, were separated today. This was a novelty. "As soon as it is midnight, I will return" – consoling himself thus and alerting a neighbour, the shehnai player left.

'But, after that, who knows what happened? See that shimmering water ahead? Who knows in what manner the boy arrived there?'

'Alone?'

'That's the thing. Both father and son were familiar with this path. They went back and forth on it often. So, following the guide of his cane, the son must have reached there. And whether it was an accident or the poor boy fell victim to some artist's jealousy

– because, just as there was a class of people who sang praises of his wonderful talent, so there was a group that criticised him – no one can say what happened but he fell into the deep lake!'

'Arr-r-r-r!'

'His father found out about it. And his heart broke. It seems he is here today.'

'Who? The boy? Or his father? Why today?'

'Today, saheb! It is the death anniversary of that boy. After the death of his son, the shehnai player refuses to take the auspicious instrument in his hands again. No matter what the occasion and no matter the fee he might be promised, he absolutely gave up the shehnai from that day on. He comes here every year without fail only on his son's death anniversary – his shehnai can only be heard on this day.'

'A bit addle-headed, or lacking in practical wisdom, or foolish, or somewhat crazy! All who are born must die. The event was traumatic, that's true. But what is to be gained from continuing to memorialise him with such crazy sentimentality?' I said with some acrimony. 'Instead of that, he could have bestowed the legacy of his knowledge on to so many other young men. If I was in the logician's[42] seat, I would put a lethal indictment on him for not increasing the country's intellectual wealth and punish him! Knowledge is hardly the sole property of a weak mind!'

'That is all fine, sa'ab!' Havaiya responded, 'but what can we know about what's in his heart? The truth is that the shehnai

---

42. Logician: A person who, on behalf of the government, went about checking the statistics on whether people were doing the work they had registered as doing with their local governments and paying their taxes.

player takes the instrument in his hands only on this one day of
the year. On this day, he is able to bring forward the one thing –
the strains of the jogiya raag that he has never before known in
his life – and, that too, in an amazing way.'

'What thing?'

'When, from the shehnai, the lamenting strains of the jogiya
spread everywhere and fill the air of the mellowing midnight,
saheb! Then you feel that it would be good if this man was a
bit more addle-headed. Addle-brained people are also a kind of
wealth, saheb! And, always, it is only particular individuals whose
brains get addled, saheb. The rest have only the opportunity to
get addle-brained. And many are not even truly addle-brained but
geniuses. An addled brain is an illness, but isn't it also a strength?'

I was about to give him an even more stern reply but then,
as if stuck to the ground, my feet stopped of their own accord.

Through the air, such despairing, lamenting harmonies emanated from the sad tunes of the shehnai player that just a single note of his falling on the ear felt like a language only the soul
understands! As if today, having the opportunity to hear that language, the soul had rendered the entire body and all the senses
helpless and had overtaken the mind.

To counter this tyranny of the soul, I began searching for wisdom. But that's when I realised that my reserve of pure wisdom
was close to nothing. What appeared to be wisdom was an argu-
mentative account of received prejudices.

But, in two moments, all that knowledge, pride and everything flew away.

That lamenting music was still floating through the air. And
not just people, it seemed as if the birds and animals and plants

too, arrey, even the moonlight flowing down from the sky, had forgotten themselves in it – or, you could say, they were seeking to find themselves in it.

Mungo Gungo

Nobody in the entire village knew his name. Everyone called him Mungo. When saying 'Mungo', the image of a thin, scrawny, small-eyed, somewhat deformed-looking human form appears before our eyes. Some kind person must have thought that it wasn't right to call a helpless stranger 'Mungo'. That person must have had some understanding of poetry so, with an alliterative playful combination that was fitting, he changed the name to 'Mungo Gungo', making the boy known throughout Bhanderiya village by that name.

At first, Mungo Gungo sustained himself by beseeching and begging. Once it so happened that, during the height of the monsoon, water was flowing in the massive reservoir of the village as profusely as in the ocean. At one end, in a part near the bank, the water was a bit shallow. Many fun-loving boys were playfully pretending to dive and drown there. What other work did Mungo Gungo have? Wherever he went, he would sit for a few hours. Today also, in just that manner, he sat watching the boys' games. Right then, one of the more jocular boys thought of playing a prank on Mungo Gungo. So he showered water on him. Mungo got completely soaked. And all the boys burst out into noisy laughter.

But then, of course, Mungo was quick to take offence. He did not have speech, so his anger would manifest itself as an animal's – unintelligible, garbled, unclear, repetitive screeches and cries. Today, Mungo added the company of pebbles and clods of earth to those shrill shrieks. As a result, seven or eight boys came out of the water and ran to catch him. Mungo ahead, the boys behind. It was quite a scene.

Mungo was not paying attention and stumbled into a pothole in the street. In that pothole, the water reached up to his waist. That was the perfect opportunity to dunk him. Eventually, the boys caught him and bathed him in the reservoir water. Only then did they let go of him.

[2]

But that evening, something happened. Mungo sat by the reservoir bank till late – until the heavenly darkness began to descend upon the earth. The reservoir waters, which had risen up to the eyeballs, were slowly becoming peaceful and clear. Who knew what thoughts Mungo had fallen into, sitting there? He stayed on.

Today, the pranksters had gone after him and caught him. And then, one of them had signalled and the others had joyfully picked it up. That's why they had swung him by his arms and legs and dunked him for a considerable amount of time in the shallow end of the reservoir. Mungo had struggled in the water quite a bit to get free, but two boys had caught him by the knees. Two had held him by the shoulders. Two had stood by the sides. 'Swim, Mungaji, swim! Otherwise, you will die drowning.' So saying, they had made him taste the world of water for a good amount of time. When he had gotten out, he was trembling. Then, the boys had gathered up twigs and lit a fire. Someone had given this, someone had given that – and in that manner, they had even given him some clothes.

But who knows what had happened to Gunga that, even after everyone left, he sat at the edge of the reservoir just staring at the water. He had no tongue, so it was not possible for him to tell anyone what was happening to him. Even if he did have speech, Gungo had absolutely no person to call his own in the village. So he remained seated by the water. Whether the waters of the reservoir understood the thoughts in his mind, only they knew. But it was as if, that day, Mungo had made the quiet and flowing waves listen to his heart's 'kai-kai' speech for a long time. Then, maybe he had rebuked the waters for making fun of a disabled person like him, or prayed to them to show him the poetry within them, or perhaps appealed to them to absorb his uninteresting life within them, or perhaps simply paid obeisance to the waters as a grateful devotee.

What he did, what he experienced, what he understood, or what he felt – only he knew. But, after that, he was seen many times by the reservoir's banks. When the boys swam, it seemed as if he too was attempting to swim. And, even though everyone laughed at his vain attempts, he would exert himself repeatedly. In time, he even brought a bowl up to the surface.

[3]

Thereafter, Gunga's fame as an accomplished swimmer grew. As if the waters had heard his pleas, when Mungo would go into them, it was as if a light would shine. Not only that, he began to be seen as good luck. He had plucked out one or two people from the reservoir as one plucks specks out of the eye. If someone's jug fell in the water, a group would come calling, 'Come on, Gunga bhai!' If someone's pot fell in, there would be a search for Gunga. Once, he had gone and found an earring from a well. Gunga was now renowned as Gunga Tarvaiyya.

When this crippled man's meaningless life gained purpose in this manner, all the many dormant desires of his speechless existence came alive too. He too felt an inclination to start a family, become a householder, make a home, settle his life. He even constructed a small room. Then the hassle of looking for Gungo anywhere and everywhere ended. Gungo could always be found, mornings and evenings, in his room. In this way, he became a member of that small village and was considered indispensable.

[4]

But the value of fame in this disabled person's life must have been quite different than in the lives of people who can speak. Sometimes, when he fished a person's only child out of the waters alive, hundreds of grateful eyes would alight on him, the boy's mother would fall at his feet, and his deformed body would receive many loving pats from the men. It seemed as if he truly experienced a joyous satisfaction deep inside his soul. A value that much exceeded the reward of five-to-twenty-five rupees that he received, and which he comprehended but was not able to communicate. It was as if Mungo Gungo's skill was moulding him. Isn't there a saying? 'The artist was creating his artwork, but the artwork was creating the artist.' Such was the rare situation here.

Once, Mungo Gungo was sitting when he heard shouting and yelling from a nearby stream. He immediately ran just as he was. When he arrived, he was told that a boy had fallen into the water. Seeing Gungo, everyone's hopes were raised. Right away, someone pointed towards a spot in the water to show Gungo where the boy had fallen. The very next moment, Gungo disappeared into the water.

Gungo had gone in; the boy would come back for sure – this was everyone's firm conviction. Hundreds of women stood at the edge of the stream, eagerly looking in. There was a large gathering of men too. Everyone was gazing steadily into the water.

But that day, unlike any day before, Gungo failed. When he was seen emerging from the water, people got ready to raise a huge roar of praise but they felt a sudden panic grip them as they realised that his hands were empty. Arrey! Gungo empty-handed? No one could believe it. There was an untold sadness in Gungo's red eyes. He disappeared once again.

After a while, he was seen again. But, again, his hands were empty.

Everyone now abandoned hope for the boy's life. Weeping began in all directions. Women began crying with loud, heart-rending wails. The boy's father, as if broken, sat down right there, holding his head in his hands. As if he were a statue without a soul!

But Gungo went into the water a third time. He had lost the game but his immeasurable grief could be seen on his face. Now that Gungo had gone back in, the child might be fished out – but no one had any hopes that his life would be saved.

The third time, like some torrential surge rising from the

stream, Gungo was seen coming through the clear waters. A boy's body was being lifted out by his pigtails. A roar of praise, powerful enough to move heaven and earth, went up in all directions. Perhaps because Gungo heard it, upon emerging from the water, as soon as the boy's body, hanging upside-down, was handed over to the village physician, a barrage of tears began to flow from Gungo's eyes. It was impossible to know what he was going through but he folded his hands and bowed to everyone. He kept bowing for a long time. Mostly, as if he wanted to say to those grave, deep, blue, dark waters, 'Today, you saved my honour.'

The boy was immediately given proper medical attention. The water was pumped out. But there was no sign of life in him. People were engrossed in these activities and, sensing the opportunity, Gungo went away quietly.

[5]

At dawn the next morning, a large crowd of people had gathered near Gunga's room. As if it were some great festival, dhol, traansa, shehnai were being played. The women of the village had taken up a progression of songs. 'Sheri Valaavi,'[43] that Gujarati garba, was pouring in a continual flow.

That boy had survived. He was a single child and a beloved son. So the father had invited the entire village to honour Gungo in his own way. Before Gungo could find out, everyone had arrived at his door.

---

43. 'Sheri valaavi': 'Sheri valaavi saaj karu ne ghare aavone' is an old, popular Gujarati folk song dedicated to a goddess.

But, as if due to yesterday's fatigue, Gunga's room was still closed.

The couple of stray dogs that Gunga greeted on waking by throwing them bits and scraps were also waiting there for the door to open.

And, as if happy with Gunga's heroism, a young beggarwoman, unable to speak just like Gunga, had also arrived and was standing there. She had no fixed dwelling. Gunga had no one to cook his meals. This coincidence added to the joy of the villagers. To bring Gunga out with sweet merrymaking, more dhol-traansa started up.

After a while, seeing that no one was coming out, one impatient watcher pushed the door to Gunga's room.

In response, the door opened. Gunga's entire kingdom lay within. There was a mat. A torn pair of pants and a couple of other pieces of clothing were hanging. On the stove, there was an aluminium vessel. A small metal pot lay upside down beside the earthen water pot. A plate and a bowl lay waiting in ash to be cleaned.

But the people who had rushed inside immediately stepped back, as if in surprise. The person for whom this celebration had been organised, whom everyone was eager to meet, whom that boy's parents had come to felicitate – that Gungo was not there!

The question arose in everyone's mind: 'Where was Gungo?'

But no one in that village ever received the answer to that.

Ratno Dholi

In our small Pipaliya village, which other skilled musician was going to come forward? So, whether you consider him the shehnai-wallah, or the bansi-wallah, or the saarangi-wallah, or the dilruba-wallah, or the vaanjo-wallah, or whatever, he was our Ratno Dholi. But he had an extraordinary gift. At the very end of the village, at the foot of a small mountain, he lived in a small hut that he had built. In the land around the hut, he had planted a few saplings and, in their presence, he sat playing his dhol and enjoying himself.

On top of the mountain, there were many ancient rocks. If those rocks faltered and fell, then Ratno Dholi's hut would be wiped out clean. But Ratno used to say that it had prevailed under the refuge of the goddess' might. Those rocks would strike like gongs and bring to mind the ringing of clear bronze. The villagers called them stone-gongs. A large river flowed behind the gong-like mountain.

When he had no work, Ratno would sit and play his dhol. That dhol, its stick, and he himself – it was as if all three had been friends since birth. From Ratno's dhol, all his heart's sentiments came forth.

Sitting alone sometimes, when he remembered his dead mother and played the dhol, it seemed as if he was offering his heart using the sticks. When a youthful fancy came over him and he hit the dhol with the sticks, it was as if joyful ocean waves leapt through the air. Sometimes, even if there was no invitation from anyone, Ratno would wear brand new clothes, tie a scarf around his waist, put on a new silken turban, place a brass chain around his neck, and get into the mood of a dhol player, showing off his astonishing skills. It would seem as if the dhol were crying, laughing, jumping, dancing; as if it were bouncing and blooming, telling the future, remembering the past. As if calling out to those stone-gongs.

Ratno Dholi told this dhol and its sticks all the secrets of his heart. It was as if he had no words to say to or before men. If he wanted to say anything – make merry, cry, express his happiness, show his disappointment, reveal his hopes – whatever he wanted to say was through this dhol.

He was intrigued too. When the dhol and sticks were separated, they meant nothing. And when they came together, there was a language. What was this? He had become a child of the dhol. Without the dhol, it was as if Ratno was without his soul.

And, having surrendered herself to the music of his dhol, a beautiful woman had also become his. Her name was Sundari. She was a beauty indeed. With every stroke of the dhol, she would dance.

Having received Sundari's companionship, Ratno Dholi became amazing. After that, there was no earthly language that his dhol could not speak. He was himself uneducated, illiterate, but the dhol could talk of all things. One time, while playing at midnight, he brought such a wonderful spectra of heroism that the entire village, as if about to rise up against some outlaws, came out with sticks, spears, scythes, old swords. Ratno's dhol, that day, made them forget the boongiya.[44]

But, when the entire village came out to see, what outlaws and what problems? There was no such thing to be found. Ratno Dholi was alone; a dim lamp burned on his street; and he stood playing the dhol. Overcome with the colours of heroism, Sundari danced on every stroke. There was nothing else to be done.

The entire village turned back, laughing, arrey, he's mad, just mad!

And Ratno was indeed crazy. All who receive oceanic talent become like that. Sanity remains with those whose minds are as small as puddles. Ratno had received the great ocean to swim in. It seemed as if he felt the pleasures of all three worlds from his dhol.

Truly, Ratno was crazy.

But, when a crazy man gets a crazy woman, half the world goes mad. Sundari nurtured all of Ratno's many manias. When she danced, Ratno felt as if the entire universe was dancing. She brought the language of Ratno's sticks perfectly to life.

But this love-devotion of hers had also manifested a corresponding jealousy in the village. A disappointed aspirant for Sundari's hand was the leader in that. His name was Nakoji.

Nakoji would say, 'Dholi thinks that when his dhol sounds

---

44. Boongiya: A type of drum that would be beaten as encouragement for battle bravery.

and this little slut dances, all is fulfilled. But the blind idiot does not see what leaps in her eyes at all. That little slut, dancing away, has discarded all kinds of men. Ratno Dholi will be asleep inside his dhol one day and this little slut will run away, leaving him sleeping. It will be good if the dancing is stopped. Otherwise, there'll be no prosperity here.'

In a village, first, a thing chafes. Then, it combusts into a flame. Then, it is as if that itself is the main event.

There wasn't any other big incident in Pipaliya, so this became the main one. A defamation of Sundari arose from it.

And this slander crossed the line. Sundari's name began to be attached to various others. Then, anyone who turned towards the dholi's home was said to have been called for by Sundari. Nakoji had also seen Sundari wandering about in broad daylight as if Ratno's eyes had been blindfolded.

Many times, when a person thinks they are honest, they do not feel the need to resist falsehoods and slander. But there is a surprising quality about liars: if they are opposed, they become twice as forceful. If you do not oppose them, they are proved right. The lies began, so they would certainly ignite a fire.

This chafing talk fell on Sundari's ears. She heard it from one ear and let it out of the other. It came to Ratno's ears. He paid it no heed. He kept playing the dhol, Sundari kept dancing, and the village kept watching. But Nakoji was not one to lose a gambit. Would anyone ask the cause for his jealousy? Love is the reason for love – this thing must be understood in the same manner. No one wants to live with disappointment.

There was envy in Nakoji's mind regarding Sundari; but when there was no quarrel initiated by either Sundari or her husband, then the flame took the form of a blaze. Now he wanted to win at any cost.

Every person has a different concept of winning. First, he tempted Sundari. He sent her a message: 'With such beauty, what are you doing sitting with that child-like dholi? Come here, sit on this leather cushion of mine. I have the entire village's bham[45] at my place.'

But Sundari did not dignify the proposition with a response. So he worked to take control of the dholi. But he could not manage the trick. And then, asserting that such a dance-craze was not right for the village, he successfully instigated the caste-community. To fit into a village, this was the only way: drag religion into the middle of things.

The caste-community passed a resolution. The dhol could be played, but the dancing was wrong. It might make the gong-stones unsteady. So the dancing must be stopped.

Dholi would go alone to play the dhol. But, without Sundari, he did not enjoy his music. So, when some enthusiasts called him over sometime, Ratno would break the law and take Sundari there with him.

---

45. Bham: Refers to a group of families from the Dalit community in a village who get together to dispose of the village's dead animal carcasses by skinning and tanning the hides and selling the meat and bones. Bhams occupy a higher level within the Dalit or lower-caste hierarchy. Here, the word is most likely being used for the stock of expensive items produced by them.

But this law-breaking gave the village proper fodder. If the same talk goes on all the time, it will give birth to suspicion even in the kindest of souls. An uncertainty entered Ratno's mind.

Once, a beautiful night blossomed. The leaves, trees, pebbles were bathed in moonlight. The gong-stone mountain looked pristine white. Around midnight, Ratno Dholi awoke. An urge to play the dhol came over him. During the day, Sundari's dancing had practically stopped. So he decided to pour out his inner sadness tonight. 'We'll suffer the rebuke, but we'll have a riot tonight.' This sentiment rose in his mind.

Sundari lay in bed, watching Dholi get up. She saw him leave. So she got up after him. With a soft step, she followed him. She was surprised, of course, as to why Dholi had not awakened her.

Meanwhile, Ratno had gotten ready by tying a scarf around his waist, putting on brand-new clothes and wearing a brass chain. And, hanging the dhol from his neck, he was standing in the street.

Sundari stood to one side under the dark shade of a tree. Her anklets remained in her hands. As soon as Dholi struck the taut leather with the sticks, she would start dancing, she thought. Her entire body was rejoicing.

But, arrey! What was this? Dholi's hands remained aloft as if someone were holding them. What was this?

Sundari was also witness to this. Just then, instead of the sticks falling on the dhol, they fell from his hands to the ground. Sundari felt the urge to run over and hand the sticks back to him. However, her rising feet were stopped by Ratno's words to himself.

Ratno, laughing sorrowfully, was speaking as if to himself:

'Ratna! No more, no more. The one who danced is gone. The golden sculpture is gone. Now it is a brass statue. What difference does it make if she dances or doesn't dance? No more, Ratna, no more. Can the entire village be wrong? One or two can be false. No more, Ratna, no more. Bas!'

Sundari felt as if her feet were stuck to the ground. Her heart sank. The anklets fell from her hands. It did not take her long to understand Ratno's talk. A thousand scorpions stung her heart. Her Ratno's heart held this kind of secret? That was that. Sundari's mind was on fire: 'Arrey re! This is what he truly thinks of me! That's the end!'

Bas, that one wound was enough.

In the meantime, Ratno had removed his dhol and placed it on the ground. As if with broken legs, he was turning back. For a moment, his gaze moved high towards the mountain and, as if he were startled, his feet stopped.

'Arrey! Did the gong move too? I saw it move clearly. Why wouldn't it move? Is it a mere rock? No, it is a holy force of virtue.'

This sentence pierced Sundari's heart like a poison-filled arrow. She was certain: Ratno was no longer hers. She spent the entire night crying in bed.

In the morning, Ratno Dholi was stunned. Sundari's bed was empty. She was nowhere to be found.

News spread across the village that Sundari had run away.

Nakoji kept checking in with everyone, saying, 'Bhai, I had said right from the start that he has become blind and that slut is fooling him.'

Ratno nursed a deep wound. He could not understand where Sundari might have disappeared. There was no trace of her either.

The street, without Sundari, was eating him up. He searched for her all day. There was no news.

He became lonely. He abandoned the dhol, put aside the sticks. His mind kept saying Sundari, Sundari. But Sundari wasn't there.

Yet, his grieving ocean of tears did not let him rest for a moment. If he looked one way, he saw Sundari; if he looked the other way, Sundari came into sight. But she was nowhere. She was everywhere but she was nowhere.

One night, his heart made a big clamour to share his thoughts with his old friend, the dhol. Ratno came out. He walked into the street. He looked at the gongs. Suddenly, he remembered. He recalled what he had said on that day. Had Sundari heard it? She had disappeared about that time. Now he connected all the dots. His words were responsible for Sundari's leaving. He himself had made her go away. *Driven* her away!

He picked up the dhol, took up the sticks. Today, he wanted to tell Sundari the story of his separation, sadness and repentance. But Sundari was nowhere.

He paced in the street. As he walked near the trees, something brushed against his feet. He bent down. Sundari's anklets were lying there.

'Aha!' His heart felt the biggest wound of all. It was as if he had found a lamp in the darkness. He had found the missing link in the chain. Sundari must have been standing here on that day. She must have been getting ready to put on the anklets and dance. But his words must have made her put them aside.

There was no limit now to the grief in Ratno's heart. The moment he struck the dhol, it was as if sounds of the utmost tragedy rose in the air. And then the expressiveness of his sticks was such that it could make even the gongs cry. The entire village could only listen. Everyone could sense Ratno weeping.

From the next day, that alone became his language. Who knows why it came to him that Sundari had merged into the big river flowing behind the gong. She had made her resting place in the water. She had found the earth too hard.

Bas, from that time on, whenever you saw him, this Ratno Dholi would be sitting at the edge of the river playing his dhol. And, as if he was actually watching Sundari before him, his eyes would be absorbed in surprise, joy, the trance of love.

At such a time, he would suddenly say, 'Here she comes, here she comes! Aha! What a dance she has begun today. Here she is, dancing. Here, she's looking at me and laughing. Here, she's rebuking me. Here, she's running after me to beat me. Here, she's coming to snatch my dhol!'

Listening to this, the laughing sort laughed and the crying sort cried. But who could say whether his vision was real or unreal?

My Homes

Who knows what, indeed, has happened today that I am remembering my previous homes. All the many homes that I have changed and settled into and out of are floating before my eyes. Each one of them has something or the other to say.

Before all others, I'm recalling my small room. That room was barely six feet long and five feet wide. One of its doors opened onto the verandah. Another one opened onto the street. Such a small room had two doors; so, at that time, it felt like a royal palace. In those days, the existence of two doors was considered befitting a royal palace. What a time? Or, perhaps, what kind of mindset? Whatever it may be, I've stored the memory of that room in my mind forever.

Laying out a jute sack, I used to sit near one of the doors. And when, with a cup of tea, I'd open a package of one or two paise's worth of gaathiya, I'd feel like all the splendours of the world were present in this room.

But an unusual thing happened. After two years, that same room began to seem worthless to me. And, when it felt worthless, the people who lived there appeared unworthy too. Otherwise, the capricious assortment of people who lived there was not the ordinary kind. Dude used to live there. His name wasn't 'dude': it was actually Lavjibhai. But he had not married. His destiny could not find a match anywhere. Given that, and considering it to be some sort of 'company', the poor man would have amusing chats with five to seven women who lived in the neighbourhood. He would share a few jokes and, from time to time, chew a paan, or oil his hair. Based on that, the womenfolk had nicknamed him Dude.

Be that as it may, from whatever this dude earned, the room's rent of six anna, milk worth one and three-quarters or two rupees, vegetables for thirty-times-two sixty paise, and always one ser flour, whatever all that came to, and clothes – he didn't wear shoes – after spending on all these things, he kept whatever money was left in a battered trunk. On occasions and events, he would take from it to offer oil to Hanuman, fill up ant-hills, and buy garlands made of crown flowers. After doing so, he would buy items like sesame seed sweets with whatever remained and, gathering the children on Mondays, distribute among them. The dude had gained a lot of esteem with these children. They called him Lavji kaka. And they had a lot of respect for him.

Lavji worked miscellaneous jobs. When it turned seven in the morning, he would drink his cup of tea and set off. He would return at noon. Coming in, he would make his dhabo and eat. For a while, he would open the Ramayana and sit. He would stretch out a bit. At four, he would set off again. Lavji had the habit of doing whatever anyone ordered him to. He never said no to any work. No haggle about money. No wicked or immoral desires. No gossip or misrepresentation of anyone. No competition with anyone. Lavji had kept his body honed like a machine.

At first, everyone had affection for Lavji. But once, he came home late evening, bringing some Bawan woman with him. The next day itself, respect for the man diminished.

Lavji had not done anything wrong in this. Within his caste-community, even if he performed penance for seventeen years, he was not likely to succeed in getting a wife. So he had done nothing wrong. Still, everyone has their different dharma customs. Therefore, it would be fair to say that, in this gathering of people, his excommunication was called for. The old woman Jhamku stopped talking to him. Although her own son was a drunkard and the son's wife had not even been keeping house in the beginning. But Jhamku felt that Lavji had brought some itinerant and polluted Jhamku's sanctity. So even social intercourse with him was not desirable.

Jhamku stopped talking to Lavji; so Dhaniyo the potter gave up his dealings with the man too. He too stopped recognising Lavji on sight. Shanki, Monghi, and all the neighbours stopped too. In the entire neighbourhood, a line had been struck through Lavji's name. After that, he would come and sit at my place sometimes, me being his only remaining association. I thought Lavji would leave the place soon. A person cannot last at a place where he cannot find even a false friendship. And Lavji had also been talking about leaving.

This is about a particular day. I had put out the lamp in my room and was getting ready to sleep when there were two or three knocks on the door.

It wasn't difficult to ascertain who it might be. These were Lavji's knocks. No one else knocked like that. I got up and opened the door. Indeed, Lavji stood in front of me. But his face was pale and agitated. I understood. Some difficulty related to his new wife must have arisen.

Then Lavji said, 'Has she come this way?'

'Who?' I asked. 'Whose coming are you talking about?'

'Gomti's,' he replied. 'She's not to be found in the house. And she had been nervous and restless since last night, so I'm afraid.'

I knew Gomti was the name of the Bawan who was with him.

I said, 'No, no one has come here. But has something new happened?'

'Something new and something old,' he sighed. 'But he must have made a complaint or Gomti must have taken fright. So, it seems, she has run away.'

'He? Who's *he* now?'

'Why, that blind flute-wallah. Call him her lord, her husband, her master, her shelter-giver, whatever you want. But that blind man lives in the dharamshala near the station and she used to live with him. He must have come over to this side. Gomti had told me just that in the evening. And, since saying that, she had fallen into a distracted sort of agitation. That's why she must have run off!'

Yes. I remembered suddenly: last evening, there was actually a blind boy wandering about this way, playing a wonderfully sweet flute. Perhaps this was about him. I said, 'Yesterday, someone had certainly come by this way playing a flute.'

'That must have been him,' Lavji said. And, saying so, he stared at the ground for a long time. There was some struggle going on in his heart.

I said, 'Lavjibhai, that's all fine. But where did you meet this Gomti? And why did you bring her with you like this? You did not even consider that she must be like this blind man's cane.

Yesterday, I heard that blind man playing the flute along this way. From then onwards, his amazing sorrow-filled tunes have stayed in my mind, as if they've made a home there. Till now, it's as if they continue to be heard. And it feels like they will always be heard. It was like he was pouring his heart out through these notes to show how heart-rending his grief was on losing Gomti's support. That's how it seemed. Whatever you think is fine. But have you searched everywhere? Asked everyone? Perhaps she's staying somewhere in this area? And another thing. Your household goods and furniture are fine, right? She hasn't taken anything? Did you check? Check that for sure!'

Lavji laughed weakly. 'What was she going to take from my ascetic's hut? Also, if she had taken something, I would have felt some gratification. But she hasn't even taken anything. So I hope she doesn't do herself in at some well or lake. Everyone here had started to scorn her a lot. You knew that, na?'

'Had begun to scorn a lot? Who, you're speaking of the old woman, Jhamku?'

'Everyone! Once they knew, was anyone going to hold back? The whole world finds other people's flaws very big. Never mind that, on a given day, they themselves indulge in fifty black deeds.'

I saw Lavji's situation from a new angle. But I didn't understand anything about it. I asked him, 'What are you talking about, Lavji? What flaws and what issue? Was there some problem with Gomti?'

'What fault? She also was a living thing. But she knew that, in four to six months, she would have to go into confinement for one or two months. If she were with someone else, there would be no problem. But the whole scenario rankled Gomti's heart, that was the problem. It was as if she was flaunting her condition intentionally. It was as if the sound of the flute and the youth's blindness were saying to her every moment: "Wicked woman! You've done this awful deed, that's fine. But you also want to burden the poor blind man with it? Isn't there a limit to shamelessness?" Stinging from this, she began to believe that the blind youth's heart will break. So, she wanted to get away from him somehow. That's when she found me.'

'Huh? Did it happen so? Then she deliberately ... and you also deliberately...'

Lavji continued looking at me. He exerted himself to clarify: 'Has any human being ever been able to truly bear his own sting for a long time without turning to stone? Then what of this soft-as-silk Gomti? Ever since I found that out, I had been thinking that she might indiscriminately give her life away at some point. That's why I told her to come with me. "I will take care of you, protect you, and also bring you back here. If the new life survives, then I will protect it too. You will have no difficulty." On hearing this, she had felt relieved. But, yesterday, that blind flute player turned up here and, for whatever reason, she ran away. Now where can I find her? Yesterday, I had dug out my life savings from the cooking hearth and shown her. To give her the confidence that we have this much...'

'So she stole that?'

'Who? Gomti? Na re, bhai! But that's just it, right? I had dug out two hundred rupees. To my mind, they would give her some assurance. I was going to use them for her alone. And to take care of that blind man. She had seen them too. But they lie there as they were.'

'Then I am certain of this, Lavjibhai! That wonderful agony-flute has stolen her away ... not even stolen, indeed drawn her away!'

'*Drawn* her away?'

'Why not? I'm saying that, since hearing that agony-flute, the Bawan's soul must have been experiencing an unending anguish about having betrayed an innocent, trusting, young, blind lover. And exactly because of that, she ran away. We rarely know a person's entire life history. But it's possible it could have happened like that. And then, of course ... it can be said that he stole her away, na?'

But, before I could say anything further or clarify my point, old woman Jhamku's unmannerly, shrill, ugly voice was heard: 'Where is that cursed 'dude'? Brought a Vaaghran into his home. Now come out! Your well-wisher is lying there in that well.'

Lavji and I were both shocked. And just then, the voices of men could be heard outside, from the basin of the well in the distance.

Lavji ran out immediately.

For a very long time, I sat there, contemplating this matter. Many unanswerable questions were rising in my mind: who, truly, drew Gomti down the path of suicide? Social disgrace? These neighbours? That blind man's agony-filled flute? Who? But who, except Gomti, could give the true answer to that?

I have still not settled these questions. Only that, recalling this story related to my small room, I am still reminded of Gomti, of Lavji, and of that agony-filled flute. And I hear it again! Such anguish I have not come across in anyone else's flute.

[2]

After that, I left that small room. I went to live elsewhere. We used to have a gathering there. Among them, Gangadeen was considered an amazing storyteller. Gangadeen's stories were Gangadeen's stories. Even if he was gossiping, he would do it in such a way that you would just keep listening.

Once, we were all sitting together. I was there; our neighbour Nenshi Bhojak was there; Devji Karamshi Khajuriyo was sitting too; Bhagatraj Vanubha was also there. Vanubha's one and only young son had died. Since then, for the most part, he counted prayer beads. We called Devji Karamshi 'Khajuriyo' because he once ate two and half ser of dates – along with the pits!

So everyone was seated and, suddenly, Gangadeen said, 'Garuji!' He mostly called me simply 'garuji'. 'This, where you live, who originally owned the place? Do you know?'

I said: 'Na re, bhai. What would I, a visiting foreigner, know of such history? Whose was it originally?'

'So, originally, the house was old woman Devu's.'

'Old woman Devu? Who's that?'

'She's dead. And, by now, she must have returned from the heavens to earth to take another birth. But there's a story about her. It cannot be forgotten even if one wants to. As they say: even when a person goes, their story remains. This is that kind of story.

'At that time, I was in the prime of my youth. I was the first head constable in the village. Then, this village was also as small as the cup of my hands. Now it's grown in all four directions. Before, the entire village could gather behind this Vanubha's house. At that time, Devu lived here.

'I observed that Devu's youthfulness. Since then, I've seen many summers and winters go by. But I swear on my mother that I haven't seen any other woman in such bloom. Her youth was just different.

'Now, by fate and circumstance, this Devu got a husband, but he was the kind who wouldn't even say out loud that a near-dead man was dying. He was a model of goodness. His heart also was such that, if someone called out in the middle of the night, he would not have a no on his lips. Viable fields, cattle, all the conveniences. But Devu's and his nature were not compatible. Devu's youth was such, it was said that she had a hypnotising cobra-like stare.

'Their personalities did not align. Just. Did. Not. Align. And all of them were creatures coloured with a zest for life. They were hardly like us – people of modesty and decency – were they? Leaving Sajjan standing, Devu ran off one day.'

'Who's Sajjan?' I butted in.

'Devu's husband's name was Sajjan. And he was truly a good man. When the goddess-like Devu ran away, Sajjan felt he was alone in the entire world. He went half-mad. The farming was set aside. The cattle starved … did not descend to graze. Even the huts began to fall apart. The house in which you live, that was his place!'

'Oh? But the home is comfortable. It's easy to manage.'

'Arrey! Just listen. This is just the beginning of the story. Then Sajjan lost even his savings and everything.

'Now, over on the other side, it so happened that the arrogance of youth abated, the tides turned, two to four years passed. Then, with new experiences, Devu felt that, no matter what, Sajjan was a good man! So, just as she had left one man standing and run off, exactly the same way, she ran back again. Once, in the middle of the night, she came and stood in Sajjan's courtyard. In the meantime, her second husband died and she set up house with Sajjan again and stayed there.'

'It's like returning from the dead – that's what this story is about.'

'But this woman was also a true gem. And though she looked mischievous, yet there was real womanhood inside of her. We found that out afterwards.

'Sajjan had lost his capacity to earn now. Sold one or two homes and used that up. But simply sitting around like that would have emptied even Raja Ram's treasure troves. So, one day, Sajjan said to Devu, "Now I'll go to Rangoon and bring back a couple of paise income. Then we'll sit back and take it easy for the rest of our lives. Doesn't matter that God has left us without an offspring. You carry on my name and I'll carry on yours."

'"How am I going to carry on your name?" Devu said as she sobbed. "And I don't like you leaving. I feel as if we'll never meet again."

'"Arrey, don't be crazy! Don't say such inauspicious words at the time of parting. I'll be back in two years," Sajjan said. "How long does it take for two years to pass? And then, Makanjibha is with us."

'Makanjibha was, at the time, considered a rich man of consequence in the village. He'd been to Rangoon and earned a good bit of money, and had constructed a three-storey cement house in the village. Sajjan went with Makanjibha to Rangoon – from that moment to this day!'

'It's like this,' I interjected, 'human wealth is as deceptive as the colour of the sky. All right then…' I was about to get up.

'But the part worth listening to, garuji! That comes now,' Gangadeen stopped me. 'In all this, one thing of beauty happened. Those who saw it are alive and I, who knows it, am still alive.'

'What is that thing now?'

'This story's fragrant blossoming happens now. Makanjibha is returning – the telegram with this news came one day after two years. Sajjan was also coming with him. Hearing the news made the entire village happy. Makanjibha was the pride of the village. Sajjan's goodness was known everywhere.

'In the courtyard of the house where you live, Devu started a happy celebration. That day, she prepared a variety of dishes and sat waiting for Sajjan. You know the house where you live is at the end of a long street where the train stops by. In those days, the train came at noon.

'It struck twelve. The train came. I saw, with my own eyes, a man like Sajjan enter the street. But he was alone. I thought, perhaps he has left all his luggage at Makanjibha's. But, seeing him, I sat up in shock. It was Sajjan only, but he was wearing black clothes. Why was he wearing black clothes? I was surprised.

'I thought, whatever. It must be some new kind of Rangooni fashion going on. I myself ran ahead to give Devu the glad tidings. Devu became restless too. Covering the prepared food and leaving the gate open, she sat waiting in the verandah. Her gaze was fixed on the street. Any moment now Sajjan will come and I will run to him – this yearning speech of true love was pouring out from every part of her body like poetry.

'It isn't right to be in the middle of this with these two right now ... So thinking, I went off by another path in another direction.

'Over here, Devu felt that it had been too long. She could not wait any more, so she came outside. From the gate, she peered at the street. She saw a man coming too. It was her Sajjan only. But, seeing his black clothes, she felt deeply anxious. Still, she immediately ran to get things ready in the house. She became impatient to shower him with flowers.

'But what happened in the end? She just stood there waiting for him! Just stood there! Sajjan did not come at all.'

I was taken aback by this turn of events. 'Where did he go?' I asked.

'That itself is the mystery, garuji! No one is saying what happened. Makanjibha's second telegram confirmed that Sajjan was coming alone. I had seen the man coming with my own eyes. There was only the matter of his black clothes at the time that I had not understood. Devu said she had seen him coming too! She had also been struck by the black clothes. Many neighbours said they had seen a black-clothed man walking to the last house. He had even stood by the gate. But then he was nowhere to be seen!'

'Where did he go? What happened? And then Devu? What happened to Devu? When did Sajjan return?'

'Never. He didn't come back ever. That he had left was true. But he never came here. It happened just as Devu had said. They did not meet again. Ever!'

'And Devu? She must have gone off somewhere after that?'

'Arrey! Can it be, saheb? This incident had such an effect on Devu that, every day, just like that day, she prepared food daily, came out of the gate, cast her gaze along the long street and waited. She stood like that for many years. Many of us saw her do that. And there was no insanity in that either. She *knew* that no one was going to come now, no one could come now. But, whenever asked, she said, I feel that, one day, he will suddenly arrive and stand here!

'That poor Devu also died just last year. Only this story of hers has remained.'

[3]

After Gangadeen's story, I changed this home of mine too. I found a new residence. Right in the thick of population. There was one merit to it. It was on the second floor and one of its very large windows looked onto the market. Otherwise, the entire home was full of darkness, but open the window and it was all light. I often thought I could just sit by this window and keep observing the people below coming–going, the cars–horses, the endlessly ongoing industry of people.

Watching like that would be pleasurable, but what about the belly? It's hardly going to stay without making demands. So, when it was a holiday, I sat there. And coming–going, talking, laughing, fighting, joking, running, dawdling – I would watch people engaging in all these activities.

I had inherited the habit of idling away time by just watching people for the sake of watching. With this, I often got caught up in imaginative ways of observing ongoing caravans of people. At such times, I saw historical figures from hundreds of years ago rise before my eyes. As if a caravan could be seen coming forward ceaselessly from the past to the present. That caravan had no country, no province, no religious discrimination, no language difference. As if it were an unceasing, great stream of water flowing. And it moved on and on only due to the language of humanity. A people-caravan!

But, instead of talking about my new residence, I've gotten into philosophy. Living near this new home was a man named Kalyanji bhai. He had a routine. When it was 9:00 PM, having eaten, he would come out belching. He would walk a few rounds of five to twenty-five steps to and fro. And, in the end, when he went and sat at someone's home, his food would settle properly.

Once I came, he slowly began to make my place his nightly destination since I had a lot of newspapers.

'Sahebji! How are you? When did you arrive? Have you eaten?'

Such was the inconsequential beginning. Then, gradually, he immersed himself further.

One time, Kalyanji said to me, 'You, bhai, are seriously brave!'

I said, 'Why do you say that?'

'You've been here so many days, but you have no complaint. Others who came would yell by the fourth day!'

'What are you talking about, Kalyanji bhai?'

'Are you not experiencing it at midnight?' Kalyanji asked.

'I'm not understanding anything. If you could talk more clearly, I'd understand. Is it something to do with the house?'

'The old woman who lives downstairs doesn't wake you up?'

'Yes … hmm … so that's how it is? I've always wondered who cries at midnight. First, the quarrel begins. Cannot understand who is on the other side. But then the crying begins. So it's this old woman crying, it seems.'

'It's the old woman's doing only. Her own handiwork is hurting her heart. Even during the day, if we meet her face-to-face, she is like a vicious shrew.'

'But why does she cry? Sometimes she doesn't even cry.'

'There is a history,' Kalyanji said. 'This old woman had a daughter, and a good amount of money. She wished for a simple man for her daughter, who would live in their house, and be of some support to her as well. For that, she left many young men hanging by a thread of hope. But the old woman had hopes for *such* a gentle disposition that no one passed muster! If someone talked in a slightly loud tone, it would be noted in her black notebook. The next day, Narmada's behaviour would change too...'

'Narmada? Who's she?'

'The old woman's daughter's name was Narmada. And she drank only as much water as the old woman gave her. So, the next day itself, she would become cool as a clay pot and the young man would catch that very night's train! More than angry words, the cold taunts of women are so troubling that they can make the bravest of the brave retreat. This old woman looks quite frightening now. But, at that time, she looked very wise and, when she issued a cold taunt with a quiet, patient, terrifying iciness, it could freeze a man as if buried in snow. Mother and daughter had, in this manner, driven many away.

'But don't they say there is always a tit for tat? They met a great thug. He made a plan to carry Narmada away and to separate the old woman from the wealth on whose basis she was prancing about, so her sport would end. But the old woman had a lot of life experience. He was successful in carrying Narmada away but the wealth did not fall into his hands.

'The old woman took this wound to the heart so badly – don't even ask. In six months, she lay dying. It was as if she would die any day. Still, her mind was filled with malice. She did not call for her daughter at all. When the doctor said, "Vijuma! Now, at the most, you have twelve hours' time. If you want to meet anyone, call for them," the old woman sent a telegram to her daughter and had her brought over.

'But her soul lusted to take full and proper revenge. So she called her neighbour, Harkha Mehta, and said, "Harkha Mehta! That boy-like doctor keeps saying, without checking my pulse, that I am a guest for twelve hours. But my mind tells me that I am not likely to go for twelve years. So I am not going to leave. Let the daughter come. But, given my illness, if she does some sleight of hand and deceives me, and strangers' hands are filled – I don't want that to happen. Instead, let the wealth remain in Mother Earth's lap! It was hers and it remained in Mother's lap, they will say. I have faith in you. You take all my ornaments to your home. When I'm better, you can bring them back!"

'Harkho Mehto always said yes to the old woman. He also used to run errands for her. So, per the old woman's guidance, he took out all the ornaments and jewellery from their underground hiding place. The empty spot was just ordinary earth again. When Narmada came, the old woman was barely conscious. Narmada thought that, if the old woman dies this way, everything will remain in the ground. So she served and nursed her well. The old woman began to sit up. But, as soon as she got enough strength to speak, the thought that had been making a home in her mind – to strike secretly and put the daughter away in the ground – returned to take over!' Kalyanji paused.

'Oh ho ho!' I said. 'Everything about human beings is astonishing. There is no limit to their greatness; and there is also no end to their wickedness. This shows the endurance of this old woman's deeply degraded nature. Wants to die, does not want to enjoy, but she's only worried that no one else should enjoy!'

'Not just worry,' Kalyanji said. 'She was also eager to see that the fierce blow of the situation she created would hit the other person properly. Her real pleasure was in that. So, one day during a conversation, Narmada broached the risky topic and the old woman immediately spoke up, "You tell your lover that even the ashes of my stove are better than the usual gems and pearls. Fill up a pan from there and take it, ne!"

'Narmada understood. If forced to speak, the old woman would become stubborn. After that, Narmada never raised the issue again.

'Narmada left. The old woman flourished. Began walking about with a cane. Started calling to the dogs in the street. Started negotiating the prices of vegetables. So Harkho understood that he must run off now if he wanted to keep what had come into his hands. The woman wouldn't give up her jewels without a fight.

'So, one day, Harkho Mehto disappeared. The talk in the neighbourhood was that he had moved to another country to earn money. But he was gone for good. Never seen again!

'The old woman kept her patience for fifteen days or so. But then Harkha's wife too locked up the house and went off to her family home. The old woman went insane. At first, she would go there three or four times a day to curse and then return. Then she got into the habit of waking up in the middle of the night. Since then, once it's midnight, the old woman starts reproaching Harkha. And she pretends as if Harkho is responding. Then she turns her face away and begins crying. Why, that's how it happens, na?'

'Yes, that's how it has happened,' I said. 'But where is Harkho?'

'He's there, waiting for the old woman to die. And the old woman is taking care to not die before he returns. And Narmada is waiting for the old woman's telegram. Your house here is a place of waiting. A place of waiting! In all four directions, everyone is waiting.'

'And I have also got to wait, na?'

'Why, what do you have to wait for?'

'The old woman had yesterday climbed the stairs and come up.'

'What? Truly?'

'Yes!'

'Then?'

'She says to me, "I have a requirement from you." Just then, someone arrived, so she left. But now I understand what need she had of me. She must have wanted to tell me about her daughter. Or, she must have wanted to tell me about Harkha Mehta.'

'Just so!'

And then, the old woman's voice was heard from downstairs, 'Accursed wretch, Harkho! For so long, you've been sitting upstairs! Come down, you wretch! You've taken and are sitting on your mother's things…'

Kalyanji and I were both speechless on hearing this.

Today, the old woman had started her thing early.

[4]

When midnight struck, the old mother's music began. Always. On a good day, she would skip it, but in the end, I left that residence too. Now, I wanted to go where there were the least number of people residing. Based on that, I searched out a house.

It was towards the very end of the village, standing like a ruin. Nearby, there was hardly any population. And whoever was there was the kind that barely paid attention to their own lives. That house suited me just fine too. On the one hand, it stood all by itself, but on the other, it was also among people. All around it, there was empty land. In the middle, there was just a small, single-room house. In it, there was everything – kitchen, living room, bedroom. But, on each side, there was a small shuttered verandah. So, even inside the dwelling, it was like there was a private place.

For the most part, I would sit on a swing in the back veran- dah and do all my work. One day, I was sitting there when a man arrived. In his hands was a tanpura.[46] On his head, he had tied a red-ochre turban. His neck was adorned with necklaces. On his forehead was a chandlo.[47] It seemed as if he was somewhat shocked to see me. I never left the gate open anytime but, perhaps, today it had been left open by mistake. So he came to stand right in front of me and, only then did my gaze fall on him.

He looked at me and asked, 'Where is Atmarambhai?'

'Atmarambhai? There is no Atmaram here.'

'Your name?'

'My name is Manilal. But who do you need?'

---

46. Tanpura: A long-necked plucked string instrument used in various forms in Indian music. It does not play rhythm but rather supports and sustains the melody of another instrument or singer by providing a continuous harmonic bourdon or drone.

47. Chandlo: Typically an auspicious red mark worn in Hindu-based religions. It can also be saffron or white.

'Atmaramji, the musician, lived here. He owned this house – where is he? He doesn't live here now or what?'

'I live here. No Atmaram lives here!'

'But then, who owns this house now?'

'Now, as you see, it is mine.'

'Na, na. But who is the master of the house?'

'The master of the house … There, he's coming from up there. Look…'

Through the front gate, Ranchodlal, our neighbour, was arriving. The house was his. Having stepped just a little inside the gate, he stopped. Standing there in the street, he said, 'Mohangirji! Not there, not there. Now we have changed the location.'

The man standing before me went to him immediately. 'Arrey, but how can that be, Ranchodbhai? Then I might as well bid farewell from here. Where God has been seen, the pilgrimage arrives there.'

'But just come with me,' Ranchod said gently, 'just see. We have built a permanent entertainment platform as would suit a great musician … and today, there…'

'All that is well, Ranchodbhai,' Mohangir did not seem to be interested in Ranchod's decorative language. There was a bitterness in his complaint. But, after that, they both went towards Ranchod's house. So what was the issue, who was this Mohangir, who was Atmaram, whose house was this, who was this person they called 'musician'? All those questions remained suspended in their wake.

I felt Ranchodlal and Mohangir had some difference of opinion regarding this house. It pertained to some Atmaram, and that Atmaram was related to some musician issue. I worked hard to untangle the mystery, but the matter could not be resolved.

The next evening, I was sitting at leisure in my alleyway. I had planted two to four plants there and was examining how they were flowering. Just then, someone pushed at the gate.

'Who?'

'It's me, Ranchodlal! Could you please open up?'

I got up and opened the door. Ranchodlal came inside. He seemed to observe me with a careful eye. Then he also looked towards the plants. 'You've planted gulbas? Then, bhai sa'ab! Be wary of snakes!'

'I've never seen them here. Have you had any experience?'

'Had no experience. But received wisdom is that snakes are very attracted to the gulbas flower; so I warned you. Anyway, I thought, that wretched musician had bungled it up the other day, so let me go talk to bhai. And, if there's any doubt in his mind, let me go remove it!'

'Who are you talking about? The one who came yesterday – him?'

'Of course. About that Mohangir. He's a bit crazy-like…'

'Yes, I also thought the same.'

'Na, na, he's just like that. Makes a person suspicious…' Ranchodlal sat in front of me. 'The matter is like this, sa'ab! This house is Atmaram's!'

'Who is Atmaram? Where is he?'

'Atmaram is known as a great sarangi[48] player in these parts.'

---

48. Sarangi: A bowed, short-necked string instrument used in Hindustani classical music. It is said to most resemble the sound of the human voice – able to imitate vocal ornaments such as gamaks (shakes) and meends (sliding movements).

'Is that so? This house is his?'

'This Mohangir is crazy. So, forgetting everything, he ran here. Otherwise, he knows, of course, that Atmaram is no longer on this earth. He had become an amazing man. Atmaram's sarangi meant Atmaram's sarangi. All other musicians had sarangis in their hands, but Atmaram *himself* would live inside the sarangi. This sarangi of his also had a history. Atmaram's father used to tell him that he had seen this sarangi with his dada. From that time, it had been in his home. Atmaram was besotted with that sarangi. When he had that sarangi with him, he would feel as if the three worlds were sitting beside him. He was a man infatuated by his own music. But his only son died. After that, nobody ever saw Atmaram lay a hand on that sarangi. He would keep looking at it. Tears would flow from his eyes … and, would you believe it, saheb, I have seen this thing with my own eyes: the sorrowful notes of Atmaram's silent weeping would seem to rise from the strings of the sarangi as if by themselves!'

'What? Truly?'

'This is a witnessed matter, saheb!' Ranchodlal said, staring at me. 'He became a rare soul. But you know that saying, na: the snake has gone but has left the marks of its slither behind? Just so, many tanpura players like Mohangir, who considered themselves students of Atmaram, would gather at this house each year.'

'To do what?'

'I'm telling you everything. Atmaram never played the sarangi again. But his soul was in agony due to the fact that this extraordinary instrument had been in his family for about 150–200 years. It was as if it could revive the centuries-old ambience of the home. But now there was no heir to inherit the instrument. Atmaram was anguished about this…'

'There was no one worthy among his students?'

'I'm saying ... I'm coming onto just that topic. This Mohangir's belly hurts but he's beating his head ... There were a few capable young disciples among Atmaram's students; some well-known names too. But Atmaram's mind could not accept the idea. He believed that he could not place his beloved sarangi into anyone's hands ... there was no one among them greater than his sarangi. The agony and misery of this whole issue weighed on his heart. And how long would he himself live? What would happen to his sarangi afterwards? This unspeakable worry was oppressing Atmaram: What would become of his sarangi?

'Among his students too, there was competition in this matter. Some jealousy also existed. There was an ongoing eagerness for one-upmanship. But not one person's hand could make Atmaram's head give the nod. He was simply searching for the heir to his sarangi. And not one such was becoming apparent to his eye.

'This is about one particular time. Having heard about Atmaram's sarangi, some musician showed up here. His bursting youth, alluring face, highly melodious language, attractive manners ... everyone thought he would get away with Atmaram's sarangi!

'He came to Atmaram. In this very house, saheb! In that corner, a small assembly gathered. This well-known musician, who could make many lose their pride, even asked Atmaram for his sarangi to try it out for a bit. But it was hardly a sarangi in Atmaram's heart. It was like someone as dear as life to him. Atmaram shook his head, "Na, bhai! That thing is unique. It is heavenly. It is not of this earth. No one other than the heir can even touch it. The only one who has the right to touch it is its heir!"

'Atmaram's students, on hearing this, became very happy. Their minds were satisfied. But that other musician was an extraordinary man. With extreme humility, he folded both hands and bowed his head, "I know, Atmaramji! What you said, I have also experienced. I have understood. This thing is different. You are right."

'For a while, there was some other idle chatter. Then that musician left. But, when he left, he gave Atmaram an invitation as if he were Atmaram's student. His public performance was going to take place that day.

'Atmaram went to listen to him. But that musician exceeded all limits in showing his art that day! Others would make their sarangis weep. They'd get the strings mourning. This well-known musician filled every molecule of air with the essence of sorrow! Everyone felt that, today, it seemed as if the master of the planet himself was bidding farewell to the entire planet. And, because of that, an ocean of grief was overflowing from every molecule! He crossed the limit.

'Atmaram was also fascinated. He was convinced that this man alone was the heir to the sarangi. At that time, he said nothing. He came home.

'The next day, at dawn, the sarangi was lying on the doorstep of that well-known musician and Atmaram – '

'And Atmaram? What happened to him?' I asked impatiently.

'He was never seen since that day. He felt he had completed his life's work, had found the sarangi's heir. After that, whether he didn't want to stay or whatever, he was never ever seen again. Despite many attempts, his whereabouts were never known again.

'Since then, every year, Mohangir and the others assemble in this house on the day Atmaram disappeared and hold a night-long musical concert.'

'So that's why he did not appreciate your talk of moving it to another place. That's it, right?'

'Na, saheb! It's not like that either. The musician's home is mine. He himself had, on one occasion, signed it off to me. These students want to get the inheritance of that sarangi back from the one to whom Atmaram had given it up. So the musical concert is a pretext to arrange the opportunity for one among them to grab it. I feel, if that happens, wherever Atmaram might be, his soul will be in agony. He wished for the sarangi to either be destroyed or be in the hands of someone – a student or otherwise – who could preserve its 150- to 200-year-old heritage. He was married to learning, na? So, from this year on, I've taken the concert out of this house and arranged it at my house. So that these average students of his cannot cause the sarangi's inheritance to slip to their advantage by creating some legal contract. This house is Atmaram's! If crazy Mohangir's talk has affected you in any way, please let it go. There is nothing more besides this.'

Ranchodlal went away after telling his story. He went and I kept seeing the ambience of this house, the great musician's house that I had come to live in, in a different way. I felt that, truly, its aura was extraordinary.

The Prisoner of Andaman

Outside the village, there was a restaurant and Visaji sat there for a while. From here, he could see the trees of his village. He could not see the uncultivated patch of land in front of his field. But he could see, in his imagination, the big pipar tree above the well. From a low-bending branch of that pipar, how many times had he jumped into the well during the monsoon? At that time, his mother was alive. His older brother and he would sit in the shade of that pipar at noon to smoke their pipes. Oh ho ho! What a time that was! Back then, the entire world seemed to be filled with beauty. Who knows how his eyes saw only loveliness in everything? But it was the delusion of that beauty that made him lose himself one day. And, to hide that mistake, he finished off his own neighbour, Lakhoji.

For twenty years, he was in the Andamans. It was said, the government had changed. He gained freedom from the Andamans. He had come to his village. Still, his village was about a half gau away. On the way, he had spotted a restaurant. And he had sat here to get a drink of tea.

Everything seemed so new to him. How could he recognise

anyone at the restaurant? Sitting there, he kept looking at everyone. They were all looking back at him. His youth had left him. The
love for beauty had fled from his eyes. But this restaurant, the trees
near it, the cows grazing in the distance, the rabaari standing among
the sheep, his verses, the sounds of the birds coming from far-far
away – all seemed appealing, new, and life-affirming to him. He was
drinking his tea with pleasure. He was experiencing the joy of freedom in the air. His village was constantly on his mind. Amthi kaki
will be there. His friend and neighbour Mokhdaji will be there. The
village merchant, Motichand, surely couldn't be there at this time?
But, sooner or later, he would be there. His aged mother might
well have been there for some time. He recalled his older brother.
When he was in the Andamans, the brother had passed away. But
who all would he meet and, on meeting, how pleased would they
be? And what kind of talk would he offer about the jungles of the
Andamans? There, with two monsoons, there was unlimited rain.
So many things like these had filled his mind.

Having drunk the tea, he gave the due paise. He gathered
up his staff, slung his small bundle over his shoulders, took the
metal trunk into his hand. He was getting ready to leave when,
from within the restaurant, an old woman emerged. She placed
a hand above her eyes as a shade and, for a while, just kept looking at Visaji.

Then, she suddenly said, 'Vihoji murderer. Don't I recognise
him? Vihoji!'

Visaji did not recognise the old woman. But the 'murderer'
label she gave him was like a fatal blow to his heart. Still, he kept
his peace and said, 'Maadi! I don't know you. Who are you? I'm
Vihoji, maadi!'

'That I knew from over there itself. I said in my mind – whether I speak it or not – that's Vihoji the head-splitter. And then, who else would have such a killer-like face? An entire lifetime has passed by. Eh, Lakhaji! My son, where are you, my dear?' And the old woman, sobbing greatly, sat down right there beside Visaji.

Visaji was disconcerted. But he folded both hands together and bowed his head to the old woman. 'Maadi, I am your cow.[49] Forgive me.'

'You have to suffer for your deeds! For seven lifetimes, no one will even let you stand on their doorstep. Go, wretch!'

As if she were being polluted by his shadow, having expressed her sorrow, the old woman moved away.

In the meantime, all those standing and sitting there came up to Visaji. They gazed intently at him as if he were some creature on display. Visaji felt the ground weighing upon him.

Without saying anything, he left for his village. But it felt as if his legs had broken. His heart was wounded.

[2]

Visaji reached his village. He recognised the outskirts right away. Everything was just the same except for a single tree that he couldn't spot. He recognised rabaari Devji. His figure looked just the same but his hair had turned white. Visaji went up to him, 'Devji bhai, Ram-Ram! Do you recognise me?'

Resting his head on his staff, supporting one foot on the other,

---

49. Saying he is her cow is a way of saying he is the humblest of her servants.

Devji stood there as if stunned by the words. He kept staring at Visaji. For a long time, he stared. And then, as if he were remembering something, he said with surprise, 'Alya! You're not Vihoji murderer, are you?'

'Yes, Devji bhai! You've identified me correctly,' Visaji replied. But the word 'murderer' had made his voice crack.

Then, Devji asked him to a verandah at the far end. 'Come, let's go there. Here, there will be a crowd of cattle.'

Devji ahead and Visaji behind – and so they both walked on. But there was no strength in Visaji's legs. Devji had called him a killer too. The word was still hurting his head like the strike of a hammer.

Devji sat. He removed a pipe. Both started chatting.

'What is Amthi kaki doing, Devji bhai? She's hale and hearty, I hope? Has the house fallen or is it still there?'

'It's there, baapa! Your house is there too. And Amthi kaki has also been sitting there for twelve years. Whenever I come out, she's always doing the gaar.[50] These days, some white dust has arrived. Behind the peepal orchard, huge holes have opened up.'

'The merchant Motichand's shop must be doing well?'

'Of course. What troubles does he have, baapa? He stands apart from the entire village. He's built a three-storey. You can see there!'

Visaji looked in the direction he was pointing. The upper storey of Motichand's house could be seen. Behind that, there

---

50. Gaar: A mixture of cow dung, earth and water used to daub at hut walls and floors in villages.

was the kanbiwaad,[51] sutaarwaad,[52] and right after was his own koliwaad.[53]

He grew impatient to see his house, meet kaki, and see his neighbour Mokhdaji.

After smoking the pipe, he immediately sat up. 'All right then, Devji bhai. We'll meet later. I'll go meet kaki. She'll be at home now, na?'

'At this time, she'd be at home only, baapa! She'll be making rotla. Go there, baapa! They'll be freshly hot and ready. How many, seventeen–eighteen years have gone by, Visaji?'

'Can you believe it, baapa? Two months shy of nineteen!'

'May well be, baapa! It's more than enough that you've returned safe and sound. Is everything there like ours or different? There must be cows and buffaloes, na?'

'There? There, Devji bhai? Jungle! Two monsoons! Endless rain pours!'

'Is that so?'

Visaji walked towards his home. Now, if his mother were alive, if his father was there, if his older brother breathed … Love for his family arose in Visaji's heart. Old memories awoke in his mind.

He walked past Motichand's three-storeyed house. It seemed as if old Motichand was sitting at his shop's counter. Next to him, a boy was weighing something on the scales. That must be his son. Visaji could not identify the boy. Then, he had been little. Visaji's feet turned suddenly towards Motichand's shop.

---

51. Kanbi: A farming caste-community; waad: settlement
52. Sutaar: The carpenter caste; waad: settlement
53. Koli: A lower-level caste; waad: settlement

On reaching the shop, he immediately bowed to Motichand and, folding both hands, he said, 'Kaka! Recognise me? I'm Vihoji!'

Motichand was as if frightened by this advance. He sat up a bit. 'Who are you, bha! Who are you? What is it?'

'Kaka! I'm Vihoji!'

'Vihoji? But who is Vihoji?'

'Why, did you not recognise me? Of Koliwaad.'

Motichand remembered suddenly. 'Yes, yes, Vihoji murd – ' Motichand did not finish the word. But his voice pierced Visaji.

'When did you arrive, bha? You are in good spirits? You've returned from the Andamans?'

Visaji responded but there was no warmth in his voice now. Motichand had also called him 'murderer'. It was as if his name had received the eternal title of a murderer.

His head felt a heavy agony, as if someone had struck it with force. He folded both hands. 'Kaka! I'll go now. Will come back later.'

'Yes, bha! Go, baapa! Where are you going to, kaki's house?'

'Where else, kaka?'

'Yes, bha, yes. Go, baapa, go. You would have been enjoying life today. But can what's written in our destiny be erased, baapla? Go, bha!'

Visaji began walking. Having heard the reference to murder three times now, his ardour had disappeared. Everyone had forgotten him but they had not forgotten his murder. As if the murder had occurred today, the thought of it was still on everyone's minds. He was headed towards his home but it was as if there were chains weighing a hundred maund around his feet.

His happiness about returning home had fled.

He arrived at the house. There was his gate. It seemed to be shut from the inside. He rattled the door-chain. There was no response. He rattled it again.

'Who? Who is it? Eh, I'm making rotla. If you need something, come back later!'

'Kaki, open up. It's me, Vihoji!'

'Vihoji meaning? Vihoji from where? Vihoji who?'

Vihoji means who? How could he explain himself to kaki?

So Visaji himself made himself known. 'So kaki! I'm Vihoji the murderer! Back from the Andamans! Open up. I've arrived!'

Kaki came out immediately. As if lost deep in thought, she was coming slowly. In her feet, Visaji did not hear that hurried pace that accompanies the yearning to meet a loved one.

He stood there for a moment in thought. He bowed to kaki. Folding both hands, he bowed again.

'Who is it, Vihoji? So you've been released from prison, have you, bhai-la?'

'Yes, kaki. Released from prison. The new government has released everyone. Released me too!'

He entered the house with kaki.

There, he sat on the verandah. But the bird of imagination in his heart had died much earlier. The joy that had filled his heart – the love that had manifested simply from seeing the trees of his village – he hadn't seen even a tiny part of that reciprocated across a single person's face.

No one could even recall his name in any other manner besides 'murderer'!

And, even in this kaki's heart, he saw a deadly coldness. She had also not greeted him with affection. She had also felt: where has this botheration come from? She hadn't said so out loud, but aversion can be ascertained even from the eyes.

For a moment, he sat there dumbfounded. He felt that if he stopped to think of these things, he would go crazy. He began a conversation with kaki. If nothing else, at least he could experience a sort of warmth from the conversation.

'Kaki! Over there, it's not like this, ho! There are two monsoons over there!'

Sitting before him, kaki said nothing except a 'huh'. She seemed to be lost in her thoughts. She was concerned about the house. Where she lived – this house – was Visaji's. On her face, Visaji did not see even the slightest bit of welcome.

Just then, Mokhdaji could be seen coming from outside.

Seeing him, kaki said hastily, 'Mokhdaji! Vihoji has come!'

But kaki was only speaking quickly in order to warn Mokhdaji and, sensing this, Visaji experienced even more of a jolt. All his enthusiasm died. His words retreated from his tongue even more.

'Vihoji? Who's Vihoji?' Even Mokhdaji did not immediately recall Visaji's name.

'Why now, have you forgotten? Our Vihoji!'

'Yes, yes. The one who had gone to Kaala Paani[54] for murder – him?'

'Yes. Him. It must be in his destiny to see the trees of his

---

54. Kaala Paani: Meaning 'black waters' and referring to the colonial prison in the Andaman and Nicobar Islands. It was used by the British for political prisoners and dissidents during India's struggle for Independence.

village, so he has come. Otherwise, who returns from Kaala Paani? His destiny is so favourable!'

'Good, good. Good that you have come, bha!' Mokhdaji said. Even in his voice, the question and fear of 'but where did Vihoji return from?' was apparent.

All of them sat together and ate rotla. Talked about things from here and there and of far-off lands. Visaji was aware that the air was weighed down by thoughts of 'he has done a black deed'.

And kaki's chatter then seemed even more extraordinary.

Her rapport with Mokhdaji did not escape Visaji's attention. Kaki was preoccupied with the worry of hiding this, but Mokhdaji seemed to have a deep playfulness in his eyes. Visaji had returned to his village but it was as if no one was happy to accommodate him. He had been forgotten. His arrival had not brought joy to anyone. He did not have anyone of his own here. He did not sense, in anyone's voice, the love that was brimming over in his own heart. His desire had awakened for the village's houses, trees, animals, birds, everything.

That night, he went to bed outside in the alleyway but could not sleep. He lay there awake.

Late at night, he heard some murmurs from inside the house.

Curiosity rose in his mind. He did not consider it worth placing much trust in kaki. Wondering what it might be, he got up quietly. Gently, so there would be no sound, he opened the back gate. At the back of the house, there was a recess high up on a wall. It had bamboo bars that let the air circulate. Visaji went to that wall and stood close against it. From inside, he could hear voices but not understand the words. He climbed onto the earthen wall supports and looked inside through the bars. It was pitch dark inside. It was not possible to ascertain who was inside. To catch the words, he waited with bated breath.

His hearing did not comprehend much else apart from the repeated use of the words 'murder' and 'murderer'. And, like sharp nails, they were piercing his head.

He descended gently. Opening the back gate slowly, he reached his bed. He lay there quietly for a while.

The dark night was progressing. Inside Visaji too, a similar black, silent darkness was spreading. His despair knew no limits. His soul was sad. Here, he had no one to call his own. Everyone considered him a murderer. No one had forgotten the killing. He felt as if this were a foreign land. He fell into thought. After a while, he sat up in his bed. He strained his ears to check if the sounds were still coming.

None.

The night was steeped in a heavy stillness. Only, Visaji's ears kept hearing the echoes of those two forgotten words: 'murder' and 'murderer'!

He got up, collected his clothes, took the metal trunk lying below the bed and stepped forward with a soft foot. Very slowly, he moved forward. He went out of the front gate. He was remembering his home country. Kaala Paani was his true home country.

He recalled the details of that place. So many wonderful images of its jungles were embedded in his mind. There, ghee was given with rice. Instead of ghee, here was oil. There, they bartered for trade. The hands of the jungle-people trembled to even touch money!

And here? Here, instead of love there was stone. Instead of enthusiasm, you received cruel coldness.

He recalled the rivers, canals, dense jungles, two heavy monsoons, torrential continuous rains – and, taking pleasure in all that, the jungle folk.

Those jungle folk did not have any means of accounting. They did not have any memorised value counts of one for one. They brought the shell of a tortoise and took away a tin of cigarettes. And, if they brought six shells, they would still ask only for one tin! There was no calculated counting in their minds that there should be six tins for six shells. Visaji remembered those jungle people. He remembered the jungle. That was his country, not this.

That country had no coin-based accounting but they had accounted for love. There, everyone knew him. All were his. He was everyone's. With a full heart, he walked away to settle there, in his own true country.

A Happy Delusion

One time, at nine o'clock at night, I was making preparations to go to bed when someone made a sound outside. Who could it be? Wondering, I got up and opened the door.

I saw a sweet youth standing before me. The word 'sweet' could truly be used for him as he was so handsome, pleasing, and his eyes, nose, face were all lovely. With him stood a woman who, though middle-aged, could be considered good-looking. I did not know either of them. It did not seem as if they knew me either, but it appeared they had come because they had heard of me. Pulling the chairs nearby, I told them to sit, and waited to hear them speak.

The woman, as she was sitting, said to the youth: 'Say now, whatever you want to say to bhai!'

The youth said nothing and took out a large, artistic-looking cover from his beautiful embroidered bag and held it out to me.

I took the cover and began to remove the papers from within it impatiently, expecting a letter or recommendation or something similar inside. What I found was a small, attractive, handwritten monthly magazine. I looked at him as I opened the magazine.

There were pictures everywhere within it. And, on page after page, there were what we might call decorative flourishes. The decorations were attractive and the kind to momentarily hold our attention. Quietly, I looked through the handwritten magazine from start to finish. Within it, there were all kinds of subject matter: poetry, stories, meditations, essays. Just as the magazine was filled with decorations, so also these writings had adornments. A young man's love for literature was within them. To observe this on page after page brought some inner joy also. And I remembered that I too used to do this kind of thing once upon a time. The name of the magazine was also fine: *Sand-Farm*. With the name itself, he had offered a rebuke to an uncultured society.

Handing the magazine back, I asked, 'You publish this?'

'Yes.'

But I noticed a ring of self-satisfaction in his voice, hearing which, I was a little taken aback. I thought, could a youth such as this, so engrossed in his self-satisfaction, perhaps also be a slave to his own delusions? Whom we might describe as being absorbed in vanity? If he has a lot of vanity, then one will have to take great care in speaking with him. It doesn't take long for such men to get upset. And if you agree with them, they are immediately ready to accept you as their own.

Just then, he asked, 'Why, how did you like it?'

'You've made a huge effort.'

'But how did you find the writing?'

'You have a particular diligence for presenting things in an attractive way,' I replied.

He didn't seem satisfied with the response.

And then, that woman, who had been sitting silent all this

time, said, 'He wants to get this printed, bhai! He's been telling me for six months!'

'How are you related to him? What is his name?'

'His name is Manmohan. I'm his mother. I have built the tower of my hopes on him, bhai! He was *this* small when his father passed away. And then he was emaciated. I've worked day and night to just barely see him to this stage. And now this…' The woman's voice became choked with emotion. Her speech slowed down. She could not talk any further.

But, even from this little speech, her difficulty could be seen clearly. This widowed mother must have raised her only son by working day and night and taking on who knew how many challenges. And the son, instead of earning something now, must be running this handwritten monthly magazine. And if it's good literary art, then he must have faced rejection frequently for it. It seemed that he now had a hankering to have it printed. This lower-middle-class woman must barely manage to keep 500–700 in savings. The fear of those savings disappearing in the printing of his magazine must be weighing on her head. As a last resort, she must have thought to show it to someone who could say if it ought to be printed before actually printing it, which is why she must have brought him here now. This inference could be made clearly from her talk.

Then Manmohan said, 'Once this gets printed, there will be no problems.'

'But will you be able to afford the cost of a one-time print?' I asked. 'There is a lot of writing. It will be of large dimensions.'

'How much will it cost?' the mother asked.

'It'll be … about 500. There is a lot of content.'

'There, see! Had I not told you? We spend 500 rupees to print and then who will buy it? What if no one buys it?'

'Arrey! Is that likely, Ma? This first edition will be unique; not to be found anywhere. Ask bhai, how is the content?'

Now the matter became even more clear. The boy was the mother's one and only. So she had spoilt him while raising him. She had been at his beck and call and done everything at his behest. But the boy was either quixotic or delusional. There was pride from the happy delusion that he was accomplishing something significant through this magazine. It was obvious there was a fear that, if this delusion was broken, the mother-son relationship would also break. The boy's delusion, if nothing else, certainly melted one's heart. He was preparing his magazine with appreciable labour and love. In his mind, he probably thought this love alone would bring him victory. And this love alone was excellence. He was attributing a substantially high value to his own enthusiasm. And, in this, it was likely that he had forgotten what was of real value to him. Or, the honesty or maturity needed to ascertain that value was not within him. His mind had fallen entirely into this delusion, it seemed.

So I said gently: 'Look, bhai Manmohan! This material is good. Your effort is genuine. Your points are fine. But it is worth understanding your mother's points. If it takes three–four months to get established – how does it harm anything till then? Generally, it is difficult for a monthly magazine to get established before two years.'

'But then it will cost twofold instead, na?' Manmohan insisted. 'Once this is out, I am certain it will get established. It might happen like we hear happening to Europe's and America's

famous books. Not *might*, but *will* happen,' he said with considerable firmness. 'I have complete confidence here,' he placed a
hand on his chest, 'Ma needs to have a little patience.'

His mother had understood his crazy delusion. But she was
looking at him with the utmost love and sadness. The scene was
one to melt the heart. How each could understand the other,
that was a most complicated question. The mother did not want
to hurt her son's heart in the slightest. She was ready to spend
the last of her savings. But what if, even after spending that, the
son did not awaken from his reverie? That worry-filled question
could be read in her eyes.

I was not equipped for such a complicated issue. It wasn't
even my line of work. I said softly, 'Why don't you do this —
reduce the size by half?'

'No, sa'ab! Don't say that!' Manmohan said hastily. 'I have
yet to include my father's biography in this. I want to create a
good impression right from the start. Want to make every edition superior to the previous ones.'

'But, bhai! That's your enthusiasm. Enthusiasm does not
mean success. Enthusiasm comes first, then comes service. Here
is the service. And, for that, you also need to think about Ma's
resources.'

But none of this talk seemed to be reaching his mind. He
said, 'Then I say to Ma: you let me muddle through on my own.
If this magazine comes out, she will find me alive. If it doesn't
come out, then I have no need of this world. The world has no
need of me!'

The mother seemed shaken by the words. She said quickly,
'Then you do this. Let's get this printed. I'll even sell my nose-ring

and give that to you. But after? If it doesn't work, then you'll leave the matter, na?'

'But why won't it work?'

'Bhai! Monthly magazines don't run in Gujarat. And you will remember this bitter experience your entire life. And you will be putting your ma in a big difficulty.' I spoke in as placid a voice as I could.

'I'll be fine. I've dealt with so many of his whims, this will be one more. But then my suffering will have been worth it if he will let go of his obstinacy,' the mother shrugged.

For a little while, mother and son sat there, discussing the magazine. The son wanted to print it. The mother found the son's stubbornness hard to deal with. But it was as if some other bitter life experience was stopping her from telling him off with harsh or heated words. I could feel this pathos of hers. Affection would not allow her to speak. Yet, there was no escape from speaking either. So, with some uneasiness and a faint, worry-filled laugh, she said, 'He's very stubborn, bhai! Won't concede.'

On the one hand, there was the happy delusion – which came from who knows where – of a young man's heart. On the other hand was a helpless sorrow watching the boat, that had just made a path through many difficulties to reach the shore, sinking. I moved my gaze from one to the other. Manmohan's face was radiant with a beautiful vigour. Within it, there sat a desire to consider his own totally mad passion as an ideal of self-sacrifice. The ideal on whose peak he was meandering about – from there, with just a single gust of wind, he was going to fall into a deep valley.

Such a violent fall might leave him with the gift of a bitter, acrid, sarcasm-filled, what could probably be called merciless, and unsuccessful life. I felt some sadness thinking this. The country would be short of one young man. And a prematurely old, bitter, failed man would be added. I looked in Manmohan's direction once more.

But, like the many bearded faces I had seen that, no matter what happened, having been shown the path, they didn't turn; having been advised, they didn't understand; having lost and been beaten, they didn't understand their failure – exactly such facial signs were also to be seen here. I kept looking at both mother and son silently.

'What do you want to do, Manmohan? Bhai says that it is better to not print!'

'Bhai may well say that. But I want to print it!' Manmohan responded with firmness.

'Your father had the same stubbornness as you, my son,' there was pain now in the mother's words. 'With that I ... Your father destroyed me with his death. You, my bhai! Having grown up, you're destroying me. Fine then, let's print it.'

'You will contribute your writing, na, sa'ab?' Manmohan asked.

'I will surely give it. But this is your delusion,' I now said clearly. 'This is not a service to the literary world, nor is it an aesthetic ideal to strive for.'

It seemed Manmohan did not like what I said. He did not answer.

But a lot of time had passed; so I now sat up. 'Fine then. We'll meet again.'

Mother and son sat up to leave. I watched them leaving. A thought came to my mind that, at a stage when the intellectual strength to understand the difference between idealism and delusion is yet to develop, many other deviant thoughts come together. And from those thoughts, such self-perpetuated difficulties are borne. How could one give lessons on mental strength to young people? That was the big puzzle for me.

'Fine, what will be, will be.' So saying, I fell into bed. But the same thoughts kept coming back to me.

[2]

I then forgot about the matter. This occurred after six months or so. One day, the postman dropped off a sky-coloured cover. The handwriting was not known to me. The name of the village could not be read properly from the stamp. Opened the cover. A letter emerged.

Bhai! You might remember that day, when a mother–son woke you up at night. I am Manmohan's mother. I am writing this letter to you from a small village. Manmohan did as he had intended; you may have received this news. For a month, two months, three months, I kept his work going by selling clothes, items and jewellery. But then, eventually, there was no way left to get even two paise. I did not hold back in sounding him off. But who knows what delusion was sitting in his heart? He could only be at peace if he could do work that he himself considered great. Otherwise, his restless soul would be sad the whole day and make others sad too. Fed up, I let him remain in his happy delusion. And, to somehow earn my own livelihood, I have come to settle in this village near my parents. I now have a few days left. But whatever days remain, I am ready to help him in any way I can. I have heard that Manmohan has been wandering about in who knows what kinds of places to run and hide away from the hounding of the debt-collectors. But, if he perchance comes to meet you, please would you deliver this message of mine to him? If he lets go of this addiction now, I will give away the last of my life-savings and everything else to help him. If you can help a widow in this task of getting back the young son she had raised as her support, then not only I but even God will pay you back.

From: the mother who came to trouble you at your home with her son that day.

I fell into thought. The lady had given her address. But I had not heard anything about Manmohan in the recent past. I hadn't the slightest information about which heaven of his happy delusion he might be sporting about in. I wrote out a letter of assurance. Writing that, if Manmohan shows up, I will certainly tell him come to you, I sent it off. But, after that, many days passed with no trace of Manmohan.

Subsequently, I did not receive any news about what happened to Manmohan or his mother. I decided that Manmohan must have fallen into some other line of work and his poor mother had probably managed to get him back or had lost him forever.

For a long time, there was no trace of either of them. And then, that matter was also forgotten. All of a sudden, one day, there would be only a hazy memory of the incident, that is all.

[3]

Many years passed after this occurrence. The name Manmohan was also forgotten. And no detail of the incident could be remembered. The days of a quotidian life kept passing by as they do.

Suddenly one day, at two in the afternoon, as I sat on a chair in my courtyard and leisurely enjoyed the winter heat, some man showed up. Seeing his emaciated face, deep eyes, thin body and extremely simple, almost ugly-looking clothing, I was surprised.

Before I could ask any question, he folded both hands in nam-askaar and said, 'Jai jai, bhai! I've come after so many days – not days, years – so you might not recognise me. Years ago, I had met you right here. At that time, the doorway was on the other side, right?'

'I can't recall anything. Your name? Where are you coming from?'

'My name is Manmohan!' he replied.

Swiftly, who knows from where in my mind, I recalled the ring of self-satisfaction in his voice all those years ago.

'Haan … uh … haan … oh ho, Manmohan bhai! You've appeared after so many years? Where have you been hiding? You never showed up after that.'

'How could I show up, sa'ab? I've been almost buried in the worst difficulties. But you will congratulate me. I have still not let go of that ideal. Are you receiving our monthly magazine or not?'

'Which one?'

'Why then? Our magazine. *Sand-Farm*!'

'Yes, yes. I remember. Is it still going?'

'Going and how! It has not fallen in its ranking. Its standard has not yielded. Not one *paisa* remains to be paid back to anyone. And, bas, the magazine keeps running per our principles. Now it's not even running a loss!'

I kept staring at this unusual, weird-seeming, still unyielding, gaunt man. His thin, long, wizened face showed all that he had endured during this time. There wasn't a single living mark of the sweet Manmohan I had observed that day.

I said, 'Bhai. Sit, sit. Tell me your story. Where is your ma?'

'That poor one is gone!'

'Gone? Arrey, Ram! Then you did not get to meet her?'

'I met her at the very end. That much contentment I have in life. Then, I was in Africa, na? There, I gained a couple paise. Earned. Started the monthly magazine again. Paid off all my debts. Lost everything again. Took on another debt. But now everything has settled into place. Poor Ma went in that distress. The wife also went!'

'You were married?'

'I experienced that for seven to eight years also, sa'ab! There's nothing in that either. As long as our *Sand-Farm* keeps going, we've won the war. Now it is counted among the well-known. You must be getting it, na?'

'I'm not getting it. But I've seen it. It's nice. All by yourself, you've made a considerable effort!'

'It's all right. God has given me this dharma; so I must abide by it. What else can be done? Now I've moved nearby. Today, I said, I must go meet bhai. You must come once. Please visit.'

Two cups of tea arrived so our conversation paused. But I kept looking at this earnest man. He had endured suffering inexhaustibly. Even made his relatives take plenty of heat. And his monthly magazine? It was certainly a symbol of his whimsy. But, within it, there was no vision, no life experience, nor anything that could be of use to any nation. Like some constant machine-like process, it kept running regularly. But one was blown away to see his determination in the whole matter.

After drinking tea, he took his leave. Manmohan left but, having opened up some of the pages of his life, he had inspired even more curiosity.

One day, I left in the morning and arrived at his place. He was at home. When I entered his room, a piece of gunny cloth was laid out on the floor. A small bed was arranged on one side. With a few vessels and a curtain fashioned out of a piece of gunny, he had made a kitchen. It was as if, having created his own little world, he had settled into it. In all directions, there were piles of his magazine.

I sat there, but it was as if the environment was letting out a heavy sigh. Waves of happiness could be discerned playing about too. I thought: when he was a boy, he came to my place with his mother. The happy delusion he nursed continues even now. His entire life has been filled with a happy delusion. If that image shattered, so would he.

He began to pour out to me all the hard work of these many years. There were many notebooks of poems too. He even read two to four poems from them. There was nothing in those poems. But that was the beauty of it: that he was completely oblivious to the fact that there was nothing in them. He was absorbed in the delightful world created in his mind.

More than knowledge, there was the bliss of ignorance here. And due to that, he was seeing his great, lifelong delusion as a great, beautiful dream. He was immersed in it and enjoying himself within it.

A question arose in my mind: what is reality even, in the end, other than a person's own beautiful delusion?

My mind fell into a cold churning of thoughts. What was the

accomplishment of this man's lifetime of labour? Nothing at all, was the answer. But wasn't his hard work the highest possible degree of his achievement?

Many questions began to arise. I felt sure that if that web surfaced, it would be impossible to find a path out of it. So I stopped my mind from asking questions.

He prepared two cups of tea with great affection. When he placed the tea near me in a broken saucer and a cracked cup, all the other thoughts were quelled within my mind. Only one idea reigned supreme. His non-achievement alone was great. His non-accomplishment itself was his great accomplishment.

Internally, I saluted his non-achievement.

While returning home, the entire way, I was recalling Manmohan's life story. And a stanza from one of Mirabai's bhajans arose in my mind:

> 'Chhota sa mandir banaun
> Main apna bhagwan bithaun.'
> ['I will make a small temple
> I will place my God within it.']

A question was surging in my mind: those who build their own little temples, the small people with such happy delusions – are they not really greater than those who make grand, propaganda-driven proclamations about seeking the truth? Who can say?

A Memorable Day

It was only possible to reach the tent-like hut – constructed from strips of cloth rags, there at the end of the inner lanes and bylanes – under the refuge of deep darkness. Otherwise, there was no way to go there. It was worth going there only when no one could see you. In that diverse neighbourhood, if anyone even suspected that a new person had arrived, a crowd would gather. And it would be all right for it to gather, but to get away from it would then be the hardest thing to do. Within that variegated, weird sort of people's carnival, there were such things that a listener would be momentarily dazed. All kinds of people lived there. Performers, gamblers, pickpockets, thugs, kidnappers, Chinese traders – all flavours of residents could be found there. It was a truly unique world. They had their bazaar too, and they traded in small and large items. Opium could be exchanged for cannabis. Cannabis could be exchanged for cocaine. Cocaine could be exchanged for alcohol. Alcohol could be exchanged for a woman. And those who made their livelihoods off those women lived there too. The universe there was just different and the value it placed on things was different too. A person there valued a thing based only on its appearance. And the wonder was that it was only a distance of a hundred feet from the rest of the populace. What the world called a cultured society, that society lived only a hundred feet away. And that hundred feet was considered to be a gap as wide as that between heaven and earth.

To go through there during the daytime, I kept in mind a particular street. It went past a back wall so no one's gaze could fall on it easily.

It was only by that street that the hut could be reached without being seen in broad daylight.

For many days, some profoundly sad-looking woman had been seen living in that hut. Anyone else's presence in that hut was almost unknown.

That woman's face was dull, vacuous, pallid, and seemed like that of a terribly helpless and considerably frightened wandering bird. In her eyes, it was as if there remained only a single emotionless tendency to keep gazing into a deep void.

To keep gazing, to keep on gazing, and to remain sitting. This was the only action that could be discerned. To keep staring at the ground – this was her only support; it was like her only assurance.

So an inexplicable curiosity had arisen – who was this woman? From where had she landed in a place like this? She had been there three or four days now and, slowly, the men of the neighbourhood had begun to come to her. All of them, in their own ways, had been making some sweet talk or the other there – this is what their manner of speaking, laughing, joking suggested.

And yet, the vacuity of her face had remained the same.

The gathering around her was highly skilled. They believed in biding their time, it seemed. But, if they got even the slightest indication that some new man had gotten the custom of this place, it could not be said how they all might deal with it then. They might just bury him.

So, one day, when thick clouds had appeared in the sky and the air was such that nothing could be seen in the darkness, I took that end street along the wall to get to the hut.

Fortunately, everyone was busy getting their dinner ready, so no one's gaze was turned towards this direction. Seeing this opportunity and drawn by my curious nature, I arrived there. On reaching, a throbbing fear entered my mind that it would be difficult to get out of here. But, accepting whatever might happen, I entered the hut.

In a corner, a lantern burned with a small, thin wick. Its faint light fell on this woman's face.

What seemed apparent from the end of the street was now clearly visible. Her body was delicate. Some weakness of the mind could also be discerned. Her clothes were extremely dirty, crumpled, and in tatters. Her face was pale, empty and fearful. But, despite all that, her looks were so proportionately lovely that, for a moment, it was impossible to believe that such a beautiful woman could be in such a state.

She saw me coming to the doorway by the back street. Like an oppressed bird, she simply looked ahead without speaking. I was afraid. If she screamed, I would be done for. But no such thing happened. Like a persecuted bird that looks on with helplessness, she kept looking in my direction timidly. And then, as if my presence meant nothing, she looked away towards the floor. It seemed as if she were getting some true reassurance from the dust on the ground.

But, because she said nothing, I was emboldened. Very slowly, while still seated, I began moving towards her.

Finally, I came right near her. I sat almost beside her. Gently, I asked her, 'What's your name?'

As if she hadn't heard, she gave no reply. With a fearful look, she scanned all four directions once. And, seeing that no one was there, it seemed she felt some relief. But, again, she began staring at the ground.

I felt a shiver. A frightful thought came to me. 'She can't be mad, can she?' But then I heard her response and it removed that suspicion.

'What's my name – nothing. Everyone comes, asks my name, no one asks about anything else…'

I said hurriedly, 'Lady! I've come to ask other things. Who are you? Where are you from? How did you come to such a place? How are you?'

She did not respond. Kept staring at the ground. After a short while, she said softly, 'This is what I am – the dust on this ground. I know nothing else.'

Despite such emptiness, there was a sweetness to her tone. Her articulation was clearly cultured. Someone had robbed her of her true position. Her pleasing, melodious voice was such that it could have spread a serene breeze in some happy family.

'But where do you hail from?' I asked.

'What will you do knowing that? What will anyone do knowing that? Once something falls somewhere, it stays.'

'But tell us and we'll understand. Where have you come from?'

The woman placed a hand on her forehead. 'This doesn't leave anyone alone.'

'But what caste are you, lady? At least tell me that. I'm a Brahmin.'

'I'm also a Brahmin,' she replied suddenly.

'Arrey! Truly? How have you come here?'

Again, she placed a hand on her forehead. And, again, she said the same thing, 'This doesn't leave anyone alone.'

Whether the matter of fate was true or false, I felt she was not employing the term casually. This woman could probably only tell her story using fate as her bolster and support. So I said, 'Lady, fate does not leave anyone alone. It hasn't left you alone either. But fate also has its ups and downs. If your story can be somewhat understood, then who knows, in time, the leaf covering your fate may fall away. Some path may be found. Fate might be overturned.'

She cast a frightened, oppressed look in all directions. From the huts nearby, the sounds of dinner preparation could be heard. It didn't seem as if anyone had the leisure to even look in this direction. She stared at me. In my pocket, even then, my constant companion, the Parker pen was sparkling. A diary and some papers were visible too. Who knows if seeing these gave her some confidence? But she said softly, 'Bhai, this body is of Brahmin stock. But my actions are all those of Chaandaal stock.'

I said, 'Lady, we are all Chandaal. And, really, we're all also Brahmin. If you tell your story, then maybe you'll get some peace of mind for a couple of moments at least. In time, someone is bound to show up...'

'They are all ready to convert me. And if I don't turn over, they will crush me to pieces. Some 1500 to 2000 customers have already come.'

I was shocked. This one poor woman was trapped here. There were thousands of policemen in the city. Thousands of karyakarta.[55] This was a known place. Constables could be seen here ten times a day. But everyone in this neighbourhood had become reckless. They knew that every person has a price. Anyways, how was jail going to change anything besides not allowing one to listen to the radio?

With a 100 mounds of oil, there may be darkness in the British Raj. But, with 1000 mounds of oil, there was darkness here right now. And no one had any free time to even look under the proverbial lampshade, past the bhak-bhak speeches. This settlement had been here for the last thirty years. It must have been destroyed at least ten to fifteen times. But it would emerge again immediately the very next day. In that time, some twelve to eighteen police superintendents had also come and gone. But I recalled what one rogue had said to me while talking about his daily schedule. The police superintendents would all always ask the rogue for five to ten ser butter for their wives and children. And sometimes, they would catch someone and inflict punishment, but they had mostly gone rotten from the bottom to the top – they seemed strong on the exterior but were the filthiest inside. Yes, they knew how to make good speeches.

So I was still sitting there but my chest was thumping. Only those who knew what this place was came here.

Whether the woman had gotten a measure of my thoughts or not, she said urgently, 'Bhai, if you want to hear my story, then, fine, you may listen. But then you must leave this spot quickly otherwise

---

55. Karyakarta: In this context, the meaning is 'social worker'.

your safety will not be guaranteed. My sense of security has held fast to this support.' Again, she looked towards the dust.

Truly, I felt that, in her helplessness, the woman had found this a refuge. It was as if she considered herself safe by staring at the dust.

Without lifting her gaze, she spoke in a soft, grief-ridden voice, 'I am a Brahmin's daughter. Of Bhildi village. My parents died, leaving me at a young age. I was raised by my mama-mami. They had a spoilt son who had been raised with much indulgence. Mama-mami had never ever said no to him for anything. He was half stupid and half crazy. I had no one else there to play with or talk with. Due to that, we both became closer to each other. And then, bhai. No one can compete with this…' She ran a hand across her forehead.

I understood. I cut off the story right there. 'What happened after that, ben?'

'Some lower-caste people resided a little distance away in our neighbourhood. Like Koli, Vaaghri, Khaat, Khaatki. I caught the eye of one of them. He devised a plan. He pressured mama. Said, "I'll take care of it, but only if you hand her over to me afterwards…"

'Mama initiated a trade-off. Took 1500. Handed me over to him. And, with that 1500, mama arranged for his son to clear matriculation.'

Now this was the limit. Hearing this story, I was bewildered. I couldn't help asking, 'Ben, are you telling the truth?'

She took a bit of dust from the ground into her hand. Flinging it, she said, 'I swear on this. This may be dust to you but, in this great crisis, it has been my only support, and in what way, don't even ask.

And there is also a reason for that. I will tell you later. I cannot get the same reassurance anywhere else as from this dust. I now understand why the goddess Sitaji allowed the earth to take her in.'

A tone of deep sorrow entered her voice. She paused for a moment. 'But I have seen how this world is abundantly filled with both nectar and poison. This low man acquired me for 1500. But this same man's older brother turned out to be the greatest of all humanitarians in the world.

'After about six months, he came to our place for some work. He used to live abroad. The younger brother told him with delight. I was listening to that. But that humanitarian pushed his thaali aside and said, "The food of your house is like dust to me. You have done a terribly deceitful thing. Hand her back to wherever you have brought her from."

'"But the rupiya?"

'"Rupiya? Arrey, you ass! What are you going on about rupiya-rupiya? Here, take rupiya!" And he really made a pile of 1500 right there.

'I just kept staring at that man. I thought, if that man could somehow take me away to his place as a servant!

'And, in the end, he also said, "If you do not return her, I will consider eating food as a sin as of today. I will eat dust." And he actually tossed a pinch of dust into his mouth. "Now this is my diet," he said.

'That man has shown me the greatness of dust.

'Then what was to be done? I was handed back to mama. But, to mama's mind, I was like a snake being reared in his home. By hook or by crook, he got me out of his house. And I have now fallen into the hands of these people. Now, I will go wherever fate takes me. But, bhai!' She cast such a frightful look in my direction that I froze.

Some man was coming in our direction from the hut ahead. There was a vessel in his hands.

'This one who's coming ... to feed me unfit food ... you run off or you will certainly be caught by him.'

'But, ben, your name? At least tell me your name!'

'Kamla!' she replied. And she stood up hurriedly to push me out the back door.

She thought that if she stood, no one could see me. Now there was no time left to say anything and it was absolutely impossible to stay.

I simply ran from there.

My chest thumped until I came onto the street. I felt as if a thousand eyes must be watching me from the huts, so I clenched my fists and just set off in a run.

[2]

Some days of our lives are memorable. It seemed this day was also going to be such. I was leaving in a hurry. My intention was to catch, if possible, a bus. So I made my way forward along a short, narrow lane.

But, even as I took two more steps ahead, a speeding auto-rickshaw collided with me. Making a noise, it stopped. Those sitting inside also looked at me with surprise.

The rickshaw-wallah also said, 'Arrey, sa'ab, pay some attention. I would have been decimated just now.' Then he got down to take the fare from the departing passengers.

But, as if they both knew me or something, the passengers

sitting inside – a thin, tall, somewhat delicate-seeming man and, standing beside him, a shapely, charming (who couldn't be called pretty-looking but, based on a first glance of her clean, attractive, simple dressing style, one thought of calling her virtuous) elegant, real Gujaratan lady – advanced towards me after paying the rickshaw-wallah and sending him off.

'Murabbi! How are you here like this?' So saying, they both stood in front of me.

I could recall many instances when my memory had failed to recognise men and women I'd actually known. So, not showing either acquaintance or dis-acquaintance at all, I kept looking at them. 'I was out this way ... just had some work.'

'But this part of town is wicked. Half the city's crimes occur right here. So many bad Delhi lenders live here. What can we do? It's our ancestral home, so ... This, along here is our home. Please come, saheb. We just ... Your books...' And he said other such things as he saw fit. In the meantime, the woman opened the door that faced the street and turned on the electricity.

As soon as there was light, that man's face was recognizable to me. Once, I had met him on a journey and, per chance, he had been reading one of my books. At that time, he had not known me. So he had asked me a question about an irrelevant-seeming matter. I now recalled that.

Then, someone came to fetch me at the station and, realising that I was the writer of the book, this man had even extended an invitation for tea. I remembered the entire incident.

I said, 'We've met once before, right?'

'Why, have you forgotten? At the station?'

'Yes, right. I've recollected,' I said.

I started climbing the steps to enter the living quarters with him. Once inside, he asked me to sit on a cushioned seat. He went to another room to finish some work.

The room he was seated in was bathed in soft, beautiful light from sky-blue lamps. It appeared as if there were only three other rooms in the house. The kitchen seemed to be further inside. The sound of the stove could be heard from there. The room nearby seemed to be the bedroom.

But, in the faint light of the lamps, I cast a look over the entire living room. And my heart danced for a moment as if it had seen some delicate, beautiful thing.

This home gave a glimpse of a lovely, peaceful, healthy, love-filled, self-sufficient kind of existence. The living room was clean, pretty, fine, proportionate, and I saw furniture and artistic decor that was in keeping with Gujarati culture.

There were no portraits hanging with photographs torn out of the latest monthly magazines and there wasn't some sculpture placed on the table at the very end to indicate a modern lifestyle. There wasn't even a table or a chair there. They were both placed in the very back of the room, as if they were of no use.

The desire to make a clumsy declaration by creating a fake impression of one's familiarity with art, as is often seen among the middle classes, could not be found anywhere there.

And yet, looking around in all directions, who knew how but it could be ascertained that the delicate hands of the lady of this house possessed a gift to recognise beauty.

From the olden eras of Gujarat, beautiful utensils of all sizes were set in an arrangement in front. But it was so elegantly positioned that an onlooker would not find it out of place in that room. It seemed like a lovely extension of the living space. In one corner, the fragrance of rose and jasmine emanated from a flower vase. Whether this small family had only one faith or for whatever other reason, there was a single portrait of Shrinathji hanging on the wall opposite as if he were looking over the entire room with a love-filled gaze. Or perhaps my weird, fanciful, capricious, foolishness-filled, reclusive nature was rejoicing in almost every kind of useless and meaningless crazy thing. However it may have been, but I felt that the room's decor was more joyful because of that single portrait. The toys that were hung in other places as false and artificial declarations of 'artistic' decor never gave even a single life inspiration – only that they were flashy to the eye and gave visitors an air of heavy ostentatiousness. Instead of that, this one portrait seemed to exude a more exalted air. In a similar way, the arranged boxes, small items, wooden furniture, seats, all made the room look polished and becoming. It felt as if the lady of this house had poured the very essence of her life into the decoration of this room.

I sat there, looking over all this beauty when the decorator of the home arrived with two cups of tea. Her face seemed to have the true happiness of hospitality. The man also arrived and sat before me. An unmissable impression of gentleness could be seen on that simple man's face.

'You have made this house very beautiful and fine, with a Gujaratan-like, cheerful character!' I said to them both.

The joy that spreads across an artist's face when someone recognises his talent, that is the joy I saw emerging on their faces. I immediately realised that art and life were both wholly interwoven here.

Those awful middle-class working people who bought sugar in packs of two and half ser and on occasion ripped out portraits from monthly magazines and ran to get them framed with bribe money, received salaries ranging between 250 and 1000, had a half-baked education, were like slaves of even the slaves of the British – such people had truly wrought the destruction of art just like they had destroyed the mother tongue.

They needed English for their jobs; so, without even knowing the language, they never tired of falsely praising it. Now, they need Hindi to fill the holes in their bellies; so they don't tire of falsely commending it. As if their poor mother tongue is simply some unnecessary appendage in their lives.

Instead of homes decorated like counterfeit shrines of art, how delightful was the ambience created here by this couple? Here, no one had extracted art from life and hung it onto a nail to gaze upon. So it was true that such art could not be seen here but, due to the environment where both life and art were as one, it seemed to me that art was being lived here.

I stared at that lady. She hadn't the slightest awareness that she had done any extraordinarily artistic house decor. There was not even a discernment that this was an artful composition. She had been doing this from an easy, natural flow of innate talent. Her lack of consciousness was itself a great accomplishment.

I felt a desire to take a peek into their lives. I said, 'Bhai! Gulaab bhai … if it's not a problem, please tell me what work you do.'

'What problem can there be, saheb?' he replied. 'I don't do any kind of special work. I've been going to a couple of old places for a long time to supervise general, miscellaneous tasks. By the grace of god, they have confidence in our honesty; so, whenever they have any new work, they always hire me for supervision. From that, I'm able to manage household expenses. Otherwise, *she* preserves the home's prestige … who am I?'

'Oh, let it be, let it be. Embarrassing me for no reason – you are the one running the house! God and my husband here have gifted me some tranquillity of mind; so I do some mirror-work embroidery. Can you call that any kind of work?'

I was surprised. In a corner of the city, in a small, secluded residence, without making any kind of declaration, here lived a family that was, moment by moment, making its own existence more and more abundantly beautiful with simple, clean, lovely adornment. Shaping life in every moment. The matter was plain. Their existence was also plain. But, given that, its consequence was not irrelevant.

If the meaning of life was somehow about a spiritual journey, then it could be said that this couple was truly undertaking such a journey. Wasn't the fulfilment of our existence, within our lives, in this alone? There was certainly no ostentatiousness here. But, in that scene and that moment, a hate was born in my heart against all kinds of advertisement, people's tendency to exhibit themselves, pretentiousness, bustle, disorder, and useless activities. Hate also rose now against those commonplace loquacious, lecturing art-lovers.

I thought of this couple that valued art in the manner of a spiritual journey – which was the true meaning of art – as more art-loving than a thousand art-lovers. Besides anything else, this life was being lived meaningfully. Or it was as if they had found a particular way to thrive in life and the significance of this was no small matter.

I said, 'Ben, what did you say about the mirror-work?'

'Arrey, it's just that, when I get some free time – just to entertain myself, with my little know-how – I do some embroidery
work. He goes and sells it someplace and, from that, we get a
couple paise. Our miscellaneous expenses and any health-related
expenses are taken care of with that. That little support is useful for our health and wellness. But how can it be said that I have
maintained the house because of it? That's just his nature to make
me appear important. Otherwise, in our small household, what
is there to maintain anyway? There's no child or dependent that
there would be any unexpected expense. And we have removed
all the impulsive types of socialising expenditures. Then what
expenses are there? God gives two human beings enough to eat.'

The air of this interesting, faith-filled marriage touched me.
I was barely there for a half an hour or an hour. But the experience was such that it became forever memorable. Even their talk
was all related to a calm, quiet, pure living. This is why I found
this corner of the world so different.

When I rose to leave, both of them came all the way down to
see me off; and, with affection, they stood with folded hands to
bid me farewell.

'Again, saheb! Now please, definitely come sometime. If you
could spare us time someday, we can have a meal here.'

That lady said, 'We tend to recall your *Chauladevi* at least ten
or twelve times a year, if not more!'

Gulaab bhai added, 'If some beautiful woman like that comes
into our sights, we even say immediately "there goes *Chauladevi*".'

I said, 'Ben! It seems that fanciful whims are also an artful,
spiritual necessity in life. So Chaula must have entered my soul,

that is what I feel now. Setting that aside, I congratulate this part of your home and your beautiful decor with all my heart. I will certainly come sometime – if I'm going past this way. But what is your name? Please tell me that. I still don't know by what name I should call you if I happen to go by this way.'

'My name is Kamla,' she said.

On hearing the name, I was shocked. The experience of meeting Kamla just an hour ago was still fresh. I could not resist comparing the two namesakes.

Such disparity? The question arose in my mind. And yet, instead of that Kamla evolving into this kind of Kamla, the latter one had been created. And who else were her creators? Were they not all of us? And 'us' meaning? 'Us' meaning who?

Customs, social traditions, 'us' meaning our communal existence. Moreover, people – the pillars of our societies, statesmen, philosophers, politicians, social workers, religious leaders, teachers – in short, the entire social hierarchy. So it is us alone developing these constructs and then, again, it is us sitting to wonder about these Kamlas. Such delusions and deceptions?

Blind-alleyed, terrible, illusion-filled maze!

How many Kamlas must have been produced in this maze? And how many must it have destroyed? And yet, there is this particular quality. We non-violent people oppose the violence-filled atom bomb. And, just by standing in such opposition, we believe we lay claim to a spiritual elevation.

Oh, what a maze!

When a Devi Ma Becomes
a Woman

We twenty–twenty-five breakfast customers would appear at Gopikabai's mess between 9:30 and 1:00 AM. There was no work-related fellowship between us because, among those who came to eat, some were clerks, some miscellaneous working types. Many were also students. Some were from small factories. And some came because they enjoyed Gopikabai's cooking and, even more than that, her lovely nature.

In Gopikabai's countenance, there was such a kindness-filled, pleasing enchantment that any man who spoke with her even for a few moments would forever remember the charm of her facial expressions. Even the word 'charm' was not accurate for her. Charm is dependent on beauty. But what people consider beauty was hardly the kind to be found in Gopikabai. And yet, a wonderful loveliness played in those facial features. She laughed, looked at you, simply said a merry thing, made some sweet joke about life, arrey! Gave you a gentle reproach – but whatever activity she would be doing, that beauty would not leave her alone for even a moment. Many a time, no words could be found to give a true description of her beauty. Because it didn't simply exist. It emerged anew every moment due to Gopikabai's actions in each moment.

This Gopikabai had no kinspeople. That is to say, she had absolutely no relatives or loved ones. And, in another way, just as there were no kinspeople, there were no strangers either. To her mind, there were no customers either, people who just paid to dine there. She took pleasure in cooking. She enjoyed serving the food. She enjoyed feeding others. As if the hallowed title of Annapurna[56] was for her alone.

All her diners came to eat there between the aforementioned hours. After that time, rarely anybody came to eat. So, in the afternoon, after taking some rest, Gopikabai would sit with her Tulsikrit Ramayan. The peaceful rhythm of her slow, sweet voice would flow throughout the room. For a couple of moments, she would forget everything. She would forget herself. She would forget her mess. She would forget her household affairs. Everything. If someone showed up during this time, he was sure to mistake her for a goddess and wouldn't be able to resist folding both hands and bowing to her. A lovely, auspicious mark of sandalwood would be honouring her forehead. Nearby, on both sides, lamps would be glowing. In front, there would be a portrait of Ma Annapurna. And, sitting there, Gopikabai would have forgotten herself in Ram, Lakshman, Sita, Hanuman, Tara and Mandodari. Many times, some customer would come to confirm their attendance or absence for the evening meal but, seeing Gopikabai, the

---

56. Annapurna is the goddess of food and nourishment in Hinduism; also, one of the many avatars of the goddess Parvati.

topic of conversation would be put aside and they would fold
their hands, bow, and take their leave. Gopikabai would have to
remind them – why had they come? Then that man would stop
to tell her his concern.

So this Gopikabai – if you want to call her a hostel-waali,
you can call her that too. If you want to call this business of
hers a business, you can do that as well. But, within it, she had
spread her own fragrance in such a manner that whoever came
there would believe they were committing a crime by calling her
a hostel-waali. No one had heard anyone call her a hostel-waali
or bai or hostel-waali bai or Gopikabai. They only called her
Annapurnaben. And many spirited young students addressed her
as Annapurnadevi. Those among them who found that name too
long began calling her simply 'Devi'.

And, truly, she was like a goddess to us customers. If there
was any festive occasion or major holiday, some sweet would
have been made. Then, a small gathering would assemble around
Gopikabai after eating. At that time, the goddess-like respect for
her that everyone nursed could be seen clearly. A beedi-roller
would come there – a man who did not, generally, belong to the
better classes. But even he would remain civil in her presence. And
he would be constantly careful that his own merrymaking did not
slide below a certain level.

In this way, she had been enshrined the devi of a small family. Her countenance was so calm, lovely, and beautifully enticing.
The subtle lustre of that gracefulness also emerged in her manners. Her speech had the same attractiveness. Even in the jowar
she made, there would be 'a certain amount of sweetness' rolled
in so naturally that the taste of it lingered long in the mouth.

Nature had seemingly put a line of modesty in her hands. Even her appearance would be like that. It didn't seem too conceited or too sober. Pretty in a dignified way, yet showcasing the allure of both her body and clothing fully.

Once, a student joined our gathering. His name was also somewhat weird. Everyone called him Naveen bhai. And later, everyone forgot his original name. And this name, Naveen, stuck firmly. This Naveen bhai had come here from the village to study at the college. Who knows what it was about his gaze but, whenever he looked at anyone, he could only look with a slanted, sideways gaze. It was later that we found out that his gaze was an indication of his character. Fault-finding was the biggest feature of his personality – the kind that could take a person's small flaw and view it as much larger. After further acquaintance, it was discovered that this Naveen bhai was the kind who believed that even the least respectful attitude towards someone else or an acknowledgement of another person's virtues was, in his mind, akin to slighting his own person. So, from the time that he arrived, he would uncover some shortcoming or other even in Gopikabai's cooking. On the first day itself, he had asserted that there was extra salt in the dal. When he said very softly into his neighbour's ear, 'If it's too salty, you're hardly going to eat it, na?' it might have seemed like an ordinary thing at the time. But, like that, slowly, Naveen bhai's conversation became about making regular revelatory announcements of some fault or other.

Weak willpower is a naturally inherited trait in some people. Believing that acting per one's own wishes might sometimes be counted as obstinacy or considered as stupidity, and eventually just for the sake of remaining sweet-tongued, there are always those who articulate agreement with the person in front of them even if they forget the matter afterwards. In this manner, at first, some people seemed to agree with some of Naveen bhai's talk. Thanks to that, talk began to circulate that Gopikabai had won everyone over due to her entrepreneurial skills. Otherwise, she was also a profiteering wheeler-dealer. Her cleverness was praised. But the positive sentiments towards her began to crumble.

This Naveen's mental state was also perverted. If a thaali fell, he laughed. If a lota tipped over, he laughed loudly. If a ladle scalded someone, Naveen would derive some sort of amusement. Seeing the descent of any thing or person gave him pleasure, it seemed. Seeing someone's belittlement gave him joy. He could not bear anyone receiving respect. Due to this mindset of his, once he sunk so low that, seeing it, we regulars were frightened. We felt this man was just a terrible barbarian.

[2]

It so happened that a head constable, an acquaintance of Naveen's, had recently come to town. He had a considerable reputation. He had come in search of some criminal and was to stay awhile. From time to time at our place, a good number of people disrupted our rows of bicycles. And this head constable had a good connection with the local police. So, as if doing us all a big favour, Naveen had this head constable checked into our hostel. Then the constable also began to come to the mess to eat regularly.

In appearance, the man was forceful and strong. Due to his large eyes, massive forehead, awesome face, and the kind of voice that could leave a man trembling where he stood, our first impression was that he was some hard-minded, tough man. But gradually, this impression changed. His own carefree attitude was the cause of this. Though he was a big man, he took part in our joys and jests like a child. His frank nature was adored by all. Furthermore, with his habit of doing some or the other favour for everyone, he established his position within our community. Naveen would always be quietly whispering with him about something or the other. No one understood what that private talk was about but, having done it, they would both laugh. And, laughing so, they would give each other a clap. That head constable would come on time and leave on time. He rarely touched on questions that might create disagreement with anyone. But, if he did, he would not leave off without having established his opinion as the right one. From this, a kind of high opinion of him became firm in everyone's mind, that there was no harm in believing the head constable was always right.

Once, we were all sitting and Naveen raised a matter. 'What do you suppose ... about this Gopikabai? She looks like a goddess but what do you think of her?'

Hearing this, everyone was rendered speechless. No one from among us had, to this day, ever raised such a question about the lady. To pose such a question about her was like breaking a beautiful idol into pieces. So, no one responded to Naveen's question at the time. Everyone cast their gaze downwards. No one said anything.

'Why has no one said anything? Our people, yaar! This is the big affliction. Once they start worshipping something, they just keep worshipping it. If they start criticising it, then they keep criticising it. But it is this Gopikabai's resourcefulness itself that tells us that she is bound to be deficient in some way or other. She's also a woman. Young. Alone. To cut a long story short, let me just tell you … she must have some secret family affair. Also, hear this, she must have her own affair now and, over time, she must have had other affairs too! Without that, there would not be so much sweetness in her. The lovely skill with which she is able to play with each of you twenty-five men also shows that she is just like all the other hostel-waalis. She is a woman shaped by her own affairs. She is uncommon, there's no denying that. Otherwise, whatever you see in her is a projection of your own minds, not of her life.'

'So what are you trying to say? Do you know who you are talking about?' one of us said. He had become a bit hot-tempered.

'I've said what I wanted to,' Naveen replied, calmer than the person who had responded. 'And you have heard what I have said about Gopikabai. Now what do you have to say?'

'You are an absolute liar,' said an emotional student.

'And fault-finding,' another added in assent.

'You are revealing yourself,' a third said.

With even more calm, Naveen spoke about Gopikabai with a terrible contempt, 'I've heard what you said. And you've heard what I said. Either I'm wrong, or you are. That decision – this head constable will give us.'

'Arrey, me? How will I hand out a judgement? I am just your guest for a couple of days.'

'Not so, head constable, not so,' Naveen said. 'All of these folks are as if unknown to worldly ways. Whose reputation is stained and how much, they have no comprehension of this. So this task is your responsibility. You are our head constable. You search it out. What is the story?'

'But what do we have to do with that?' the head constable said.

'My nature is somewhat punctilious. If I go after something, I will keep at it till I find what I need. I've just got that habit now.'

'So the task has been assigned to you. You need to give us a report on the fifteenth day from now.'

'You, Naveen bhai! You are yourself base!'

'I accept that. I am base. But I want to say another thing. This is no baseness. And, from it, there isn't going to be any damage to anyone. Let's do this – for fifteen days – for exactly fifteen days, let's zip our mouths. Then, the ghee will fall into its rightful vessel. Tell me, do you accept?'

'Accepted, accepted,' three or four young men spoke up in unison. In their minds, Gopikabai wasn't a bai – wasn't a woman – she was a devi. 'And if your story turns out to be worthless, then?'

'Then we will leave this hostel,' Naveen said.

'Agreed, fine.'

'Agreed.'

Once the agreement was made, everyone became sombre.

[3]

It was exactly the fifteenth day. The head constable sat in a nearby, open dharamshala. Naveen was also there. One after another, everyone was arriving.

The head constable's commitment was ending today.

No one was saying anything. The head constable was also quiet. Naveen was absolutely quiet.

It seemed as if everyone had arrived. One man glanced all around. Wordlessly, he counted the heads. Twenty-five. The twenty-sixth was Naveen. Stepping forward, Naveen got to the open door of the mess. Then, with a soft step, he returned. He said something in the head constable's ear. The constable stood and went forward. Everyone watched him going up to the hostel, which was on the top floor. The entrance from the road was open.

Inside, the entry door to the top floor was closed. Yet, everyone saw the head constable going up. After a while, the head constable returned. Without saying anything, he gestured to everyone. It was a sign to follow him slowly and softly.

Everyone held their breath. Faces became stern. A silence like that of the speechless sky extended everywhere. That head constable seemed like a terrible blaze of fire in that silence. Without speaking, walking so softly that his footsteps could not even be heard, he was moving ahead.

Very slowly, very slowly, as if on the silken paws of a cat, the head constable began to climb the stairs. Naveen was behind him. Everyone else was following in the wake of the head constable's footsteps. They moved forward in a way that they did not make a single sound.

Eventually, they reached the top floor. There was a long corridor. At the far end of it, there were two rooms. One room was where Gopikabai sat and read. The other was the kitchen. In that kitchen, there was a rather faint lamp burning.

There, in that long corridor, as if with bated breath, everyone stood quietly for a while. No one's gaze could fall in their direction. They all stared steadily into the inner room.

Two minutes, five minutes, ten minutes – time seemed to be ticking slowly. The head constable had, quite some time ago, left them there and gone into the inner room.

In the faintly burning lamplight, the head constable's wavering silhouette appeared and disappeared once or twice, wandering about. In the end, it became invisible in one corner.

After a little while, a shadow could be seen emerging from a nearby room. Slowly, very slowly, as if darkness had stood up and was walking, so that shadow was walking.

That shadow entered the inner room and, from the bit of light that fell, it could be seen that it was Gopikabai. She also became invisible in that corner where the head constable's shadow had disappeared.

A moment passed. That lamp burnt out.

In the corridor, Naveen appeared to be coming towards the twenty-five men standing like stones, like dumb, stunned, frozen tears. His cruel pleasure was evident from his gait.

But, before he could come and say anything, the heads of these twenty-five men had drooped onto their chests. Without saying a single word, without a single sound from their moving feet, those twenty-five men – like walkers of the dark night, like shadows of awakened ghosts, like death – were slowly, very slowly, descending the stairs. Not one among them was saying anything, nor making any sound while walking. Not betraying even a slight understanding.

Their idol had been crushed. A dream had been shattered into pieces. The great rock of faith in their lives had become like grains of sand. Like the living dead, they descended the stairs.

[Based on a well-known story by Maxim Gorky.[57]]

---

57. The famous story Dhumketu has referenced here is 'Twenty-Six Men and a Girl'. It's about lost ideals, where the eponymous twenty-six men see the girl, Tanya, as a paragon of virtue. When a new soldier arrives and, to prove his point about her, seduces her, the other men are left crushed and upset. Gorky's story ends a bit differently.

The Golden Necklace

This is a story from fifty to seventy-five years ago. Told and heard. At that time, in a small village called Bhandaariya, there lived a famous craftsman. It was said there was no other craftsman like him in a hundred villages of that region. He had one specialty: he made gold necklaces. And no one else's craftsmanship could measure up against that of his necklaces. An onlooker would not be able to stop staring. That's all it was. But, because of it, there was always a clamour of work at his place. There would be plenty of business going on. So that no one would learn his art, he never let a grown man work alongside him, only a couple of young boys. When he was working, he was celebrated. Everyone considered a craftsman like him to be god-like.

This artisan, Bhagwaan Soni, was also very honest. Just as his handiwork was uniquely his own, so also, if there was even a tolerance deviation of a quarter in any item, that would be the end of it. His renown was such that there would never be any deviation on any day.

But, later, Bhagwaan became a bit of an addict. He had started taking a bit of opium. Occasionally, he also had liquor. He was a

craftsman. But, in a way, he was afflicted. He had a small physical defect in one hand. And he limped too. One of his eyes was
large and the other was small and he was also dark-skinned. So
he was dark, crippled, and maimed – all of it. He was generous
but his shortcomings were such that, for a long time, he was not
even able to set up his home and family. So, it could be presumed,
that was also the reason why he became an addict. Then, when he
married late, he did not marry with any good augur.

His wife, Lakhmi, desired his money more than his craftsmanship. So she would frequently tell him off for his deformities.
In so doing, she would get money off him and give to her relatives and loved ones. She would behave as if she were doing him
a big favour by looking after his household affairs. Even when she
talked of his craftsmanship, she spoke with contempt.

Due to this, Bhagwaan slowly began looking for a new love-
life. So he came to be in the company of Kaali – a Koli by caste,
ebony in colour, and even named Kaali. This woman had a natural sweetness as if there were pitchers of nectar on her tongue.
Kaali was alone. She had no dependents. She settled in to take
care of Bhagwaan's various needs. As time went by, Bhagwaan's
household was kept running in that manner. Many times, Kaali
would sit and gaze at his artisanship. She wouldn't say anything but, due to her presence, new works would emerge from
Bhagwaan's hands.

When talk began about this affair, Bhagwaan's and Kaali's
relationship had already manifested in such a wholesome way
that people had considered it just useless repetition to talk of it.
And Lakhmi was only concerned with money. As long as she had
a bag of money in her hands, it was fine.

While Lakhmi was bitter in her speech, she remained vigilant about her self-interest. She saw that Bhagwaan now closed
shop at 3:00 or 4:00 PM and went to sit with Kaali. Sitting there,
he talked till 7:00 or 8:00 PM. All the talk was weak, worthless,
and like that of young boys. Talk such as once there was a king
and once there was a queen. So Lakhmi decided that this fellow's
business was about to fall apart. And his body did not have the
strength to do physical labour. The money had been used up so
he could only eat his next meal if he got money out of her. She
deduced that it would soon be time for her to do hard labour. So,
for a while, she became agreeable with Bhagwaan and made him
fashion two necklaces for herself.

'But Soni ma'jan! Now look, ho,' for the first time, there was
sweetness on Lakhmi's tongue, 'make it special. So that people
will not be able to take their eyes off it. And, in five to twenty-five
years, everyone will look at the necklace and wonder which divine
craftsman created this exquisite piece. Who knows, this artisanry
of yours might be put into … what is it called, an exhibition –
might be put into that.'

'Arrey! Just you wait and see this thing I'll make for you. I'll
make it so that anyone who sees it will be dumbfounded!'

'Craftsmanship. Craftsmanship is something that God has
given only to your fingers. The entire world's craftsmanship has
been bestowed onto your fingers. For everyone else, god has only
given plain fingers. Long and weak!'

In this manner, she had praised his handiwork for the first
time in her life and believed that her necklaces would be made
such that they would feed her rotla during times of scarcity.

Whether this Bhagwaan was there or not, if she sold them, she would be able to eat without needing to work. This was in her mind. She praised Bhagwaan's craftsmanship so much that he truly felt deep within his soul that he would make something that, even when he wasn't there any more, would speak of his craftsmanship. But, along with that, he understood that Lakhmi was being insincere. So he simply paid attention to his craft. And he made a truly extraordinary necklace. He gave Lakhmi not one but two necklaces. If you looked at one, you forgot the other – such was the beauty of each.

While he was making the necklaces for Lakhmi, Bhagwaan was also making a jewel for Kaali. This necklace became even better than the other two. He gave it to Kaali. While doing so, Bhagwaan had laughingly said that, if some craftsman makes us such a necklace, then we should fall at his feet! And, really, that necklace had turned into that kind of item.

After that, Bhagwaan passed away. His craftsmanship was also forgotten. That there was once upon a time such a crafts-man – this was also forgotten. In due course, there was a new wind blowing and, in it, there was talk of collecting the items of all such strays who had become craftsmen. And to preserve them together in some location so that, in the future, people might con-tinue getting inspired by them all. At that time, this was a new trend. Some British officer had taken up this responsibility and he had a true love for craftsmanship. So this Bhagwaan's name was made known. His craft work was with Lakhmi. The people doing the collection called her. The price she asked for was agreed upon for the items.

Lakhmi was relieved; at least she had secured her rotlo. In her mind, even then, there was contempt that the saala disfigured one had kept her high and dry throughout his life. After dying too, he would have left her with nothing if it hadn't been for her wisdom in getting the pieces made.

In that manner, the matter was settled. The necklaces were taken. The decision about where they would be sent to be kept safe was confirmed. The plan to send them off with a couple of local men was also decided.

Those local men had some suspicion in their minds. They had someone test the items for purity. But now, if the matter got spoilt, it would invite the British officer's anger. So, after having the necklaces tested, they looked at each other.

'What do you think?' said one of them eventually.

The one who was a craftsman responded in a whisper: 'Saheb! Will you believe it? This chap, Bhagwaaniyo, must have made several others weep in this way. If this issue gets out, many others will come running here. And then our good names will get ruined. In short, this is simply a brass toy! But it can't be said now, so what's to be done of it?'

'What? Brass? Arrrr! Then ... then, if we deliver this, the first attack will be on us!'

These two were mighty perplexed. The matter could not be revealed to anyone. If they revealed it, and it spread, then hundreds of Bhagwaan's customers would run to get their items valued and that would cause a lot of trouble. And sa'ab would also get angry. Jobs would be lost and fraud charges would be loaded onto their heads.

If they delivered without saying anything, then, in time, what if they were the first to be attacked with an accusation? Someone could take them severely to task that they had delivered brass instead of gold.

Now what could be done? Both of them fretted. No solution came to mind. Agreeing to decide in the morning, they slept off their mental fatigue through the night.

In the morning, they started up and, while drinking tea, they were thinking about how to resolve this matter, how to bring it up, how to prevent sending this item.

Just then, they heard some rattling outside and were startled. Peeping out, they saw an ebony-coloured woman standing there. They were surprised. 'Who's this?' they asked. At that, she entered.

She had no understanding of how to speak. For a few moments, she just stood there.

Then those men asked: 'What is it, bai?'

'My name is Kaali!'

'Sure. But what's your business here? Why have you come?'

'Do you not recognise me? I'm Kaali!' Kaali thought that, because of the fame of Bhagwaan, everyone must know her. Now she realised that was not the case.

She began to speak. 'I'm Kaali. The wonderful piece I own by the craftsman Bhagwaan is exquisite and exclusive. I had come to tell you that. Do you want to see it?'

'Yes, yes, we want to see it!' The two men felt that she had been sent by god to show them the solution.

Kaali placed her necklace in front of them. The craftsmanship of the jewel was so extraordinary, they both kept staring. It was way more superior than those brass ones. And it was the real thing, of a hundred tach.[58]

'If you want to get rid of it, we will give you whatever you say. We will get it valued by a good man!'

'I do not want to take anything for it. And I don't want to sell the necklace either!'

'But who are you?'

'Me? What I am of his, he knew it. And I was the other who knew it. The talk is that you want to display his craftsmanship somewhere. So I came to tell you that, if you want a work of his real craftsmanship, keep this. Then his name will continue on. It will remain known among people. I have brought this here so that his name continues to be known. But it is not for sale!'

'Then it is just to be given for nothing?'

'No, it is not for that either. In exchange for this, give me what you have. You take this. The only condition is that only we know of this matter!'

For a moment, both of them looked at each other. What she had couldn't be fake, could it? What if that was why she had come? But no, her necklace was real.

'But what is the reason for doing that?' they said. 'What we have are these necklaces from his wife, Lakshmi. We'll put them in the collection for viewing. Everyone will see them and Bhagwaan's name will continue on!'

'If you put my item, his name will become immortal among people. Look at his craftsmanship! Look at it and test it.'

---

58. Tach: An ancient Indian unit for measuring the purity of gold.

Both of them now thought that this Kaali was a simple labourer. She had come to speak with a true heart. She did not seem to know that these other necklaces were made of brass. For now, the problem would be off their hands. If anything happened afterwards, they could deal with it later.

They immediately agreed to her proposal and gave Kaali the brass necklaces in exchange for the one she owned. Then Kaali went away. She didn't seem to realise that something was amiss.

After she left, both men fell into thought. It was fine, she did not know, so the matter had ended there. Afterwards, who was going to listen to her?

But they stopped talking because Kaali was turning back towards them. Both felt a panic as there was the possibility of an explosion now.

And Kaali did cause an explosion. 'I have come back to tell you that this issue must remain between us, ho. That necklace I gave is of pure hundred tach gold. That item, he crafted with love. Within it, he has put the secrets of his heart's affections and desires. That item should remain with his name. Not these things. Not what you have given me. This is simply brass. He himself had told me that. His name should not be disgraced, that is why I came. I had only come to tell you that. This matter should remain buried. Craftsman Bhagwaan's work and fame should remain like absolute pure gold among people.'

On hearing this, the men stood. Before they could respond, Kaali disappeared. They quickly had a search made in the valley below but it was as if she had become invisible. As if she had come to say simply this much!

The Dispenser of Justice

Someone is sitting there as the dispenser of justice, bhai! This is a thing I have come to learn. Then if anyone wants to say anything different, let them say it.'

In the middle of the afternoon, we, two or three people, were going along a path towards a village after having crossed the Bhaadar river. Keshavji was an acquaintance from my old village. There was a chief constable, Raghuji. I was a teacher in a nearby village and had made it a habit to get to some or another big city every Saturday. Today also, I had arrived in the big city, having met Keshavji and Raghuji on the way. So, as the afternoon descended, all of us set out to return to our village. But the heat from the sun was oppressive. And it was doubtful that the bundled watermelon from the banks of the Bhaadar would remain unspoilt till arrival. So we sat under a pipar tree at the edge of the path to eat the watermelon. And, when some topic came up, Keshavji said, as if speaking from his own experience, 'Someone is always there as the dispenser of justice. Always. Always.'

Right in front of us lay a desert-like maidaan. Wherever you looked, there were only rolling stones. There was absolutely nothing else – not even the stump of a plant or tree. It was absolutely without any greenery. Like a terrible desert, the maidaan lay like a void ahead. One might think that land was cursed.

Keshavji's gaze rested on that maidaan. At the far end, there was a small border, near which was a small shrine. Just there, two to four trees could be seen. Otherwise, the entire maidaan felt terrifyingly godforsaken. A lone person passing by on an afternoon would be dumbfounded by its emptiness. There wasn't even a crow calling anywhere!

Keshavji kept staring at that maidaan. He seemed to be recalling something. There was a conversation going on among us about god and the balancing of justice. With great gusto, he now underpinned it further: 'I am telling you, bhai! Someone is always there as the dispenser of justice. Always. Always. Then, whether we want that justice or not, whether we live to see that justice or not, that is another matter. See that border visible there? There's that small shrine-like thing near it, which was made by one of the area's lower-caste Koli women. This is God's justice. It's my recollection. Raghuji! You must remember, na? That Jhamkudi?'

'Arrey, yes! That woman, she was the bold kind who could catch birds in flight. But god made this happen through her hands only. To erect a small shrine in such desolation. This is what it is called – God's justice!'

I kept staring at both of them, for I could not understand any of their talk. I said, 'What is this about?'

'On that day, bhai! You must have been about knee-high – this is about those days.

'Yours, mine, everyone's original village is Bhamarda. It's only now because there is a school in Jarakhiya that you have landed here. And we also left Bhamarda and came here.

'This Koli woman was from Bhamarda, but from the area's lower castes. Brazenly caught birds in flight. At that time, it was the age of the baapu darbaar.[59] Bhamarda baapu's kaamdaar, Narbheyram, was a bitter man. At that time, whatever the darbaar said was the law and whatever the kaamdaar said was the rule. The kaamdaar held sway.

'A poor Brahmin lived in the village. So poor, don't even ask. On a wealth basis, he was certainly very poor. But he was also so impoverished by nature that he wouldn't even say a dying man was on his way out. If he was going somewhere and a cat crossed his path, he would return home. If he met a black dog, he would sit to chant prayers. If he met some cattle head-on, he would move aside rather than push the cattle away from the path. If someone said two angry words, then he would go to their place for three days to ask for forgiveness. In short, he was so beggarly by nature that anyone who told him off would themselves later regret it. His disposition was so meek.

'Only one thing had made a home in his mind: I am poor, I can't say anything to anyone. Arrey! Even if the village's untouchable Dhed said anything to him, he would listen quietly and sit and weep after the Dhed left. That's the kind of maharaj[60] he was. His name was Gokul.

'One time, Gokul maharaj was found to be at fault. The mistake

---

59. Darbaar: The ruling caste or clan in feudal times.
60. Maharaj: The term used by Gujaratis to refer to a Brahmin priest or cook.

was to do with hunger – but an offense is an offense. And, at that time, tyranny ruled.

'What happened is that a cow belonging to the darbaar's mistress, Rani Baajibai, got cut up at the railway tracks. This cow was worth seeing. A huge Desan.[61] She looked as if she had been dressed up in much beauty. When she walked, it was as if some royal queen had ventured out. Per lactation, she gave twenty-seven ser milk. On all four legs, she had silver anklets, while golden bells hung around her neck.

'The day this cow got cut up, there was a strike in the village. But Gokul maharaj lived at the far end of the village. The darbaar himself had, by way of kindness, given him fifty yards of land at 1.5 pie per yard. Gokul had three boys and a blind wife. He would himself go seeking flour as alms[62] and, at noon, would come home and make rotla. His wife would have made urad vegetables. Between noon and 2:00 PM, everyone would eat. In the evening, he would circumambulate the Mahadev temple. In the afternoon, if anyone wanted their astronomical chart looked at, he would see to it. Such was his life.

---

61. Desan: An indigenous breed of dairy cattle, also called Gir, Bhadawari, Gujarati, Kathiawari, Sorthi and Surati. It originated in the Gir forests of South Kathiawar in Gujarat and is also found in Maharashtra and Rajasthan. This breed is known for its hardiness and disease resistance and yields a lot of milk. Its distinct horns are curved in half-moon crescents. It has a striking colouring – white with dark-red or chocolate-brown patches, or all black, or all red.

62. Alms: In earlier times, Brahmins did not do manual work to earn money. They subsisted on alms and charity. In return, they gave horoscopic advice, made astronomical charts, conducted pujas, and even cooked for wealthy patrons.

'Gokul didn't know there was a strike in the village. So, per his usual "in the name of god" alm-seeking, he set out at the mercy of god. His custom was to start asking for flour in the Koli community first. There, he initially met Jhamkudi. Who knows what happened but Jhamkudi, who had never done it before, invited him for a group Brahmin bhojan on that very day.

'Gokul abandoned his alm-seeking and went home. He fetched all three boys and led his blind wife along. And, at Jhamkudi's, laddoos were made. Everyone ate. Filled with happiness, Gokul maharaj returned home.

'But he had barely reached home when this Raghuji Nayak's father, Gigoji Nayak – who at that time ran errands for the kaamdaar – came to call him.

'When Gigoji Nayak came visiting, no matter who it was, they would tremble.

'Gokul also felt a terror in his stomach. Definitely, someone had said something to the kaamdaar. For the kaamdaar to call for him, it must be serious.

'Trembling, he arrived at the kaamdaar's. Jhamkudi was there too. She was extremely shrewd. Why would there be any shame in her eyes? Or any fear? She told the kaamdaar off clearly: "Anyone else is free to leave the village, sa'ab! I will absolutely stay in this village. And this was a strike for the darbaari cow. But, even if there is a strike for the darbaar's son, I will still feed Brahmins. My dharam comes first and house and family after!"

'The kaamdaar had chided her for having fed a Brahmin today, on a strike day.

'Jhamkudi stood there, completely impudent and shameless. Flames blazed from her eyes. The kaamdaar also felt that it would not be possible to get the better of this villainess. So he gave her a reprimand and, with a command to never do this again, told her to leave. Then, Gokul maharaj came, all trembling. So Jhamkudi remained standing there.

"'But why are you trembling about this, ma'raj? I fed you and you ate. If it's anyone's fault, it's mine. What is it to you?" Jhamkudi gave him courage.

"'My fault is first, baapa! Baapla! My crime is first, ba! I made the first mistake. I should have said no. I have committed an offense against the darbaar," Gokul conceded defeat. He was shaking.

'Until now, the kaamdaar's pride had taken a beating, thanks to Jhamkudi, with the peon, clerk and village-folk listening. So now, the kaamdaar started roaring at twice the volume: "Ma'raj! You will have to leave the village. Understood? You won't observe the strike for the darbaari cow, right? Leave the village. Run off tomorrow itself!"

"'Arrey! But, baapa! My giver of food and shelter! Forgive my mistake. I was raised by the darbaar. I have been given land by the darbaar. I have made a huge mistake. If you tell me, I will fast for seven days!"

"'Fast-bast is fine. Seems you've seen this Popabai's[63] behaviour here. But, here in Bhamarda, there is a lot more to see, ho!"

---

63. Popabai: A reference to a folktale about a pious woman who fasted regularly and lived a minimal life. When a king kidnapped her to marry her, she cursed him that his entire kingdom would get destroyed. He then took her back to her hut but drowned on the way and died. Justice was dispensed. Here, the kaamdaar is using Popabai to refer sarcastically

'"There is, baapa! There is … it's my fault!"

'But the kaamdaar had to recover his lost reputation. And that could be done only by threatening this weak man. So he roared even louder!

'"Arrey! Who's there in the courtyard? Gigaji? Is Gigaji there?"

'Gigaji was this Raghuji's father. He immediately made an appearance.

'The kaamdaar issued a command: "Go to Gokul ma'raj's. Put a lock on the house. Such beggars will insult darbaari commands? Drive this beggar away from here. Go, ali Jhamkudi, go! Take care! If you ever do anything like this again…"

'Jhamkudi left as though nothing had happened.

'But this fright was too much for Gokul maharaj's weak heart. He arrived home and could not sleep the entire night. For three days, he lay hungry and thirsty. And then who knows what happened, but he died on the third day!'

'What? He died? Arrrrr!' My horror escaped my lips.

'I have witnessed this story, bhai! Not heard. He died. And the boys were left bereft. The blind wife took a cane and went out to beg for flour as alms. At that time, Jhamkudi gave her some serious help. She turned out to be a warrior's daughter. The kaamdaar was a bit scared after this death. He had made arrangements to send them all to another village. But Jhamkudi waged a battle and kept the blind Brahmin woman and her three boys fed and sustained. And kept them in the village. Didn't let them go elsewhere.

---

to Jhamkudi as a pious, fasting woman. As we see later in the story, Dhumketu is indulging in some clever foreshadowing here.

'Since then, a thorn remained in the Koli woman's heart. She believed that the kaamdaar had killed the Brahmin. She developed so much enmity against the kaamdaar's cruel nature, don't even ask. She did not let it go.

'She was quite shrewd. She could fell flying birds. She had scalped such learned ones that no one could know about.

'One day, in this very maidaan, at the edge of that border, that shrine was made. Jhamkudi had it built. Every summer, Gokul maharaj's water-stand is placed there for travellers and passers-by.

'She had made a resolve – if I don't kill this kaamdaar in a terrible way, then I am not Jhamkudi Koli. It is because of his threats that the poor, meek Brahmin lost his life.

'And, will you believe it, bhai? One day, Jhamkudi began a huge religious festival here at this border shrine. Almost 200 to 500 people came from the village. There was a brahma-bhojan. All the big nobility of the village had also been invited. The kaamdaar was also among them. And, when everyone was scattered about, she absolutely had Narbheyram kaamdaar picked up from within their midst.'

'Picked up? Meaning? Killed? Who did it, Jhamkudi?'

'That is the beauty, bhai, of that woman! God only knows who picked him up. At that time, there was a loud cry from the outlaws, who were also among the crowd. A murky, dim darkness was descending. And everyone was on their way back. In that, four to five riders also left this maidaan with loud explosive noises. A fear spread among the people. Some ran this way, some the other way. And, in between all that, it could be seen that the kaamdaar had tumbled over in his horse-carriage. It was said to be the handiwork of the outlaws and then there was no further trail of that talk either. So I was saying, bhai! That there is justice in God's house. Consider this an accident or God's justice given through a scheming woman like Jhamkudi – or however you want to consider it. But, that day, I heard so many say this, bhai! God does not forget. The kaamdaar had to give his own account right by the shrine of the poor Brahmin he killed for no reason.

'And then, as the local gossip spread that the kaamdaar had joined the world of ghosts, everything here became desolate! Going past here in the afternoon even, a man trembles. Alright, come on, let us go…'

'But then what about Jhamkudi?'

'What would happen to her? For as long as she lived, she looked after the Brahmin's blind wife. We'll talk about that some other time.'

I got up and kept gazing at the maidaan. Truly, it seemed as if someone must definitely be roaming across this maidaan at night. It looked so uniform, empty, like a deserted burial ground. As if there was simply no life in it!

The Creator of Life's Ruins

The cripple did not do any work. He was capable of doing something, but he just didn't do anything. He was lame in one foot and weak in the body. Still, if he wanted, he was capable of being helpful around the house in many roundabout ways. But his disabled state had shown him the fun of lazy pleasures. And he became accustomed to them.

If he had controlled his disposition somewhat, he might have given some relief to those around him. But no, Langda bhai was deriving a kind of new, weird pleasure from his physical short-coming. Just as he had physical defects, so he had become odd in character too. He needed to do some kind of talking all day. And, because he needed to talk, he also needed someone who would listen. His conversations would be chock-full of rumours. On top of that, he would pile on exaggerated stories of how heroic he had been before he was crippled. Listeners would get bored but Langdo never ever tired of talking about himself. He would be sitting all day on a broken cot in the alley. And, sitting there, he'd be gossiping away. There would always be someone or the other there to listen to him. Eventually, if there was no one, the neighbouring children would show up to sit in Langda kaka's presence because he would tell magical stories about thieves, ghosts, spirits and giants, and his own exploits when he had gone lion-hunting and what not.

Langda would sit on the cot in the morning and stay there all through the evening. His meals, bathing, washing, sleeping – everything would happen there. Sitting there, he would issue commands. His wife, Mangu, and daughter, Kesar, both would always be standing attentive all day at his service. If they made one small mistake, Langda bhai would lose his temper. And, if he lost his temper, then he would just strike out freely with his cane. Thanks to such behaviour, everyone at home had cried out for help. But Langda bhai didn't care about that. He would just sit there and issue orders. He assumed that the management of the house happened as if with divine intervention. His wife and daughter had to run around so much – he did not care about this at all. In fact, he did not care about anything at all. He himself did not work, fine, but he also kept everyone else present in his service. So, the mother and daughter were both fed up with him. What else could be done? If they left Langdo stranded, he would mostly settle down. But, in the characters of both the mother and daughter, there was a certain natural tendency to not even think of doing such a thing. This tendency is what had given Langda a fair amount of leeway. Both of them would silently obey the man's commands and get shattered doing their own work while also taking care of Langda. He had now grown accustomed to that life – hurl commands sitting about, and throw his cane if an order was disobeyed. The cane had come to suit him well.

His wife was all right but his daughter was so dignified and mature that even the neighbours would not tire of praising her nature. Langda's household continued to run in this manner. If that daughter hadn't been there, then all these many antics of Langda bhai would not have been allowed. It was as if nature itself had put sweetness and love in the girl.

Langda had this other trait – consider it a great virtue or a great flaw. He would sit on that cot and keep an eye on the entire neighbourhood. He would set up a conversation in such a fine, suitable way that the listener would not think of doubting his story in the slightest. He had every tiny little detail about the entire neighbourhood at his fingertips. Langda would tell everyone a story that such-and-such bhai was going to ridicule you in this way, but I said two words of advice to him and he complied. The listener would feel that, even if Langda kaka sat all day on the cot in the alley, he paid attention to all the people in the neighbourhood. And, until this thing of his got caught, the listener would feel that Langda alone had protected him. Langda also, sitting there, watched every neighbour's comings and goings, and kept an eye on even the most ordinary matters. Someone has gone to the edge of the village to leave cattle, to bring cattle back, another has gone out arguing, the third has some dispute, another has some loan issues, this one brought up someone else's past, that one's daughter-in-law has run off, that other one's daughter-in-law is going to run off, there's discord among brothers in that house, that house has women quarrelling, those ones have guests at their place, those have a merchant pressing for dues at their place – Langda bhai would know everyone's story!

This was the main delight in his life. As long as it was an aimless kind of curiosity, this trait was not harmful, nor did it create much friction. When he slowly realised that such matters could also be put to use, that they could allow the 'arbitrator' to make some income passively, this trait began moving into deceit. As long as this delight was about bringing happiness to his soul, it was fine. But ever since Langda felt that, saala, these things could also bring money, he began to descend even deeper into them. He began contriving new schemes. His idle mind began to find its own path from such schemes. He felt they had a potential to earn him money.

In that neighbourhood, there lived an old woman – Sumal Doshi. Her son was Jaaglo. The woman had gotten the boy married with much celebration. Then, who knows what happened that she would regularly fill the son's ears. Anyway, the boy was of a weak mind and influenced quite easily. Given that, one issue arose. The son's wife, Manchudi, began to look for an opportunity to run away. Langda bhai had gleaned this bit of information.

When she went to fetch water, left for work, came anytime to ask for something – from all this, Langda bhai figured this customer could hand over, at a minimum, 300 rupees. If one knew how to get it.

In this world, whoever knows how to bring together the fool and the crook, that person can forever live off extortion money – such is the wise way of this world. Langda secured the trust of Jaagla's wife such that she would be straightforward with him.

So, when Jaagla's wife slowly began to speak to Langda bhai with a free mind, to sing about her sorrows, Langda bhai began to search for some layabout.

He had found a task – one that made money. He had found an idle man. Whenever Jaagla's wife came, that man would also arrive to get some advice or other from Langda.

Once it so happened that Jaagla was goaded in casual conversation by this bhai himself: 'Look, if you can hammer in an iron nail near such-and-such banyan tree in the middle of the night, then you are a true daredevil. We'll give you 100 rupees. Otherwise, I'll go and hammer it in. And you give me fifty.'

There was no substance in this. But which life doesn't have non-substantive issues become and remain driving forces?

So, the impressionable Jaagla thought there was great heroism in this matter. But Sumal Doshi found out and she let forth loud lamentations. The matter was suppressed for a while. But the way Langda bhai had arranged this matter was that, when Jaagla bhai would be off to do the hammering work, then Manchudi could run off – with that other bhai. In exchange, that bhai would give Langda kaka 300 rupees. And Langda kaka would set forward someone else's name, point in a false direction and get the matter crushed and buried. All this was to be done sitting on the cot. Langda liked this profit.

This is how it happened. Langda sought out Manchudi. 'Baapa! The husbands today – they simply can't do anything. In our time, if something like this happened, the wife would remove her bangles and give them to the husband. She'd say – you wear these, I'll go and hammer in the nail. *One* nail has to be struck into a tree and you've been making promise after promise for six-six months as if some big war has to be waged.'

Jaagla's wife liked this talk. She instigated her husband. And Jaaglo also, dreaming of the heroism and how he would earn the jingling 100 rupees, came home, made the wife sit, and to put a stop to her wagging tongue, set off walking one night towards the banyan tree. He did not let Sumal Doshi know of this.

Now, there was folklore regarding the banyan tree about a ghost sitting in it. And that if a man went there, he would not be able to move away. The ghost would not allow him to leave.

Jaagla also had this doubt in his mind. But he had mustered up the courage to go there. His plan was to quickly strike in the nail and run away. As planned, he hammered in the nail and ran too . . . but he lost all courage. Who knew why, he felt as if he couldn't move away at all. He began to feel as if someone had held on to him. That suspicion was, of course, in his mind. He thought that the banyan tree's ghost had caught him – so his scream rang out. He did not even have the courage to look around himself. He just tumbled to the ground and lay there.

Half the night had passed and Jaaglo had not come home, so the Doshi set out to search for him, making stops along the way. She came to Langda kaka, but he held his hands to his ears: 'There's a fault in my hearing, bhai. But they say he had gone in the direction of the banyan.'

'What! To the banyan? Oy, baaplya!' so saying, the Doshi just ran.

And, on the other side, that layabout turned up to take Manchudi away.

Who knows what happened, but right at the last moment, Manchudi changed her mind. Whether Jaagla's inauspicious destiny had stunned her or whatever, that idle bhai went back home high and dry. But Langda bhai's fee was like a lawyer's fee – had to be paid upfront. So the bhai came back from his house to meet Langda – to get his money back.

However, Sumal stood there making a racket. The neighbours

had also gathered. So, at that time, he did not linger. But he could not stand that Langda should get away with his money.

Here, Sumal was babbling: 'He's got such a high fever, Langda baapa! There he's lying at home! I said, I'll call some known person to treat him. Do you have any such in mind? Putting all else aside, you know the idiot did not even see in his rush that his own pyjama string had come under the nail and that no one was holding him back? In his impatience, the nail had been struck on his own string. If he had only seen that, nothing would have happened. As soon as he felt a tug, he failed to see anything else. And he tumbled and fell there! Karam! What can we say to karam? My karam, what else?'

Jaaglo, prattling on about the fear that induced the fever, went off on the third day, leaving Sumal weeping.

The entire village was in grief. Having lost her one and only son turned Sumal into something like a lunatic. She lost all interest in life, became vacant-minded and empty.

Whatever happened to Sumal, Langda bhai sat with the folded 300 rupees under his tattered blanket. Every day, when it struck four, he would throw a rupee with a clink. 'Alya! Is tea to be drunk alone? Go, Kesari, and get peda and gaathiya!'

Mother and daughter did not discern this secret of Langda bhai's for a long time. They surmised the money must have come from somewhere.

So Langda Ram's feast carried on. Sumal's home got seized and locked up by her creditors. But that navraram[64] would press Langda for his money. The cripple would make the idler drink tea, eat

64. Navraram: A sarcastic name for the idle ('navra') man.

peda-gaathiya, and tell him to be patient: 'Ghee will eventually fall into its rightful container. You remain patient. Just wait and see...'

'Arrey!' But Manchudi runs to beat me now. And speaks of cutting me into two pieces!'

'She herself will come to your place. But let a bit of time pass.'

Langda made a new scheme. He now took pleasure only in making devious schemes. Sumal Doshi would tell Bhojal Rabaari about her happiness and sorrow. One day, when Bhojal Rabaari set out, Langda called to him: 'Cattle-herder! Poor Sumal has been harassed and ruined. The poor thing's home has been seized and locked up. But on whose account, do you know?'

'Who else, Langda baba? What our karam can do, no one else can do. Such is her karam. Otherwise, why would Jaaglo go to do the bidding of such a layabout? Karam! What karam can do, no one else can do!'

'Karam it is, cattle-herder! But dharam is also there. You must know about that, na?'

'About what?'

As if he wanted to speak softly so that no one else would hear, Langda slid closer: 'Look, bhai cattle-herder! The fault is in my hearing, alright? Only god knows what's true or false. But was whoever said "we must suffer for our sins" wrong? Sumal is suffering thanks to her own doings. The actions of the hands are hurting the soul – that's what has happened. It's karam and it's also dharam – that's what this is called.'

'Why do you speak so?'

'Then? The entire region knows – who killed Jaagla's father? Nobody will say, but everyone knows in their hearts, na? That was Sumal's doing. The whole area knows. Then God had her name cast aside. My girl Manchudi has also been here only for twenty months. Sumal only had cast some incantation over Jaagla. And, with that, Jaaglo went to ruin. Otherwise, how was the poor banyan-waala going to kill him? Usually, he's the one always crying. So many know this. Someone sits and cries in the banyan. Likely, it must be Jaagla's father!'

Langda bhai knew that, once he set a story afloat, it spread with the speed of wind. And a flowing story does its own work.

So it came about that, whenever Jaagla's mother and Jaagla's wife quarrelled, they piled fresh accusations on each other's heads. Talk of Sumal began everywhere in the neighbourhood. The sorrow was forgotten and talk of suffering for one's doing took on a much bigger shape.

The noisy, constant chatter about her deeds made Sumal suffer and cry out for help. Once the doubt creeps into the mind that others are gossiping about oneself behind one's back, then one's own mind eats one up. That is what happened to Sumal too. So now she moved heaven and earth to get this incantation-wielding Manchudi out.

Langda bhai first told the navraram about this while eating peda-gaathiya, and explained how the opportunity could be seized.

So, one day, the navraram and Manchudi seized the opportunity and took off. Langda bhai digested the 300 rupees. He sat on the cot and threw up a rupee with a triumphant clink. And he would keep saying, 'Saalu, how will the tea go down the throat by itself?' and keep eating peda-gaathiya. Then, he would occupy his mind in looking for another such scheme. He had now seen the earning potential in it. He thought of it as a business.

But, ever since Sumal had heard about the matter from Bhojal Rabaari, she had felt a pressure from her head to her toes. The issue that she didn't even seek to recall, everyone had forgotten, she had also forgotten, had been buried deep into the seventh nether region of the earth – Langda had dug it up to keep his peda-gaathiya safe. Now Sumal wanted to show Langda. She began to slowly and confidentially instigate the mother and daughter. 'What you are eating is my Jaagla's destroyed pyjama string. Langda bhai thinks that no one knows, but the one above knows everything. This money will erupt from every pore of yours like a disease!'

Such talk does not need any basis in reality. You till the soil once and the ground itself is such that it keeps growing. The talk goes from one mouth to another. And, as it progresses further, it also gets four extra furrows ploughed through each time!

So, one day, when Langda was leisurely chomping on the peda-gaathiya, Mangu suddenly said: 'What you're eating, that's not peda-gaathiya, alright? You think no one knows, but nothing is hidden from me. But who will speak? What you are eating are Sumal Doshi's son Jaagla's meat and bones!'

'Arrey! Get away, whore! You've been encouraged by that Sumal. But she's the kind that consumes her husband! God took revenge for that. What do we have to do with it? Did we tell Jaagla to invite such a fate? His karam, what do we have to do with that?'

'But where did you get 300 rupees from?' Mangu persisted. She now wanted to get everything out in the open.

'Arrey! Get away, slut! I got them from wherever! For one, you want to eat from my earnings. And then you want to shower accusations on me?'

'What accusations? Your handiwork will consume you and all of us. Who's saying no to earning money to eat? This money is ill-gotten! With this, our house will get seized and locked up! The one above knows everything.'

With that, the matter escalated. This quarrel then became a regular one. Sumal also played a proper part in it. In this way, a bitterness began to emerge in the life there – the kind that births life's ruins.

In society, one person's life always has an impact on other lives – favourable as well as unfavourable. Langda's actions had led to such repercussions that, in one way, it was as if he had brought about the ruin of lives. His work would have continued in that manner but for his wife's and daughter's sound judgement. They believed this money to be of sinful means. A tale they'd once heard about Prahlad reminded them that it remained to them alone to bravely give Langda clear direction. With perceptiveness, they thought that such actions of his made them complicit too. They alone must guide Langda. It was nothing more than the fact that the cot was destroying Langda. Sitting on that cot, he would continue to make such schemes and keep himself going with the money gained. His tongue had a charm. Around him, all the neighbours were simple-minded. So that his own mithai could continue, who knew how many more homes he would push into ruin and have locked up? He had the means to do it. His redemption would happen only if he got some kind of work. Idle hands are the devil's tools. A disabled person can do limited work but, if he doesn't contribute at all, his idleness only sparks mischief in his mind. As he had done to Sumal Doshi, he would do to several others. All those sins would attach to them too.

So this mother and daughter, led by such forthright understanding, took courage one day, made a decision, and told Langda
in clear words: 'Look, today, you have to go to work. If you don't
work, we will no longer feed you sitting there. We don't want to
use your sinful money.'

Langda replied: 'What are you feeding me, anyway? I'm the
one earning money. That's how your household runs!' So saying,
Langda reached below his tattered blanket to pick a rupee.

There was nothing there. Mother and daughter had colluded
to take the money away. Langda had sat on that money and continued with his mischief. He would only face the truth when that
money was gone. Mother and daughter had devised a plan to get
Langda on the straight and narrow.

Seeing the money wasn't there, Langda became anxious. He
tried to fling the cane. But, today, the mother and daughter had
become emboldened. They just caught his hand.

'Look, your money came from evil. True or false?'

'Just leave off, truth-waali…' Langda struggled.

In the meantime, Jaagla's mother showed up there too. The
three women had conspired together that, whatever happened,
they would straighten Langda out today. As soon as she got
there, she took Langda to task: 'My child-like son was devoured.
My home was seized and locked up. And, Langda, you go about
with impudence. Having seen money, you've become wide-eyed
crazy. But you're not likely to see that money now. We have
seized that money. It will now be used on Jaagla's behalf, understood? From today, I am going for all-day labour work. There's no
one at my house. To ensure no one steals anything, I am assign-
ing you the work of safeguarding it. In return for that, you will

get eight annas in the evening. The day you don't earn those eight annas, you won't get your rotlo! Your wife and daughter are also coming to accompany me and do labour work. We're all going to work full time. So you'll have to make the rounds between both these houses two to four times daily and safeguard the locks of both houses. This is your job. Speak, do you agree? Otherwise, you keep sitting on your cot and no one will make rotla for you any more!'

'Now quit being over-smart,' Langda said.

Then, as planned earlier, Mangu and her daughter assembled their bundles and were getting ready to walk away as if about to leave the house to Langda.

The man now truly felt he was going to be stranded.

The power he felt he had based on that money had disappeared.

So, from the very next day, if he wanted to get his rotla, he would have to teeter-totter back and forth between the two houses. If he didn't do the rounds, what would he eat?

Langda had no recourse but to do this work. Now he had little time for idle chatter. He didn't realise it but these responsibility-filled rounds – simply the rounds – had slowly begun to shape his life. His habit of gossiping was wearing off. The idler's business – troublemaking – was diminishing over time too.

Since then, that odd disposition of his – to get his mithai out of other people's stories – that lazy pleasure also began to vanish. It could be said that the small task had saved him.

Someone has said correctly that society is shaped by individuals. But an individual is shaped by work. So, when the easy ways of making money are gone, humanity enters one's life.

When a little work came into Langda's life, although late, something like humanity grew within him. Perhaps he was beginning to learn life's first lesson now!

The Worst of the Worst

Whomever you ask in the village, everyone will give only one response. Who is the worst of the worst in the village? That's Makno Bharthi. He'd be sitting all day in the village square. He'd do his puja in the square, ring a couple of bells, and then he would be free for the rest of the day. He had no source of income, yet ran about busy as ever – such was his work. So it would seem as if he was hustling-bustling about all day. He would either be playing with cowrie shells with the boys, cutting cards with someone, or be sitting puffing a beedi. When one was done, a second, and when that was done, a third. He would smoke continuously.

At that time, royalty still governed and the village folk had built a space in the threshing area for this square's Makno Bharthi to do puja. At harvest time, enough grain would be collected for twelve months. Then why would Makno bhai care about work? The Bawa Maknoji sometimes even went to beg for flour and sometimes just sat and let out beedi fumes.

He was like an 'ekla ram' – a solitary soul. But everyone knew that, within his establishment, certain businesses were conducted.

Sometimes, there would be a gambler's den being run. At other times, bhai would be sitting brewing tea for some ascetic. And, in all that, he would have a hard cash interest. So this Makno bhai had received the honorific title of 'the worst of the worst'. But he paid no heed to it. Whatever everyone said behind his back, nobody did or said anything to him directly. And, if someone said something to his face, then Makno was so outspoken that he would sound off about seven generations to that someone. He would dig up a vast history – things that the listener himself would be unaware of – about that person's family that the person's tongue would be sewn to silence.

Across the entire village, Makno had everyone's account at the tip of his tongue. Everyone knew that he was the worst but, due to his outspokenness, he was also considered the most honest of the honest. These two contradictory attributes endured for him: the worst of the worst and the most honest of the honest!

There was no connection between the two, but this contradiction blended into the very air of that village. In that square, there would be puja, bells would be rung, and gambling cards and chequers would be going on alongside. Bhajans would also be sung and slander about the entire village would also be going on.

The darbaar of that village was somewhat easily influenced and also spent money with a free hand. His loans had grown thick and fast like the hair on his head. Eventually, he met some class three educated Jagjivan bhai. That Jagjivan bhai advanced him money to pay off his debts and, making a firm arrangement with the saheb of the province at that time, got a surety for that loan to be paid off by the darbaar. And he became the kaamdaar himself.

Jagjivan bhai was the kaamdaar of kaamdaars and the darbaar

of darbaars. His authority was even greater than that of the darbaar, for he was the creditor while the darbaar was the debtor. So
the talk would run that whatever Jagjivan bhai did was correct. No
one could utter a syllable in front of him. If they did, they would
not do well. Because everyone, from the peon to those recruited
at the top, was from Jagjivan bhai's own men. He alone possessed
the sovereign powers of creation and destruction. There was no
talking against him. The speaker would have to leave the village.
Such was everyone's understanding.

Now, one time, it so happened that an old Brahmin in the village – extremely poor, and also of such an impoverished disposition that even the wickedest of the wicked would shudder to cause
him pain – was found to be at fault. And Jagjivan bhai's wrath
descended on this old Brahmin, Mayashankar.

The incident was that, in the darbaar-garh, some old woman –
a relative of the darbaar – had passed away. She had suddenly
breathed her last in the middle of the night. Immediately, an offi-
cial day of mourning was declared for the entire village. But, from
the previous day, Mayashankar had received an invitation for a
feast at Khaant Bai Jaasal's, who was good, simple and affectionate towards all. It was the death anniversary of her only son; so
she had invited Mayashankar, along with his entire family, to cook
and join the feast. The invitation had been extended the previous day. So Mayashankar had also arrived at her place early in
the morning to do the cooking. The information about what had
happened in the darbaar-garh came much later. Mayashankar had
completed almost half the cooking by the time it came. He had
crushed the pancakes and prepared the churma. All that remained
was to pour on the ghee.

Given the situation, he quietly called his family and had them finish eating quickly.

Then, trying to ensure nobody found out, they left early for their home.

At noon, Jagjivan kaamdaar's peon, Prabhaat Gohil, suddenly showed up at Mayashankar's. He called for him, saying, 'Come on. Kaamdaar sa'ab has sent for you.' He himself had told Jagjivan kaamdaar about Mayashankar.

Jagjivan kaamdaar was a kaamdaar of his era. In those days, it was considered a terrible sin to disregard authority even slightly, and such disregard was surely not to be tolerated.

Seeing Prabhaat Gohil at the entrance to his home and hearing that the kaamdaar was calling for him, old Mayashankar's legs trembled. He turned pale. He was terrified thinking of the terrible punishment kaamdaar Jagjivan had in store for him.

In this sort of matter, the kaamdaar would bluster heavily – like a lion set free – even if he was dealing with eight or ten of the village's most wretched workers. And his bluster was so forceful that even the hearts of the great and mighty would tremble with fear at least once. Mayashankar asked Prabhaat Gohil fearfully: 'Bhai! Why is kaamdaar sa'ab calling for me? What could he need from a poor man like me? Do you know anything?'

'Bhai! What do we know about such governance work? We're just the paper-pushing servants. He called me and asked me to fetch Mayashankar ma'raj. And I came to call you.'

'But has any crime or mistake been reported? If you know...'

Prabhaat began half in jest and half in mockery. 'What crime or mistake could have been reported? Without committing any crime-mistake, will it be reported? But he might be calling to set a time and arrange for a brahma-bhojan.[65] So come along, it's hardly far off.'

'Where is he – at his lodgings or at the darbaar-garh?'

'Lodgings, lodgings – kaamdaar sa'ab's lodgings. Come on now, good man! You'll be back in no time at all.'

Mayashankar called his seven-year-old son, who, in this time of distress, seemed to be a source of strength to Mayashankar. 'Sadashankar! Beta! I'll just come back without any delay. The kaamdaar sa'ab has called for me so I'll just go and come back.'

'But why has he called for you, do you know? Or are you going to get butchered for no reason?' Mayashankar's older sister enquired. She was a widow and had been taking care of the man's son since his wife had died.

'I'll just go and be back…' so saying, Mayashankar set off to meet kaamdaar saheb Jagjivan bhai. But there was such a fear inside of him that even his footsteps were falling unevenly.

[2]

Oil smeared over half his head, cat-coloured eyes, a hard face and a short physique – such a kaamdaar Jagjivan bhai was sitting on a mattress and cushions and reading some document. Mayashankar had, in such-and-such manner, cooked a feast when it was the time of darbaari grief in the village – the document was an anonymous complaint regarding that very matter.

---

65. Brahma-bhojan: An ancient Hindu custom of offering food to Brahmins as they were seen to represent God on earth. This ritual is considered sacred and still plays an important role in several Hindu ceremonies.

Mayashankar arrived there, offered his salaam to the kaam-daar saheb, and stood to one side. Prabhaat Gohil went and sat outside on the bench.

'So then…' Jagjivan bhai raised his head from the document, 'You have come, ma'raj?'

'Yes, sa'ab! If you call for me, I have to come, na? I will be a bit late for the katha.'

For a while, the kaamdaar did not say anything. As if gazing at some murderer, he was considering Mayashankar from his head to his toes. This sizing up was even more chilling than his talking. And Mayashankar was so weak of heart that, seeing the adminis-trator's roving eyes alone was making him tremble.

'Ma'raj! You have been called today because you have to leave the village today itself. Understood? You are a god above all gods, isn't that so?' Jagjivan bhai – Vaaniya administrator – his voice while speaking felt even more fiery than a cannon.

Mayashankar shuddered. He understood the situation and folded both hands. It was about him at the feast. 'Kaamdaar sa'ab! Me'erbaan! Please forgive this beggarly Brahmin's fault-mistake. It will never ever happen again.'

'Now you're not going to be staying in this village, ma'raj, are you, that you will be able to throw dust in our eyes again? Leave the village today. Your fault-mistake is forgiven. Start walking away from this village. Otherwise, I will have you thrown in jail. I am letting you go knowing you as a Brahmin.'

'Arrey! But, sa'ab! Kaamdaar sa'ab! Please have some pity on a poor old Brahmin like me. God will reward you in return. Where will I go off alone, with my family and children here? Forgive me this one time. I touch your feet with my hands. Two generations of my family have lived and died here.'

'Ma'raj!' Jagjivan bhai roared just once. 'Bas, now leave the village before sundown; or it will not end well. Do not knowingly make me throw out a Brahmin's belongings in the night with my own hands. You are a god of the earth. I touch your feet. Now, go in peace…'

'Arrey! But kaamdaar sa'ab…!'

In response, Jagjivan kaamdaar called for Prabhaat. 'Prabhaat!' He had made himself clear. Jagjivan kaamdaar's brutality was well known.

Mayashankar conceded defeat. Tears fell from his eyes. Where could he go now – even the thought made him tremble. Before he could say anything, Prabhaat Gohil showed up there.

The kaamdaar looked in Prabhaat's direction. 'See ma'raj out. He's old, na – give him a little support and escort him outside!'

Hearing the kaamdaar's words filled with terrible sarcasm and ridicule, a wave of laughter rippled all around in the vicinity.

That laughter, for a man as weak-minded as Mayashankar, was filled with a gravely wounding mockery. Not jest – mockery.

Mayashankar returned home with a crushed soul.

'So you went there? What did the kaamdaar say?' Seeing him back, his sister asked immediately.

But there was no strength in Mayashankar's legs, and he had no energy to talk. He said softly: 'What else was he going to say? He asked me to leave the village!'

'What?' the sister also cried out. 'Leave the village over such a small matter? But any fault-mistake?'

'Is there any god above God?'

'But did you meet the darbaar?'

'Darbaar, Sarkaar, whatever you consider it, right now, it is Jagjivan kaamdaar. Who is going to oppose anything he says? Fine, it is God's will. Make a bit of tea for me. Let's have a last bit to drink…'

'Arrey! What are you like, bhai? Being a man? What kind of crime have we committed? Let's talk to the village. Will the people not rise in our defence? What kind of crime is it? We ate, is that our crime?'

'That's all very well. Make me some tea. I'll drink it. It's God's will.'

The sister made the tea. As if he were drinking tea for the very last time, Mayashankar drank it with an empty mind. He ran a hand over the heads of his three boys silently and then covered himself up to his head and fell asleep.

At four in the afternoon, his sister went to call him. In the short while that he had been sleeping, she had gone and spoken with many merchants, leading men and Kanbis about their situation. Everyone supported her in private but no one was willing to rise up against the lion-like Jagjivan kaamdaar. She was now convinced that they'd have to leave the village and had grown sad. That era was such that there was a big, God-like absolutist governing authority across every one and a half to two villages, whose power was bigger than even the rural government. And everyone had become so accustomed to it that the issue of challenging its dictates or even discussing it in private was considered off limits.

Like the weakness that exists in every level of a scaffolding before it comes crashing down, there was a flaw pervasive in every layer of society. If anyone had stood up, he would have been considered the true son of his mother. But why would anyone here stand up? To wake Mayashankar up and talk to him, his sister began to shake him. But, as if the man would never recover from the terrible wound, he did not sit up. He had left the world. Leaving everyone with no support, he had gone away. For two days, everyone in the family sat crying. What else could be done?

Jagjivan kaamdaar also came to know of this. And whether he then felt regret or whatever, he buried the talk about the family leaving the village.

[3]

Some days passed after that incident. One night, exactly at nine o'clock, Prabhaat gave Jagjivan kaamdaar the news: 'Bawo Makno Bharthi has come to meet.'

'Bawo Makno Bharthi? That village square waalo? What does he want? He is a useless man. Who is free to meet with him? And that too at this time?'

'I told him. But the bawo is sitting there in serious obstinacy. He says he will go only after meeting.'

'But what does he want?'

'He's not saying anything.'

'Ask him what he wants. What is his business? Whatever the business, ask him to come in the morning!'

Prabhaat Gohil went to Makno Bharthi.

Makno Bharthi was just standing there, silent. He listened to Prabhaat Gohil's talk. Then he said softly but with a deeply sonorous voice: 'So Prabhaat Gohel! You are a paper-pushing servant. Like me, one who tires his legs running about. You tell kaamdaar sa'ab that I am the square-waalo bawo. I don't have a house in the village, don't have a field at the border, don't have any honour among the people, don't have any connection at the Darbaar. I want to meet the kaamdaar sa'ab and I want to meet now. If he says morning, then I'll come in the morning. But, in this, his honour will suffer, not mine. What do I have to lose? Now think through all these things and come back with a reply. Go. Otherwise, I will gallop away just as I came and you will stand watching helplessly.'

'But what do you want?'

'Arrey bhai! You are arguing in vain. I have work with kaam-daar sa'ab, not with you!'

'But if he asks me what you want, what response should I give?'

'What I said. My work is with the kaamdaar sa'ab. With him alone. No other person needs to know. The work is neces-sary. It is fully to his own benefit. That's why I've come at night. Otherwise, don't I know how to come during the day? Now go, get me a reply.'

There was some leavening now in the matter so kaamdaar Jagjivan bhai, after a while, gave him the permission to come.

Makno Bharthi came there and stood. His tall, well-built, black-as-ebony body seemed even more frightening at this time than during the day. He was renowned, of course, as the worst of the worst. So, assuming that he must have come to hide or cover up some misdeed of his, the kaamdaar decided to approach the conversation with an air of pomposity and superiority.

'What do you want, Bawaji? Don't you have any cognizance of night and day? Or do you just come galloping at any time?'

'I'm aware of night and day, sa'ab! That's why I've come now. At this time, no one will know the matter. If I come during the day, you will feel the stigma!'

'What is the matter, just speak up!'

Makno Bharthi came closer, up to the edge of the kaamdaar's mattress, then sat there, said softly: 'The thing is, sa'ab! To be told only to you. To be heard only by you.'

'Yes, then just say it. There's no one here. What is it about?'

'The thing is, sa'ab...'

'Arrey! Are you a man or an ass? The thing is, the thing is – you keep saying that! What is the thing?'

'The thing is, sa'ab, that it seems that the poor Mayashankar ma'raj has died!'

'The whole world knows that, Bawaji! What have you come to say about it?'

'The thing is, sa'ab, that his poor sons are starving to death. There is Mayashankar's older sister in the house. She's aged. So, sa'ab, you have to give me 500 rupees – now. I have to get them to her.'

'Have you lost your mind?' Kaamdaar Jagjivan was stunned on hearing this. The situation was an altogether new one.

'Sa'ab! Kaamdaar sa'ab! The thing is, I am not settled in one place, so I have come to meet with you. All those who are settled, they're sitting in their homes. But this Mayashankar, sa'ab, was killed by you. I am here, the square-waalo bawo. I have to give her 500 rupees. If you consider it from the village, then it's from the village; if you consider it from yourself, then it's from yourself.'

'Seems like you're high on some bhaang-waang, Bawaji!'

'Not high on bhaang, sa'ab, but the thing is that I have come after making the decision to sacrifice myself. Consider it bhaang or whatever you like. That you killed Mayashankar, this is the truth. You have committed his murder. And so everyone believes. But everyone in the village is a coward. No one has the strength to speak up. The darbaar is indebted to you. I'm a layabout – without any business or employment – I'm all alone in the entire village. I don't want Mayashankar's boys to die of starvation.'

'Then you go toss them some jowar-bajra at their place. Why have you come here?'

'At first, my thought was just that, kaamdaar sa'ab,' Makno Bharthi's voice grew louder, 'but I said, no, they must receive justice. Justice must be done. Justice must be taken. From the entire village, not one man came out to tell you. So I had to come. You have to give them this money.'

'Have to give – meaning? Have you discovered the Brahmin widow's field that she has suddenly become dear to you?'

'Kaamdaar sa'ab! I have come here like this because, during the day, you will certainly be defamed publicly. Tomorrow, this Makno Bharthi will defame you publicly before the entire village. Then it will be too late. Think about it. Just a stone's throw away, there is the Province sa'ab's residence. The story will reach there too. Let me give the money to her privately. Our matter is done. Once the matter is resolved, then if you say, sa'ab, for the sake of your honour and to ensure that our little arrangement doesn't reach the ears of the villagers, I will stop drinking the water of this village, bas? I will also go away. I am asking for only this justice. To give or not to give – that's your wish. You think it over. I have decided to sacrifice myself on this matter. There will be no change in that. Think.'

'I have thought it through, Makno Bharthi! You will rot behind the bars of a jail cell for nothing, understood? If you don't want that, walk away just the way you came.'

Makno Bharthi stood. He spoke with a loud, firm, sharp, sincere voice: 'Kaamdaar sa'ab! This Makno, he'll die at your place, but he will not leave without getting justice. You will have to give the money. You killed Mayashankar. Answer me – once I go out of here, the matter will not be in my hands. Your name will reach the province-level administration. Those who have given surety for the darbaar will go back on their word. Think about it. There is still time. Tell me. I don't have a home in the village, a field at the border, I'm the worst of the worst. But you think about it, it's your honour that will suffer. Not mine. Where do I have any?'

Jagjivan kaamdaar had fallen into thought at the mention of the province. Because of his threats and misguided punishment, Mayashankar, being of a weak mind, had died – this he himself understood too. He saw the benefit in changing his footing.

'And you're going to give the money to her only?'

'Prabhat Gohel can come with me. But, if that happens, your name will be sung. Have faith in me. From the entire village, no one has raised even a finger to help. Hypocritical followers of truth, all of them. They've become villainous as foxes in their own backyards. Then they will gossip about you. But if you place your trust in me, the all-enveloping darkness of the night will tuck the issue away.'

In a little while, Jagjivan kaamdaar, becoming utterly weakened, brought the 500 rupees. He had understood. It was best to keep a distance from this worst of the worst.

And Makno Bharthi immediately went out to deliver the money.

The next day, when Prabhaat Gohil went to look for Makno Bharthi at the square, he wasn't there. The gods were there, unworshipped. The bells were silent. The gong had not been struck.

Everyone was gathering. There were rumours running rife – last night, the kaamdaar had called him out, so it seems he had run away; how many days can bad businesses be kept secret?

Then, who knows how, and from where, and in what manner – no one knows that – the children were listening to the story of Makno Bharthi. Some old man was telling them.

In that story, it was said: in this small village also, there was a great man who made history. No one was brave enough to seek justice and he, alone, had the courage to do so. Since then, Makno Bharthi's cushioned seat in the square has remained empty, for no one considers themselves worthy enough to sit on it.

This Makno Bharthi!

Today, this Makno Bharthi is no more. Jagjivan kaamdaar is no more. That darbaar is also not there. Prabhaat Gohil is not there. No one's there. And that village has also changed.

But this story has continued among the children. And it has remained so.

And Makno Bharthi's story raises other Makno Bharthis as if from thin air.

Old Custom, New Approach

[1]

It was the tenth round today. There was a heavy despair in his mind. He thought: I wish I could meet the saheb today at least! Just about managed to get matriculated, but getting a job had been an experience as impossible as making water flow up a roof's eaves to its cross beams. Today, he had passed by the saheb's house three times between 7:30 AM to 9:00 AM. But how could you call it a house? It was a large, grand mansion. To get from its bottom stair to the saheb's living-room, you had to go past three peons' security gates. But, despite the ten rounds, he had not caught sight of the saheb's face yet. Once the reply was that the saheb was drinking tea, come later. Returning later, the saheb would not be there. Another time, he was busy with work. On another instance, he was at home. The fifth time, he was not free. In that manner, the young man had done rounds one through ten – and not one round had been, to this day, successful. So, today also, he kept his hopes in check about this eleventh round bearing fruit.

But, just then, near the stairs, he met a childhood friend

named Bhanusingh Vijaysingh, who had studied with him once in a Gujarati school.

On seeing him, Bhanusingh immediately asked: 'Arrey, Lakhman! How are you here? What do you need? Do you have some work? Whom have you come to meet?'

'Who else? The saheb!'

'Who? Bhagwaanlal bhai?'

'But of course!'

'What do you need?'

'Bhai, God has made us bump into each other today, so I hope I will finally see the saheb's face today. Otherwise, I've done ten rounds and they're not letting anyone go beyond the fifth stair! The saheb is always busy at work!'

'The saheb always has a lot of work. He also works at night. But correspondence – ohoho, there are piles of correspondence. Everything happens here via correspondence. It's as if no one talks with their mouths. The correspondence speaks. Letters speak with letters. People avoid other people, this is called administration. That's how it is here. It's fine. It will go as it must. What is it to us little people? But say, why did you want to meet the saheb?'

'A decent job. What other concern will matriculated and B.A. and M.A. and BSc. people have? If I can get a job, I can earn my rotla – that is why I have come!'

'So how many days have you been here?'

'Today is my eleventh round. Count and see; I've been here for ten or twelve days. The hostel cost is too much to bear and my money has depleted. I think I must return to my village Nagnesh. But what will I do after I return? What do the educated do in villages? There's only dust and cattle there.'

'So you've come to get a job! Passed matriculation! But come, let's eat some paan-baan at that shop and have a chat.'

[2]

On their way to get paan, Bhanusingh asked: 'Lakhman, how much money have you brought?'

'Enough for the hostel expenses. But that's finished now. Today, I have just a rupee and a half left in my pocket. I will probably have to borrow for the train.'

'Then your work is not likely to get done, bhai! Here, sacred cash is the most popular. If you give the sa'ab money, then he will give you a job.'

'Arrey! But I am of his caste-community. If you just get me a meeting with him…'

'All right then, I'll get you a meeting. I'll do it today itself. But listen: this sa'ab is a bottomless vessel. No matter how much water is within, even if it is all filled up, it will not be enough. Without giving money, your work will not get done. Tell me then, can you arrange the money?'

Lakhman felt that Bhanusingh was afflicted by some prejudice. They were caste brothers. So, when they met, Bhagwaanlal bhai would certainly melt. And, definitely, something would be done. Right now, new jobs had opened up and they needed men. So he said, 'You just get me a meeting. Then, I will manage everything.'

'Fine,' Bhanusingh knew that experience would make this one wise.

When they returned, Bhanusingh went inside and spoke. And saheb Bhagwaanlal bhai called Lakhman in immediately. Lakhman went inside.

[3]

In conversation, when he said to the saheb, 'Saheb, I'm of your caste-community,' the saheb responded with as much pride as if he were the best member of an ethical society: 'Look, Mr Lakhman, we are living in a new era. Our democratic government does not consider caste-fast. If you are of my caste-community, and you have come on account of that, then there's the way out. Otherwise, write up an application and you will be called for an interview.'

Looking glum as if he had drunk castor oil, Lakhman left on the verge of tears. The talk in his village was that Lakhman had matriculated and who knew where he might rise in rank. And here, there would be an application, then another one, then an interview, then pass-fail, and even after that ... zero ... a zero in his fate.

In the meantime, Bhanusingh came out. He put a hand on Lakhman's shoulder and asked: 'Why, Lakhman, where did he say the appointment would be?'

'Arrey, bhai! My legs are just broken. Instead of this, if I'd learnt my family's line of work, at least I would get my rotlo today!'

'But what did the saheb say?'

'To make an application!'

'But did you not talk about the caste-community?'

'Of course I did. But, because of that, he immediately showed me the way out. This feels like the entire custom has turned upside down. Now, no one can take anyone on. He must also be accountable to someone, na?'

'Now, shall I show you the way?'

'Yes, show me, na?'

'If you want to get a job, na, then come back after making provisions for 150. The saheb has filled several positions with that amount. He must have made 500 already today. Do the math! So now, go home and return after making a provision for 150.'

'But which tree should I pluck them from?'

'Alya! You've been given advice. Gold is useless. The body is embarrassed by it. True beauty is constituted by good virtues. Go, sell a couple of the wife's jewels. That will give you 150. Otherwise, there's no likelihood that your voice will be heard in the bustle of interviews. We are not as educated as you, but we have experience. This is known as everyone's "Swaraj". Abide by the ethics and go home. But, if you feel that a lack of ethics pays better than ethics, then come back and see me. But meet me only if you have 150 in your pocket. And 150 multiplying into 500 – keep doing that math as you go home.' Bhanusingh laughed and patted his shoulder. 'Don't lose hope, bhai! This is how the world works, and it will continue to work this way. Come back after five to fifteen days.'

Lakhman returned home with a crushed soul and broken feet.

But what was he going to do by going home? The educated must get jobs; what else can they do? Education ruins you for anything else. To make hundreds of thousands of people weak, there was education worth tens of millions.

So, in about five to fifteen days, Lakhman got tired. His vision, in the end, came back to rest on employment. There was nothing as much fun as a job. From eleven to five. In between, tea. This is what pushed him back there. So, pawning his wife's jewellery and armed with 150 rupees cash, he departed again to meet

Bhagwaanlal bhai. There was heat in his pocket so, this time, there was heat in his legs too.

But he thought, I know the matter now. Why do anything that will get Bhanusingh's mind working needlessly? Let's just meet Bhagwaanlal bhai directly.

And, with that thought, he arrived at the office at 7:30 in the morning. It was a Saturday. The saheb had arrived early. Lakhman vowed to himself that, if his work got done, he would offer oil worth four annas to Hanuman. And if he could not get that oil, then he would offer mustard oil. On the strength of that vow and the courage of that 150, he entered the saheb's office.

So that the private talk could happen in private, he went all the way to the saheb's desk and roused the saheb whose head was bent over files: 'Sa'ab! I have come back. And this time, sa'ab ... I'm a poor man, sa'ab! Having pawned my wife's jewels, I offer you not the entire flower perhaps, but a petal...'

The saheb saw the bundle of cash in his hands. And, despite casting a glance around to make sure no one could see, he said with an air of superiority: 'Mr Lakhman, you are living in the fifteenth century. This is the twentieth century. And that too, under our ethical government! You take a look there.' The man drew Lakhman's attention to the board hanging there: 'Act ethically, ensure others act ethically, and insist upon it. Mind yourself!'

'I am not handing you over to the police because you are a caste-community brother. Otherwise, be careful about ever approaching me in such an uncouth manner. You have no knowledge of the correct way. Leave! Arrey, Bhanusingh...'

Bhanusingh came running from the room next door.

'Take this uncouth one outside. And show him the correct way. Go! Be warned about ever coming to this office for such unethical matters! Go! Bhanusingh, take him away. Show the fool the right way. Now leave ... Oh, why are you still here? Bhanusingh!'

Bhanusingh came forward. He placed a hand on Lakhman's shoulder and said: 'Bhai Lakhman, come. I'll see you out.'

Once outside, Lakhman said to him: 'I did as you had told me. Yet, it resulted in a zero only!'

'You did not take the right path. You've done a stupid thing. Can such a matter be addressed so? You go away for now. Come back in exactly fifteen days. But, when you arrive, come and meet me.'

[4]

Exactly on the fifteenth day, Lakhman appeared again. He had received such a fine education that, besides this, he could not think of anything else at all. These people who blindly pour money down the drain, are called educated experts by everyone. So this poor, handicapped youth returned with 200 instead of 150.

But now he had understood.

So, this time, he went to Bhanusingh's, who took him to the saheb's home instead of the office.

There, he made Lakhman sit. Then he went inside and had a word with the saheb and, returning, told Lakhman: 'Sa'ab's wife is coming. She will meet you. Do as she says. I'm leaving now. But you don't say anything. Just listen to whatever the lady says.' So saying, he went away.

After a little while, the saheb's wife came. Sufficiently large, fair, robust. Chewing paan, she came and sat there.

'Why, who, you had some work?'

'Yes, ji. I do.'

'What?'

Bhanusingh had warned him not to say a thing about work-ferk and to just offer up the money. Lakhman removed the envelope and put it in her hands.

The saheb's wife, Rupali ba, spoke as if she was granting him a favour: 'Come after three days. Sa'ab's time for leaving for the office is 10:45. Come at exactly that time and meet him.'

Saying this, she stood up immediately. Poor Lakhman went home wondering whether he had been robbed.

Exactly three days later, he came like a starving wretch with some fancies in his mind. This time, he had resolved to offer Hanuman oil worth a half rupee instead of four annas. And, for that, he had even kept a half rupee ready in his pocket. From here, he was going to go directly to offer the oil.

The saheb was in a hurry to leave for the office. He saw Lakhman there and, immediately, in an impatient, harsh, and rather loud voice, he said: 'Why have you come here? Go, now don't come here again!'

'Arrey but, sa'ab! I'm a poor man!'

'Is the government sitting here to run a dharamshala for you? Leave!'

But today, on hearing his voice, the stately Rupali ba emerged from inside. She stood there for a while. Then, as if she had given them both a fair hearing, she said: 'What is this loss-making habit you have developed? This poor wretch is making the rounds. So get his matter settled, na!'

'But do I have to give answers to somebody or not? Here, sitting at home, you think of giving out buckets from your ocean of kindness…'

'Arrey, I'm saying, take the poor thing on, take him on. He's got bellies to feed, na? Where else can the poor thing go during such inflationary times? The government is now going to give everyone daily wages – you yourself were saying so. And those over seventy will be able to retire and live well!'

'That is about the seventh, eighth, ninth or tenth yojna. You don't understand anything about yojnas and you're banging on for nothing as if deaf and blind.'

Rupali ba laughed: 'I am not banging on anything as if deaf and blind. I am talking about an agreement. If you do good for him, then God will do good for you. In the end, God is everyone's refuge.'

Bhagwaanlal bhai immediately got what had transpired. He understood. What was supposed to happen had already happened. This was the meaning of 'God'. So he said to Lakhman: 'Go now, bhai, you go. You've given your application, na?'

'Yes, that I have given.'

'Then it's done. After eight days, everyone will come for an interview. You come too. And come for sure. God will also see to your needs. Go. But stop making the rounds here, alright?'

'Yes, alya! Don't dig up the roots of a sweet fruit-bearing tree. Go now,' Rupali ba added.

And Lakhman, saying 'Hey Bhagwaan!', ran to get a half-rupee's worth of oil to quieten the fear-driven thumping of his heart, which had been swayed by impractical wisdom. In addition, he was going to run to the cinema in the evening to celebrate his job. And, from there, he was going to bring back ethical principles — from the cinema.

But, as he was running to offer oil to Hanuman Dada, a new solution had occurred to Bhagwaanlal bhai in the office. So, having called Bhanusingh in, he was saying: 'Alya, Bhanusingh! Do you know how to do anything? Let's get a few principles-shrinciples of ethics drawn up and hung all around the office! Everyone will be happy to see them!'

And, in that office — where first a photograph of George the Fifth had been hung, then one of Tilak maharaj, and then one of Gandhiji — ethical principles were now hung around on all the walls.

Glossary of Terms

Alya: Slang; used to address a younger male.

Anni: An old one anna coin; 1/16th of a rupee.

Bha/Bhai: Though bhai literally means 'brother', it is common in Gujarati culture to call men bhai or bha, including relatives who are not brothers and those unrelated to oneself.

Bhangi: Was (is) considered one of the lowest castes – those who do the most menial labour and are, therefore, unclean and untouchable. Today, they are mostly referred to as Dalits.

Bawa/Bawan: a Gujarati sub-caste that, in old times, were mostly itinerant, wandering sadhus or ascetics. The caste is considered a lower-ranked community of people – mostly wandering mendicants or gypsies.

Dhabo: Rural slang for roti.

Gau: An old unit of measurement that translates to 3.2 km today.

Ghatika: An ancient measure of time – a period of 24 minutes.

Ghazal: A romantic/love poem or song.

Kaamdaar: The darbaar's prime minister, administrator or diwan.

Maund: A unit measure of weight used during colonial times. There were different variations of maund measures in different Indian regions. In Gujarat, it equated to 40 seers or 28 pounds.

Nayak: Chief.

Paavli: A paavli was a four-anna coin. An anna was 1/16th of a rupee. So a paavli was 25 paise.

Pie paisa: A pie paisa is an old Indian currency. It was the smallest unit of currency in India, Burma and Pakistan until 1947 and equalled 1/3rd of a paisa, 1/12th of an anna, or 1/192nd of a rupee.

Pol: A pol (pronounced as pole) is a walled and gated housing cluster, which comprises many families of a particular group, linked by caste, profession or religion. These first came about in ancient times in Ahmedabad and still exist today with people living in old, ancestral homes.

Rabaari: The name of a community of wandering, landless cattle-herders. The rabaari tribes are from the semi-desert Kutch region of Gujarat and are a pastoralist community.

Ratti: A traditional Indian unit of measurement for mass. Based on the nominal weight of a ratti seed, it measured approximately 1.8 or 1.75 grains. It has now been standardised as 0.1215 gram.

Ser: An ancient Indian unit measure of weight, usually taken as one-fortieth of a maund and amounting to 46 grams.

Shroff: A sub-caste within the Vaaniya caste. Typically, this sub-caste consisted of bankers and money-changers.

Surti: An inhabitant of the city of Surat in Gujarat, India.

Vaaghri/Vaaghran: A caste-community in Gujarat and Rajasthan. During colonial times, they were considered a criminal tribe. While they are a Hindu community, they used to be a landless group of people and considered of a lower caste that did menial tasks/labour. Vaaghran would be a woman of this tribe and the word was/is used as an insult or epithet.

Vaaniya: The Bania caste of merchants and shopkeepers.

Translator's Acknowledgements

Thank you, first of all, to Vaishaliben Patel and her family for granting the copyright permission to translate these stories by her grand-uncle. I hope this book does justice to his memory.

I am grateful to Manubhai Shah, Dhumketu's publisher at Gurjar Prakashan, for connecting me with the writer's family.

This book would not have come into being if literary agent extraordinaire Kanishka Gupta hadn't called me within a couple of hours of a cold email. Beyond having a keen sense of what readers want, he's one of the strongest supporters of his writers.

Rahul Soni, executive editor at HarperCollins India, saw the potential in the book proposal and took the time to have several insightful discussions about it, for which I'm deeply grateful.

Prema Govindan is a rockstar editor whose superpowers of enduring patience and laser-focused perceptiveness helped whip these stories into shape. This first-time translator will forever be in her debt.

This is my third time working with Harshad Marathe, who designed this stunning cover. In addition to his incredible artistry, he's a careful researcher and works hard to get every single detail right. It's inspiring to work with such a talented creative.

Last, but not least, thanks to my husband, Praveen Ahuja, who deserves an award for putting up with all my literary anxieties and reminding me of what's most important in our lives. It is a blessing to share this journey with him.

Dhumketu was the pen name of Gaurishankar Govardhanram Joshi (1892–1965), one of the foremost writers in Gujarati and a pioneer of the short-story form. He published twenty-four short-story collections and thirty-two novels on social and historical subjects, as well as plays, biographies, memoirs, translations, travelogues, literary criticism, etc. Dhumketu was a contemporary of Rabindranath Tagore, Munshi Premchand and Saadat Hasan Manto, and his contributions to Indian literature are just as wide-ranging and groundbreaking.

Jenny Bhatt Jenny Bhatt is a writer, literary translator, and book critic. She is the founder of Desi Books and teaches creative writing at Writing Workshops Dallas. Her debut story collection, *Each of Us Killers: Stories* won a 2020 Foreword INDIES award in the Short Stories category and was a finalist in the Multicultural Adult Fiction category. Her literary translation, *Ratno Dholi: Dhumketu's Best Short Stories* was shortlisted for the 2021 PFC-VoW Book Awards for English Translation from Regional Languages. Her writing has appeared in various venues including *The Atlantic*, NPR, BBC Culture, *The Washington Post*, *Publishers Weekly*, *Los Angeles Review of Books*, *Dallas Morning News*, *Literary Hub*, *Longreads*, *Poets & Writers*, *Guernica*, *Electric Literature*, and more. Having lived and worked her way around India, England, Germany, Scotland, and various parts of the US, she now lives in a suburb of Dallas, Texas. Find her at https://jennybhattwriter.com.

Thank you all
for your support.
We do this for you,
and could not do
it without you.

DEEP
VELLUM

PARTNERS

pixel ||| texel

EMBREY FAMILY
FOUNDATION

ADDITIONAL DONORS, CONT'D

Mark Haber	Scott & Katy Nimmons
Mary Cline	Sherry Perry
Maynard Thomson	Sydneyann Binion
Michael Reklis	Stephen Harding
Mike Soto	Stephen Williamson
Mokhtar Ramadan	Susan Carp
Nikki & Dennis Gibson	Susan Ernst
Patrick Kukucka	Theater Jones
Patrick Kutcher	Tim Perttula
Rev. Elizabeth & Neil Moseley	Tony Thomson
Richard Meyer	

SUBSCRIBERS

Margaret Terwey	Nicole Yurcaba	Jarratt Willis
Ben Fountain	Jennifer Owen	Heustis Whiteside
Gina Rios	Melanie Nicholls	Samuel Herrera
Elena Rush	Alan Glazer	Heidi McElrath
Courtney Sheedy	Michael Doss	Jeffrey Parker
Caroline West	Matt Bucher	Carolyn Surbaugh
Brian Bell	Katarzyna Bartoszynska	Stephen Fuller
Charles Dee Mitchell	Michael Binkley	Kari Mah
Cullen Schaar	Erin Kubatzky	Matt Ammon
Harvey Hix	Martin Piñol	Elif Ağanoğlu
Jeff Lierly	Michael Lighty	
Elizabeth Simpson	Joseph Rebella	

AVAILABLE NOW FROM DEEP VELLUM

SHANE ANDERSON · *After the Oracle* · USA

MICHÈLE AUDIN · *One Hundred Twenty-One Days* · translated by Christiana Hills · FRANCE

BAE SUAH · *Recitation* · translated by Deborah Smith · SOUTH KOREA

MARIO BELLATIN · *Mrs. Murakami's Garden* · translated by Heather Cleary · *Beauty Salon* · translated by Shook · MEXICO

EDUARDO BERTI · *The Imagined Land* · translated by Charlotte Coombe · ARGENTINA

CARMEN BOULLOSA · *Texas: The Great Theft* · *Before* · *Heavens on Earth* · translated by Samantha Schnee · Peter Bush · Shelby Vincent · MEXICO

MAGDA CARNECI · *FEM* · translated by Sean Cotter · ROMANIA

LEILA S. CHUDORI · *Home* · translated by John H. McGlynn · INDONESIA

MATHILDE CLARK · *Lone Star* · translated by Martin Aitken · DENMARK

SARAH CLEAVE, ed. · *Banthology: Stories from Banned Nations* · IRAN, IRAQ, LIBYA, SOMALIA, SUDAN, SYRIA & YEMEN

LOGEN CURE · *Welcome to Midland: Poems* · USA

ANANDA DEVI · *Eve Out of Her Ruins* · translated by Jeffrey Zuckerman · MAURITIUS

PETER DIMOCK · *Daybook from Sheep Meadow* · USA

CLAUDIA ULLOA DONOSO · *Little Bird,* translated by Lily Meyer · PERU/NORWAY

RADNA FABIAS · *Habitus* · translated by David Colmer · CURAÇAO/NETHERLANDS

ROSS FARRAR · *Ross Sings Cheree & the Animated Dark: Poems* · USA

ALISA GANIEVA · *Bride and Groom* · *The Mountain and the Wall* · translated by Carol Apollonio · RUSSIA

FERNANDA GARCIA LAU · *Out of the Cage* · translated by Will Vanderhyden · ARGENTINA

ANNE GARRÉTA · *Sphinx* · *Not One Day* · *In/concrete* · translated by Emma Ramadan · FRANCE

JÓN GNARR · *The Indian* · *The Pirate* · *The Outlaw* · translated by Lytton Smith · ICELAND

GOETHE · *The Golden Goblet: Selected Poems* · *Faust, Part One* · translated by Zsuzsanna Ozsváth and Frederick Turner · GERMANY

SARA GOUDARZI · *The Almond in the Apricot* · USA

NOEMI JAFFE · *What Are the Blind Men Dreaming?* · translated by Julia Sanches & Ellen Elias-Bursac · BRAZIL

CLAUDIA SALAZAR JIMÉNEZ · *Blood of the Dawn* · translated by Elizabeth Bryer · PERU

PERGENTINO JOSÉ · *Red Ants* · MEXICO

TAISIA KITAISKAIA · *The Nightgown & Other Poems* · USA

SONG LIN · *The Gleaner Song: Selected Poems* · translated by Dong Li · CHINA

JUNG YOUNG MOON · *Seven Samurai Swept Away in a River* · *Vaseline Buddha* · translated by Yewon Jung · SOUTH KOREA

KIM YIDEUM · *Blood Sisters* · translated by Ji yoon Lee · SOUTH KOREA

JOSEFINE KLOUGART · *Of Darkness* · translated by Martin Aitken · DENMARK

YANICK LAHENS · *Moonbath* · translated by Emily Gogolak · HAITI

FOUAD LAROUI · *The Curious Case of Dassoukine's Trousers* · translated by Emma Ramadan · MOROCCO

FORTHCOMING FROM DEEP VELLUM

MARIO BELLATIN • *Etchapare* • translated by Shook • MEXICO

CAYLIN CARPA-THOMAS • *Iguana Iguana* • USA

MIRCEA CĂRTĂRESCU • *Solenoid* • translated by Sean Cotter • ROMANIA

TIM COURSEY • *Driving Lessons* • USA

ANANDA DEVI • *When the Night Agrees to Speak to Me* • translated by Kazim Ali • MAURITIUS

DHUMKETU • *The Shehnai Virtuoso* • translated by Jenny Bhatt • INDIA

LEYLÂ ERBIL • *A Strange Woman* •
translated by Nermin Menemencioğlu & Amy Marie Spangler • TURKEY

ALLA GORBUNOVA • *It's the End of the World, My Love* •
translated by Elina Alter • RUSSIA

NIVEN GOVINDEN • *Diary of a Film* • GREAT BRITAIN

GYULA JENEI • *Always Different* • translated by Diana Senechal · HUNGARY

DIA JUBAILI • *No Windmills in Basra* • translated by Chip Rosetti • IRAQ

ELENI KEFALA • *Time Stitches* • translated by Peter Constantine • CYPRUS

UZMA ASLAM KHAN • *The Miraculous True History of Nomi Ali* • PAKISTAN

ANDREY KURKOV • *Grey Bees* • translated by Boris Dralyuk • UKRAINE

JORGE ENRIQUE LAGE • *Freeway La Movie* • translated by Lourdes Molina • CUBA

TEDI LÓPEZ MILLS • *The Book of Explanations* • translated by Robin Myers • MEXICO

FISTON MWANZA MUJILA • *The Villain's Dance* •
translated by Roland Glasser • DEMOCRATIC REPUBLIC OF CONGO

N. PRABHAKARAN • *Diary of a Malayali Madman* •
translated by Jayasree Kalathil • INDIA

THOMAS ROSS • *Miss Abracadabra* • USA

IGNACIO RUIZ-PÉREZ • *Isles of Firm Ground* • translated by Mike Soto • MEXICO

LUDMILLA PETRUSHEVSKAYA • *Kidnapped: A Crime Story* •
translated by Marian Schwartz • RUSSIA

NOAH SIMBLIST, ed. • *Tania Bruguera: The Francis Effect* • CUBA

S. YARBERRY • *A Boy in the City* • USA